A COMMON ORDINARY MURDER

A COMMON ORDINARY MURDER

A NOVEL

DONALD PFARRER

RANDOM HOUSE · NEW YORK

Copyright © 2008 by Donald Pfarrer

All rights reserved.

Published in the United States by Random House, an imprint of The Random House Publishing Group, a division of Random House, Inc., New York.

RANDOM HOUSE and colophon are registered trademarks of Random House, Inc.

ISBN 978-1-4000-6690-2

Printed in the United States of America on acid-free paper

www.atrandom.com

2 4 6 8 9 7 5 3 1

First Edition

Book design by Victoria Wong

dedicated
to the well-beloved Annie

A Word of Thanks

I owe a debt of gratitude to the officers who served on the 3rd Relief, 5th District, Dayton Police Department in 1983 and '86, and especially to their commander, Lieutenant Tom Tunney, who allowed me the privilege of riding and walking with his street cops for forty-eight nights.

My agent, Julia Lord, is a steady source of clear thinking and good cheer. I'm glad to be on her client list.

I also wish to record my gratitude to the late Gloria Emerson, a brave reporter and generous friend. It was she who steered me to the incomparable Robert D. Loomis at Random House.

Bob Loomis is a category of one. Indelible memory, colossal energy, and a drive to find a better way—he is a superb editor-critic. He doesn't try to write your book, he just wonders why you didn't write it better. And so you try. To say that I thank him is to say too little. But: Thank you, Bob.

—DP

Contents

A COMMON ORDINARY MURDER

Father and Daughter

Charles Carden defined strength as fearlessness in the face of death. Tonight he was strong.

In fact he was elated, he was bouncing in his chair and shifting items all over his desk for no good reason. His usual state of mind, his idea of "normal," was to think of his life as a book entitled *Destination Death*. Greedy as he was for more life even after seventy-five years, he knew with a biblical certainty that greed is always thwarted. "We are animals," he would say, as if speaking for all mankind, "therefore we die."

"So why do I feel so good?" he asked. He usually spoke to himself aloud, a habit that had begun to draw stares on the bus. And the word "bus," or rather the image of it, made him uncomfortable. Now it came rolling back upon him, the memory of finding himself riding the bus yesterday—with no idea where he was going. Looking at the passing streets he understood well enough that he was on the 5 Route to downtown, but why? It was a queer experience to recall so clearly one moment that followed upon an earlier one that was lost.

Something like that was happening right now. He was happy and didn't know why. It's a pity to miss out on a good thing, but the secret of his happiness was locked up in the memory vault. "Sometimes they come out," he said to encourage himself.

Then he asked: "If I'm happy, who cares why?" But—if you can't connect one action, decision or intention to the next, your life has no direction. "Except you know what," he said as a man might say to prove he could joke about it.

What lay between him and death was his present life. The horizon no longer receded if he walked a mile nor would it if he walked ten. But this minute was the same as any other in one respect, that it was the essential life. And—

"Marie!" he shouted—his daughter, his reason for living, his joy of joys, his living link to the departed Agnes. He had good reason to want memory and continuity, and Marie was the reason. Fear death?—no, not for his own sake. But for hers—yes! He feared and hated it because by dying he would leave Marie alone in the world—no brothers or sisters, aunts or uncles, or even cousins, and she had just parted from her boyfriend.

Thinking of Marie he thought about shaving. Marie used to scold him for dressing sloppily and letting his whiskers grow, so he touched his chin and found it smooth shaven. And now he smelled shaving soap. Was this only a memory of long ago, when he used to lift her and sit her on the sink where she could watch him shave? He taught her to say "soap" and "shave." He would soap up her face and drag the dull side of the razor through the cream, while she watched in the mirror with solemn concentration.

He felt now that the vault door might swing on its rusty hinges—that he might recover the reason he had shaved and dressed in his pinstriped suit. He glanced down at his legs and at the worn carpet slippers that hung on his purple feet. If he had shaved *in the evening* there had to be a reason.

A diary or journal of some kind lay open on the desk. He turned to it with a powerful curiosity. He saw with admiration the bold, flowing style of the journal-writer's script. He could see the eager flow of ink from the writer's pen and the bright lip of silver on the letters as they faded into black against the page. Then he surprised himself with a question:

"Did I write this? Is this my journal?"

And he started to read, but even before he read a single line the name Ronski jumped out at him and suddenly he was back at Ash Gully. He and Ronski were sitting side by side on their helmets eating K rations and drinking cool water. They had just refilled their canteens and the novelty of the cool drink was like champagne in the mouth. They laughed. Charles Carden remembered that they clicked canteens like two Frenchmen in a restaurant with white cloths on the tables. Just then Ronski jerked. Charles Carden felt the shock wave hit his right ear, the sound and the shock arriving at the same instant—so you don't so much hear it as feel it—and Ronski's blood or something splattered its warmth on Charles Carden's cheek. Ronski pitched forward and his open eye pressed against the ashes. Charles thought: "The Japs!"

Heaving his body to cover Ronski's he found his face touching the back of

Ronski's skull and a ghastly image of the bullet hole sent him rolling off. He scrambled for his carbine and fired off a complete magazine, more or less at the sky. The chagrin, the shame of this tormented him still. "I lost my mind then," he said, fingering the pages of the journal nervously. To empty his magazine at nothing! The platoon opened up and maybe they got the bastard and maybe they didn't, nobody would ever know.

Charles Carden turned the page and read: "I can endure anything. The question isn't death, the question is life. Why do it? Is there supposed to be a reason?"

"That's me," he said, for he was sure now. "The question is life." That was his kind of talk.

This entry had been written on 10 November 1946 and Charles knew that he was in law school then on the GI Bill, preparing to live life and earn his way. He hadn't met Agnes yet; Marie was not yet born; and even though his life was defined for him by these two women as wife and daughter—and by Ash Gully—even though it was true that he was the writer—still—he—

Hooked in his crooked fingers he saw a pen. He stared at it. By his right hand lay an envelope addressed to the city council. "To the Honorable, the Common Council, City Hall"—in letters scratched out by an arthritic hand. "Damn it!" he said. His pre-owned hands seemed to testify against him. Spotted, almost green beneath the liver splotches, ridged by reed-like bones, with fingers bent every which way and disfigured by lumps—and these lumps hurt!—used-up hands hanging on rods of wrists protruding from the cuffs of an ancient suit—could these be his hands? The suit was blue, pinstriped with gray, and slick with wear. Could the owner of this rag, of these skeletal hands stretched over with parti-colored skin, be the man who wrote the journal in such graceful script?

He turned back and read: "Ash Gully, a bending of contour lines on a Marine Corps map of Okinawa—a ravine blasted to hell by napalm and mortars. Here we rested, Ronski and I talking in whispers.

"I was the lieutenant and undoubtedly the bullet was meant for me. His eye looked into the ashes and lost its luster. His legs acted out his death spasm. He was a man running to catch up with his death."

Charles Carden heard the squeaking of the chair wheels, or thought he did. He sat in an old swivel chair that rolled on little wooden wheels. He even visualized the wheels pierced by steel axles—and yet—here he was, belly against the desk—

"Hell with it! The question is why did I shave. Have I got a date? Ha ha ha!"

Anybody observing him would have heard the mirth in the laughter and seen big teeth discolored by decades of coffee and cigarettes. He couldn't drink coffee now, and Marie had made him quit the cancer sticks years ago.

There was a flash of that, Marie pleading, "Daddy, please, please, *please!*" Somehow this upset him—seemed to raise a question. What question? He felt in the holey pockets of his suit coat but found no matches or Chesterfields. Still, feeling around for his cigarettes was a trip down memory lane.

The fact was he still craved his Chesterfields. That was something else he couldn't shut off—cigarettes—and his mind. He had a friend, Lee Sherman, who used to say, "Can't stop the old think machine."

Then, zip. His brain was telling him, as if he didn't know, that Marie's name had been Carden from the start. "We named her Marie Julienne Carden. But mine used to be *Cardonne.*"

Bouncing in his chair and yelling "That's it, that's it, that's it!" he flipped pages till he came to the entry about his change of name.

It was about three years after the war. He was graduating from law school and had registered for the bar exam. He went to his father and said, or at least this is how he wrote it down—:

"Pop, I'm going to Americanize. I know where I'm headed, and I'll go there as Charles Carden. C-A-R-D-E-N. Hope you don't mind."

The old man growled, but the son had been saving the 2000-pounder till last.

He said: "And also, Pop, I've worked out a new philosophy."

"What's that?"

"What's a philosophy?"

"No, you monkey, why do you need a new one? You were born with one."

"That's just it, Pop. I quit going to church. I quit after Okinawa and I'll never go back."

"You call it a philosophy to break away from your religion?"

"Yes sir I do. I call it—the name of it is 'Don't kneel, stand up.' I call it 'March!' I call it 'Face the Music.' "

"You'll face hell, is what you'll face. You'll find you can't stand up in molten lava or hear the music for the howls of agony, for Christ's sake!"

Thus his father on Charles Carden's philosophy. But what Charles had seen in Okinawa—not just Ronski, although there is nothing quite like seeing your bullet hit somebody sitting right beside you—what he had seen and smelled—napalm especially but artillery and naval gunfire and bombs and machine guns and rockets and "all that shit"—well, it all called for something new and strong.

Speaking of music, he thought he heard somebody sawing on a bass fiddle.

It was nothing like his father's piano playing. His father didn't really play, he beat the instrument, did everything but kick it, and out came a theme from Tchaikovksy or the opening bars of Beethoven's Fifth, which the old man put into words: "Drive slow, save tires." He exulted in the war.

He told his son: "Charles, your philosophy is dog shit. Don't tell me about Okinawa or your man Ronski's brains. They don't mean what you think they do. You act like you're the first man to discover the horribles. You're the Christopher Columbus of horror. Balls!"

"I never said I—"

"Take the whole world, from the stars right down to the lungs of a butter-fly, and there's only one explanation. You haven't got an explanation, Mon-key. All you've got is an attitude."

"I'd rather have an attitude based on truth than a—"

"Truth! You found it? I never knew you were so humble. Your truth is a ticket to chaos. Go on, go there and see how you like it. It'll make you home-sick for Okinawa."

But he did know what Okinawa meant. He also knew that from now on he would identify himself as the man whose bullet hit Ronski. Never before this could he define himself with such precision. And if his father had really been as bull-headed and superstitious as the father in the journal, then he, Charles, was a fighter against the forces of darkness. "That's me," he laughed. "The truth shall make you pee!" With fear.

He found an essential sentence in the journal. He knew where to look. It said: "Dad was right about the attitude." And he said aloud: "Am I as strong as he was?"—thinking of the journal-writer as another man, a strong man, not afraid.

This shaven boomerang jawbone was without a doubt the jawbone of the man some of his neighbors called "The Solitary Crank." And this room was the crank's study, stuffed and stacked with books and political pamphlets heaped up in piles on the floor. What reason could the Solitary Crank have for shaving?

He was born in 1910 and graduated from Kenyon College in the Depres-sion when jobs were all but unattainable. He worked on farms for three or four years till the war in Europe began to revive the American economy and he could get a boring desk job at NCR. When the Germans invaded Poland in September 1939 he could see his fate written in the headlines of the *Jour-nal* in the morning and the *Daily News* in the afternoon. He joined the Ma-rine Corps and was commissioned a second lieutenant. He fought through the Pacific War all the way to Okinawa.

So it was clear to Charles Carden what kind of world this is. And this law student, writing his journal after the war when he should have been reading cases, was a man of intensified identity, because of Okinawa.

In those days anything that worked well, such as a Parker fountain pen, or a room that was warm and dry, and lighted at night, seemed like a blessing. A soldier, in this case a marine, who has endured hunger for many days as if hunger itself were a kind of sustenance, who has lived in wet clothes, which can only be dried by the heat of his own body, who has stood on the firing step looking with straining eyes out into the black jungle—such a man understands how clever and useful a chair is; how good it is to switch on a light and never worry about drawing fire or ruining your night vision. Such a man appreciates clothes that don't stink, and low-cut shoes as light as feathers.

He has seen in the jungle something invisible, that changes the magnetic forces of life. For Charles Carden the Solitary Crank to be carried back to the law student's room, and to be sitting on his swivel chair in the Crank's Den, both at the same time, and to know it, was to comprehend that he was older than he ever expected to be. Yet he knew what it was like to be young.

Youth meant Agnes and then Marie. He now turned unerringly to the entry dated "8 August 1957. Marie born. Marie, you are a living baby!"

"That's it!" he cried and he was flooded with joy. "She's coming!" Coming tonight, this girl who gave a body and soul to the only argument for the existence of God that he hadn't exploded. His daughter, Agnes's daughter. He cried out again "Marie!" and shouted nonsense—"hoo hoo yipee." He bounded in his chair and the thing squeaked again—and he heard glass breaking—or something like that—so he listened.

Here was a favor granted by tight-fisted nature to the old farts of the world, an interval of lucidity in which to exercise the splendid powers of reason, memory and prediction, and to know you are doing all that effortlessly. He predicted she'd knock at any minute; he sat erect and listened.

Words raced through his mind: "I have a daughter named Marie who has not forgotten me. She's on her way from California. She may be at the airport now. She may be in a taxi right now on this very street!"

He could all but see her, the princess of his life, and he thought maybe he heard her knocking—but this knock, clatter or scrape, whatever it was, came from the back of the house.

"She'll knock in front," he said aloud. He wished he had fixed the bell. He imagined her taking her glove off to rap on the door and he saw her face, the eyes he used to gaze at when she was an infant, her noble features—"Yes noble!" he insisted. "Princess Marie."

Here before him lay the dust rag he used to clean his books. He had but to touch it and his hand went dry. And the question was: had he been dusting this old journal book?

Did it gather dust or did he read it every day? "Maybe I haven't read it for thirty years," he said and shivered—and realized he was soaked with sweat.

He was in Ash Gully, threatened with death. But death is natural and necessary. He could see just how natural by looking at his hands, which he now did.

And these were the hands that had wielded a scythe for the Ohio Department of Highways one hot summer before the war. The blade swept through the weeds with a sound like—Carden thought: "No, that's the wrong sound." And again he listened to a sound he couldn't identify; then to a new one like a scrape, which could have been the whetstone sliding along the knife edge of the yard-long blade—but no. "That's not it either," he thought, listening, visualizing the yellow dump truck with "Ohio" on the door. He thought of his careful effort to protect his thumb as he slid the stone down the blade. He had imagined his thumb sliced by a chance motion of his unskilled arm; this imagined cut came to him now and he laughed at it. "God, what a baby, what a child I was."

That was pretty much what his father said.

"Charles, you must be thirty-five but you have not yet grown up. I thought the war would make a man of you but you are as naive as ever. You've dressed yourself up in a man's clothes, I mean that so-called philosophy, but inside you're still in the first grade."

"Thanks, Pop. I just wish you'd been with me in Ash Gully."

"One guy gets killed and you deny God? We are creatures, Charles, not gods ourselves."

"At least you've quit calling me Monkey."

"That was your mother's pet name for you. I just wish she had lived till you could appreciate what a great woman she was."

"I doubt she'd say 'Monkey' in the same tone you do."

"Charles for Christ's sake, you're so sensitive. I thought the war—"

"I know what you thought, Pop, and what you think. I just can't believe it anymore and even if I could, I mean if it were true, your myth, I'd say 'Keep it,' I reject it." And Charles Carden thought: "I'm supposed to thank God for sending cancer to torture Agnes to death. That's what he wants me to do."

His father had never said exactly that, only that we can't fathom God's will.

When the old man said this Charles replied: "We can't understand what's most important, is that what you're saying?"

Said the father: "Right. And you're saying that you understand what has baffled the most learned and thoughtful men and women, saints and philosophers, since the beginning of history."

"No, Pop."

"Yes, Charles. Your man Ronski is dead. So is everybody else who ever walked the planet except those of us who are about to join them. So what? God created nature and we are a part of that, but you reject it. OK, son, I'll never call you Monkey again since you insist on misinterpreting me. But you can't reject nature. That is an insane idea."

But Charles said, as if it followed: "Tell me, Pop, why does one man blow out another's brains. Is it because it's natural?"

His father said, "Jesus, he's incorrigible."

Charles left his father's house and rented a room near the law school. By way of parting his father said, "Goodbye, Charles Carden. I'll pray for you."

Charles thanked him but never went back.

Turning the page Charles read:

"Give me the man who wrote that what Dad calls 'the horribles' is legitimate grounds for suicide—but don't kill yourself! Look into the abyss of suffering and watch the worms writhing down there, and say, 'I am one of those! And I will live!' Jump the abyss and live. Don't ask why, just jump."

This was a mind he could respect—whoever wrote this journal. He said aloud: "I wish I could write like that."

He slid off, and for a minute was fascinated by the image of himself sharpening a scythe by a yellow dump truck. Then he remembered shaving, and Marie, and was happy. He was enjoying his lucidity, but the intervals always came freighted with a threat. Suppose he lost it just when Marie arrived. She would see the monkey loping around in his worn-out clothes asking the same questions over and over, and this spectacle would operate on her conscience and maybe she'd decide she must sacrifice her freedom. "I have to come home and take care of him." The end of her life in California. This possibility sharpened his anxiety, as on a whetstone. He looked around aghast at the den of the solitary crank.

He was sitting at a rolltop desk facing an array of cubbyholes stuffed with rolled-up leaflets, pamphlets and posters stretching back from the most recent presidential election, Reagan over Mondale, 1984, to the early part of the century. In a drawer at the center of the array he kept the best campaign buttons in his collection, including Joe McCarthy and "Joe Must Go," Wendell L. Willkie, FDR and a little brass shield from the campaign of James M. Cox, candidate for president on the Democratic ticket in 1920 and an Ohio man. From cornice to baseboard the walls all around were covered with posters and portraits—Dewey, Truman, Taft, Ike, Bricker, Nixon, Johnson, Goldwater, Stevenson, Hoover and Frank Lausche among them. Burlap strips, each one studded with colorful campaign buttons, hung in ribbons of red, white and blue among the portraits.

"Nothing crazy about that," he thought. "Everybody's interested in something. I just happen to be interested in all these—dead—struggling—politicians with their dreams and ambitions."

But then his gaze traveled over the floor and made him uneasy. Amid the heaps of books and magazines little paths led across the room at all angles, and the paths had narrowed over the years till they were so clogged he could hardly navigate them. "I'm a screwball but at least I know it," he said.

He turned a few pages for the pleasure of it—but this is what he found: "They call him 'Heavenly Father' and they call him omnipotent, but they don't grasp the fact that a father is not omnipotent; he can't always protect, rescue and defend. That's the pain of it."

Charles Carden jumped to his feet, and the chair went squealing back and smashed a pile of magazines, blocking one of the crank paths. He cried, "That's true! God damn it!"

He tramped out of the room, following one of the paths as naturally as a blind man who knows his way by instinct (although he could see well enough in a small circle), and felt his way along the wall to the front door. He parted the curtain that gave on the porch, and she wasn't there, so he turned on the light, thinking, "How often have I turned a light on for Marie." Then: Agnes. He stood there stunned with her intimate presence; and then she was gone, and he made his muddling way back to his desk. He pushed the chair.

"A father is a man who has a child, whom he loves, whom he protects . . ."

And he thought: "I live a single continuous life blessed with the love of Agnes, the love of Marie."

But the crank paths looked like a maze. He scanned the room with his tunnel vision and could never see it whole, just a circle moving among the paths and the heaps. If you crawl in a maze, if you breathe trapped air like somebody stuck in a capsized ship, then you are not free. If after denying the religion of your childhood and "standing on your own feet" you are actually crawling in a maze then you are—a damned fool—both a fool and damned.

He sat down, as if a little comfort was due to a man about to enter hell. But he also laughed, and his laughter covered the rasping for a moment, then he thought: "What rasping? What thumping?"

He sat back in his chair and the springs screeched, and made the thudding stop, the hammering. "Good." He leaned forward, and screeched back again, and his hand went to his chin and he asked: "I shaved today? What for? I've got a date? Ha ha!"

He thought: "If your mind fails in Ash Gully, what then? What good is a senile old coot in the arena of life and death? You say, 'If my life defends truth I can bear anything.' Are you kidding? Agnes's agony? And what if something happens to Marie? Nobody can *bear anything.*"

He turned—because he heard a door open. A beam of light struck so deep he could feel it behind his eyes. It was the kind of pain, not entirely unpleasant, that he had felt when coming out of the afternoon movies as a kid. The light danced closer.

Could it be his neighbor Everett? Everett was always coming over to fix leaky pipes or blown fuses. But he was a black man and the man Charles now saw standing in this very room was white.

And why the flashlight?

Suddenly there were two of them. He saw them as if through a tube, as he saw everything, but within the tube his vision was actually quite clear. Now they had turned on the overhead light. Carden kept the house dark except for his desk lamp and he wondered who they thought they were, running up his electric bill.

But he didn't protest—in case they were neighbors. "Maybe I invited them!" he exclaimed.

There was a big ugly one and a little pretty one; he saw that much as he swung his circle of vision from side to side. The big one wore a belted black leather coat with zipped pockets on either side of the chest. This ape kicked a pile of magazines and sent them flying all over Charles Carden. It almost seemed that he stuck his face down the telescope of Carden's vision. He appeared to be sliding face first down the tube and leering with great stupid eyes. He shoved Carden back in his chair with one hand and flicked his head to rearrange his greasy hair. He had wide-set eyes of no particular color and his nose was turned up, showing two big black holes. "A pig," thought Carden.

Somebody piped: "Pig!" and Carden got a sharp slap across his cheek.

Now the little one thrust his face into the tube. This one could have sung soprano in a boys' choir. He was vain of his Prince Valiant haircut and he raked his bangs to the side with one curved index finger. He said: "Just tell us where the money is, Gramps. And the jewels. Got any jewels?"

"I only have one jewel," Carden said—or did he just think it?

A high-pitched voice said: "He's got a jewel!"

Carden felt a sense of menace, danger, a malevolent force—He knew they were robbers but that wasn't it. He wasn't afraid of these galoots, these bone-headed cretins. He was fearless, he'd proven that in the war. And these brutes—put them on Okinawa in the blaze and thunder of battle and see how fancy they'd be. They'd pee their panties and whine for momma—or daddy—or—

The horror pierced him to the heart, a horror unknown since Agnes's death agony, when he stood beside her helpless.

"My jewel!" he thought—or said.

Marie could be getting out of a cab right now, or climbing the steps to the porch, lifting her hand to knock.

She'd know the bell was broken; she'd take off her glove to knock on the big wood panel of the door.

A harsh bang both inside and outside his head jolted Carden but didn't stop his thinking. His mind still did its work, and it showed him now a dream picture of Marie reaching out to knock.

Carden cried: "God—Jesus—stop her!"

CHAPTER 2

District Commander

"Now Stevie," said Sergeant Hughes, "I'm no lawyer but—"

"No, you aren't," Steven McCord cut in. He knew his man. If Sergeant Hughes said he was no lawyer it meant he was ramping up to give legal advice. If he was no psychiatrist it meant—etc. etc.

Sergeant Hughes went right on: "And a month from tomorrow I won't even be a cop."

"You'll be dying of boredom," McCord predicted, wishing for some of that boredom for himself.

The Department was forcing Sergeant Hughes into retirement for two reasons, length of service and heart trouble. "So I figure," Hughes said, "I can speak freely to my so-called superior officer."

"You?" cried McCord amazed. "Speak freely?"

"And since I was your training officer when you were a wee babe trying to arrest every rogue in town, and since—"

"Yes, I remember those days. I was a baby cop and thought you had all the answers. And you had hair then, a picture rises before my eyes, hair and no paunch."

"So, Lieutenant, cut the bullshit and I'll tell you something, OK?"

"When did you ever ask to tell me anything? Haven't I been choking on your advice for twenty years?"

"I'm asking now, to get your attention."

"Here's your answer. No. Don't tell me anything except what you know about this COM, and I'll go out there and kick a detective in the butt."

"So here's what I think," said Sergeant Hughes waving that aside. "Here's my question. Forget the COM. What courses are you taking in this part-time study program that keeps you out of the office half the time and leaves the shitwork to me?"

"I told you, law courses."

"Right, but I mean—rules of evidence, criminal procedure, what?"

"Ohoho, Sergeant, you are smarter than I thought. Now I see where you're going with your nastiness about lawyers, the most innocent profession there is. Since I already know what's next, why don't we just drop it and you brief me on this COM."

"Tell me, what courses."

"Well," McCord answered, thinking deeply, squeezing his forehead between his thumb and forefinger, "there's one course where they teach me stuff I can't understand, and another where they teach me what I already know."

"So you're ashamed to answer. Did you ever look that shame in the eye and ask yourself why—"

"I never ask myself anything except why I became a cop."

"God help you, Stevie. Do you see where you're headed? I do."

"Good, then I can ask your advice about how to live my life, so just stand by. Don't call me, I'll call you."

"Now Stevie." Sergeant Hughes lifted his white eyebrows in two interrogative arcs.

Knowing what this little ceremony meant, McCord nodded assent, and Hughes got up with his usual deliberation and went to the door and closed it. He never quite straightened his body when he walked and never moved fast. He returned, sat, and set his dangling foot bobbing up and down off one knee. Leaning forward he embraced the other knee and looked his lieutenant sincerely in the eyes.

Before Hughes could speak McCord said, "Did you know you've got pleading eyes? Big, blue, juvenile eyes that must have melted your mother's heart."

Hughes paid no attention. He said: "The point is—the disaster is—you? A criminal defense attorney? A traitor? Turn into a snake at your age and crawl on your belly for money? What's Nora got to say about this? Just tell me honestly what Nora—"

McCord dismissed this with an angry gesture and Hughes relented. When the lieutenant was getting ready to get mad (he never quite blew up), the sergeant could see it all over his face. His eyes maybe didn't change color but they took on a stabbing intensity.

"OK, OK, sorry," Hughes pressed on, "but ask yourself if—if Nora smells a rat maybe you are the rat she smells."

"Hey Hughes, what's with the animals? You hate snakes and rats? I sort of like snakes myself. Rats, no. Bats, yes, I find bats sort of charming. They are God's creatures like you and me, and you keep preaching at me—

"What I was about to say," Steven McCord continued after pausing as if to think, "is that lawyers are better than cops. Lawyers are paid in money. Cops are paid in false satisfaction, the illusion of self-worth. Lawyers get real stuff, boats, cars, houses, women, good liquor."

"Except for my Janey you got the best woman I ever met," said Hughes, aggression in his eye.

"Yeah, yeah, you think I don't know that? But just take a look. Lawyers never have to chase rogues down dark alleys or go into whorehouses or drug dens and they don't have to clean up the puke the low-lifers leave in the back of their cruisers."

"When was the last time you had to—"

"Long time ago but I can still smell it," McCord said. "In fact that was the first time I asked myself what I was—"

"Thought you never asked yourself anything. You just said— Anyway there's no water around here."

"Huh?" said McCord.

"You said you'd sell your soul for a boat."

"Forget the boat. I'll get a Mercedes."

"Unreliable," said Hughes authoritatively. "My cousin had one. A pile of junk."

"Your cousin should be driving an F-One-Fifty."

"Listen, Stevie, if I came into this office and saw you with your sleeve rolled up and a razor in your hand what would I do?"

"You'd save my life. You're still my training officer. And I'd be so grateful I'd treat you and Janey to dinner at McDonald's."

"Stop this shit. Use your imagination and picture the scene. You in a shark suit wrecking the jury selection process, confusing the ones that do get selected, filing for a continuance every other day."

"That," said McCord sharply, "is up to the judge. If the motion doesn't have any merit then the judge—"

"Come off it! The judges are the guys who can't make it as lawyers. I could quote you by the hour on how the defense lawyer is a worse insect than his client because at least the client can say he murdered on the spur of the moment."

"Which he did not."

"But the defense lawyer paces the floor in the wee hours thinking up new ways to subvert justice."

"Justice," said McCord as if he meant it, "is the outcome of an adversary proceeding. That's the only kind that exists. The rest is bullshit. Anyhow you seem to think there's only one kind of lawyer, the one you call a shark."

"I could quote you yourself on that."

"Quotes from my blowhard cop days."

"So you're not a cop now?" asked Hughes.

"Not for long. And listen yourself, Huge-es." He pronounced it "huge" with a separate s. "Who said I was going to join the civic-minded gentlemen and ladies of the criminal defense bar? Did I ever say it?"

"Obviously not. You'd be ashamed."

"I fuckin told you—just—who said I was—"

"I said it."

"So you know what's in my mind and I don't."

"That's pretty much it, yeah. I see where you're headed even if you don't. You're telling little lies to yourself and pretty soon it'll be too late, is what you're hoping. You want a Mercedes, a boat, a home entertainment center with a—"

"I never said anything about a fucking—"

"And you're studying criminal procedure. Am I right?"

"Depends where you're going with these dumb questions."

"The point is where are you goin? A rich lawyer, OK? You don't know anything but crime and criminals. You can't make money as an assistant DA, so there's only one answer."

"Answer to what?"

"Don't keep running away from it. You're heading for the criminal defense bar and yeah, I do know what's in your mind."

"Jesus, he's a shrink. And a great gas bag."

"Thanks. Now you're up to personal abuse of a subordinate in violation of Department rules."

"Turn me in, Crybaby."

"I'll turn you in to your wife, is who I'll turn you in to. If you won't listen to Nora your sorry ass ain't worth saving. I can give up and let you go to the dogs."

"More curses on defenseless animals. Where does this animosity come from? Now listen. There are dozens or scores of careers within the profession of law."

McCord spent a professorial minute naming some and Hughes seemed to listen with care. They were in McCord's office in the shabby old house, an ex-funeral home, that the city had renovated to provide a headquarters for the 6th Police District, Lieutenant Steven McCord commanding. Sergeant Hughes was in uniform. McCord wore attire suitable for giving speeches to the Rotary Club. In fact few Rotarians operated businesses in the staggering 6th. (Why open a business to benefit the neighborhood robbers?) But McCord was sometimes called upon to give speeches to business groups downtown. The chief would call and say, "Do this Rotary thing for me, Steve. I want to put our best foot forward." For this reason McCord was sometimes called "Best Foot" and "Rotary Cop" at the weekly meeting of district commanders.

The lawyer dream had entered his head after he gave a speech to the Civic League. A man his own age but wearing a shark's suit had approached him and enthused about his speech, then said: "Why are you wasting your time carrying a gun around? You could make ten times as much practicing law." McCord had never thought of making ten times as much so he didn't really listen, but the idea stuck. That same night McCord thought he'd seen the light at the end of the tunnel.

When he had enumerated twenty different lawyer functions he pressed again to find out where Hughes got the wild idea that he was planning to defend criminals instead of arresting them.

Said Hughes: "Just as well you didn't tell me. I could've had another heart attack."

"I never said it to you or anybody else."

"I get it. You'll be an ambulance chaser instead."

"People riding in ambulances sometimes need and deserve a lawyer. But just listen for a minute, because I'm going to say something new."

"Ah!" Hughes exclaimed. "He's gonna do—what they call—trusts and estates, taxes, real estate. The terrific stuff. Think of the thrills. Not a snake, I was wrong, thank you Jesus, just a fuckin drone."

"Will you listen?"

"Can't. I'm having a mystical experience, I'm seein my old rookie spellbinding a jury, the men saying 'What a brain on that guy' and the women gasping, 'My idea of a real man,' and he's master of the courtroom, defending an innocent citizen accused of murder by rogue cops and a degenerate DA. The jury comes back with a verdict of Not Guilty. The judge wipes his eyes, the lady jurors faint and the defendant hugs our hero till his chest creaks and the press comes thundering over the rail and our hero—"

"Everybody accused of a crime is guilty, is that your point?" McCord demanded with anger in his voice.

"No, matter of fact that's not my point, counselor."

"But you do have a point so what the hell is it?"

"You're going to be the world's first honest defense lawyer—or let's say the first one who's both honest and rich. Cause nobody has ever done it up to now. And please don't tell me we need criminal defense lawyers, I know that."

"We do," McCord said anyway, "unless cops are gods."

"No, Stevie, the one who thinks he's God is the lawyer who says he can tell the innocent client from the guilty one. So you'd represent only the innocent? I'm givin you a minute to answer, and you ain't sayin puppy shit."

"OK, puppy shit."

"See what I mean? Stevie, listen, you can't be a selective advocate like that. And if you could you'd fuckin starve. The pukes we arrest, if they didn't do one thing they did two others."

"Some did, some didn't," McCord said judiciously.

"Ninety-nine point nine percent."

"I haven't decided anything. I'm studying law and thinking about it, that's all."

"You're not going to be a lawyer?"

"Oh I'll be a lawyer all right, and never again will I clean the puke out of a cruiser."

"Oh I see!" Hughes burst out naively. "You want clean work."

"Right. I'm getting out of this dirty business before I turn into an old dragon like you."

"You should be so lucky. I got Janey, I got—"

"Christ, man, I'm not knocking Janey. I love her and you know it."

"So you should. But lemme close my eyes and see a movie of your future. Yeah, sure. You'll be the top lawyer at NCR because you've got such impressive experience in business. They'll make you vice president and general counsel at Mead Paper cause you know so much about paper. Top pig at Bank One cause you know so much about banking.

"Yeah, yeah, Stevie, I see where you're going now, sure, a million opportunities, a million lawyer jobs out there for a forty-five-year-old man who—"

"Forty-two," said McCord.

"—who has never done anything in his life except be a cop."

"Two inspiring years in the Army."

"I can see it now, your first job interview. This silver-tongued oldster in a thousand-dollar suit says, 'Now Mr. McCord, we are so impressed by your years cleaning up the puke in a squad car that we saved the corner office for you and here's your first assignment. Ready? We want you to handle this billion-dollar merger of the Hong Fat Chinese Food Conglomerate with Acme Sheet Metal and Tool. It's your baby. OK?' Yeah, I can hear it now, your first little task."

McCord said, "There's always the DA's office."

"Yeah, assistant DA, but you could make just as much where you are. In a year or two, Stevie, Best Foot, you'll be a captain and captains make pretty good money and they don't get their hands dirty."

"By money," said McCord patiently, "I mean life-changing money."

"Oh. You want a different life."

McCord said silently: "Exactly: no blood on the walls." He got a flash of himself driving a Mercedes and it embarrassed him. Aloud he said: "Now tell me about this COM. Somebody's got to do the police work around here."

Sergeant Hughes briefed Lieutenant McCord on the latest Common Ordinary Murder in the 6th and McCord said:

"I'm going out there. Can you watch the shop?"

"Sure," said Hughes. "Say hi to Bonehead for me."

"Oh Christ, is Reitz on this?"

"Reitz and Tim."

"Good. I can talk to Tim."

"Tim's friends with Nora, right? Ask what Nora's gonna say."

"Watch the shop," said McCord slipping his suit coat over his revolver in its shoulder hanger. "Call if you need any advice."

The gun against his ribs, the badge folded in leather in his suit coat pocket—there was a time when these two things completed him. Now they weighed him down like anklets of lead on a swimmer. He couldn't make it to the top, to the air.

The body McCord twisted while putting on his coat was well equipped with the powerful but vaguely defined muscles of a frequent swimmer. They were not heavy like a weight-lifter's muscles nor sculpted sharply like a body-builder's. They were good for the use to which they were put by the owner. Nor was he a big man. But growing up in the East End had taught him that big is not always tough. By processes he scarcely noticed he came to see that he didn't have to fear anybody.

A snob might say that his kind of intelligence was mere shrewdness, even cunning, but the people he competed against for rank and stature in the Police Department would not necessarily agree. The promotion board had been advancing him steadily and the chief and the head of operations had consistently sent him where the need was greatest. The officers he worked with, most of them, respected him because he usually knew what to do and what to leave undone. And some men he had known for many years were his closest friends regardless of rank.

One of these was Sergeant Gil Hughes, boss of the 2nd Relief in the 6th District. Another was Tim Sloan, an evidence technician from Downtown who had formerly worked for McCord as a street cop in the 6th.

When McCord arrived at 128 Laurel Street Tim Sloan called his attention to something interesting. It was a window screen with a wood frame, leaning against the foundation at the rear of the house. The top of the frame was covered with a thin deposit of snow.

This suggested to Tim Sloan, who suggested to Steven McCord, that the killer or killers, who had gained entrance via this window, had gone in before the snow fell; and since there were no footprints, rear or side, he or they had left the house while the ground was still clear of snow.

McCord stood with Tim staring at the frame as if it might be persuaded to reveal something more.

McCord said: "It was pretty cold last night, eh, Tim?"

"Freezing," Tim Sloan agreed.

"OK then, you know what I'm thinking," said McCord.

"Yeah."

"Will you call or should I?" McCord asked.

Tim said he'd call. It was in response to his call that, a half-hour later, an evidence technician arrived with a broom and began sweeping away the snow covering an empty parking space beside the garage. An alley ran behind the house; the garage and parking space abutted the alley.

McCord had been studying the garden, to see if it would reveal anything about its owner. It lay next to a walk leading from the back door to the garage. So McCord, squatting by the garden, could glance up and watch the policeman swinging the broom in long, slow strokes. McCord wanted to know if the owner of the house, an old geezer named Charles Carden, had been as decrepit and helpless as some of his neighbors said. And—so long as he was studying the geezer's garden he wouldn't be looking at his body. He knew exactly what was going to happen when he looked at the body.

The Meals on Wheels volunteer who reported the old guy's failure to answer her knock had said in her written statement that Mr. Charles Carden had been a danger to himself. "He should never have been allowed to live alone," she wrote. McCord wanted to know: "Allowed by whom?"

There were berry canes falling against each other in the garden and weathered tomato stakes angling into the ground. The rows between ran in two directions. The old guy had evidently planted several kinds of vegetables in short rows.

McCord sometimes thought of a "scene" as it might appear from 35,000 feet, difficult to locate among the thousands of houses spread over the city, but then the eye seemed unbelievably penetrating when one examined a detail from six feet away, or one foot. What is a detail? How do you choose one? What questions do you ask? He kept going back to the miniature mountains heaped up by the gardener's spade, where the snow was starting to melt. He concluded there was nothing to be learned here except that Mr. Charles Carden could drive a spade to its full depth into the earth and that his mind was equal to the task of planning, planting and tending a garden.

Now it was a question whether McCord could rise from this squat as a younger man would, in one smooth motion, or make a big production of it. With pain in his football knees and a reddening of his face he got up, stretching his legs and arching his back.

He crossed a strip of grass to the concrete walk and his shoes glistened. He went slowly along the walk between garage and fence and entered the alley, where he saw a row of uniformed police officers moving slowly in a line abreast, with heads bowed like a council of wise men, except that two were women. The day's cars had packed down the snow in the alley.

Charles Carden's house stood in a neighborhood very like the one where McCord grew up. This alley, the house and entire neighborhood had been built in the early twentieth century when labor was conscientious and cheap, and food, coal, and clothing even cheaper. In that bygone era a man working one job could support his family by himself, working like a Turk so they could live like Americans. His wife could stay home and raise the kids, which was probably good for them whether or not it was good for her. There was nothing pretentious or extra, but neither was anything essential missing. There were yards, garages, fences, porches, posts for the clotheslines, and alleys to hold it all together, to serve as raceways for the kids as they grew up and started to learn what freedom was. That the old man had stayed here while the neighborhood decayed placed him in McCord's category of volunteer victim.

It did look like a COM, in which a life connected to few others, perhaps no others, is brought to a bloody end for no reason by an attacker who stands for nothing.

"Why is a retired lawyer living in a dump like this anyway?" That at least was an interesting question. He was surely living here because this was his home. McCord had spent the last twenty years defending the right of such people as the old man to commit suicide in just this way.

The line abreast passed in review before him. Two or three of the officers looked at him and one said, "Nothin."

"Right," McCord said, meaning, "Keep looking." But everybody knew it would lead to nothing. Four other officers would soon begin a new canvass of the neighbors, during dinner hour, and that might turn something up. Somebody might have seen a known rogue or a stranger. People are nosy with a nosiness that crosses the color line; they are sometimes even kind with a kindness that affirms the common humanity of black and white, and they like to talk. Few will keep quiet if they can say something about a murder.

The officer with the broom laid it down carefully and crouched for a closer look at the muddy ground. McCord joined him.

"Pretty clear," said the officer.

"Very clear," said McCord.

The officer touched the mud with a fingertip and said, "I don't have much time, with this sun."

"Go to it," McCord said.

He went around to the front and mounted to the porch. He noticed that even if he tried to walk quietly his heels made a hollow boom on the boards. He opened the door and met Tim Sloan.

Tim was using the sunlight in some way. He was such a methodical investigator he might have been waiting for it to move, so he could follow it across the wall. He would certainly be here long after everybody else had left, and not just for the overtime. He didn't need the money, being a bachelor with no costly habits. What he wanted wasn't money. Whatever it was, he seemed to think he might find it in this hallway.

A year ago while Tim Sloan was still on the street he responded to a domestic violence call. He knocked on a woman's door and the boyfriend shot at him through the screen. He felt the shock wave on his cheek—"You're dead, or maybe not." The boyfriend burst through the door and ran around the house. Tim chased him and stopped at the corner, wisely. No boyfriend anywhere but maybe he heard breathing.

Tim was a gun nut, with his own private collection, but of course the Department insisted that every officer carry the .38 revolver. Tim knew how to improve on that. He loaded his own ammunition, using power powder, and he capped every other round with a soft bullet—not necessarily in compliance with regulations. He always aligned the cylinder to place a soft bullet in first firing position. That proved a problem as he stood at the corner, because he wanted a jacketed bullet for penetration. He rotated the cylinder, which he had practiced doing silently, and brought a jacketed round into position. He fired through the corner and the citizen on the other side howled in pain and rage, and crumpled.

Thus did Tim Sloan, author of ten thousand traffic tickets and the only officer on the 3rd Relief who faithfully reported unlit street lights, add a silver stripe to his reputation. When Tim drew up an accident report you could print it in a textbook. If he said a word, he had a reason to say it; if he had nothing to say he never said it. He did, however, sprinkle Latin phrases from the law books into his speech—i.e., per se (his favorite), e. g., ipso facto and *res ipsa loquitur*—"the thing speaks for itself."

Tim was tall and large. He wore a black jumpsuit, gun belt and shoes. He had black hair and slow-moving gray eyes. He spent his evenings fiddling with guns, watching movies or reading crime novels. He could not solve the sex problem. From time to time he ventured into bed with a woman, sometimes a skilled professional, and he understood why people of different sexes lived together, but he would never trade solitude for marriage. Nora McCord invited him for dinner several times every year.

"I got two people in here I think," Tim said touching his "doctor kit" with the toe of his shiny black shoe. He told McCord that whoever had ransacked the old man's study was wearing gloves but that here in the front hall he, Tim, had brushed several fingerprints on the door and adjacent window frame, including what he believed to be one complete set, and he doubted they were the old man's prints. His search was not yet ended.

Staring solemnly at McCord Tim lifted his thumb over his shoulder and said, "Gloves." He pointed to the door and said, "No gloves."

McCord went down the hall, glancing into the living room and dining room. Reaching the so-called study he saw Detective Sergeant Richard Reitz surveying a great mess of books and papers on the floor, a technician and an old man in a pinstriped suit sitting in a chair. He didn't linger on the old man but turned away and went upstairs.

Here was another ransacked room but this looked as if it had been turned upside down whereas the study had been turned inside out. To place this distinction before the detective sergeant in charge of the investigation McCord would speak through Tim Sloan. He'd say something like: "Tim, I don't think the mess upstairs was a search. I think it was a fight."

As District Commander, McCord could influence the investigation but not direct it, not, at least, according to the book. The Detective Bureau, which was based Downtown and reported to the Inspector of Detectives, not to McCord, was in charge. But the crime occurred in McCord's district, and ultimately it was his reputation at stake. There were just a few too many of these COMs going on in the 6th and pretty soon the Superintendent of Operations and his staff, maybe even the Chief of Police or the mayor would take notice.

So McCord seldom stood idly by. He paid due deference to the Bureau's people, but he used to be a detective himself, and he knew how to drop a hint or pick up an idea. The Evidence Section, a branch of Technical Services, assisted the detectives and so did the Coroner's Office, an independent agency of the county, not the city. McCord had friends in all these agencies.

But he had to operate subtly. If he said directly to Detective Sergeant Reitz downstairs, "Hey Dick, here's what I think," Reitz's mind would shut off and nobody would ever find the switch to turn it back on. Reitz would look at him as he'd look at a monkey trying to talk English. Reitz simply could not think what McCord suggested he think. But Tim Sloan, McCord's source inside the investigation, loved Nora McCord's cooking and even loved the McCord kids. Steven McCord could help and to some degree guide the investigation by sending men to canvass and search, by providing whatever other manpower the detectives might want, and by speaking to Tim Sloan, who would speak to Detective Sergeant Richard Reitz.

And McCord could stand to the side and breathe. He was doing that now. Detectives believe that District cops who hang around murder scenes are moved by a prurient curiosity. But McCord was not curious. He was showing his flag. "I'm the district commander and you dicks better work this case or I'll remember you when I make captain."

Actually he had no desire to make captain. He wanted out; he wanted bloodless freedom. It was a strain on the nerves, it seemed almost obscene, to think of a new life as a lawyer while standing in the upstairs room watching an evidence technician and a photographer poking around—and seeing a disordered bed and an upset dressing table and mirror.

The technician asked McCord whether he should take the bedding and McCord said, "Up to you."

Not a helpful response but it couldn't backfire if the man took it to the lab, the lab found nothing, and berated the technician for wasting its time, and the tech said that Lieutenant McCord had told him to test it. Didn't the lieutenant think the Bureau knew its job? That would, or could be the outcome. So McCord just breathed.

The bed was torn up, the blankets twisted and the pillows thrown across the room; the vanity table lay on its side with a cracked mirror on the floor. This was the kind of thing McCord was sick of looking at. To look at it was to re-enact it in his mind.

He saw, for instance, that the bed had no sheets and none could be seen lying around. He thought this room was unused. The place had a musty smell. Maybe it was a guest room or the room of a departed son or daughter; he thought a daughter, considering the dressing table and mirror. The furniture was cheap but the place, before last night, had been tidy and simple.

He stared at it, letting a spontaneous process begin. He wondered why any action at all had taken place here. The old man had been killed at his desk downstairs. What happened here? If the room was unused who was here? Why had the killer come upstairs? If he came in search of valuables why were the dresser drawers unopened? Maybe it was a search after all, but a hasty one. Maybe there was some pressure on the killer—a knock on the front door or a ringing telephone.

McCord went down the hall to another bedroom. He saw a stack of books on the night table, a glass of water and a bottle of aspirin. The bed was in the same kind of rough order as the garden. There was a rocking chair by a floor lamp with a pull chain—and McCord pictured the old guy rocking and reading; wearing his pinstriped suit.

The house had been home to a family but a quick glance showed that the last occupant had closed off one room after another till he was living in his bedroom and bath upstairs, his kitchen and study below. McCord had seen this pattern before—and he followed a tangent: Why would a semi-smart criminal risk the penalties of burglary and murder for the measly rewards to be found in the house of an old coot like this one? Yet they did it all the time; they robbed and sometimes killed old people in their homes, probably because it was easy.

Now the image of the wrecked bedroom rose up again in his mind. He walked down the hall to see the real thing and a flash lit up the doorway as he approached. He stood there and compared this room to the little sanctuary his daughter Jill had created. Jill's bedroom was crowded with various mementoes, pictures and posters, so it was colorful and gay. And so had this other room been, maybe, at some time in the past.

McCord couldn't picture the action. He didn't know who to put in the picture. All he had was the question, What happened in the wrecked room?

At last he went down to the study, the murder room. The mess on the floor could never have been contained in the old rolltop desk and the file cabinets; there was too much of it. McCord concentrated on the floor. These papers and magazines and such had been stacked in piles, some of which still stood; the rest had been strewn about, kicked about, he guessed.

The walls with their festoons of ribbons studded with campaign buttons fascinated him, and for a few minutes he found himself reading a kind of history of politics, but of course he was just putting it off—so finally he looked directly at the old guy sitting there with his head a little to one side, a lamp cord around his neck, and his throat slit. The blood cloud on the geezer's chest was turning from red to dark red and with time would turn black.

McCord felt compelled as a matter of honesty to look at the no-light eyes, but you can't look "into" such eyes. They are surface eyes. Had they been in working order the old man would have seen—leaning a little forward and staring at him with dark, insatiable eyes—a man whose expression seemed to show a touch of impatience, as if he wanted a quick answer.

This was the inevitable moment McCord had been so anxious to delay. He heard his own voice inside his mind: "I don't feel anything." This was a corpse, not a man.

He thought what an honest voice it was, and how revealing, that it should send a message about his real mind, not the one that knew it was being watched. Here's a guy who's been terrorized, beaten, slashed and robbed—"and I feel nothing."

McCord was good at professional detachment, which is absolutely essential. "I'll take credit for that." The choice is to be detached or deranged.

He had an idea: "I'll tell her," he said, surprising himself. The trouble was he had never spoken to "her" except for five minutes' small-talk at the fundraiser for Great Valley Hospital, which he had attended as part of the Department's community relations program. While talking with "her" he tried to keep his eyes off her body; and after they parted he spent the rest of the evening searching the crowd for her or dragging his eyes off her. So now some wild power in his brain was proposing that he confess to her that instead of ordinary human sympathy he had a hole in his soul. "Stupid," he said aloud.

Then he went back to the case before him. "Broke into his study—tied him up and choked him with a lamp cord—cut his throat. What else?"

He told Sergeant Reitz that the District officers in charge of the alley search and the canvass would report their findings, if any, directly to him. He left the house and listened to his steps thudding on the boards of the porch. He had a vision of the geezer's hair standing up as if in the wind and his eyes bulging. What was this, comic relief from some grotesque region of his brain? Then he saw the face of "a woman not his wife," a vision so sharply detailed that a rational man would have concluded there was no need to go see her since she was fully present in his head.

"What?" he asked. "Tell her—that?" She'd think he was bonkers.

He went back to the parking space beside the garage and asked the technician if he'd gotten a good impression of the tire treads and he said yes. The mud under the snow had been frozen hard, and he got a very good impression before the sun softened it.

"Fine," said McCord.

Returning to the street side McCord trotted down the concrete steps to the sidewalk where an officer opened the cordon to let him through. The little crowd of neighbors, shivering in the wind but enjoying the murder, parted and McCord walked down this path. What the crowd saw was a boss of some kind, a strong, stocky man, on the short side but built like a football player, with a quick, almost a lunging stride. The striking dimension of his face was its width; his forehead was like a brick; his eyes were well lighted, serious, and—maybe—unfriendly. His jaw was set hard. He seemed to think that by mashing his teeth together he could solve a problem. He bored through the crowd. He was thinking of the picture painted by Sergeant Hughes, of himself saving an innocent man from jail. But in his rerun of this scene the satire was washed out, and what remained was a valiant, selfless and worthy action.

As this impression deepened in his mind McCord began to criticize it, precisely because it was going so deep, and he was in danger of believing it.

He thought: "So I'm a hero, for Christ's sake. Absurd!"

A few strides later, opening his car door, his inner voice threw this in: "Get out of this god damn business before you turn to stone."

He reached the station too late for 3rd Relief roll call so he had his secretary post a notice that he would award fifty points to any officer who opened a lead in the murder at 128 Laurel. The point system was a thing of McCord's own contriving. An officer got twenty-five points for executing a capias, fifty for a felony arrest. At five hundred he got a paid day off.

McCord conferred with his secretary, bade her good evening, talked briefly with the duty sergeant—Hughes had gone home—and then went into his office, put his feet on his desk and began reading law.

His subject was the rules of evidence and he already knew it pretty well. Naturally he understood the exclusions as impediments to justice but he also knew that justice was not the object of the exercise. At best it was a happy accident. There was a game to be played here that was more profitable than the one he'd been playing for twenty years. He studied with an energy suited to his ambitions but also with the natural facility of one who enjoys studying.

When McCord graduated from Stivers High School he volunteered for the draft, to get the Army out of his way. Then came insufferable boredom and his attempt to brighten barracks life with courses supplied by the U.S. Armed Forces Institute. He read *Crime and Punishment* and the character of the prosecutor fascinated him. But he didn't think of himself as lawyer material. It never entered his mind to aim that high. He was out of the Army and into the Police Academy before the country began the heavy commitment of troops to the Vietnam War, so he missed the test that history was preparing for the population cohort just behind his own.

He was still a rookie when he married Nora O'Leary and their first baby came a few months later—six, approximately. He remembered how eager Nora had been, at age eighteen, to "go all the way." He'd thought she was too Catholic for that but she soon taught him his mistake. But for the wife and baby he might have joined the Army or Marines for Vietnam. If the peacetime Army was enervating maybe a fighting Army would be a real experience. He was all for experience in those days. He stayed with the police, so if he had a test to face it wasn't going to come in the rice paddies of Vietnam.

He served five years on street patrol, which is a test in itself, was promoted to sergeant at age twenty-six and served three more years, in the district he now commanded, as sergeant in charge of the 3rd Relief, the platoon on patrol from three to eleven. Next he spent three years in Internal Affairs, then four as sergeant of detectives in Homicide, starting at age thirty-two.

In this history the most disturbing tour was not Homicide but Internal Affairs, investigating and ruining, in two cases the jailing, of his friends. Cops are isolated in their social lives, and look for friends among other cops; but an IA cop is not free even in that confined universe; he is powerful, and alone with his power.

The Department sent him to public administration school and made him a lieutenant at age thirty-six. His first job at his new rank was to coordinate the installation of a new communications system; important work but a bore;

then he helped reorganize Technical Services and wrote a new protocol for
the Detective Bureau, a job he enjoyed. He liked thinking that the detectives
would be doing things his way, more or less, for years to come. And he liked
to write. It came easy; there was no labor in it. Then he worked Downtown as
assistant superintendent of operations, then as field lieutenant, and finally as
a reward they gave him the 6th District, a little less than three years ago.

Throughout this career he studied at night or shifted his duty hours to at-
tend classes in the daytime. He stood at the top of the list in his examinations
for sergeant and lieutenant, and got a bachelor's degree from the local branch
of the state university.

But from here on promotion was political, and the jobs were different.
First you had to prove to somebody you didn't respect that you had changed
yourself into somebody you didn't know; then if you got the job it would turn
out to be an insult to your old self and degrading to your new one. From
below, at least, the jobs at captain and above seemed to reward patience with
power, but if you didn't care about power or simply weren't addicted to it,
they proposed to exchange something worthless for your life. As for money,
which presumably had its own kind of value, there was more to be had elsewhere. He had begun to notice what money can buy and to imagine himself
buying it. Up to now he'd been content to remain in the condition into which
he was born. In fact he'd done better than his father.

Two or three years as a lawyer and he'd surely outgrow the satisfaction he
had always taken in the natural superiority of cops over lawyers. Looking up
from the page he hit upon a question: If being a cop was superior why did it
eat you up? In cold fact he knew what he meant by superior. "You may not
touch that old guy. If you do I'll kill you." But they went on touching, and
McCord didn't kill them. Maybe then this superiority that had been his personal style of narcissism for twenty years was an illusion.

He underlined a sentence in red; he circled an index word. When he
came back to this chapter he could scan it at a page a minute. He knew this
method moved him too fast, but it was only law.

You can't prove guilt this way, that way or the other way. He was etching
the exclusions in his memory and knew exactly how the prosecutor of Raskol-
nikov would react to the rules of evidence in the American system.

It occurred to him there was no point in killing the old man's killer if a
body is just a body. In that case money and power were the whole game, as he
had suspected all along. Or at least in the last two or three years.

Somehow this led to: "Why be a drone all your life? OK, strike that 'drone'
and make it a foot soldier."

He stopped and thought again of "a woman not his wife." He got a jolt just from saying her name: "Lindy Alden."

It was dark and time to go home but instead he went to the murder house. The sound of the address in his head, 128 Laurel Street, pulled him. Walking across the porch, listening, he imagined the killer stiffening when he heard footfalls of the kind McCord was now producing—and a wedge of fear in the killer's heart—followed by an iron determination to do whatever was necessary. Doing what the situation dictates he must do, the killer saves his body and destroys his reason for existing.

McCord found Tim Sloan in the study, sitting in the old man's swivel chair reading some kind of journal or notebook.

"What have you got there, Tim?"

"It's the old guy's diary. Sergeant Reitz went through it but I thought I'd have a look."

"Is there anything in it?"

"Just his thoughts."

"I mean anything relevant."

"I don't see how there could be, per se. It's pretty much old stuff, sort of the story of his life, you know?"

Tim held the volume the way he held his target pistols, with care, with a respect for a well-made object. Eyes sensitive as his hands, he looked up and asked: "Did you see the upstairs bedroom?"

"Yes," said McCord. "What did Reitz make of it?"

"He thought there was a struggle up there, i.e., I'm fighting for my life."

"Fine," said McCord. "I was going to ask you to suggest that very thing."

"I did. And anyway they weren't black, I don't think. Can't be sure but if there's any black man's hair in this house I'll go back to writing up busted street lights."

He spun around in the chair, lay the book on the desk and opened his doctor kit. He handed McCord a clear plastic envelope with a white card inside.

McCord held it at various angles and finally saw a hair—very long, perhaps eight or ten inches, light and gently waved.

Watching with satisfaction as the lieutenant's mouth drooped and eyebrows raised Tim Sloan handed over another envelope, also containing a hair and a blank note card to serve as background. This one was dark and shorter than the other.

"I think this one's a man's," Tim said and paused.

"And this is a woman's?" McCord ventured, re-examining the curved blond hair.

"That's what I think. I got to think something."

"Where did you find these?"

Tim smiled and lifted his thumb toward the ceiling.

"Both in the same room?"

Tim said yes.

McCord asked: "Do you know how many sets of prints you've got?"

"I'd guess one, possibly three. I don't know."

McCord saw the upstairs bedroom again and felt his mind darkening.

Tim Sloan snapped his doctor kit, and no sooner had this big slow man in a black jumpsuit and black gun belt risen from the swivel chair than McCord saw the old man sitting there with his head sagging on one side, with his bright inquisitive eyes fixed on the man whose eyes were fixed on him.

McCord took up the journal and turned some pages, reading a sentence here and there, coming to a page that was blank except for these words in the center: "The doctor predicts Agnes will live less than three months." On a later page, also blank but for a single sentence, McCord read: "She is suffering and Marie cannot understand." Reading further he learned that Agnes, the wife, had died and that the couple had a daughter named Marie.

McCord decided that someday he would bring his own daughter, aged fourteen, to a place like this and say, "Look at him. See him clearly."

She would protest, "Why do I have to look at something so horrible?"

And he would say, "This is our world. See it clearly."

To Tim Sloan McCord said: "Did you plan on taking this?" — tapping the journal — and Tim said no.

McCord said, "I think I'll look into it."

McCord flipped a page and his eye fixed on: "Tolstoy says, 'Resist not evil.' I say, 'Resist with all your might.'"

When McCord left the house the old man was still in his eyes and his own stony reaction still in his mind. He had decided to go to Lindy Alden. He thought: "By God I'll tell her." He checked his watch: already late for dinner. But Nora was used to that. He started the engine. He had looked Lindy Alden up in the phone book two days ago. He even knew her building — not a very safe one, in fact. He had been dispatched there more than once on "family trouble" calls during his years on street patrol. He could drive there, say hello, and be home in another hour, having done nothing really wrong. Stealthy yes, but harmless. Except of course that he wouldn't tell Nora. Why plant a false suspicion? And his schedule was so erratic, with his cop job and law courses, that Nora—true and lawful wife—wouldn't suspect—anything. He set the car rolling.

Anyway he couldn't tell Nora what he planned to tell Lindy; Nora would take it as an opening for an argument, leading inevitably to: Why don't you go to God?

McCord had toured the City of God when he was young and he came around to the belief that it was built on blinding fear and blind hope. If Nora wanted to earn angel wings it was OK with him, but he had left all that among the discards of his youth.

He experienced a sane moment and said, "Go home, Moron." But he didn't. He intended to look at Lindy again, see her eyes and speak with her, and if he said something unexpected or inappropriate, since he'd forgotten how you talk to a woman in whom you have a certain interest, at least he'd be able to see how she handled it. He had no future with her anyway because for Christ's sake he was married to Nora and had two kids still at home and one in college, and anyway he loved her and he had never stepped out on her.

As to starting a conversation, he was sure you don't say: "Hi, I just looked at an old buzzard with a slashed throat and didn't feel a thing." A brilliant opening, no doubt.

He had two facts: she was a nurse, and she wore no ring on her left hand.

Here came another chance to turn toward home, the intersection was coming up, and he passed it by, on course for the Normandy Arms apartments. His hands were unsteady on the wheel and his brain was in revolt, but this wasn't a brain event. The storm inside, like surf pounding against a sea wall, told him how scared he was—but—scared of what?

Maybe all he wanted was a little adventure, freedom, gratification without consequences. But he'd been gratified just last night by the only woman who knew his every desire and need—so why—

Or maybe the old geezer was—

His fertile brain produced, purely for the entertainment value, a picture of a tuft of white hair that he saw in the geezer's lap before Tim Sloan scooped it up. Obviously the killer had grabbed the old coot from behind, jerked his head back, slashed him, and flung the head and handful of hair forward in one derisive thrust.

McCord worked by imagination. He never ignored scientifically derived evidence but his inner method was the fantasy. He had developed this art in his years as a detective and saw no reason to change it. Many of his "visions" were wrong but they moved him forward—or, to be honest, they moved him somewhere that sometimes only felt like forward. Now he was in a fantasy with two players, himself and Lindy Alden.

It was six-thirty in the winter dark. The light was artificial, red beads floating ahead in his lane and glaring white on the oncoming side. None of it illuminated his spirit. He pulled over and let the traffic stream by him, thinking at once of two scenes—one at home where he was expected, and one in the other place where he might not even be recognized. He sat there with the cars humming by.

When he was a kid he and his friends talked about "Heaven or the Other Place." The "other place" he contemplated now was a place no prudent man would go. McCord was not a prudent man, and though his heart was struggling in its cage he drove on and parked his unmarked car, a plain gray sedan, outside the Normandy Arms.

This was a building of some sixty apartments arranged in two wings and a center span. The Normandy had been erected in the 1920s to provide starter housing for young couples. As the building aged, so the neighborhood declined; nothing was properly maintained, and the streets gradually turned grim and dangerous. But the apartments were spacious by the standards of the mid-1980s, and well lighted by double windows in the living and dining rooms. The place was still a pretty good buy for what it gave, which was not prestige.

He went to the central door and scanned the name cards. Finding Lindy Alden's he tried the door and found it unlocked. He mounted to the third floor and walked down a corridor of worn red carpet that had lost its color except at the edges, hearing thudding music from either side, until he came to her door. He stood precisely in the center to make himself visible through the spy hole—and he knocked. He thought he heard movement inside, but the door remained closed. He stood there believing she was watching him.

He thought: "What will I say?"

The door opened two inches on its chain and a feminine voice said: "Yes?"

He wasn't sure it was her voice. He couldn't see her face, and this intensified his sense of being out of line. He said his name and reminded her where they had met. A silence followed—till he heard the chain slide, and saw the door swing—and there she stood—and he was not disappointed.

He would have admitted that she was no movie-star beauty, that other men might not even notice her at a party or on the street. Over the days since he had met her he often wondered if it wasn't her imperfections that fascinated him. She was not smiling now, but he knew that when she did smile he would see the off-balance, ironical quality that had such an effect on him—as if a straight, normal smile would convey too little information, but hers—the smile he had been seeing in his mind for three days—could express irony, pleasure, reproach, sympathy, doubt, goodwill and—goodness! She seemed good! Of course if that were true she'd shut the door in his face and she wouldn't be standing there in her robe.

Was he making up all these smiles? Was there a real woman somewhere in all this?

Right now she looked as if she understood him all too well. He felt he had to apologize. He rattled on that she probably didn't remember him and he recited a fragment of their small-talk. He concluded: "I just wanted to say hello."

To which she replied: "Hello." And did not step back.

She was looking up to meet his eyes, because he was the taller, and this "looking up" had nothing of submission in it. A few hours later, when he had already begun to assign her the starring role in the new life he was planning, he remembered this moment almost with fear; he might have said "I'm making a mistake" and turned away, and never seen her again.

Instead he risked everything by saying: "I've been thinking about you since we met."

What he saw then was not her "ironical" smile but a kind of sympathy in her eyes, as if he'd complained of a headache.

Then she did smile and said: "I've been thinking about you too—but—I assumed you were married."

"I am," McCord said.

She seemed to absorb that information, and to figure out what it might mean. She said: "But your mother told you there were good girls and bad girls."

This shocked him a little but he said: "Well, I figured that out for myself."

"And you prefer bad girls."

"I don't say 'girls.' Sexist pigs do that."

"Women, then," she said in a voice that warned him not to try humor.

"I just wanted to look at you. You're bouncing from one side of my brain to the other."

"I'd be happy to hear that if you weren't married. Please don't tell me your wife doesn't understand you."

"She understands me pretty well."

"Or that you and she have an agreement."

"Like an open marriage? No, we don't have an agreement."

"Then why are you here, Mr. McCord?"

"I don't know. Well I do know but it's—To be honest—" He saw how ridiculous it would be to "confess" that he was a heartless clod, so he didn't.

"I'm sorry," Lindy Alden said, "but I'm meeting someone for dinner."

"A man," he thought, and wasn't happy.

She stood calmly and met his eyes. He looked at her unself-consciously, forgetting Nora, family and everything else, seeing only her and knowing, for the moment, nothing but her. She was a woman about six years younger than he, about thirty-five, with elliptical cinnamon-colored eyes and brown hair so dark it was almost black, white teeth not quite perfectly aligned, a strong jaw and full lips. She was wearing a green silk robe, and her freshly combed hair was wet. He imagined her pulling back the shower curtain and pressing her hair from front to back, and the little ripple of water this would send running down her neck. Accustomed as he was to his wife's fullness of figure, he saw this woman as light, with subtler curves and smaller bones. The wrist that showed between her sleeve and the doorknob, which she still held, was thin and tinged with red, maybe from the heat of the shower.

Lindy Alden said: "I don't go out with married men."

He thought: "Good," but didn't speak.

The color in her face deepened and she said: "You are embarrassing me."

McCord felt a stupid smile spreading across his face and he said: "OK," and turned and walked away.

He heard the door click shut. He was walking down that faded carpet, passing closed doors on either side, and the junk music was thudding against the wood—and he did not see or hear any of it. All he could see was her smile and all he could hear was "I've been thinking about you too."

CHAPTER 3

The Liar

D riving home he couldn't evade the eyes of the geezer, fixed on him with a mocking twinkle as if to say: "What are you going to do, Lieutenant Bigpants?" Why this should pop up now he did not know— unless, thinking of his home, of Nora and the true structure and meaning of his life he somehow went sliding down the path to 128 Laurel Street.

Thus in his thoughts he half-consciously connected his wife and his duty—or at least his job. He was already a cop when he asked her for their first date twenty years ago, a cop when he made her pregnant, and when he stood by her hospital bed while she gave her breast for the first time to their first child—Robert, now a student in college. Steven knew that to Nora his identity was wrapped up in the police uniform and way of life—which was not any ordinary way of life but one they both regarded as a commitment that set him, his wife and his family somewhat apart from the community in which they lived, and which Nora served as a senior civil servant in City Hall.

And this tendency of his to associate Nora and his job had been strengthened in recent weeks by her obvious dislike of his plan to quit the cop shop and become a lawyer. She did not oppose him. She had said so a good ten times, but her saying "I am not against it" was the measure of her undeclared skepticism.

About two weeks ago she had remarked on how uneasy she felt about a loan Steven had taken out to help Robert through his second year in college. When he told her not to worry, that lawyers make real money, she threw him a strange look, almost of disappointment. But all she said was, "We have enough, Steven." But McCord was thinking that they also had two other kids, at least one of whom would be entering college while Robert was in medical school—if he could get in. He was a smart kid; he'd get in. Steven thought but did not say, "No, we don't have enough." Of course that depended on what you meant by enough.

It was unlike Nora to worry about money or to withhold full support for a project so fundamental as law school. He thought maybe she was growing more conservative since the death of her sister last winter. Nora had nursed this beloved sister, ten years younger than she, virtually around the clock for three months, taking a leave of absence from her job, and the ordeal had drained her. To Steven it seemed she sometimes spoke from weakness, as if this cruel death were partly her fault or that she could have prevented it by an even greater exertion. She wore her sister's robe now every night and morning.

As he turned the car into his home street McCord had a bastard thought, which expressed itself as: "So she loses her sister and now you're going to cheat on her." He denied it but some inner voice had said it. Worse, he had recently caught himself wondering whether she wasn't a little boring—because she was good—good wife, mother, sister and aunt. "She is good, you god damn fool," he exclaimed silently, "and if anybody's boring it's you."

Going over all this as he drove through the darkness he rounded on himself: "Who are you to accuse her, you bastard." Calling himself a bastard disturbed his sense of entitlement. He hadn't touched another woman in twenty years—but—he was ready to lie if that was the price of seeing Lindy Alden again. He realized he was waiting to see what developed with Lindy Alden. What if this Lindy figure kept crashing around in the attic?

There was a dark place in his thinking: If he lied steadily, could he do it and keep his personality intact? Would he cope with shame by rationalizing the lies?

"Lawyers are an indispensable part of the system," he said aloud as if he was already deep into self-justification—or just reacting to Hughes's prejudices.

And he suddenly thought again of Lindy Alden, this woman he scarcely knew. "She's a mirage," he decided.

He knew what Nora wanted even if—or because—she never said it. Stay in his job, buck for captain—go on, and on, and on. She was a moralist in control of her life and expected him to control his.

"I can start a new life, a clean slate." Let the Detective Bureau do its job on Laurel Street. Study law; run the District, sure, but study law.

McCord slowed down. His car moved through darkness. He could imagine Nora sitting at the kitchen table with her adding machine and papers before her. He would have to enter this honest place with his dishonest mind on the alert. But then he protested: "Christ, I didn't touch her!" From this outburst he jumped to:

Whether Nora was "good" or not she loved him with an undying love, and nothing else that could be said about it was half so meaningful as that word "undying."

Trying to be honest he said to himself, as if a wise counselor had entered the conversation: "And you love her. Don't forget it."

It was true and he did not forget it. That was the problem.

An alley ran behind McCord's house, pretty much like the one behind Carden's. His headlight beams lurched up and down as he cruised slowly between rows of trash cans. Reaching his garage he knew without quite seeing that the paint was peeling off the doors. They were closed and Nora's Chevy would be inside. Making the turn into the space beside the garage he saw Nora through the kitchen window, rising at the sight of his lights. She wore her sister's old red robe. McCord cut his engine.

He stood beside the car in the cold, looking at the peak of the house against the opaque pink sky, suffused with city light. The windows on the second floor, where Jill would be studying and Danny would be building a model car or doing a puzzle, had a romantic yellow tint. "Danny isn't preparing for anything." This thought passed through his mind leaving a shallow impress of anger and disappointment. Danny would graduate from high school in the spring. Nora passed across the kitchen window and didn't look out. McCord waited to see if she would go back the other way, and she did.

The air hummed with the blended, indecipherable sounds of the city where he did his work. Nobody is more aware of a city as a social organism than a policeman. At this moment the sound was soft, unbroken by shouts, sirens, crashes or the shattering of glass. He stood a few seconds more, and the house seemed to rise into the red haze without getting any higher. It had a steep, pointed roof. It didn't make him feel that it was his house, rather that he was its man. A house need not be excellent or rich. This one sheltered his family.

He opened the back door and stepped onto a boxlike landing with a square linoleum floor. To the right a set of wooden stairs went down; to the left three clean carpeted steps went up to the kitchen. It had been his custom for years to take off his shoes before going left, considering the kinds of places he walked in during duty hours. He removed his shoes, walked into the kitchen and kissed his wife.

"It's a pity, isn't it," said Nora McCord, glancing up from the stove. Her eyebrows lifted, but so subtly that perhaps he was the only person alive who would notice.

"What is?" Steven asked getting a bottle of beer from the refrigerator.

"That lieutenants aren't paid by the hour."

He said, "Yeah, or politicians." He called her a politician. She was assistant to the City Clerk, a post of considerable influence Downtown.

"Then," said she, "you'd be almost as rich as some lawyers."

"Hardly," said Steven taking a bottle of bourbon from a cupboard and drinking from it. He chased this with beer and asked what she was cooking, but he was thinking that a little money wouldn't kill him. "But I don't want a little," he thought.

"Not cooking, just heating up," Nora said. "Spuds, sausages, tomato gravy, as you can see."

"Gads, my favorite dinner!"

"And your salad's in the Frigidaire."

"Blessings on your ass, woman."

He went down the hall and looked at himself in the bathroom mirror and experienced neither shame nor epiphany. The face looking at him was rugged, flushed. It was an emphatic face. If a man could design his own face, this is the one McCord would design for himself. With a face like this you could stare down practically any man anywhere. He urinated and swung his dong, sending the last drops into the air, then washed his hands. Here in the mirror, surely, was the face of a man who was willing to lie. "I am a liar and this is my face. Therefore this is a liar's face." This was a deduction without a detonation at the end of it. Maybe if you're always true and honest life runs along too smoothly. He was tired of being honest.

"What was it?" Nora asked stirring the pan.

He drank and looked puzzled.

"What kept you?" As she stirred the red gravy and poured it over the spuds she looked at him with large, very dark enigmatic eyes.

McCord couldn't quite understand this unusual inquisitiveness. "An unimportant murder," he said.

"A COM, as you might say?"

"Yes."

"Of course it's terrible that someone was murdered," she said putting down the spoon but not looking at him, looking intently into the pan with troubled eyes, "but why should you stay out late on account of it? What's the Bureau for?"

"The Bureau will fuck it up. It's my district. Laurel Street. I ordered a recanvass. I talked to Tim and made sure the stupid Dutchman got started right. I'm sick of it."

"I've been noticing the symptoms of your sickness— Is Reitz really so stupid?"

"Yes."

"He seems bright enough to me."

"Symptoms of what?" Steven said.

"Whatever it is that's making you tell me every other week that you're sick of it."

"Sorry to repeat myself. That's the enemy of marriage, repetition."

"I want to know what you're thinking."

Steven didn't pick this up. He said: "Reitz is a comedian when he's half drunk at a party. On a scene he's in too big a hurry to get home and get sozzled."

Nora repeated calmly: "Dick Reitz seems very intelligent to me. Whether he's careless I do not know." She twisted the gas to off, filled his plate and put his dinner on the table.

Nora too had been late coming home but not so late as Steven. She had eaten her own dinner, which Jill had prepared and left on the stove, only a short time before, and that was why Steven's dinner was so soon heated. She had cleared the dishes from her end of the table, wiped it and spread out her papers.

Nora's boss, the City Clerk, was appointed by the City Council to organize its business. He was an out-of-office alderman in need of a living, who had been given his job on condition that he hire Nora McCord to do it for him. Nora had previously served for several years as clerk to the Public Works Committee. Her new boss had lost his seat on the Council in the same election that elevated her old boss, the former chairman of Public Works, to the presidency of the Council. It was he, the president, who placed Nora in charge effectively of the entire agenda of the City Council. The City Clerk, meanwhile, her nominal boss, was set free to smoke cigars and leak the contents of his brain to his friends in every corner and corridor of City Hall.

Taking his seat at the kitchen table, suddenly ravenous, McCord observed his wife's printer-calculator and paperbound New Testament. Both were small enough to fit in her briefcase. He ate with a will, and lifted his bottle, and asked: "When did you get home?"

"An hour ago," she said.

"Too bad you don't get paid by the hour, huh? O'Leary?" He often called her by her maiden name.

Nora didn't answer or even look at him. Either she was already concentrating or deliberately ignoring him. She opened a file and gave it what Steven called her devouring stare. Her back was straight, even arched, and she leaned slightly forward holding the file in both hands. The red robe was tight at her waist and loose at the bust, falling in two folds over her breasts, which enjoyed their freedom in a loose flannel nightgown, white with a pattern of small red roses. Her black hair had started to turn but her complexion, her lively eyes and sympathetic features, and her figure were invigorating to look at, and Steven never tired of looking. Even the glints of white in her hair were all right with him. To him she was young because he always saw her as she had been at age nineteen; and the white streaks in her hair declared the length and durability of their marriage. For the moment they were two people, Nora reading and Steven eating, watching her, and Lindy Alden did not exist.

She closed the file, leaned back and said to him: "Sick of murders, at least of COMs. A sex murder or a dismembered millionaire might arouse your interest, though."

"Doubtful," said Steven.

"And I gather, sick too of living on a lieutenant's pay."

"For sure, O'Leary. And you're not?"

"We have enough, Steven."

"Enough and no more. What happens when Robert's in medical school while Jill's in college?"

"And yet, you are not planning to buck for captain."

"Certainly not."

"Strange," said Nora as if to herself.

He didn't respond.

"If you are going to be a cop," she surmised, "you want to be closer to the street. Captains are chained to the desk. Is that it?"

"Yeah, the street without a god. Reality Street."

"All the things that make you sick."

"Right," he said. "So there I am. Fucked."

"You are not fucked. You are doing work that must be done. I don't know many people who can say that."

Steven asked: "What's this all about anyway?"

"About your being sick of your work. But if you're so tired of it why did you stay at the scene after Tim left?"

He sensed something wrong and he drew a blank. After a second he repeated: "Stay at the scene?"—and it sounded evasive in his ears.

Nora said: "Yes. When you're so famously sick of your job."

"What do you mean 'stay there' or whatever? I came home. Here I am." He drank from his bottle and looked her square in the eyes and feared he wasn't doing this right.

Nora put down her file folder and said, "Tim said you forgot to sign for some piece of evidence and he'll come to the District tomorrow morning to get your signature on it."

"Yeah, I guess I forgot that," said Steven. "You mean Tim called here?"

"Yes," Nora said—and they were still in one another's eyes—"he called just as I opened the door."

McCord shrugged and said, "So I'll sign the thing tomorrow." He maintained the stare but he shrugged again, once too often; but he didn't break the stare—and neither did Nora. He knew he had one great advantage, that he had never cheated and she knew it.

But she pressed on: "It took you an hour to drive home?"

"I cruised around the District," he said plausibly.

And maybe this satisfied her. She moved her calculator and a set of papers into place.

Steven said: "Anyway, I'm not sick. If I'm tired of murders it's a sign I'm well."

She looked at him as if considering her reply, then bent to her work. She began tapping numbers into the calculator, as if she had suddenly found herself to be alone, as if he'd walked out of the room. He watched her, and he felt the rebuff, and wondered what it might signify, then went on with his dinner. Her head was down, her heavy black hair fallen forward, and she was concealed from him. Was she pondering that lost hour? She kept tapping and the little device kept whirring, feeding a ribbon of paper curling itself on the table. She paused, lifted the ribbon, scanned it with great seriousness, then bent to the machine again and tapped away, her dark eyes darting from the notebook to the paper. Working, she was like a beast of prey consuming her catch.

"We are in a crisis," she said looking him full in the eyes, and Steven started, and felt the oncoming conflict, and hardened himself for it.

Nora added: "And you—it means exactly nothing to you. We are heading for trouble and you simply don't care."

Steven met her ominous gaze but he found that it took courage to do it. He had twice faced a maniac aiming a gun at him, without a flicker, but this took courage, or gall. He held the stare and waited.

"Well?" she said.

And Steven replied: "Well?"

Nora lifted the little ribbon of figures and gave it a shake: "Our bond rating is going to fall. It's just a matter of time."

He asked carefully: "That's the crisis?"

"From A to B. And you sit there eating your dinner."

"Didn't you just eat yours?"

"But I was worrying. You don't even care."

"Actually I'm worried as hell. I don't think I've ever lived in a B town. What's it like?"

"We'll soon find out. So—" She leaned back, folded her arms under the twin objects of his admiration, and said: "Laurel Street?"

"One-twenty-eight Laurel," he said with relief.

The address was about ten blocks away.

"Anybody we know?" she asked.

"I didn't know him."

She asked: "Have you ever tried to talk with a man who says as little as you do? It's so stimulating. So, Steven, a murder of a white man or black?"

"White," he said taking another forkful of spuds and sausage covered with gravy.

"Old, young, middle-aged?"

"Pretty old."

"White hair," she speculated, "skinny, little pot belly, blotched hands and bleary eyes, robbed of a pittance and killed for no reason."

"You should be on the case," said Steven.

"You know," she continued without irony, "I don't think I want to know his name."

"Fine with me," he said. "How's Jill?"

"Fine, fine, getting psyched up about the game."

"Did you hear from Bob?"

Robert, their older son, the college student, sometimes called his mother and even stopped at City Hall to talk with her.

"Not today," said Nora. "OK, tell me his name."

Said Steven: "Carden, Charles Carden."

She went perfectly still and looked burningly at him, and her eyes filled with tears. From the way she looked, he might have been the murderer himself.

The theory of devils got support from what happened next. Her whole body jerked and shivered and a sob burst from her throat. Her face, before she could cover it, turned crimson and collapsed in grief. Another sob broke from her—and she uncovered her face and looked fire at him. Her body leapt as if struck by a lash, and it was then he thought that devils are said to inhabit the bodies of their victims. She buried her face again, her hair falling forward and covering her fingers, and she wept with a soft convulsive stream-like sound.

McCord got up quickly saying, "Nora, I'm sorry, I'm sorry."

Nora heard the scrape of his chair, and her own sobbing. And this sudden storm was a surprise, which she thought she must be able to control, but it overwhelmed her, took her exactly as if it were a devil and squeezed the sobs out of her even as she felt Steven take her shoulders in his hands to steady her. She heard his words of comfort and presently she felt and heard his whispering near her ear. The sound was so close it had a pleasant sharpness to it, like the sound of water falling on a stone. But some irresistible power shook her gasping body. She groped for his hand and kissed it and pressed it to her cheek, but she couldn't stop sobbing.

Steven lifted the hair from her forehead—she felt that—his fingertips brushing her brow. How strange that a single click of knowledge, of a man she had known only in her capacity of city employee, should loose these convulsions in her. She kissed Steven's hand and consciously stopped rocking back and forth, holding herself motionless, still pressing his hand to her face— trying to breathe slowly and deeply, missing an occasional breath for a new sob, but she was gaining on it. She tried, she forced herself to a new rhythm of breathing, and then she saw that Steven was kneeling by her chair and looking up with his patient, sympathetic blue eyes, waiting. Seeing him she thought: "God bless this man."

She took a handful of his hair and pushed his head from side to side, and said, "Get up, you big palooka, I'll be all right."

In the bathroom she rinsed her face, held her cupped hands full of cool water against her eyes, and saw the old gent, overdressed in his museum clothes, crossing the lobby at City Hall with quick jerky steps that conquered arthritis and space at the same time, his briefcase in one hand and a bunch of papers clutched against his chest with the other. He was looking anxiously at the numbers over the elevator doors. She rinsed her face again and drank to cool her throat.

"I've talked to him hundreds of times; we were friends, in a way," she told Steven. Her throat closed, stopping her voice. She opened the Frigidaire and took out a container of ice cream and held it up, with a question. He declined, looking into her eyes with concern. She ate the soothing ice cream, and though her face was calm he thought he saw a wild shine in her eyes. Her cheeks were bright red.

She told him that Charles Carden had been the voice of the voiceless in City Hall. He came nearly every day to the committee meetings from which by law he could not be excluded. Few aldermen would grant him an individual meeting, and these few had dwindled in recent years to one or two.

She told Steven that one day Mr. Carden unwrapped a bundle of newspaper at a Public Works meeting, revealing a broken Coke bottle. He allowed a silence to draw itself out before asking: "Do your children play in broken glass? The children on the West Side do."

The ice cream cooled her throat. She ate slowly, speaking of Charles Carden. She said he had organized a neighborhood association to oppose the destruction of houses for a freeway corridor, to promote clean alleys and repavement, to require the trash crews to give quality service in poor neighborhoods. The freeway had been built anyway, splitting the neighborhood in two.

"I spoke with him only last week," she said. Her spoon was suspended; she seemed to be looking into the past. Then she smiled at Steven and helped herself to another spoonful of ice cream.

That night after Nora closed her book and turned off her lamp Steven got out of bed, closed the door, stripped and joined her. He began to unbutton her nightgown at the throat. In the dim light from outside he could see that her eyes were open.

Whether moonlight or street light, light reached her eyes, which also possessed a light of their own.

He took her warm breast in his hand, kissed her cheek, kissed her breast and looked at her face, not with any guilty purpose, just to see this lovely face, perhaps to experience the quiet joy of seeing her eyes close, as a sign of acceptance.

Nora's eyes did not close. Tears filled them and spread their light, and sent it spilling over the lids, and down to her temples in broad lines of silver.

He thought: "She cares more than I do. Well, sure—she hasn't seen a hundred murders. But—she cares, and I don't." He removed his hand, as a trespasser. He knew that a hundred or a thousand murders were no excuse.

The Enemy of the Good

Lindy Alden felt an agreeable sensation forming around this Steven Mc-Something. She liked his ballsy request that she stand still and let him stare at her. And she admired his quick retreat before she could even think of closing the door on him. Obviously he wanted what he wanted, and Lindy Alden admitted that, knowing him better, she might very well want it too.

Pausing at the mirror in the front hall she glanced at what she called her "gifts." She was a realist about her looks, the good and the not so good. Since the age of twelve she had known that boys and men gaped, whispered, laughed, whistled—and a few begged—because of this body. The one thing they apparently could not do was ignore it. Too bad about the face, though.

As she entered her bedroom to dress for the evening she caught her mind playing a trick. She was thinking of Steven McSomething's eyes. She christened him Warm Eyes. The trick, if that's what it was, consisted in just this concentration on his eyes. She had zero awareness of his body—except for an impression filed away for later contemplation. But the message of his eyes stirred her in the depths of her own—body—and it happened that she had just at that moment taken off her robe. She was looking at the dress, panties, bra and half-slip she had laid out on the bed before her shower—at the shoes on the floor—

So it was almost as if she felt his eyes challenging her as she stood naked beside her bed.

But this "trick" was not as pleasant as it might have been. The eyes, the desire, the suggestion of masculine potency—all came from a married man.

And she had resolved after her divorce from Harry Kalzyn not to trifle with married men or allow them to trifle with her.

Lindy had been a popular girl in high school, so popular she found herself pregnant three months before graduation. But in this whole career no boy had ever called her beautiful. By that word they seemed to mean lovely in the face, the eyes, the complexion, the smile. And she knew instinctively that it was not beauty that drew Warm Eyes to her door.

She had a gift of which she was unaware, the changeability and mobility of her features. All she knew was that her figure made them dizzy; but the dizziest fool turned out to be the girl who let this terrific body run away with her. Her mother, who had never offered any instruction whatever on sex, was shocked when Lindy, aged seventeen, told her the happy news. She insisted she marry the boy, gangly Joe Rutherford whose face was still pimpled, and Joe was more or less willing, since to him marriage meant only one thing—total access to her body.

It was this more or less accidental coupling that brought her her son Edward; and Edward was the reason she had called her second ex-husband, Dr. Harry Kalzyn, and asked him to meet her this evening.

The dress she had chosen for the meeting with Harry was still spread on the bed. It was a pale gray with maroon pinstripes, suggesting a man's business suit, and it was the same dress she'd been wearing when Warm Eyes picked her out of the crowd.

Putting this back in the closet she chose instead a one-piece belted wool dress in blue that Harry always spoke of as if it were a living animal. He called it her breathing dress. Why dress to please Harry? He already knew her body better than she did, and this meeting was strictly business. She intended to make it short, one drink, two at the most. Then she'd come home and throw together a dinner, watch the news on television and go to bed early. She had been sleeping irregularly and kept seeing incisions, swellings, discolorations—all the exterior signs—in her sleep, or just before sleep while she passed through the twilight zone. Occasionally she heard the cries of the sufferers, especially one particular girl who'd been wheeled into the ward two days ago—a redheaded child-woman of sixteen—with no luck and less courage than she needed. A career in nursing had taught Lindy that you need one or the other.

So Lindy was short of sleep and she looked forward to the relief of slipping into bed with a book, reading for half an hour, then surrendering to oblivion.

Her body craved oblivion but something else besides, oblivion's opposite. Dr. Harry Kalzyn would of course be eager to offer it. But she would resort to the solitary solution, actually no solution at all, before she'd let herself be entangled again with Harry. Get tonight's business done; drive one more nail into the coffin of their marriage.

"I love you, Harry, but we are divorced. I do not love you in a marrying way and certainly not a remarrying way." She had her lines memorized. Her message was: "Edward is my son, not ours."

There was one person in the world to whom she could cry out that she was lonely—and that person was Harry. But if she said it to him he'd misinterpret it. So in fact there was nobody. "I am lonely. I want—I want!" She couldn't quite say it. Warm Eyes, however, either knew it was true or hoped it was. How could he know? Was it so obvious?

Dressed in her warm coat, hat and gloves, trotting down the stairs, she thought Warm Eyes might be a stalker so she paused on the landing and peered down the second-floor hallway. She scanned the ground floor too, and the dark place outside between the bushes and the wall. It would be a pity if such an appealing man were a sex maniac.

The night had turned cold and she ran to her car, fumbling with her gloved fingers till she separated the right key from the bunch, and jumped in. If she had dangled her legs in ice water they couldn't have been colder. "Why didn't I wear sensible clothes?" she asked herself. Of course the drop in temperature took her by surprise, but—she admitted it, she had dressed sexy for Harry.

She shivered, started the engine and set off for the southern suburbs, saying: "Harry, I respect you and I am grateful. Now please quit talking. You always talk when you're desperate but you can't make somebody love you by talking."

Entering the Oak Knoll Grille she saw him immediately, leaning sideways out of a booth. He thrust his feet out and walked toward her with a huge smile. He kissed her without overdoing it—but while helping her with her coat he let his hands linger gently on her shoulders, and she was glad she couldn't see the spaniel look on his face. Still, she had a catch in her throat when she turned and smiled up at him while he was saying, "Lindy, I am so happy to see you." She said she was glad too, which was true. In her mind she said a little desperately: "We are divorced. I divorced him. I was right. I'd do it again." But maybe only after some pretty deep thinking about the future. She'd been focused on the past.

They sat in the high-backed booth facing one another across the table and she found, as she did every time, that he was actually very handsome— an energetic, sincere-looking, excellent—human being. And the question zinged through her brain for the ten-thousandth time: "Why did I leave this man?"

Leaning forward, taking both her hands, Harry started right off. It was her meeting, she had called him, but he took the mike, as she knew he would.

He was saying—bobbing their hands up and down in rhythm with his sentences: "I saw Jake yesterday and he's very encouraging. He says there's every chance I'll be fully capable if we're just patient and if we keep trying."

"Not we, Harry, you," she said. You had to be quick with Harry.

Jake was his urologist. They had been classmates in med school and roommates during residency. When Harry said "fully capable" he meant capable of pleasing her.

Harry shook his head and squeezed her hands. He said: "I wonder if we haven't placed too much emphasis on mere sex. Don't you ever wonder that? We've had all this time to identify the real problem, and it occurs to me that we had an adolescent view of it, that a marriage can't endure without a kind of Olympic Games of Sex."

He released her hands and leaned against the backboard and smiled. His smile had a blazing, surprised quality as if he'd discovered this striking new possibility and would wait for her to catch up.

A waitress showed up and Harry asked: "Do you have Wasa crackers? OK, let's have Wasa crackers, Brie, white wine for the lady and a double scotch and soda for me, and ice water please."

Harry then turned to Lindy and said: "Not that a woman in your position has to accept impotence. I am not impotent. I have some prostate difficulties like half the men in the world and I'll be fine, that's all.".

"Harry, you are making too much of sex."

"Exactly my point."

"No. Your point is that I made too much of it. Now you are. You were wrong about me and you still are. And wrong about age. I never thought you were too old for me."

"I am not an old man, Lindy, not by a long shot."

"It's not your age. It never was."

"Oh but I think that was part of your grievance."

"What, that we liked different music?"

"Your generation does not know what music is. But no, I was saying that you saw certain effects of my condition and you ascribed them to my age and concluded I was a goner, while you were still a young healthy woman, which you are, but I think your flaw is you sometimes want too much of the wrong things."

"I'm sure I do, Harry, but a young stud is not one of them."

"I never said that."

"Harry, can we talk about something else?"

"There's a great variety of ways for people who love each other to express their love physically," he rattled on. "Leave it to one side that physical acts are only one means of self-expression, that love is told in many languages, and the chief among these is what we call empathy, sympathy, understanding, forbearance, generosity of spirit."

"And I have none of those."

"Oh no! You have them all in abundance, Tulip, but when my troubles came you focused all your attention, which came to mean all your dissatisfaction, on one secondary aspect of our marriage, S.E.X. You're a modern woman and we live in a culture drenched with sex and self-forgiveness, everybody needs six or seven orgasms a week that blow their minds. If you don't die in your orgasm you're not living."

"You're saying I was, I don't know, abnormal," Lindy protested. "You're making me mad!"

"You left me when we ran into trouble." Having said this somewhat sharply he came to a dead stop and stared a hard, glaring, demanding stare at her.

Lindy said: "It was all falling apart for lots of reasons and I admit sex was one, even before your operation as you seem to forget, but there were others that I tried to tell you about and you, actually, you never really listened. You kept insisting you'd get better, and maybe you will with your next woman."

"You are my next woman. I haven't been with any woman since you left me."

"Maybe you should find one."

"Oh—I should? Does that mean you—I mean, obviously you've got another man. Do you?"

"That's not your business."

"I hope he's not married. The city's crawling with married men looking for something on the side."

"Harry, listen. I called so we could talk about something. Can we do that now?"

"Depends what it is, Tulip. We already covered the important topics, A, I am not impotent and B, I am not nearly as old as you seem to think. And C, new subject, you have destroyed the good to go off searching for the perfect. Did you ever read any Greek philosophy?"

"Sure, volumes and volumes."

"Well some Greek said you shouldn't let the perfect become the enemy of the good. See the point? This life is a vale of tears, suffering, chaos and want, loss and grief, with a few good things to be treasured, not tossed into the trash can. Our marriage was good. I never was much of a gymnast, but look at what you get—a really fine house, a good car, leisure if you want it, freedom, you don't really have to work at all but I don't object if you do."

"Thanks."

"Ah, she's so dry. And then there's Edward."

"That's why I called you, Harry. Here's what you've got to do: stop sending money to Edward. He is my son and I don't want you to spoil him with tons of money."

"Hey, college kids need money. Computers, stereos, plane rides in the spring to ogle the ladies cavorting on the beaches of Florida."

"Harry, stop it. Do not send him another dime."

"Why ever not? He's my stepson, since you asked me to quit calling him my son."

"He's not either one."

"God, so dogmatic. Maybe we should ask the man himself."

"What—if you're his stepfather?"

"No—yes. If he wants the money."

"He does want it and that's why you've got to quit sending it. How much are you giving him?"

"Oh God, let me see, maybe, uhh, two hundred a month."

"That's criminal."

"Criminal!"

"You're trying to bribe him."

"Well, bribe, I mean—" He brightened up with a new idea. "You're pay-ing, I mean after the scholarship money, you're paying tuition and room and board, right? Out of your rather modest means. You wouldn't let me pay the whole freight although I begged to do it on my knees more or less, so—are you bribing him too?"

"I'm his mother."

"And for several years I was the closest thing he had to a father, if you please, Miss Tulip, and it is not *criminal* for a father or even a stepfather or an ex-stepfather to help a kid through college."

"OK," said Lindy, "so you agree to quit sending the money."

"I what?"

"I'm glad we cleared that up. You and I are divorced, which you don't seem to have noticed, and Edward is my son, and I don't fucking want—"

"Such language!"

"—want you to give him a penny of your money. So stop. Just stop, damn you."

"Because you say so."

"Because you're spoiling him! I'm responsible for his upbringing and I—"

"You're as old-fashioned as Herbert Hoover's Aunt Minnie."

"So what? I'm his mother."

"I already knew that and now I also know that so far as you're concerned I'm nobody. I have no connection whatever to Edward, and if I want to help him in some useful and harmless way I have no right."

"If it was harmless I wouldn't care."

"Because I'm nobody. Can't pay his tuition or send him to France for the summer, no, he's got to get a job here in town at McDonald's where he'll earn pennies and waste his time—and can't send him to Middlebury for the summer language program because he'll learn more making change at McDonald's because you are the mommy and I am birdshit."

"Next item," Lindy said grimly. She had long since pulled her hands out of Harry's grasp. "I have not returned your flowers because I was touched, and I thank you, but—"

"You're welcome, finally."

"—but stop, please, stop sending flowers on my birthday and our anniversary. I love flowers, Harry, and I really—"

"I know you do. I know you quite well, Tulip. I will continue to send flowers because you appreciate beauty, flowers to my once and future wife, the girl I love."

"Stop, stop, stop. Can't you see it's over?"

"Can't you see it can never be over? I do not harass you, I do not stalk you or telephone you or follow you around the corridors at the hospital, but I love you, you are the loveliest most finely formed woman I have ever seen."

He was grasping for her hands and she let him catch one, and it was a happy hand once caught.

"And I will always love you, and I know the depth of your sexual hunger, Tulip, and if you're sleeping with a married man you are making a terrible mistake."

"What makes you think I am?"

"As I said, I know you. The depths and all that."

"Harry, Sweetheart, if I were it'd be none of your beeswax."

"OK, see? In saying that, you more or less confirm my suspicions which are based on intimate knowledge. Call it a jealous obsession, who cares? Are you?"

"Harry, stop this."

"I take it as a fact that you are needy. That fact reinforces my belief that you are going through a period of disorientation and bewilderment after our divorce."

She would have said he was right but he was running on, saying:

"I ask you, since you tell me you made a stupid mistake marrying your first husband, and later claimed I was a mistake too, why in God's name go around sleeping with married men who treat you as an object? You know they always do one of two things, they go back to wifey or dump wife and mistress both, and find a new woman. The mistress serves to detach their emotions from the wife, that's her role, not a starring one. So they marry a brand new woman and the mistress is left howling alone. Did you hear, alone?"

Lindy did not bother to contradict him. She took his other hand and drew his hands close, leaned far forward and looked beseechingly into his eyes. She didn't want to speak, didn't believe speech was necessary. She held his eyes in her gaze so long that he said, in a voice that was a little shaky:

"Do you remember, Tulip, you once looked at me like this and said, 'Harry, my Harry, true doctor of my spirit, all I want is to look into your eyes this way.' Do you remember?"

"Yes," Lindy said with difficulty.

"And you said, 'Doctor of my spirit, lover of my body, teacher of my mind, what are we trying to say when we look at one another this way?' And I said I knew, but it was knowledge beyond the kingdom of words, that words were like little tin soldiers marching in a cardboard castle, they maneuver, form and re-form, march and countermarch, but they are in the end only words. For all the rest, Tulip, we have music, we have our eyes, we have our bodies, we have our companionship and we have our son. I said all that. Do you re-member?"

"Yes," she said kissing his hands and allowing him to raise and kiss her own, which he did with a familiar warmth that touched her.

Tears were rising to her eyes and he saw them. But now she saw him moving in for a kiss. She drew back, and saw his pain. Her throat closed on itself and she fought to suppress a sob.

The waitress brought their order and they didn't speak for a while. Lindy sipped her wine and it tasted astringent. Harry took half his scotch and soda in one pull, then began building cheese sandwiches. He offered her one and she shook her head.

Lindy said: "Harry, you have never in all our arguments about our marriage, never mentioned what you have done for me and for Edward. You have never taken credit."

He stopped chewing and looked off to the side. His eyes, deep brown and slightly bulging, turned to her, then he turned his head toward her as well, so now he faced her directly and with his whole presence. She felt the force of his generosity and her shame that it wasn't enough.

"You transformed our lives," Lindy said. "Our life together was actually pretty grim before I met you. I know what a difference you have made for both of us and I'm grateful."

"Right," he said with a crack in his voice. "My wife and son."

"You didn't buy my love. It was pure generosity and I love you for it."

"And you didn't give yourself," Harry said, "as a way of buying my help. Did you?"

"I accepted your help for myself and for Edward."

"But you're not saying—are you—?"

"No, Harry dearest, I'm not saying what you think. Only that when you proposed to me and said, 'Let me be a father to Edward,' I—"

"And a husband to you."

"Yes. I did see the advantages, Harry."

"That's OK!" he said with a sudden burst of energy. "That's perfectly OK. I saw the advantages too. Why would anybody get married if they—I mean, should a man go out and find the ugliest most selfish woman in town and marry her precisely to get nothing he wants in return? Ha! Jesus! Marrying you I married youth and hope and beauty and joy and honesty, you name it. Of course! I took all that into my arms. Advantages, for God's sake."

"You are a generous and trustworthy man, Harry. Nobody has better cause to know it than I do."

"But gratitude and respect and so forth are not love. Right? Is that what you're trying to say? Paying your way through nursing school, giving Edward every advantage a kid could have, that's not like money that you buy somebody with. Love that's for sale is a whore's love, right? If I thought I could buy you with all that I'd be calling you a whore, wouldn't I. So if I did it, what little I did, like, say, sending Edward to camp to learn to swim and sail and ride a horse, if I say to myself, 'Now she'll love me, now we'll be together for the rest of my life,' you'd call that criminal, right?"

"Wait," Lindy said with sudden worry. "I said 'criminal' in a different way. I didn't mean—"

"You meant I was trying to bribe him, you used that very word, so I suspect you must think if I paid your way through your RN and your MSN I was buying you, your love or at least your body. I mean, Christ Almighty, isn't that what you think?"

"You know it isn't. I was angry about the money which I have repeatedly begged you to quit, and I slipped and said something I didn't mean."

"If you say it, how am I supposed to know you don't mean it? Are you sure you're not saying exactly that? You can't love me anymore because you let me turn you into a whore and now that I've got this handicap you're sorry."

Her legs were weak and she was confined by the table. She slid awkwardly to the open end of the bench and stood over him in the aisle.

Bending down and speaking in a whisper so as not to be overheard by the people all around Lindy said to Harry: "I am not a whore, and you are not the kind of man who would buy a woman. Please. No more flowers for me and no more money for my son."

"And why did you divorce me?" Harry whispered with bitter vehemence. "That's what you've never explained."

She started away. But she realized she was forgetting her coat. And she had to answer. Returning she bent down to him again, and in the face of his terrible pain she whispered:

"You give me what I don't need. What I need, you can't give me."

She kissed his forehead and walked toward the door. As if fearing a distraction she aimed deliberately for the brass bar, but her vision blurred as the tears flooded her eyes.

CHAPTER 5

The Body Beautiful

A fter seeing his wife's tears Steven McCord could not think of Charles Carden's death as a Common Ordinary Murder. And since he thought that Sergeant Reitz had bestowed too little attention on the old man's journal he decided to look into it.

When he woke up at three in the morning, as he almost always did, he took the book downstairs and turned on the lamp in the corner of the living room where he had set up his study table. He had no hope of falling asleep for an hour or more. He began to read. The hour passed quickly, and his reading vindicated Sergeant Reitz. Most of the entries dated from the 1940s; the recent ones, mid-1980s, tended to reiterate the writer's favorite dictum that he must struggle against chaos. McCord decided that when Tim Sloan came to get his signature in the morning he'd sign a chain-of-custody affidavit and give the book back. The old man had written some striking sentences, especially about his war experience, but nothing that would help a detective.

But when Tim came to McCord's office McCord found himself signing for the book, formally taking custody of it, and slipping it into the accordion-bottomed briefcase that stood by his desk.

Tim asked if he'd started reading and he said he had.

"Anything in it?" Tim asked.

"Not so far," said McCord. "Philosophy, religion and death. He had one or two fixed ideas toward the end."

"Yeah?" said Tim.

"He said he didn't understand why his wife had to die."

Tim made no comment but seemed to wait for an explanation.

"He knew she had suffered and was dead—he said he knew it—but couldn't accept it. He said he wanted to ask his daughter if she thought he was crazy, because sometimes he'd say to himself, 'She can't be dead.' "

McCord tilted his chair and planted his feet on a pile of papers in the middle of his desk.

Tim asked: "Has the coroner located the daughter, or any relatives?"

"Not yet," McCord said, thinking: "I accept death as the primary fact. I look at the old coot's body and say, 'That guy is dead.' " To Tim he said: "You know my concern. All I want is a good aggressive investigation."

"Yes sir."

"I'm sure Sergeant Reitz'll give us just that."

"Yes sir," said Tim Sloan.

"It's not like I'm playing detective. I still want everybody Downtown to think I'm an easy guy to get along with."

"Right," said Tim in the same flat tone.

"But, Tim, you know Mrs. Nora McCord. That woman is a human being. Turns out she was a friend of Old Man Carden. I happened to mention last night that we had ourselves a COM on Laurel Street, Mr. Charles Carden, and if you could have seen her face—

"She's not a woman that skims along the surface of life, and this old guy meant something to her. He used to come to her when she was clerk of Public Works and she'd give him plans and maps and so forth, and they'd talk about I don't know what—life.

"He was a do-gooder, Tim, and there's nobody Nora likes better. She's got to believe do-gooders actually do some good, you know?"

"Sure."

"I mean maybe they do. Life is so fucking complicated. I can see how it'd be possible, barely, that an old coot like him might make a difference somehow."

"Yeah. Sir."

"And if he didn't, you know, so what? He lived his life. I mean, a lawyer, he could have joined the criminal defense bar and sprung drug dealers and bargained murderers down to a traffic violation. You know that, Tim. The worse you behave in that racket the richer you get."

"Absolutely."

"Anyway she knew him and cared about him. And you know, since he was always raising hell at City Hall and was a lawyer and so forth, maybe this isn't a COM after all. See what I'm sayin?"

McCord stopped and after several seconds Tim Sloan said, "I see."

"It's still the Bureau's case," McCord reiterated as if hoping for corroboration.

"Yeah, Reitz's case."

"It is my district. Your old district."

"Nora's district," said Tim. "Ha ha ha."

"More or less. Pop! I had an idea once," said McCord with new energy. "It came by pure accident. Is your brain like that? All the best things happen by accident? I saw this whole Sixth District as if I didn't know anything about it, not the streets, the rogues, whores, the businesses, nothing, not where the boot joints are, where to get a hamburger at two in the morning. Didn't know if the people were black or white. I knew one fact, that inside this district people kill each other. There are people in here with nothing better to do than rip some old man's throat for maybe ten dollars and a ballpoint pen. While I was thinking this way I came up with a name for the place. Murderville. Did you ever think like that?"

"Not per se," said Tim. He spoke in the tones McCord liked to hear. Tim was steady on his wheels.

Waving a memo McCord announced: "We got a witness. Some Tyrone visiting his grandmother on Laurel Street the night of the murder, he saw a cab slow down, saw the brake lights come on."

Tim Sloan asked: "What cab company? Did he say?"

McCord scanned the memo, which reported the results of the second canvass of the neighborhood ordered by McCord on Day 1. He read aloud: "Green. That'd be a Cliff cab, right?"

"Yeah."

McCord buzzed down the page and said: "Tyrone Halyard, black male, DOB eleven eleven sixty-one, address Seven Thirty-Three Highplain Avenue. Know the house?"

Tim said he didn't.

"Do you know, Tim, did Sergeant Reitz interview this Halyard?"

"I can find out. I'm going Downtown," Tim volunteered.

"Could you?"

"Sure, sir. Get back to you."

"Thanks, Tim."

Alone in his office, McCord pulled out the geezer's journal and flipped a few pages. He stopped, laughed aloud, and decided this was too good to pass up. He telephoned his wife at City Hall.

"Since you hate lawyers so much," he began.

"Wait!" Nora interjected. "I'm happily married to a man who's studying to be a lawyer."

"And you disapprove. You'd rather be a cop's wife."

"I never said that."

"Of course you didn't."

"I am glad you called," she said. "Your voice can clear up the air in my head."

"Anybody calls you an air-head, O'Leary, I knock his teeth out his asshole."

"Ah, my hero. But I never said I disapproved of the lawyer idea."

"OK. Why's your head in a fog anyway?"

"It's the City Hall effect."

"Yeah but how's our bond rating today?"

"Like everything else," Nora replied, "barely holding on."

"Anyhow, the reason I called, you'll like this. Quote: June Fifteenth, Eighty-two. Are you with me?"

"Not at all."

"This is from Charles Carden's diary. Can you take it?"

"Certainly. You're reading his diary?"

"His journal, his thoughts over the years. Quote: Newspapers reporting the distilled wisdom of graduation speakers all over this tortured country. None of the orators however is delivering the real message of law school today. Which is: Listen, kids, you've got your training, get out there and wreck society. End of quote."

"Ha!" she cried. "How I loved that man."

"Don't forget he was a lawyer himself," said Steven.

"I've never opposed you on this and I don't oppose you now," she insisted.

"Opposed, no," Steven agreed. "Supported, also no."

Nora took that up. "I've only observed that the hardest challenge lawyers face, since you claim you enjoy a challenge, is justifying what they do."

"Some lawyers anyway," Steven corrected her. "Everything else is easy after that."

"Sorry, but I think that's often the case. There are lawyers on the good side too, but I suspect—"

"That'll be me, defending the innocent and indigent."

"You could do that where you are right now. I always thought a cop was supposed to protect the weak from the strong."

"Sure, that's the whole point. Be a hero. I actually know one or two heroes myself."

"And I know one too."

"Tim."

"That makes two," she said.

"Naaaah."

"But I don't think you're studying law to be a saint."

"I am not. I've got a better idea, you and me on the beach at Waikiki."

"I think you want more than a vacation. I think you've decided the crusade is over."

"Is there anything wrong," he asked cautiously, "with going forward? With taking the next step?"

"If you put it like that," Nora conceded, "no, of course not, but step toward what?"

"I'll tell you when I know," said Steven. "OK, new subject. Are we going to the basketball game?"

"Just a minute, Steven. I am very glad you called, in case you think otherwise." She sounded defiant.

"I'm glad too," he said. "If you think I'm a quitter I might as well know it."

"Please, Steven, don't."

"Don't what, read between the lines? Isn't that where you put the meaning?"

"You know, Lieutenant, it isn't just the lawyer thing."

"Then what else is it?"

Nora said in a different voice: "I don't know, Steven," and by putting his name at the end of that disavowal she sent a little tremor through his guts.

He thought maybe she suspected what wasn't true, not yet anyway, and he saw the face and the queer smile of Lindy Alden.

"OK, enough," he said. "Are we going to the game or not?"

"Of course we are. What a question."

He hung up, and some hidden voice spoke from the shadows: "Lie to her and you won't get away with it."

And Lindy Alden stood before him, in her green silk robe, under a dim light, blocking him, not quite smiling.

Turning another page McCord came on this: "I try to dodge and deny but sometimes it hits me on the head—that I am wasting my life."

Thinking how Nora would react to this, McCord smiled and marked the page.

He put on his coat and went to see Sergeant Hughes and said: "I'll be gone for an hour, Pop."

"Goin to school, eh?"

"No sir. I had a brain wave. I think I'll interview a witness in the Carden case."

Sergeant Hughes leaned so far back in his chair that he seemed to be look-ing down on McCord. "Did you ever hear of the Detective Bureau?" he asked.

"I'll write a memo for Reitz and call it 'supplemental activity.' He's a good bureaucrat. He'll appreciate that."

"Oh sure. He really enjoys people messing in his job. Why don't you just work on that pile of paper on your desk, Stevie?"

"Sorry. Gotta boogie," McCord answered. "Watch the shop."

Most of McCord's District lay in a triangle with its apex pointing toward downtown. The slanting sides were, on one side, the big river, and on the other Jonathan Creek. McCord now drove to Highplain Avenue, which ran beside a levee, and the levee ran beside the creek.

Here the slabs of pavement lay in jagged patterns covered by a thin layer of tarmac. Some of the houses were burned out and boarded up, like corpses with closed eyes. All the houses were on the right; and on the left the levee rose high enough to block McCord's view of Jonathan Creek. Whatever height the street possessed over the water had been concealed by the con-struction of the levee after the big flood of 1913. Highplain now looked pretty low.

Seeing this wretched street he wished the old man had written one more sentence. What do you do after renouncing false hope?

Highplain was the kind of street McCord sometimes walked, especially at night, in order to get a certain jolt. He would walk and look and take it in, and feel a truth coming home to his heart, because in some incomprehensible way it confirmed him. This was a wild guess, but maybe the feeling of some-thing solid in his chest came from entering a zone of danger where he was ca-pable of defending himself. Or else: the sight of deprivation, hardship and struggle told him something he needed to know, or reaffirm. It was his "clar-ity"—the same conviction he had felt while looking into the wrecked room at 128 Laurel—the belief that he was absorbing a harsh but true lesson about the meaning of life. He did not use that phrase derisively.

Locking the gray sedan he walked to the only person in sight, a little boy who was the framework on which someone had draped a collection of rags.

The boy spoke first: "Hi man."

"Hi mister," returned McCord.

The boy held a puppy on a length of clothesline. The puppy sat by his master's knees, regarding him with intense, moist, submissive eyes. He shifted his paws and looked up at McCord, then back to the boy, and yawned with a nervous squeak, straining jaws and neck, and ending with a twist of his head.

McCord, down on his haunches, held out his hand for canine inspection, and talked to the boy.

"How old is he?"

"He six."

"Weeks?"

The boy didn't understand so McCord went on, asking: "Housebroke?"

"No. He plop inside. Mama say she frow him in the crick."

"Hmm. I hope she doesn't."

"She wone," the boy assured him.

"He's a boy, right?"

"Boy name Chollie."

"Hey Chollie," McCord whispered and scratched the dog under his chin, which he lifted for the man's convenience.

"Why do I always forget?" he thought—forget how easy it is to squat and how hard to get up. And: "Am I getting a headache?" McCord's headaches were like the slow insertion of a steel spike into his head through the right eye.

The boy asked: "You d'lanlor?"

"No, I'm a policeman," said McCord scratching the dog and settling in to this lucky meeting.

The boy sat on a crooked curbstone of sparkling gray granite. He wore a pair of old, big leather shoes and had neither gloves nor hat, but didn't seem cold. The sun warmed him as it warmed the fur McCord was stroking.

"Them's plain clothes?"

Said McCord: "They sure are."

Glancing at the unmarked car the boy asked: "You uncover?"

"Yep."

"Well Jimbo say them white-ass po-lice crack yo noggin." He hunched into his clothes, his neck seemed to extend itself from the heap, and he looked at McCord with a look caught between anxiety and hope. McCord was what he called a new man, not an old one, and he looked good. But the boy wasn't sure.

Still stroking the dog, looking into the child's pristine, clear brown eyes, McCord said, "No, the police won't beat you." He decided not to go into the question of good and bad cops.

McCord stood up with little pains shooting through his knees, and a quick, thick throb in his head, right and forward of center. It passed.

He asked the boy's name.

"My name Bill."

McCord gave a cool wave of his hand and said, "I'm Steve. Bye, Bill."

McCord sensed that Tyrone Halyard wasn't happy to see the badge McCord held out for his inspection. He froze, then took a doubtful step toward McCord, drawing the door shut behind him. McCord thought: "He'd rather stand there and shiver than let a cop into his house."

McCord rattled off a phony description—a white male about forty years old, heavy features, six foot four, two hundred thirty pounds, Cincinnati Reds windbreaker—and solemnly asked Halyard whether he'd seen anybody like that on Laurel Street the night he visited his grandmother.

Tyrone Halyard replied that he had passed just such a man on the sidewalk about three blocks from the murder house. McCord's private explanation of this lie was that the man was sucking up to the cops to cover his eagerness in shutting the door. So—one lie. McCord then went over what the man had told the officers doing the canvass, and he repeated that he had seen a green taxi come to a slow stop.

"Saw his brake lights," he said. "Fronna the murder house."

McCord thanked him and went toward his car feeling depressed and somehow bitter. People lied to him all the time, so what did it matter? But it did. His imagination went to work anyway, showing him a green Cliff cab stopping at the house, and the nonvisual part of his mind conjectured that this happened while the murder and robbery were in progress.

"Mr. Po-lice!" the boy called with irony worthy of a man of thirty.

McCord smiled and said, "Hi, Bill. Hey Chollie."

Going to his car he faced the city skyline which rose above the levee like the spiked spine of a prehistoric reptile, from the age when monsters of a more primitive order roamed the earth. His next step was to find a telephone. He drove to the Church's Fried Chicken at Majestic and Galena and parked near a pay phone on a pedestal at the edge of the parking lot. He called Tim Sloan and said,

"Tim, I just interviewed a liar."

"Par for the course," Tim said.

"Yeah but let's take the next step. I am mighty pissed, Tim."

Tim Sloan waited.

Said McCord: "Here's a rogue who lies out of pure contempt for— justice—ha ha!"

"Yeah, justice, ha," Tim responded.

"He fuckin lied for no good reason except he hates the truth, maybe."

"Wow, Lieutenant."

"Sorry. Pay no attention, Tim. OK now let's see if he was lying about the cab. Can you tell me," McCord asked, "did Reitz find the cab driver yet?"

Tim said he'd find out, and he put down the phone.

McCord heard the receiver touch the desk. He heard a car slide, skid, into a space just behind where he was standing. Doors slammed and there was laughing and black gang talk. Turning he saw two men in their twenties among the kids hanging around the parking lot. The sun had sunk down the sky and was bright but cold. The two men kept looking toward McCord. One stared with bold, hostile eyes. Two or three dudes sauntered by his car looking in the windows. There was no police gear visible in the car—except the radio. They meandered close enough to overhear his conversation. Two moved behind him.

"Lieutenant?"

"Yes, Tim."

"I got the file. Reitz interviewed the cab driver last night. "

"OK."

"He took a woman from the airport to One-twenty-eight Laurel."

McCord received this dark knowledge in every nerve. He said to Tim Sloan, "A woman of what age?"—calculating Marie Carden's approximate age.

"Twenty-five or thirty," Tim Sloan continued, "nice looking, light brown or blond hair, white, tan raincoat. You want the rest?"

McCord thought: "I already know the rest." To Tim he said: "What's the driver's name?"

"Basil Samuelson."

"What are his hours of work?"

"Uh—da dadada da—noon to ten P.M."

"Tim, will you do something? Call the cab company and see if the dispatcher can bring him in."

Waiting, McCord turned. The two men were standing ten feet away.

He checked his watch and finally gave up on the idea of lunch. He dug in his coat pocket, found his aspirin bottle and swallowed three aspirin tablets dry—but knew they would have no effect. Wherever his headaches came from, aspirin couldn't go there. If it was coming—and maybe it wasn't—it would come and he'd be in a dark room for two or three days, getting up only to vomit. He stared at the two men and they stared back with hate in their eyes.

Tim came back on the line and said: "He got the driver. He'll be at the garage in fifteen minutes."

"Do you want to meet me?" McCord asked.

"I could," Tim assented.

"I'll see you there."

Next McCord telephoned his secretary for messages, then asked for Sergeant Hughes.

"Nothin, nothin," Hughes reported.

McCord said: "If anybody wants me, say I'm talking to the Neighborhood Priority Board or some bullshit. Beep me if you have to."

Hughes started to protest but McCord overrode him saying:

"Send a crew to Church's at Majestic and Galena. There's a couple of parasites bothering the kids here."

The two parasites dropped their eyes and turned away.

McCord hung up and went close to them and said: "If I were you I'd leave."

The image of the boy with the puppy came into his mind and he thought: "Well how *would* you raise a kid on Highplain?"

He drove across the old bridge over Jonathan Creek, an arch with rusting re-rod exposed in the decaying concrete. This structure spanned the narrow gap between levees. McCord followed a circuitous route through an adjoining District, then crossed a modern straight bridge over the big river. Here the levees were farther apart and the river spread itself over a wide, flat bed.

There was a huge old iron screw and wheel at the levee side, rusted and jammed, a mechanism to admit or release water. He could clearly remember asking his father what this thing was for, and his father's saying the Ohio State football team built their muscles by coming down here once a year to turn the wheel. "Ha! I had a father," he said aloud. He smiled and saw the same image he had seen as a boy, the whole team in shoulder pads and cleats crowding around the wheel. He had loved his father.

He drove south on the "highway" (which in this city meant freeway) to the industrial flats and to the old car barn that Cliff Cabs had taken over from the transit company and remodeled.

Driving, he was thinking: "She arrived before, during or after. If before, why did she leave? Why come from out of town and leave so soon? If during, did she come while they had the old man tied? Was she an accomplice? Accomplices seldom come in taxis. If after, she would have reported the crime. She arrived during." And he added his usual caveat: "I could be wrong."

His car kept moving but his mind halted on a picture: a young woman carrying a suitcase up the steps to the porch and walking on those hollow, resounding boards.

McCord saw the murderer come alert, take off his gloves, turn on the porch light and open the door. McCord's mind wheeled back. He saw the murderer take off his gloves a finger at a time while peering between the curtains, looking at a lone woman with a suitcase. Whether the man smiled, or his eyes blazed with something McCord did not want to name—both possibilities were displayed in the picture. He saw the man pocket his gloves and open the door.

There were new windows set in the old walls of the car barn, and entrances massive enough to receive a trolley car. He drove right in, saw a police cruiser at the end of a rank of cabs, and parked beside it. He walked across a clean cement slab to the office which stood against a wall like a box with windows. He could see Tim inside talking with a man in a gray sweatshirt with "Fairmont Dragons" on the chest, a dragon shooting smoke.

As McCord entered, the Dragon man keyed a microphone and chattered out a string of addresses, stopping now and then to write down a driver's response. Tim Sloan meanwhile handed McCord a folded paper which proved to be a copy of Sergeant Reitz's memo on his interview with Basil Samuelson, the cabbie. McCord retired to an unused desk to study it, and Tim declared to the man in the Dragon shirt:

"I buy started tomatoes."

"Me too," the man replied. "And I buy onion sets. I line'm up on the window sill this time of year or a little later. I ain't done it yet. Got to go to Siebenthaler's."

"Everything else," Tim continued, "I start from seed. Except lettuce and peppers. I'll plant by the middle of March this year, a month from now."

"Well and good, but you could lose it all."

"I never have."

"Frost," the man explained.

McCord folded the memo and put it in his shirt pocket and looked around, thinking of the melting ridges in Carden's garden and feeling a vague unease. He had worked in neighbors' gardens as a boy and still couldn't understand why anybody who could buy vegetables at a store would plant a garden and stoop around in the blazing sun pulling up weeds. The thought of the sun reminded him of his headache, if that's what it was, and he focused his mind on his head to learn if he was in trouble.

In his early teens he had found that when he did this he always felt something akin to sickness or pain which, when he jumped back into the real world, would be forgotten. Discussing this with a doctor friend in his adulthood, he had learned that some people agreed with him, that you always have a headache of greater or lesser severity. The doctor said:

"I had a patient just yesterday who said, 'Well sure, my head aches all the time, but everybody's like that.' And I said to him, 'No! Everybody's not like that!' The guy was stunned."

McCord remembered the all-powerful sun hovering above as he crawled along a row of onions in somebody's garden.

The dispatcher rotated in his chair to take a phone call and then repeated a series of addresses over his transmitter, wrote in his ledger and chanted more addresses.

A man-mountain appeared in the doorway, leaving, however, enough space around his body to admit a flow of engine fumes from the cab bay. The fumes empowered McCord's headache.

The new man had a "Here I am" attitude about him. In his genes he was obviously 90 percent white, but society would identify him as black. He had tightly curled red hair, facial features that suggested Africa, olive skin and brown peck-like freckles even on his lips. He stood tremendous in old blue overalls. One breast pocket was stuffed with a dozen varicolored pens and pencils. He was not shy and he was not in a hurry.

Ignoring Tim, who was in uniform, he said to McCord: "Basil Samuelson, sir," the "sir" signaling distance, not subservience.

McCord stood, endured a piercing pain behind his right eye, and said: "I'm Steve McCord, Mr. Samuelson. Thank you for coming in."

"You are a police officer."

"I am the commanding officer of the Sixth District, sir."

The man's hand and McCord's met, and McCord felt the thickness of it. He could have been gripping the fat end of a ball bat.

McCord said, "This is Officer Sloan."

The light orange eyes of Basil Samuelson shifted without interest to Tim, and the two shook hands.

"Shall we go to your cab?" McCord suggested.

Samuelson turned without a word and led them through the cavern toward a row of cabs near an open doorway, where the light was part fluorescent and part daylight. His walking technique was to set his center in motion and then find a way to keep his legs under the moving mass. This he did with a measured ease, like a dancer, but his fingers wiggled frantically as his hands swung along at his sides.

As if he performed re-enactments every day, and without protesting that he'd already been through this with Reitz—and maybe he hadn't—he opened the trunk and reached in for an imaginary suitcase. He placed it at Tim's feet.

"She tipped me generously and I thought, 'Should I carry her bag up the stairs?' because there are stairs. At first I thought yes I would, then I noticed a second set of stairs to the porch, you know: one set to the yard, the other to the porch. I decided no. I do not strain my heart, Mr. McCord. I cannot afford to do that.

"She must have guessed my thoughts because she said, 'I can manage it,' and I said, 'Thank you, Miss.' I say 'Miss,' not 'Mizz.' I am not some share-cropper from Alabama, Mr. McCord."

"All right. Go on, sir."

"Well, I looked up and down the street for danger as I always do wherever I find myself. I saw nothing and nobody."

"OK."

"Up she went. I could see the suitcase was a burden to her and I almost changed my mind."

"You got back in the car?"

"I stood in the street to see her into the house."

"Describe the house please."

"Describe it? Remember, I saw it in the dark. It was two stories high, big, ordinary. I recall nothing exceptional about it. A typical wooden house of its age and place."

"Were there any lights?"

"Didn't I say that before? There was a light somewhere deep inside, not at a front window at all. There was a porch light."

"Was there a light in the cellar?"

"How should I know?"

"There are cellar windows in front."

"Not visible from where I stood, I shouldn't think. The house is elevated. Are they visible from the street?"

"I don't know," McCord said. "Are you sure there was no light in the cellar?" What he wanted to do was prompt an allusion to the second floor by putting pressure on a lower level. Sometimes that worked, sometimes it didn't.

"I am not sure. I have no knowledge."

"Let's do the lights again. Do you mind?"

"Not at all."

"What lights if any did you see? Pretend this is the first time you've heard the question."

The man entered into the spirit of it, seeming to look up at the house. He said: "Ah. I do remember that I did not see a house number. She said, 'This is it.' I had slowed and she said, 'This is the one.' There was no light from the front windows, just a weak light from deeper inside, as I said. I have nothing to add or subtract from what I said before."

"Wasn't there a light on the second floor?"

"No, sir, I am certain of it." He closed his eyes, lifted his face, and his eyelids trembled.

McCord watched closely.

Basil Samuelson lifted the delicate light-brown lids and looked full into McCord's eyes and said, "No, sir, there were none on the second floor that I could see from the street."

"Please go on. She is carrying her bag up the stairs from the sidewalk to the yard."

"She went up to the porch—she stood there awhile after knocking, I heard the knock—the door opened—she went in. First some words that I couldn't understand, then she went in."

"You heard her voice and how many others?"

"Hers, yes, and one other. A man's, but not a deep bass voice, not like yours, Mr. McCord."

"Did they kiss? Were they happy to see each other?"

"Hmmm, that's not easy. All I can say is, there was a conversation lasting a few seconds, then she went in."

"Did the man take her suitcase?"

"I don't know. You'd think I'd have noticed but I am unable—I can't visualize—she hesitated. That I definitely saw. I expected her to wave to me but she didn't. Maybe she didn't realize I had watched her to the door. There was a silence, she hesitated, then went in."

McCord could see her hesitation and her going in. In his chest or gut, somewhere inside, he could feel her hesitation.

Basil Samuelson turned from the scene on the porch to Steven McCord and said: "The other officer told me nothing and I did not ask. But I would like to know, did this young woman come to any harm?"

McCord said: "There was an old man in the house. It was his light you saw. He was murdered. We know nothing about the woman beyond what you have told us."

Tim Sloan then elicited a detailed description of the woman and her suit-case.

McCord was echoing: "She hesitated." His eyes and those of Basil Samuel-son met.

The man-mountain's eyes were troubled. "I would hate to think . . ." he began.

Bidding him goodbye, thanking him, McCord shook his great thick hand and saw the pocket full of colored pens and pencils, and looked into the man's baffled, worried face.

"We don't know anything about the woman," McCord said, thinking: "We know too much."

Each in his own car, McCord and Tim Sloan drove to 128 Laurel Street where Tim collected the bedding from the upper room and took it Down-town.

In less than two minutes McCord found what he was looking for, a photo-graph. A girl of Jill's age was posing for her school picture. He did not linger over the sight. He did not look closely at her face. He tried so hard to make his eyes brush past her face that he couldn't help seeing her expression. She was unafraid, already fully alive and ready for more. Or else he saw what he was trying not to look for.

Basil Samuelson had only twenty dollars to show for his day's work so far. He had probably missed one or two fares talking to Mr. McCord. He drove to the new hotel downtown but the cab line was too long. Nonetheless he pulled in at the end and idled his engine. He had hoped for a chance to think, to med-itate on the disturbing possibility that he had driven the young woman to a place of danger. What he wanted was to drive to the airport because he could think better while driving on the highway. But it was too far to go empty. As he idled he began to imagine he was breathing fumes from the cab ahead, that his heater was sucking in carbon monoxide, but he couldn't back away because a new arrival sat right on his rear bumper. He tried to smell the fumes, saying to himself: "You cannot try to smell something."

He was restless. He pulled out of the line and drove to Main Street, which he cruised both ways, from the veterans' monument at the river and back to Fifth; then he drove to the bus station where only two cabs waited and joined the line.

Basil Samuelson said to himself: "I should have asked. He would have told me." Should have asked if the murdered man was white. He assumed he was.

Many old white people still lived on Laurel and surrounding streets. And the young woman was white.

At the age of about eight Basil Samuelson had stopped praying for God's intercession in matters already closed. He saw that there was no point in praying that he'd find a letter from his grandfather in the mailbox if the mailman had already completed his rounds. The letter was there or it wasn't. When he grew a little older he resumed praying for what he wanted, so long as he believed it to be worthy, whether the matter was closed or not. If God could put it into his grandfather's head to write a letter, he could arrange for the letter to be in the box regardless of when Basil said his prayer. The important question was worthiness. He ought not to pray to get a hit in a ball game because that was selfish. Was Basil praying for the right things?

There was another factor to be considered. That was God's foreknowledge of all things. God knew Basil would pray before Basil did, so the timing of the prayer was of no importance.

He slipped his engine into gear as the line moved forward. He gave no thought to exhaust fumes. "Please," he prayed, "do not let the murderer be black."

McCord found a phone and called Police Liaison in the Department of Motor Vehicles. He gave Lindy Alden's name and address to a clerk and she told him the make, model and license number of Lindy's car. There was some risk in making this query but he made it anyway.

All he wanted was to see her again. He knew what would happen if he showed up on her doorstep. She'd peek through the spy hole and see a nuisance or a nut. He'd have to retreat, and that would be the end of it.

So he drove to the hospital where she worked and cruised the employee lot till he located her car, and he waited. He guessed she started work at seven-thirty and quit around four-thirty. He parked in a nearby row and waited twenty minutes—and here she came, walking rather slowly as if she were tired, wearing a calf-length coat over green scrubs. The wind was whipping at the skirt of her coat as she opened her purse and took out her keys. She looked across the roof of her car, so McCord saw her in profile—and then she ducked in, and drove away.

He did not follow. He would never do anything to frighten her. But his imagination showed him the routine that would lead to the wet hair and the green silk robe. Then he imagined her preparing dinner, watching the news or going to bed early. And he saw her sleeping. All this was clear as life to him.

An aisle runs through the men's locker room at the YMCA health club, a strip of blue carpet unfurled between rows of gray lockers on either side, leading to a mirror. Sometimes walking the strip lifted McCord's spirit to a false high. Seeing his nearly naked body pass under the lights one after another, and the play of light and shadow on his shoulders, chest and abdomen as he neared the glass—seeing, with an emotion that was almost joy, the muscular planes of his chest and hard hollows on either side of his abdomen—he couldn't tell whether this firm, sculpted body was promise or fulfillment. Did it mean he was so alive he could do anything, or that this was his peak and he'd never do better?

He carried his pager, a metal block like a polished weight to be thrown in an athletic contest; he wore a blue swimming suit designed to cover his butt and enclose his genitals with not a square inch of fabric to spare; and he forgot, during this parade, that flesh is corruptible. This glorious form implied that life itself could be glorious; and the other implication, that this body would someday be riddled with bullets or cancer, was pushed aside and forgotten. So was the headache.

In the shower room he put his pager on a dry bench and immersed himself in a cool metallic drizzle. He saw the paunches and little afterthought buttocks which seemed to have been patched on the middle-aged men standing under the other nozzles. One man, bald, pink, fifty, with a "bad sack" that hung so low you couldn't see his cockandballs, if any, smiled at McCord and said hello. McCord returned the greeting and tried to remember who he was.

He adjusted the water to a cooler temperature and let it hit his face, then turned to play it over his shoulders and back. This ritual completed he retrieved the pager and went into a frigid corridor past windows astream with condensation, his skin burning with cold, and so through a heavy metal door to the natatorium. A sheet of turquoise water extended fifty meters ahead to a diving tower and three boards of various heights. There were few swimmers in the pool but a team was practicing diving at the far end.

McCord whistled and the chamber magnified the sound. The lifeguard, standing across a corner of the pool, turned, gave a sign of recognition and held up his hand. McCord sailed the pager across the water and the man caught it expertly and dropped it into the deep pocket of his jersey. McCord dived and started under water, swimming ten long strokes before breaking the surface and shifting to crawl. He stroked along with a geyser of foam struggling at his feet as his arms knifed rhythmically ahead. His body rolled with every second stroke to free his mouth to take in air. He caught a glimpse of the big chamber each time, then returned his gaze to the blurred green world below and the black lane lines on the bottom. He swam near the right side to avoid the divers when he reached the other end—and having reached it he shoved off the wall backward and began back-crawling down the same lane. His choice of strokes was no accident. Swimming on his back he could watch the divers as he retreated stroke by stroke toward his starting point, and half these divers were of the female sex.

One was said to be training for the Olympics but several were so good McCord couldn't distinguish the Olympic aspirant from her teammates. The girl now poised at the end of the one-meter board stood erect and easy on the balls of her feet, her back to the pool, arms extended straight before her. The lights overhead cast a small shadow below a muscle in her upper arm. He could see her body subtly change its shape with each breath. She stepped back in one easy movement and turned straight down in another, and then she seemed to hesitate in the air—and in a third motion her fully extended body entered the water straight as a sword. While still under the surface she must have tilted her head so that the velocity of her upward stroke, with a gentle influence as deft as the hands of a sculptor, swept her hair back from forehead and temples, toward the slender neck. She emerged to her shoulders and sank gently till the water circled her neck. She looked toward her coach, a young man in a white sweat suit who stood at the pool's edge opposite McCord's lane. With imitative bends and twists of his body he began his booming critique, but McCord himself had no criticism to offer. He stroked away and watched the girl lift herself out of the water, bend to one side and tug at a stretch of material covering one buttock, then bend to the other side. She remounted the ladder for another attempt and McCord regretted the distance his powerful stroke was placing between them.

He wanted to say to Charles Carden, whose journal betrayed an obsession with chaos and an attempt over twenty years to define it: "This is not your 'plain choked with rocks.' This is not chaos."

He watched the girl mount the ladder, pause as she listened to her coach's final comments, and pull herself with strong arms up the last step and advance along the board.

The old man's whole argument, one might say his philosophy, flowed from one idea: "This is not love," where "this" meant his friend Ronski's getting his brains blown out in the battle of Okinawa. "For God so loves the world that he allows one man to blow out another's brains. The god they invented out of their hunger for love is not a loving god." This was more or less what Charles Carden wrote. McCord was swimming crawl and couldn't see the girl's next dive but he could imagine it, which was almost as good. To him her body and her grace implied—if not a loving god—a loving nature.

Completing another circuit he flipped against the wall, twisted his body and shoved off facing upward, reaching back to grab his first stroke away from the divers. A girl was spinning in the air, and entered the water with hands reaching out, back arched and toes pointed neatly upward, to make a splash so unobtrusive it seemed to ignore the laws of physics, if such laws exist. Another young woman sprang aloft from the three-meter board, folded her hands on her stomach and rotated back with her body at full extension, falling fast and rotating slowly, and dropped into the water feet first with a calm smile on her lips.

He was pulling too hard to smile in sympathy—but her smile invoked its opposite in McCord's imagination: he saw the old man in his chair, with his hair standing in the breeze—the electrical cord, the sagging mouth, the neck, the blood.

"There was no breeze," he insisted but the hair waved and stirred. He knew what the old man's body looked like under its clothes, not a taut curve left, tits instead of pectorals, bones instead of biceps.

Charles Carden wrote: "If you reject your religion you are not free. You are in chaos."

"And if you keep it you're a child," McCord replied.

"You are left with pure physics," Carden wrote.

"No sir!" McCord cried. Something more than physics animated these divers.

Another took to the air and her body entered the plane of the water as a narrow beam of light. And when she emerged and stood breathing just a little heavily, her breast rising and her cheeks as red as the stripes on the flag, seeming to think about her dive, or herself, McCord repeated:

"You call that pure physics?" And he asked almost in anger: "Is Lindy pure physics?" He saw her—as if she stood poised on the highest platform, her arms extended toward him—

Then by accident McCord put two things side by side, Charles Carden and himself. "If Carden is nothing, I am nothing," he said.

Then his mind took a wild leap and said: "If I am nothing, Jill is nothing." He saw his daughter's face. He stroked along and said: "Ridiculous!"

This Is My Daughter

McCord was drumming his fingers on the kitchen table, staring blankly, not seeing the geezer's journal lying open before him, thinking instead of the phone call he had made to find out Lindy's license number. While making that call he had sped along under a nervous compulsion; but in reliving it now, hearing again his own voice and the voice of the woman from Motor Vehicles, the sounds poured a chill white fear into his heart. He looked around to establish his presence in this old kitchen. He knew that Jill and Danny were upstairs, that Nora would walk in at any minute and they'd all go to the basketball game—as if nothing had happened.

"Well nothing did happen," he said half-aloud. "Depends what you mean by 'nothing,'" he added. Seeing Lindy walk to her car was not nothing. He could still feel the thrill.

To ground himself he reached for the wall phone and dialed the Detective Bureau. Sergeant Reitz answered his phone for a change and McCord asked without preamble what the airline check had yielded.

The answer was it had only just begun.

"Do you have a name?"

"We're just using the name Carden," said Reitz.

"You could try Marie Carden or Marie anybody. I saw 'Marie' in the old guy's journal."

Sergeant Reitz said he would.

"Do you want me to have some people check the civic clubs and neighborhood groups out here?"

"Check'm for what, sir?"

"Names, friends, acquaintances, enemies, anything."

"Sure. Whatever you like, Lieutenant."

"I've got to remember it's already happened," McCord thought after hanging up. "Nothing is happening to her now. The world does not go backwards."

His fingers were drumming again. The light in the kitchen kept the darkness out, but in doing this service it admitted the idea of winter. It was an antiwinter light and denoted early sunsets, windblown pellets of lead-like rain, and drenching waves of noise when a car went by. His gaze slid across the opaque sheet of darkness at the window. He heard and could not avoid hearing a voice—as if he were standing unseen on the walk at 128 Laurel looking up at the porch. The door opened and a man said: "Oh, your dad asked me over to fix the drain. Come in, come in, he's got the trap apart."

McCord said, "He wouldn't say 'your dad' and he wouldn't say 'trap.' Maybe he's a smooth-talking son of a bitch—smart, quick. He did lure her in." This set McCord off on a search for a more realistic speech.

He heard the timer ticking on the stove. He became aware of the thick and pungent atmosphere of the kitchen, a variety of cooking odors. Jill's dishes made a neat stack at the sink and her radio beat out bass vibrations upstairs, the sounds of the alien teen subculture reaching him through the walls and ceiling. Danny was not to be seen but was probably upstairs too, wasting more of his life. Nora still wasn't home. He was now sure there had been a woman in the house on Laurel Street and that she was Carden's daughter Marie.

He pulled up short like a guy in a Western yanking on the reins. "No, idiot. You have no facts. You don't know anything." He kicked a chair into line and lifted his feet and drank his beer.

The only thing worth getting out of his work was the sensation he called the "clarity." He had the bad habit of congratulating himself on knowing what the world is really like. And when he watched Marie Carden go into that house he captured another piece of the truth.

His eyes went big. "Jesus!" he said and the crime went on before his believing eyes. "Keep your eyes open," he commanded. "If you turn away from this—" But he did not turn. He saw the evil in the light of truth, a sharp and stabbing light.

"It must be good," he said, good, that is, to see the truth. But the truth doesn't just sit there, it glares back.

The table, a span of heavy maple saturated to its molecules with fifteen years of McCord family history—disputes, jibes, laughter, a rare scream— thudded steadily under his drumming fingertips. He drank his beer. He could smell it, taste it and feel its chill flood his mouth. He had left the bourbon under the sink. He was dying to embrace Lindy Alden. He believed that Lindy could change him by what is called giving herself. Staring at the window he raised his beer and took another drink. There was a sheet of outer darkness across the window.

"In chaos nothing has a reason for happening or not happening." He re-read this sentence in the journal. But chaos did admit of one rule, that the done thing is never undone; a cut throat is cut forever. A woman seen walking across an open space in a windswept parking lot, thinking, pausing to gaze over the roof of her car, is seen forever.

Jill came in and set a backpack on the table and reached up her father's pant-leg. She pulled the hair of his calf and McCord said:

"Fie, brat."

"Daddy, it was so gross in biology today."

"You butchered a frog?"

"No, it was awful. Billy Howell was talking to Betsy and me, we were lab partners, and he coughed and pew! He shot out this gigantic blob of dragon slime."

"Beautiful," commented the father.

"He covered it with his hand and screamed, 'Get me a paper towel!' "

"Did you get one?"

"Of course, it was—"

"You let that snot-gobbing Billy Howell order you around?"

"*Daddy*," Jill said in exasperation, "he had to cover it up."

"You could send him and you cover it."

"Brilliant, Dad."

"You know what this makes me think of?"

"Oh no," Jill moaned.

"I can't help myself. Puke-snot-booger-spit."

"You forgot fart, Dad. Fart, wee-wee—"

"I don't use that kind of language in front of my children. Did you get enough protein with your dinner? I mean you'll be playing basketball and—"

"Yes," she sighed with infinite boredom. "Daddy, why do you always ask the same things?"

"Because it's my duty."

"Where's Mother?"

"Saving the city's bond rating. Is Danny coming?"

"*Danny!*" Jill screamed.

There was a muffled response from high up.

Danny entered from the hall and Nora from the back landing at the same time. A hasty conference ensued. They agreed that Nora should be allowed five minutes to change clothes, that they would drive Jill to the gym, where she had to report by six-fifteen; and Steven, Nora and Danny would go to Wendy's for a Big Classic. Steven insisted on this because he had eaten twenty thousand Big Macs during his years on street patrol and would shoot himself before he ate another. The parents and Danny would then return to the gym in time for the opening jump at seven o'clock.

Nora started out and Steven said "Hey!" She bent and kissed him; he grabbed her hand and squeezed, and she swept out of the room, the fringe of her raincoat swirling and her leather briefcase shining. He couldn't help admiring her style, but the swirling coattails reminded him of a different woman.

"Danny," he said, "did you oil your mother's briefcase?"

"Yeah," said Danny.

"That was nice," the father said.

"You *told* me to do it, Dad. Obeying orders isn't *nice*."

"It was still considerate of you, old man, and as the lady's husband I thank you."

Right now there was nothing to do but Danny had a way of just hanging around all the time, of seeming undecided or indifferent or both. He sat and slumped and his feet came out the other side of the table. He was seventeen, three years older than his sister but egregiously last in order of promise among the three children. Bob at age twenty was earning A's in college and was bound for medical school. Jill, aged fourteen going on fifteen, though probably not Bob's equal in that overrated set of endowments that make a superior student, was even better equipped for life than her brother. But the mother was perhaps strongest of all.

Nora McCord had made a good enough record in high school but promptly forgot it, it meant so little to her. She was educated not by college but by her life as a Catholic, by the theology, the rituals and rigor of a demanding religion. She was educated, if that is the word and process, by childbirth and child rearing, and lastly by her political and bureaucratic experience at City Hall. She passed on to her daughter a quick understanding, a ready Irish tongue and a secure confidence on values. Both mother and daughter knew what was important. For Nora the important things were in God's hands. The hand of man was manifestly unsteady. To Jill the supremely important hadn't been revealed in its full actuality but the girl seemed to understand this and to know whence it would come. There was no torment in her soul, McCord believed.

This girl, his daughter, eluded him as she seemed always to elude the lightning. She walked as if down a corridor lined with brass; lightning struck and the brass blazed, and Jill walked right along. She was probably embracing the religion of her mother, in which she was being trained, but her father's calm, vocal rejection of it didn't worry her. If she believed he was heading for hell she didn't show it. He liked this about her.

The reassembled family was leaving when Jill let out a scream and dropped her pack. She alone had noticed that the timer had ceased ticking. Nobody had heard it ring. She opened the oven, peered inside and declared with relief and triumph: "It's OK, gang, just a little extra brown on the edges."

"Did you make a pie?" asked Danny. "I thought I smelled—"

"You do smell."

"That's what I've been smelling," Steven said. "A pie, you peach."

"It's not peach," Jill said cryptically.

Using a towel she carefully removed the bubbling, menacing pie, set it on the counter to cool, and recovered her pack which she swung deftly over her shoulder. The four McCords went out the back door into the darkness, and down the narrow walk to the garage.

Driving down the alley Steven said, "I can still smell it."

"It's Daddy's brain tumor," said Nora.

"Is it apple or apple-cherry?" asked Danny with deep seriousness.

Jill said it was apple. "If we lose," she explained, "I stuff calories. If we win we all celebrate."

"Jeez," Danny lamented, "she'll throw the game and hog the pie for herself."

"I'll be damned," Steven continued, "I was ten feet from an apple pie and I could have eaten the whole thing."

"Dad is a zombie," said Jill. "He doesn't smell it when it's there, and he does when it isn't."

Danny let out one of his repertoire of imbecile sounds, to pull his father's chain.

"What do you really want, Danny? What are you doing after graduation?" If McCord could get through the evening without asking these questions it would be a triumph of willpower.

"Daddy, you don't *have* to," Jill complained but Steven insisted on walking with her from the parking lot to the gym door.

He patted her shoulder and wished her luck and she was gone. As the door swung shut he could hear "Eee! Team! Jill's here. Hey you guys!"

This made him feel strange but good, that she was so eager to enter this world, so natural to her and so alien to him.

"Dad," Danny protested, "my god, do we really have to go to Wendy's, I mean god."

"I'm sick of McDonald's, you know that."

"Yeah but I'm not, Mom's not. Jeez, my god, can't we compromise?"

"No. I'm dad, you're kid."

"Jeez, dorcus."

"What do you mean dorcus?"

"Just—dorcus, dork."

"*Dork* means prick, are you calling me a prick?"

"Dork does not mean prick," said Danny with a scholarly intonation.

"It sure does."

"It did in the stone age maybe, now it means *sucks*."

"You're saying I suck?"

"Steven," Nora interjected, "you are being a dork."

To Danny Steven said, "And what do you think *sucks* means for Christ's sake?"

"Steven, leave it," said Nora. "This whole conversation sucks."

"Whine whine, can't we compromise? I go to McDonald's by myself, you drop me off."

"We're eating together," Steven said. "Bob's gone, Jill's gone, we're eating together."

"My god, Dad, they're not dead."

Steven turned into First Street in the center of his District, only a few blocks from the station, and slowed at McDonald's.

"Atta boy, Dad!"

He pulled into the drive-through, looking aside at Nora, but she turned her face to the window. He knew the smile she was hiding.

He said to Danny: "Don't ever tell your kids your father was a hard man."

"I'm not having kids," Danny said. "They take too much of your time and you have to give up your autonomy, don't you agree?"

"When did he start talking like that?"

For answer Nora said: "I'll take a Quarter Pounder with cheese, small fries and ice water. Don't forget there's a pie at home."

Despite the prospect of a pie Danny ordered a chocolate shake, a Big Mac and double fries. Steven relayed these orders, their car crept along and emerged a few minutes later bound for Wendy's. When Steven had gotten his Big Classic he parked in Wendy's lot and they ate in the car, listening to a Linda Ronstadt tape.

"Gads, she's always whining," Danny whined.

"She sings of loss," said Nora.

"I love it when she sings 'You're No Good,' " Steven declared. Then turning to Nora he proposed: "Quit your job. We could eat real food every night, spuds, vegetables, real meat. Why not quit?"

"Because men today can't be trusted. Some of them are no good."

"Yeah," said Danny. "They're desperadoes."

"That's a different song," Steven said. "Anyway, O'Leary, you can trust me. Twenty years, you know."

"Can I?"

"She values her autonomy, Dad."

"Listen, you know all about autonomy except what it feels like." Steven was yielding to an impulse, regretting it even as he continued: "And you'll find out soon enough."

"Right, but what am I going to do after graduation?"

"I wish I knew," said Steven.

"Me too," said Danny.

Without turning to face Danny, Nora lifted her hand and said softly: "Careful."

There had to be two assailants. One moment he was watching the game, the next he was thinking he'd been wrong about the mess in the upstairs bedroom. *Original thought*: Two could have overpowered her and pinned her down. But she had broken free. Therefore there was only one. Work on the idea of one. *New thought*: One alone could never have forced her up the stairs if she had seen her father. Therefore she had been dragged or carried up by two.

He saw one fallacy and suspected there were others. But as soon as he saw it he realized why it wasn't bothering him. The fallacy was that a single assailant could have compelled her up the stairs with a gun or knife. The reason it didn't bother him was that the evidence of the struggle was also evidence that the threat of gun or knife didn't work on this woman. And now McCord saw why. She had seen her father in the chair. She was beyond the reach of any threat. She went mad with grief and rage.

Now he knew she came to the house after they killed the old man, or that they killed him in her presence. He could now set forth a complete sequence from her knock at the door to the struggle in the bedroom, the seminal idea being that she went mad with grief and rage.

Next he viewed his new scenario skeptically. It contained at least two fantasies, that she was Carden's daughter and that she "went mad." The two of course were related. He didn't know exactly how he had built up the new scenario but it flowed smoothly—like a fantasy, or like reality. But were there two?

Why take her upstairs? This question had been calling for attention for twenty-four hours. Now he opened his mind to it. This was not the same as having the answer but in fact the answer came immediately, in words. "They were planning to stay the night." They wanted to prolong her agony and their pleasure. He paused to examine that strange word "pleasure." They wanted a bed instead of the floor, and they didn't want the old man's company. Maybe they thought they could make her forget him and submit. This idea stunned him.

He tried to remember if there was a couch in the murder room and couldn't.

Jill was bringing the ball up the floor against a full-court defense. It was late in the second quarter and the score was Holy Family Freshmen 22, West High Freshmen 18. Jill and her Holy Family mates were the Chargers, the opponents were the Vikings, although half these particular Vikings were black. There were several black girls on the Charger squad, the children of parents, Catholic or not, who had given up on the public schools and paid a stiff tuition to get their kids an education.

Jill dribbled to midcourt, faked out a defender and passed to a teammate. This girl, wearing like Jill the blue uniform of the Chargers, dribbled toward the key but got tangled up by Viking defenders. She brandished the ball over her head, finally got rid of it, and then the girl who received it got similarly entangled by a tall black girl in the red of the West High Vikings. The Charger forward passed back to Jill near midcourt and, to break the deadlock, Jill tried something foolish. She sprinted down the right side, dribbling far too high, lost the ball to a trim little redheaded guard from the Vikings, and could not catch her as she sprinted downcourt to the Charger basket and scored on a layup. Jill's face and neck turned crimson.

The little arena resounded with the cheers and whistles of the Viking fans, including parents who shrilled out a collective cry of triumph, while Jill, having received the ball from out of bounds, once again dribbled up the floor, casting a series of guarded, reconnoitering glances across the whole floor and down to the key. Nobody opened, and she plainly didn't know what to do. She passed to a girl who was well guarded by a tall opponent. Luckily the Viking player couldn't deflect the pass, the Charger forward caught it, snapped it back to Jill and opened herself to the center, where Jill hit her with a perfect pass as she entered the key. The Charger girl shot and missed. The Vikings got the rebound and the Chargers chased them in a thundering reversal, and succeeded in tying them up as thoroughly as they themselves had been tied up a moment before.

Jill's lips were parted with exertion. Her damp black hair clung to her temples and there was an arc of wet curls around her nape and another above her forehead. There were red splotches on her throat, and her legs were quite pink. He could all but see the blue shining in her eyes, which seemed to be smarting with sweat—yet all seemed clean, healthy and pure.

While the teams were off the court at half-time McCord commented that Jill was playing a hard aggressive game. This simple statement felt forced and insincere. A true statement curdled as if false. That was the effect of one harmless lie. Nora stared at him for a second too long before she smiled. Her large dark eyes under brows as black as Jill's rested, as it were, on his own eyes—and rested longer. He saw that he had entered into a new order in which he would never know whether she suspected him.

The buzzer sounded and the teams issued from separate doors, trotting in single file to the center of the court where they slapped hands, then to their benches, while the arena filled with a waterfall of mixed sound.

Jill's hair looked fluffy and almost dry. She seemed fresh and energetic, and mature. Her figure was almost ready to find a woman's form.

She played the third quarter with amazing stamina and skill. Her father whooped and her mother and brother tramped the bleacher boards. At the end of the quarter the score was tied again and both sides were fighting exhaustion. Jill stole the ball and sprinted clear of all defenders but missed an easy layup at the end of her dash.

Now the clock moved toward zero and the gym resounded with a continuous throbbing of treading feet, shouts, whistles and the blaring of the Chargers' bugle. The Vikings took a four-point lead and then the Chargers closed the deficit to two points. Next they tied the game, with thirty seconds on the clock.

Jill repeatedly moved in to fight for rebounds, leaving her zone undefended and causing her father a keen anxiety. She stole a rebound from a taller girl, passed the ball out of the melee under the basket, then broke clear for one second, long enough to take a leading pass and start a dash toward the center line.

Two Vikings converged on her and somehow all three girls tumbled on the boards with a wild tossing of limbs and bodies and knocks and bangs that could be heard all over the gym. The referees' whistles screamed from the rafters, and then the whole place fell silent. The officials, the two teams and the coaches crowded around the pileup, blocking the view. Then came the usual obscure ministrations to the downed and the injured.

When the two Viking girls got to their feet the crowd applauded. When Jill rose unsteadily it greeted her with a gift of tumultuous glory. Nobody who has ever been cheered like that, at any age, could ever forget.

She limped to the foul line, and silence again closed down on the arena. She was crying like a little girl, her face all distorted with hurt and shock.

The score was tied with the clock stopped at three seconds.

She set and reset her feet; she bounced the ball. She looked up at the basket, and took a deep breath, and gained control of her face. It was set in solemn concentration. She bounced the ball again, and with a little curtsy of her knees she took her shot and missed.

From the crowd there came a mixed reaction of groans and respectful applause. The game went into overtime and the coach took Jill out. The Chargers won in overtime by four points.

When Jill came out dressed in street clothes and carrying her backpack over one shoulder, her wet black hair was combed straight back, parted on one side; her skin was fresh from a shower, her eyes were tired but not unhappy, rather large with a complex emotion.

Half in happiness, half in disappointment, she smiled at her father and let herself be gathered in by his embracing arm. He squeezed her against his chest and kissed her wet hair. It was crisp and cold in the winter air.

"Great game, great game," said Steven. He had yelled himself hoarse and could scarcely speak.

His words were simple, short and inadequate, but he could not say more. He was dumb with love.

Still embracing her, carrying her pack in his free hand, finding some way to walk in step with her, he escorted her to the car.

A few kids crossing under the lights in the parking lot greeted her, and a passing parent complimented her on a hard-fought game. Another asked if she were all right.

"I'm fine, thank you," said Jill.

"She's fine," McCord said.

He couldn't assimilate the idea that she was his daughter, couldn't treat it as a fact of fourteen years' duration. No, it was utterly new and miraculous. "This is my daughter!"

In the car Danny and Nora congratulated her and asked if she were OK, and they speculated on whether the two Vikings had deliberately knocked her down. As McCord put the car into gear Danny said:

"Hey, jeez, like, you know, man—pie?"

A Woman of Consequence

When McCord awoke in the morning the language of confession was running suggestively through his head. "They cut his throat. I didn't feel it."

Since you can't force emotions like sympathy or horror he believed that in one sense he was blameless. But a man who doesn't care that he doesn't care would be a man McCord did not want to be. He wished he could expose this problem to Nora but he knew how she'd respond. Sooner or later she'd fire off what to her was the only important question, "How do you go on without God?"

Then there was Lindy Alden. Was he going to pound on her door and holler, "Hey, I came to confess"—through the wood?—because she certainly wouldn't open up. She'd probably call the cops.

Everything was getting complicated and it was partly because of Lindy's dancing in his brain. When he thought of it that way he realized he was trying to push the blame for his fascination on to her—that she was "dancing"; but he knew where the fault lay.

Probably he was searching for something intellectual to do, so he found himself thinking about the case. "This dingleberry goes to the scene and one of three things happens. He brings something with him which he leaves behind; or he alters something; or he takes something with him." And McCord thought: "He left tire tracks and prints." And McCord formed an image of the wrecked room—of the wreck the killer left behind him—but McCord didn't say "wrecked room" or apply any other phrase or description. The image alone was all he could handle at that moment.

It was already seven-thirty and he had to go to work and prepare for two law classes—his way out!

He found Nora at the kitchen table holding a coffee cup suspended halfway to her lips, reading something in the morning paper, swinging her foot, devouring the news with her eyes. He knew she was wearing a short nightgown under her sister's robe, and he knew where the gown stopped. Between the panels of the robe her calf appeared, an ideal shape that changed with every swing of her leg.

Looking up at him she said: "Good morning. Frog or prince?"

"I'm the guy who knows he's zero. Quote: nada and nihil. End the quote," said Steven.

"Absolutely zero?"

"Yeah. That's my 'identifying attribute,' that I'm nothing and I know it."

"Sounds rather froggish. Where does this come from?"

"Charles Carden's journal. He says if you can't find the spirit in the world you'll never find it in yourself. You are on a plain strewn with rocks, and there's slime on the rocks. But the moment you say 'I am a blob' you become self-conscious and can't be a blob. The satisfaction you feel comes from knowing that you have to start over, which means you *can* start over. Therefore you should live your life."

"Why go through all that? Why not live it from the beginning?"

"Because in the beginning he lived according to a myth, and that's no good."

"But Charles told me," she said with a meaning look at him, "that he was a daily communicant."

"What's that?"

"Somebody who goes to Mass every day."

"Jesus."

"A daily communicant cannot see himself as a blob. The two don't go together."

"Maybe he goes to church out of desperation."

"So do I," said Nora, "and many others."

"Well, Carden wasn't a blob, I don't think. He was hit by this lightning bolt about the plain and the rocks and everything—remember it's a plain strewn with rocks, and you're—"

"Yes, I'm the slime."

"Not you, O'Leary. You're a beautiful woman. Don't forget Carden had a bad war. I think that's where all this comes from, humanity not being human."

"So was he the slime or not?"

"Of course not, he was a flourishing human being. He wrote that himself."

"Ah, yes, how clear it all is. Have some coffee, Lieutenant, don't stand there with your palms turned back."

He poured coffee and drank the first cup standing, then poured a second and took an apple, coffee cake and a carton of milk from the Frigidaire.

"The Crime Lab called," she said watching him.

"Oh boy."

He returned the call and that was when he learned about the bedding. He couldn't decide whether to tell Nora.

He ate breakfast; the milk especially seemed to do him good, or the coffee. Nora asked, "Was that about the Carden case?"

"Yes," was all he said.

He didn't know how many bodies he had seen; the "thousand" was just shorthand. In theory one is the same as a thousand. Maybe he derived no meaning from it because he had sacrificed his soul. He was a champion playing a role for the benefit of society. He was consumed by his role, while the others, the ones for whom he worked, were freed to live normal lives. The man who sees a thousand murders is the scout they send forward. If he comes into the circled camp to tell what he has seen they turn to the fire, eat their sizzling steaks and drink their boiling coffee, and they don't listen.

Nora was talking.

"I'm sorry," Steven interrupted, "I didn't hear what you said."

"You didn't hear me?" asked Nora—and Steven saw a trace of sarcasm in her smile.

"Wait. Yes I must have."

Her sentence played again in his mind: "How do you go on without God?"

Facing her, he met those patient, perhaps skeptical blue eyes.

Not for the first time, she let that question suspend itself between them. After a minute of silence she smiled, and there was no irony in it.

In order to leave the table she had to pass through the narrow space between Steven's back and the window. She turned sideways and he felt her hands on his shoulders and imagined that she drew her body erect as she slipped through. She pulled at his hair and asked from behind him:

"So—you were cruising the District?"

His mouth went dry in an instant and a pit opened in his liar's stomach— but he protested inwardly that she couldn't know where he was during the hour after he left 128 Laurel Street. Staring ahead, keeping his voice under control, still feeling the pressure of her hands on his shoulders—and the pressure was increasing—he said:

"Cruising—when?"

He half expected "As if you didn't know," but she said: "Don't you remember?"

"Remember what?"

"You and Tim left Charles Carden's house and you cruised around alone. Don't you remember?" she repeated.

He wished he could see her face but was thankful she could not see his. He answered: "Oh, yeah."

"Yeah," she echoed—a word she never used. "For an hour," she added.

He shrugged and felt how she resisted his raising of his shoulders.

"You could have come home to us," Nora said. "With all the overtime you put in plus your law classes we see little enough of you."

"Cruising the District every once in a while is my job," Steven said, hoping she didn't know how seldom he did it.

Nora tugged at his hair—and went upstairs.

He noted that the drive from the station to home took twenty minutes. He was telling her he spent forty minutes at the end of a long day cruising. Not impossible; not likely.

Nora returned dressed for City Hall and stood smiling down on him, looking fine in a fitted burgundy wool suit and black silk blouse with an open throat. She wore a gold cross against her skin. He saw her as beautiful with radiant love. He felt this radiance concentrating physically on himself. She showed no sign of suspicion.

"I cared for him and respected him," she said, "and if he was struggling to find a new faith I respect his struggle. But there is no new faith."

McCord said: "That's for sure."

"Now," Nora said, and paused, "tell me."

"What?" he asked, thinking: "Forty minutes."

"What you found out from the crime lab."

"God, O'Leary, do you really need that?"

"Just tell me, Steven, and I'll decide what I need."

"Well there's an upstairs bedroom down the hall from the old man's room, and we think there was a struggle or a fight in that room. But the old man was downstairs and it looks like he, or they, pounced on him and killed him down there—I mean at his desk, so he was never in that upstairs room during perp time."

He stopped, and Nora waited, standing above him in her fitted suit, black blouse and gold necklace. By lying he had invested her with a new majesty. He might believe she was the same woman, the one he knew naked and clothed. But the belief was not as strong as his sense of her being right while he was wrong, and that was new.

"So maybe there was somebody else in the house," Steven said. "Tim and I think maybe somebody was—fighting. That's why Tim dragged one blanket off the bed and another off the floor. There were no sheets. We'll haul in the mattress today."

"Go on."

"The lab found semen, a little blood that we missed on a dark blanket, some hair, fibers, shavings of human skin. By-products of violent rape."

"I see," said Nora while looking down upon him with those great, sensitive, dark blue eyes.

McCord said, "Yeah, so do I."

He sat there a few minutes after she'd gone, then dumped the remains of his coffee into the sink, got his briefcase and raincoat from the hall closet and left the house. He drove downtown, arriving at the Safety Building early for the weekly meeting of district commanders.

There was time to stop at the Detective Bureau. From the young man who was assisting Sergeant Reitz he learned that the airlines had not yet responded to the query about passengers named Carden or Marie, or initialed M, originating in Los Angeles.

The district commanders' meeting lasted two hours, quite enough time for McCord to appreciate the complexity and falsehoods he would have to deal with if he pursued Lindy Alden. He didn't know how to go about that task but he'd find a way. Somehow he felt he had a right to this. He paused to ask consciously what exactly he meant by "this." A right to what? He left that behind him and his mind plunged on—and he said in his mind, "I want to know that woman." Because she was beautiful and because she had said: "You are embarrassing me"—the words, and the way she looked while speaking them.

When the meeting ended he went back to the Bureau. Reitz and his assistant were out but the secretary had a copy of a memo for him. A Northwest plane had brought in a passenger listed as "Ms. M. Carden."

He stared at the paper. Now he knew. The body that left him cold set "Ms. M. Carden" afire with grief and rage.

Nora backed her car out of the garage. Before starting down the alley she glanced toward the house in the hope of seeing Steven at the kitchen window waving goodbye, but he wasn't there. The old patterns had been disrupted and the new pattern was that there was no pattern. She slipped into a dark and frightened mood.

It was the combination, the working together of the report from the crime lab on the bedding and her deepening suspicion that Steven had lied about what she called the lost hour. In the midst of her ghastly visualization of a woman's suffering she was forced to listen to the demon in her ear whispering, "He's lying."

"You have no evidence!" she cried aloud. Yet the very term "evidence" suggested she was thinking with a prosecutor's mind. She cried out again: "I have no reason." But she did—a small slender one, but a reason. If Tim Sloan had said that he and Steven left the Carden house in separate cars, and no more, and if he then asked her to tell Steven that he forgot to sign for the old man's journal, she'd be content. But Tim hadn't said that. He said Steven was "headed home." That sounded like a quote. She guessed it was a ten- or fifteen-minute drive from the 6th to home. Tim had called around ten till five. Steven didn't show up till well past six. Seventy minutes later.

If this were all, she would never have noticed. But she had broader grounds for suspicion. For several months, maybe a year, maybe two years— she didn't know when to date the start of it—he had been showing a sharpening discontent with his life—with their life—starting probably about the time he took his first course in law.

"I'm so twisted that I—"

She meant so twisted that she was ready to believe that the whole business of studying law had a hidden purpose, to make his routines so confusing that she'd never know when to expect him home.

And he'd started complaining about his career with a new bitterness. Of course they all groused about the job, the city, the politicians, the clueless judges, the forgiving parole system and all the rest; but Steven's gripes went to the very bottom. He had lost his sense of purpose. His job, his life, perhaps his marriage, his family—all that to her seemed enduring and good—burned him! Dried him up. He kept saying "Get out or burn out."

"All right, Steven," she had said, "I understand. It's a hard life if you care about people's suffering."

"Wrong," he retorted, "I don't care. I don't give a damn."

Pulling into the parking garage near City Hall she had no recollection of the drive. Twenty-five minutes ago she was in the alley, now she was at work. She slid her briefcase off the back seat and slammed the door, making a huge boom in this shell of steel and concrete, then another when she slammed the front door. The ramp under her feet seemed to tilt her forward.

As she walked, her memory presented one of the many times the old man had spoken of his daughter Marie. He had said, "She's coming to see me." That was about two years ago. Nora would never again see the happiness in his eyes that she saw that day. Nora said aloud: "I ask you, Father, please, do not withdraw your grace from me and my family. I am not worthy, but please."

She might have gone on, but that way blasphemy lay. She knew no fear stronger than the fear of losing her faith. This, together with Steven and the children, supported her life.

So she tried again, to pray with true humility, just to do the thing that should have been natural and easy, to pray for the female victim, whoever she was, that her suffering be not too terrible to bear, a prayer that this young woman not be destroyed by what the lab findings told—but Nora could not utter that prayer. What she thought was: "Do not help me to understand murder and rape. I do not wish to understand." Was this defiance or cowardice?

She crossed a windblown intersection and entered the great atrium of City Hall. She went directly to her office feeling suddenly quite cool in her perception of a bleak and pointless future, if she should lose Steven and her faith in one blow. Someone would survive those losses but would it be herself?

As to faith, she knew it was a gift of grace and prayed for hers to be strengthened. The phrases "a plain strewn with rocks" and "the slime on the rocks" streaked through her consciousness, and she thought: "Life without faith." Why should anyone contemplate it?

Yet she was a fortunate woman. Millions in this or any country could only dream of a life like hers.

True, she had sustained three heavy losses, the deaths of her parents and of her younger sister Carol, whose robe she wore at home. All three were present in her mind. Carol's death especially, by reason of its cruelty, mocked her faith. But that faith had survived even Carol's helpless screams, even her dehumanization by painkilling drugs. Why this should be so, Nora did not ask. Here was a chance to offer submission to God's will but Nora passed it by; she went on with her thoughts.

"That my parents should die is hard to bear. I miss them and wish they were here with me and my children, but I accept that parents must die, and we must go on alone. But not alone, since in time we create new families."

She began to veer off into memories of Carol, thoughts of Carol's husband and children—but she pulled herself back and pressed on, following where her thoughts led. "My life up to now has been blessed." She was thinking of Steven, Robert, Danny and Jill, and of her professional success, of which she was keenly aware—warning herself against pride.

She knew the satisfaction of being among those in City Hall who are noticed. If she walked into a meeting in progress, if she appeared behind the dais in the Council chamber to speak in whispers with the Council president, if she entered an alderman's office—she was noticed.

This was pride, and therefore sinful, but there was nothing to be gained by denying it. She tried to compensate by love, the charity that St. Paul preached. And since this came to her as a gift of God, since she truly did love and since charity was in her heart, she did not worry too much about being a person of consequence at City Hall.

Nor did she exaggerate her role. She was a functionary, a servant of the men and a few women who had the power. If she was important it was only because they were. If people noticed when she entered a room it wasn't because they feared her. She had no actual power over anybody except her personal staff. It was just that people believed, correctly, that Nora McCord knew the City Council, its members and its business, inside out. Formally powerless in her position as a civil service employee and deputy to the City Clerk, she ran the office that drafted resolutions to be presented to the City Council for debate. The Council, then, debated in language submitted by Nora McCord.

It was the City Clerk's staff—Nora's staff—that forwarded to the committees the various communications from outside—from citizens, pressure groups and government agencies, including the Police and Fire departments. She could direct these to the committees of her choice in cases where discretion was called for. She maintained steady liaison with all the standing and special committees of the Council and enjoyed good relations with the most important chairmen including Finance, Public Works, and Licensing.

And other paths to power existed, hazardous but sometimes useful. There were aldermen who could not take their eyes off her. With these men she was discreet, conscious, careful and skilled at the light touch.

To the Deputy City Attorney, whose principal, like Nora's, was gregarious and lazy, she was a reliable ally when they chose to make common cause. To the President of the City Council she was a friend and an operative placed (by him) where she could guide action. And she was also the wife of a man everybody expected to be promoted to captain of police.

Without tempting fate she could admit that she was flourishing—she noted her use of Charles Carden's word. With three healthy and intelligent children (who took no drugs), a husband who loved her—she still believed—and a job that exercised her talents, she was deeply engaged in the life of the city, where knowledge, connections and personality were the currency of all transactions. And she believed. Without egotism or pride she knew that belief was a blessing. Her task in return was to discover God's will and follow it in her life. But she had thought only a few minutes ago: "Do not help me to understand murder and rape. I don't want to know." Nora was fully aware what this implied about her professed desire to bend to God's will.

Pausing, she realized she had just affirmed Steven's love. But why? She suspected he was lying about the "lost hour" and telling the brutal truth when he said, "I'm sick of it." Sick, that is, of his life's work. If she asked what he intended to substitute for it he gave confused and contradictory answers. She could not believe he'd go over to the defense side; but neither had she ever heard him express an interest in any other aspect of the law. To him "law" seemed to be an escape, not a calling.

Sick, she thought, of his work—lying—changing—rejecting the routines and structures of their life as a family—

She told herself to be rational, to trust facts, not emotions. Yet she doubted that her emotions could be radically wrong. She knew the man so thoroughly.

She searched this knowledge for a reason why he should lie and found only one. And now for the first time she brought to full consciousness the worst change of all—that he no longer met her halfway in the daily business of married life. In bed he was still a powerful but considerate lover. He still made love for her happiness as well as his own. It was in the rest of life that it seemed he had ceased to cherish her. He did not look at her and smile, or touch her when he passed, as he used to do.

When she called in her assistant for their nine o'clock conference she prolonged the talk, to divert her mind. And she asked the assistant to shut the door on the way out, a most unusual request. Nora McCord's door was always open.

How happy she would be—the word "happy" flashed in her mind—if by "crisis" she had meant the drop in the bond rating. She did not mean that. She sat at her desk and considered for a moment whether she should pray, but she was impatient, almost angry with prayer. "Angry" at the idea of prayer! She was not mad, and she was not strong. She was afraid. She said aloud: "What is he doing?"

Pushing her chair back she lowered her head between her knees and waited for the flow of blood to restore her equilibrium. When she sat upright again she found that what she wanted was to lie on the floor with her knees drawn up, close her eyes and pretend she was living in the innocent past, before Steven began his law adventure. Live in the lost world of mutual faith.

She wished it was a simple, pathetic case of middle-aged adultery. How she would scream and rave. How she would pour contempt on the other woman as a whore and on Steven as a clown—because she knew it'd be a younger woman. Oh, if he were fucking a predatory female of thirty, better yet twenty-five—Steven following a twenty-five-year-old floozie like a puppy dog! She even began composing tirades against her idiot husband and his floozie, and what a release it was. She amazed herself with her power of vulgar invective and the range of her vocabulary. She had not spent four years in a high school in the East End for nothing.

A disaster, yes, a terrible mess, embarrassing, grotesque, sickening! It wouldn't be easy or quick but the point was she could forgive. First she'd kick him out. "Go! Take your pathetic mid-life crisis with you. Out, you laughing-stock, you liar."

She was getting into this. The invective flowed like—she paused to choose the most elegant phrase—like water in a sewer! That was elegant enough for the pussy-whipped middle-aged philanderer.

"What next, Steven, a motorcycle? Hair dye? Go fuck her but don't let her see your sagging ass or chin wattles. Oh you fool, I know it"—knew he didn't really have wattles—yet—but it was true his butt didn't stick out as it used to; which in a woman would have been a sad loss. "Wait till she's forty in a mid-life crisis of her own, and you are sixty, sixty! and do you think she'll stay home then? Oh, Steven, you had better be very very rich."

When she had exhausted herself with this tirade the furies whirled around the true source of fear: if it was a "mere" question of adultery her forgiveness could—would?—be wasted on a changed man. Because he was somebody else. Forgiveness is for those who need it.

She was half ready to concede that the original Steven was probably capable of falling for what they called "young stuff."

"Save my marriage!" she thought with alarm. Yes, she could forgive him. What joy mingled in the pain and humiliation—to forgive him and heal the wound not of her own creating. "I love him!" she cried.

How could she love him if she didn't know who he was? A man throwing away his ideals for money and status? Maybe the man she loved no longer existed. But he still loved her, that was certain. Her faith in his love co-existed with her fear that he was increasingly disinclined to show it. The word "cherish" coursed through her confused thoughts. "He loves me, I know it, but I do not feel that he cherishes me as he once did." She did not pause to look at the logic of this. What she saw clearly was that his continuing love—if it was love—could not reverse the changes in his—something: soul, mind, heart, ambitions. And it wasn't just the law classes or his sudden absence of interest in promotion. "I don't even think it's the money," she said, constantly revising her thinking, although this new subject of his talk was utterly uncharacteristic. There were lunatic intervals when she thought he was actually considering a career as a criminal defense lawyer, after years of ranting against that particular breed of spider. His contempt for useless or socially damaging careers had been the bedrock of his personality. He'd turn to her after an especially stupid or degrading television commercial and ask how anybody could do that "work." And that was a mild spring breeze compared to his fury at the defense bar. Only a year ago, when he was still himself, he had said that a certain famous and rich defense lawyer was morally inferior to the savage murderer he was defending.

It was no use arguing that every defendant is entitled to a lawyer, that the whole system depended on the clash of adversaries. He readily admitted that. But he said the defense bar was set on perverting the jury selection and trial processes. A lawyer so engaged is trying to get rich by making the country safe for drug lords, rapists and murderers—at least rich ones. Such a lawyer is not playing an essential part in the justice system but working to destroy it for money and power.

Nora had said, with what must have been obvious sympathy: "Steven, there is truth in that, but what does it mean for you?"

She wanted to enter the mental territory where such questions are decided. It could be stated in one question: What is the best way to live?—for Steven, and for the McCords as a couple.

It was necessary for her to date this conversation. After some thought she placed it at six months ago. As recently as that he had been the same flawed, mercurial, cold-as-ice, flammable man she had fallen for when she was fresh out of high school. If he had burned out like so many others, or turned to alcohol, or—golf!—she laughed aloud—"Go play golf, Steven, see if it helps."

Still laughing she strode across the room, opened the door, gave a reckless wave to her assistant and went to the coffee mess that her staff maintained in an anteroom just off the big lobby. She poured black coffee and stopped, sipped, got a little scalded on the roof of her mouth, and decided. She went back, closed the door again and called the 6th District station.

"Hi Mary Lou, it's Nora. Is His Nibs available?"

Nora then imagined Mary Lou going from her office to the sergeant's desk to the squad room—standing outside the men's locker room and shouting—

then to the "bucket room" where cops thrust their heads into boxes made of soundproofing and dictated their reports, sounding in the mass like monks at prayer.

"Hey O'Leary, how's our bond rating?"

"If I said we're cutting police salaries would you take it seriously?"

"Why should I?"

"Oh I forgot. You're heading for the door."

"If I pass the bar exam. They say it's a test of speed and I'm not so fast."

"You'll pass. I called because I've just seen the light."

"Like a miracle?"

"Yes."

"You saw in a vision that I passed the bar exam?"

"A different kind of miracle, Steven. I've decided to keep my nose out of your life. Robert, Danny and Jill are free to live their lives; we've never been overbearing parents meddling in every decision. It wouldn't work anyway." She paused, and when he was silent she asked: "Right?"

He said cautiously: "Probably."

"So," she continued, "it's stupid of me to interfere in your life decisions. Suppose I decide to switch careers, which I won't. I'm not sure I'd appreciate a lot of advice from you."

"I thought we were married," he said, and that surprised her.

She said: "We are. And that marriage must be preserved."

"Not pickled? Preserved?"

"Can this marriage be saved, is how it's usually put." She had not planned to take this route and was uneasy. Never before had either breathed a syllable that alluded, however tangentially, to divorce. "Be a lawyer, be a cop or anything you want to be." She stopped herself adding, "Just be my husband." She said: "I will gladly discuss any decision, which is what married couples do, but will not try to steer you."

"So what's new in all this?" he asked warily. "You always said go ahead if I wanted to. When I signed up for my first law class you said, 'My, how intriguing.' "

"True."

"But now you mean it?"

"I see it in a new light."

"Explain that."

"It won't be easy. But to me, from the beginning till now, you were a cop for a reason. You were cut out to be one. I was sure you were good at it."

"Thanks."

"And honest. And I saw at the beginning—Do you remember the night we went to Frankie's Forest Park and we—"

"It was Lakeside Park," he corrected her.

"Right, Lakeside. We rode the roller coaster, drove the bump cars, and we danced."

"Sure I remember dancing with you for the first time. That was the night I found out what I wanted."

"You already had what you wanted, and you were only twenty-one and because you were so young you knew you were right. You were in the Academy and nobody was ever more certain of his life than you."

"I meant I found out who I wanted in my arms."

"So did I, Steven, and we were right, both of us. About your job I mean. But that was twenty years ago."

She sipped her coffee and found it cold.

Steven spoke with even greater caution. "You're saying maybe twenty years is enough? Of the cop job."

"Yes. You've earned the right to a different life if that's what you want."

"Which is what I've said to you a hundred times in the last year."

"Exactly, and now I've come around to your point of view."

"Why?"

"It would be better than—" She hesitated but went ahead with the lie: "Better than burning out like so many of your friends." Not really a lie, she thought; the literal truth. But it concealed her real motive in speaking. "Better than growing hard, indifferent, totally cynical."

His only answer was silence.

Nora continued: "I don't think you can go on ranting against defense lawyers and lenient judges forever. Eventually I think you'll blow a gasket—tell me sometime what a gasket is, Steven—but I mean you'll rip inside, and from that time on you'll be a miserable human being."

She congratulated herself on her artful concealment of the motive and the hope: "Save our marriage!" She was deceiving him, shrouding her raw fear in the language of selfless devotion, a kind of dishonesty she had never before practiced on him.

"When you say miserable human being," Steven said, "do you mean—"

"Not that you're no good. I mean a man who is miserably unhappy."

"Well I'm glad you don't mean a no-good bastard. Since we're married."

"You know I don't."

"In fact," said Steven, "I don't know that. If I've got a right to plan a new life then you've got a right to judge it."

"I don't judge you," she lied.

"Maybe you should. If you can't make judgments in this life you are friggin lost. If you say something's a step forward, or a desperate escape, that's a judgment."

"I do not judge you, Steven."

"Better try. You said you'd discuss it. What's the point if you don't judge?"

"I think we're talking about two different things."

"We're talking about the same thing, which is your opinion of my plan."

She asked: "What is your plan, Steven?"

"Be a lawyer. Get off the god damned street."

"A moneymaking lawyer. Not assistant DA, not public defender."

"Don't know yet."

"But you seem to know what you're calling my opinion of your plan."

"I think I do, yes. You want me to be what I've always been, for old times' sake. You're opposed to any change whatsoever. You want me to buck for captain. Or hey! I got an idea! Go back to Homicide. Thrill a minute, like the roller coaster at Lakeside Park."

"If I say you should stay, then, I'm asking you to burn yourself to a cinder."

"More or less."

"If I say go, you're asking me to judge you."

"Yeah."

"All right, Steven."

"OK, O'Leary."

"I guess we're stuck." She said it lightly but she was afraid she'd cry. She put the phone at arm's length and brought her voice under control and asked: "What's new on the Carden case, anything?"

"Yeah. You don't want to know and neither do I."

She asked: "What is it?"

"Just that I think his daughter came in during the murder," Steven said, "and he—or they—I'd say they—forced her up to that room, and then—took her with them."

"Oh—God."

"Yeah," said Steven. "God."

CHAPTER 8

Probing Questions

L indy Alden was crossing the main lobby of the hospital after finishing work. Of course she was tired but she was never truly happy about leaving the Intensive Care Unit. The Unit meant work that somebody had to do; it meant focus, fellowship and swift time. But you can't work day and night, and now she was going to an apartment, comfortable as it was, that meant solitude. To Lindy that was the difference between the day and the night.

She saw him. Even from a distance she recognized Warm Eyes and felt a flush of satisfaction that he was trying again. He stood by one of those ridiculous tree pots in the center of this huge space and as she drew nearer she saw that he was holding a paper cup in either hand.

She figured that out right away. The system in the cafe was: you paid, they gave you an empty cup, and you went to the urns to draw your coffee. He looked just a little ridiculous himself holding those cups. He took a step, but only one. She could approach him or keep going. She thought he was not intercepting but inviting her.

"Warm Eyes"—yes—that was the right name for the man who had so comically asked permission to stare at her. But she also saw the kind of tough-man face you had a right to expect on a cop, plus a square forehead, boxy chest and no doubt muscular arms. He was wearing a raincoat that looked too light for this weather, and his face and hands were red with cold.

Her eyes returned to his face. Set wide in that strong visage she saw the same eyes that had dwelt on her face as she stood in her doorway. She hadn't decided whether to acknowledge him but she knew: "He wants one thing, and that's all he wants." She'd had her share of married and "undivorced" admirers.

He greeted her with a tentative will-you won't-you smile, which broadened a little when she made her turn, and spread wider when she reached out, said hello, and took a cup.

He said something about needing coffee at this time of the day and she replied with something equally inconsequential about real coffee versus decaf—and they entered the cafe, filled their cups and began looking for a table. The place was jammed so Lindy led the way back to the lobby and the bench under the potted trees. This was the most public place in the whole hospital, with practically everybody passing by—so it had that to recommend it, that it was innocent.

Lindy saw two friends, who would surely ask her tomorrow: "Who's the guy?" But the deeper question for Lindy was: who was the woman with him? Was she the same woman who had decided never again to trifle with a married man or allow one to trifle with her? The same who (speaking of "allowing") was allowing Harry, her ex, to keep showing up in her life on one pretext or another—such as today, when she found him hanging around the ICU on some flimsy excuse.

When she received the first bouquet from Harry about six months ago, and realized he was after her again, she finally faced her future, and it had two pictures: Harry again, or the desert. From that point onward she could virtually feel the odds changing against her, by the month, by the week. So maybe Harry was—the answer—again.

She experimented for a while with a declaration of celibacy. If a man asked her out she would say, "Sure, but I have to tell you, I'm celibate." Some thought she was kidding, others sheered off and still others felt obliged to take her out once, and never called back.

Harry was right: she was hungry. Nobody could appreciate that better than he. But this hunger led her down a path that ended in the question: Is it a crime to want life? That was the simple essence of her hunger, a drive to live.

Wanting life, is it a crime to seize your chance wherever you come upon it? Wanting and needing it, is it a crime of a different kind to deny your own needs? Why is it a virtue to blight your own life but a crime if, by seizing your chance, you blight somebody else's?

She had thought: "Suppose I loved a married man with children. Would his family buy their happiness at the cost of my misery? If they did, would that be a virtue or a crime? Do families have rights that are denied to single women?"

She circled morbidly around these questions, seeing them for what they were. It almost shamed her that she should put logic (she called it that) at the service of her desires, building up a justification for wrecking somebody's home if it came to that. Given her own family's history she had a personal reason to abhor the kind of selfish "need" she found herself excusing. That was when she vowed never again to step out with a married man. She believed destruction lay over that horizon.

If on the other hand she denied and stifled this taunting passion for love she'd be denying the essential truth about herself, her life, her needs and her ideas about how she should or could live. Go back? Settle for Harry for the excellent reason that he was a good man and their life together had been a pretty good life? Or insist on being faithful to her own true identity. Search for real love. "And if I find it, take it."

She lurched from pole to pole, between two identities—the woman who evidently was not much more than a mix of hunger and need, and the one who sought peace of mind in a vow that amounted to physical and spiritual solitude—the desert. Certainly she had woman friends, and there were single, free men in the city, but she knew none who could give her and receive from her the love she was eager to find in a man and in herself. But: how could she—who had made two mistaken marriages—why should she—waste her time on an adolescent dream?

She did not want to caress herself. She wanted a man to caress her, and even more intensely she wanted to caress him. And why not admit it? She wanted him to take, to enter her. She ached to give herself.

But she of all people should know what life really is. She saw it acted out before her in the ICU every day, the pain, terror, stupor, desperation, impairment, degeneration and death. So why the hopeless dream of a "real man" whose passion could combine with her own in a great frightening storm? Why go mooning after paradise if you know what life really is?

Instead she should ask herself, "What do you expect?" What she expected was suffering and death just like all the rest, but in the meantime she walked and lay in a terribly healthy body whose demands she could find no way to assuage.

She asked him about being a cop. "Do you carry a gun?"

"Of course."

"Did you ever shoot anybody?"

"Not yet," he answered with a laugh.

"Do people treat you in some special way?"

"Because I'm a cop? Pretty often they do, but I try to pay no attention. But I sometimes enjoy it, I guess."

He got in a question of his own: "What kind of nursing do you do?" and she briefly described life in the ICU.

The conversation ground to a halt, then Lindy boldly asked: "Do you love your wife?"

Showing no uneasiness or surprise he said that he did.

"But of course your story for me is that she doesn't understand you, so you're looking for something extra," said Lindy.

"No, that's not my story. She understands me pretty well I'd say."

"And she loves you?"

"Yes."

Lindy was amazed at his calm in the face of these outrageous probes. She pressed him with: "In her own special inadequate unsatisfying way."

He sat there as calm as ever, with a sympathetic smile, and shook his head No.

"Children?" she asked.

"We have three."

"All at home? You live as a family?"

"One's in college, two at home."

"And you live as a family?" she repeated relentlessly.

"Of course we do."

She believed that whatever was pushing her down this line of questioning had his sympathy. He was not just answering but, it seemed to her, encouraging her. He sat there patient and willing, allowing her to ask whatever she wished. He had a settled, calm strength about him, maybe even empathy, as if he were trying to help her.

"Help me what?" she thought. "Ruin it, kill it right now?"

"You have a house?" she asked.

His eyes did not leave hers and his voice never changed. He said yes they lived in a house. He had not touched his coffee and Lindy felt hers cooling in her hand.

Growing bolder she said: "In other words you have the most precious things in life."

She felt as if she had struck a devastating blow, but he did not flinch or hesitate.

He said: "I am aware of the good things."

She raised the pressure. "If you have all that, why are you chasing women?"

"Why do you say I'm chasing women?"

"You're chasing me, aren't you?"

"Do you have to say 'chasing'? I want to know you, I think that's obvious."

"So you're risking everything that matters in life just to know me?"

"I'm taking a risk, you're right."

"With your wife's peace of mind and your own, unless you have no conscience."

This time he didn't answer, which told her he did have a conscience. And she couldn't help it, in those features that so clearly suggested a man of authority she saw the possibility of something tender and dear. But she went ahead with whatever she thought she was doing and said:

"And you still claim you think about me all the time?"

"Yes, I still 'claim' that."

Then she said: "Since you came to my apartment I have thought about you all the time."

To this he made no response, except that, maybe, his eyes showed an internal change from those of a man submitting to an interrogation to a man who was glad to hear what he was hearing.

She came near apologizing for her aggressiveness, she almost said, "I hate to be so outrageous," but she kept silent, believing she was doing something right. She asked, "Are you totally cynical or totally honest?"

"Neither," he said. "When I saw you for the first time—"

She interrupted: "Just now, or before?"

"Before, at the fundraiser. When I saw you I began to feel a compulsion."

"Love? You couldn't."

"No. But some power rising up to my head, over which I have no control."

"You're kidding. Your head?"

"Well, maybe someplace else too."

"But we humans are able to control what we do, our actions."

"Theoretically," he said after some thought.

"So you don't love me!" she cried laughing, and a huge laugh came from his chest and shook him visibly.

"I guess not," he said.

"But you want to make love to me, I'll bet."

"Probably. I don't know but I admit—"

"Have you cheated before?"

"I haven't ever cheated."

"Oh? What do you call this little conversation?"

"I guess I'd call it a grilling."

"Will you tell me," she repeated, "have you cheated?"

"No, I have not."

"My God," she said and let out another happy-sounding laugh—and it occurred to her, it came through the screen of the conversation, that she was actually happy at that moment—"in how many years?"

"About twenty. Since I met her." Then he asked, "Are you married?"

"Well, finally," she said. "Divorced twice, a bad record. Not now married."

"Are you committed to anybody?"

"If you mean a man, not in the least," she said.

"How about a woman?"

"Don't worry, I am not a lesbian."

"I wasn't worrying."

"So," she said, "you assume every woman you meet is straight?"

He just smiled and said: "Any more questions?"

"Yes."

He waited.

"Suppose," Lindy said, "we sleep together and I fall crazy in love with a gun-carrying policeman who when I say did he ever shoot anybody says 'Not yet,' my life's turned upside down, and there I am at your mercy, all I want in this life is you, I mean, it could happen—I'm not saying it will, but—"

"No, you're not, neither am I."

"—but suppose it does. What then? Is that the point where you wake up and holler 'What a pain she is,' and dump me and go out looking for some other squeeze?"

He responded: "What if I fall in love with you and turn my life upside down?"

"I asked first."

"All right. I don't know the answer."

"How truthful," she mused, "or how cynical."

"I just don't know. How could I?"

"You're right, it's an unfair question. But are you a power freak? Do you enjoy directing traffic?"

"I never did that job."

"Arresting people then."

"Yes, I like that, most of the time."

"Arresting a whore with children, taking her away from her screaming weeping babies, you'd get a kick out of that?"

"I don't know any whores who have children."

"But you know whores!"

"A few, yes."

"OK, then just imagine one with babies."

He said as calmly as ever: "No, I wouldn't enjoy that, but we seldom arrest prostitutes."

"Are there prostitutes in this city?"

"Sure. But can I change the subject? If you want me to leave you alone, I will. But I hope I can see you again. May I?"

"I'll think about it. I'm not trying to sound smart, I simply mean I have to think. I like your looks, it's all the rest that bothers me."

"It bothers me too."

"OK," she said, "what's your name again?"

He wrote it on a sheet from his notebook.

"Steven McCord," she read, then looked up at him as he said,

"Lindy Alden. May I walk you to your car?"

"Yes, please do, but how do you know I didn't take a bus?"

"I watched you walk to the parking lot yesterday."

"Hold up there, Officer. How many other times have you watched me?"

"None," he said.

"OK, I believe you. Don't do it again."

"I won't. I apologize."

Buffeted by a strong cold wind they walked side by side to the parking lot. Standing at her car Lindy said: "So now it's home to the wife and kiddies?"

"No, now I go to class at the law school."

She pondered this and surmised: "Are you planning to quit the police?"

"Yes. I'm starting a new life."

"I get it. You're shopping for a girlfriend for your new life."

"I told you, I'm not shopping."

"Right. You have a power rising up inside you which you can't control."

He said, "I want to see you again, Lindy."

Driving home she kept seeing his face and hearing his voice, which resonated in her mind and somehow seemed to be a voice of kindness and hope.

She had been too quick in saying she knew what he was after. How simple and easy it would be if all he wanted was her body, and she would certainly give it. But what if this man wanted what Harry wanted, which was all of her.

Thinking of Harry, she remembered her love for him and felt its descendent, tender affection. That love seemed almost maternal compared to this new—sensation—this "power rising within her, that she could not control." She believed that after a few minutes' talk this Steven McCord understood her better than Harry ever had in six years of marriage.

"But he loves me," she said with pain, meaning Harry. She did not want him to suffer. "Harry's a fine, generous, considerate and loving man. This new man, this Steven—McCord—God! Face it, he makes me—"

But she wasn't quite ready to face it. She tried to turn her thoughts back to Harry—and she succeeded in visualizing his kindly, devoted, slightly bulging brown eyes.

She wanted to stop the car and give herself a few minutes to blubber over the loss of Harry. "It was a pretty good life," she cried, conscious of that "pretty good." But she didn't stop. She drove on, thinking:

"The way he looks at me!"

And she didn't mean Harry.

The White Scarf

he next day as he came out of a meeting with the Westown Business Association McCord checked his pager. He had been out of contact for
half an hour persuading the business people to award their Service to
Westown medal to Sergeant Hughes. His office had called, so now he called
back.

He learned two things, that a citizen had found a woman's suitcase bearing
the initials M.C., and that Hughes was already at the site, together with
Sergeant Reitz, Tim Sloan and the beat cops. The site was the Valley Used
Car Sales on Hale Avenue, on the northwest edge of the 6th District. McCord
drove there.

Tim Sloan, attired in his black jumpsuit, was squatting on the asphalt arranging the contents of the suitcase on a white sheet. He had pinned the corners down against the wind with rocks.

McCord slammed the door of his car and approached the group—Hughes
in uniform, the beat cops Angerman and Spars looking like wrestlers who had
put on rented police uniforms, Reitz in civvies, Tim, and a withered little
man named Davy. As District Commander, McCord had, from time to time,
signed petty cash chits authorizing payments to him in exchange for information.

Sergeant Hughes was peering into the suitcase, which lay open on the
blacktop. A bleak wind was trying to lift the sheet. Hughes turned to meet
McCord saying: "I got half the relief searching the woods." McCord glanced
at the wall of naked winter trees standing behind the back row of cars. Next
he looked at the suitcase, bright red with the letters M.C. woven in black into
the fabric.

"Fine," said McCord looking at a toilet kit of white cloth decorated with red roses and blue clouds.

"I also got six men from Fourth District and a couple from Third. Battey's in there running the search."

"Fine," McCord repeated. He walked up to Sergeant Reitz and shook hands. McCord and Reitz stepped to one side and Reitz said sotto voce:

"This dumb briar's a snitch. You know him?"

"I know of him," said McCord.

The little shambles of a man, a small body hung on a smaller skeleton, with a leather face and eyes receding so deep they couldn't be seen, held out his hand as McCord approached.

"Hi, Lieutenant. I'm Davy Crockett Hamilton."

"Hello, Davy. You've done some pretty good work for us, and I thank you for calling about the suitcase. It could be important."

"I'd like a peek in his so-called house," Sergeant Reitz interposed.

"Let me talk to him," said McCord.

All McCord knew about the old briar was that he kept a sharp eye on Hale Avenue and that his residence was a 1970 Pontiac Bonneville.

There were two rows of cars on the lot, each row with a break in the middle. The break in front admitted car and foot traffic. The one in back was filled by a shanty, the sales office. An orange cable carried power out the shanty and across the blacktop to Davy's Pontiac.

McCord took Davy's hand, and held it nearly motionless.

The briar said, as if for the first time: "Howdy, Lieutenant."

"So you found us something." McCord was examining Davy closely, with undisguised curiosity.

"Found the suitcase," Davy said uneasily.

McCord took note of the definite article; one strike against Davy.

"Called your boys," Davy added with an expectant air.

McCord obliged by thanking him again and by releasing his hand. But he continued his penetrating stare. The silence was awkward for Davy, so McCord didn't let it go on too long.

"So this is your house," said McCord. "I've heard about it. We don't have too many people in this district living in cars. You know, Davy, Angerman and Spars have told me a lot about it." These two stood by the car, four buttocks in a row flattened against the fender.

Davy said: "Ain't no house but I live in it OK."

"Have you got everything you need in there?" McCord asked.

"I don't need much." Davy was actually not much older than McCord but had traveled a rougher road. "You never seen it?" he said hopefully.

"No I never," replied McCord. Like many cops he could speak in the various tongues current on the street when it suited his purpose.

He opened the front passenger door, paused half a second and, hearing no objection, put his head inside. He said, "Jesus, Davy, you got a siren in here?"

Davy hustled around to the driver door, opened it and knelt on the black-top just outside. Reaching in he extracted a bare-ended wire from under the dash and touched it to another leading from an old cylindrical chrome siren. The thing wailed a long moan, right out of a movie of the 1940s; Angerman and Spars jumped and Davy looked up mirthfully at McCord and said: "Ha! They won't like *that*."

He told McCord that on Christmas Eve he'd been awakened by a jerky up-and-down motion of his house. Two local varmints were jacking him up. He had good tires on the front, he assured McCord, who bent down to confirm this and nodded. Davy blew the thieves away with his horn and it was then he thought of a siren.

"Ha!" he said again.

McCord asked: "And have you got a gun in there too? I hope you got a gun owner's permit."

"No gun but I got me a tire iron."

There was an electric heater on the floor under the steering wheel. The bedding was piled in a heap on the driver's seat. In the back Davy had put a wood box, full of clothing, and on top was a television. Next to the box was a pile of leather strips and scraps and a green metal tool box with a chrome catch.

Davy described how he worked. He would sit in the front seat and stretch his legs out, while leaning against the door, padded by a folded blanket. He kept the tool box nearby as he trimmed and shaped the leather into belts and holsters. He could inscribe or burn it—he had a burning iron too. He worked in the light of a gooseneck lamp screwed to the dashboard. And he had a remote for the television.

His job was to keep the car lot swept, or shoveled if there was snow, to clean up the cars, jockey them when necessary, and clean the office. He was paid three dollars an hour for a forty-hour week, and given his space and electricity free. He was also supposed to watch the lot at night, and to unreave the security chain in the morning. Passing the chain through the frames of the front-row cars each evening was his biggest job.

Davy said it was a good-enough deal and that he liked being a security guard. He said he owned nothing he didn't need. He cultivated a garden behind the shanty, and McCord glanced over the woven-wire fence and saw a scarecrow wearing a red bandanna and black fedora.

The car lot occupied all the flat land between the street and the edge of a steep dropoff, almost a bluff. The garden fence stood at the very edge, and beyond this the woods dropped downward to the floodplain of Jonathan Creek.

"Where'd you find the suitcase?" McCord finally asked.

"I showed them rookies."

"He showed us," Spars corroborated, nodding toward the woods. "We showed Battey."

"Davy," McCord proposed, "what about we search the car."

"Uhhh—you got a warrant?"

"No."

"Hmmm. Cripes."

It was a gray day but Davy squinted. Maybe he squinted all night. Little slits, and eyes probably in there somewhere.

Angerman and Spars, side by side, uniformed in windbreakers with the city seal on one shoulder and the word "Police" arced on the other, badged, armed, indifferent to the cold, leaned against the fender with thick arms crossed over their chests. They watched Davy as if they were a single, patient mammal, and Davy looked nervously at them, then at McCord, to whom he said:

"Nossir. These boys know me," Davy said. "I ain't into nothin."

"That's true," Spars confirmed. "He's a good snitch."

"I ain't no snitch. I just keep a lookout and call these boys if I see anything suspicious. I seen plenty a drug deals, Mister Man."

And McCord said: "You're an honest citizen."

"I am."

McCord said to the two officers: "Search the car."

Turning away from his men McCord walked to the rear of the lot, around Davy's garden and into the woods. He began descending through gaunt, stiff twigs of thick-grown brush and small trees, sliding, grabbing branches, going down in controlled swings like a monkey, till he landed on the floodplain. He was no stranger to the territory. When he was not yet ten years old he had ridden his bicycle out here, a great distance as it seemed, hidden the bike in the summer bushes and explored the maze of trails on both sides of the creek. The floodplain on this side had been a hobo jungle during the Depression and McCord's father told stories of shivering men crowding around a campfire, cooking catfish they took from the creek—stories of comradeship among the poor homeless wanderers, and fist fights that left the combatants toothless and senseless, stories that may even have been essentially true, as McCord now believed, which had enthralled the boy.

The alders and other swamp trees on the floodplain were inundated in seasons of heavy rain but they always rose again out of the muck, and for all McCord knew he was tramping right now a path he had trod as a boy of ten.

Seeing Sergeant Battey, leader of the search, McCord whistled. He asked to see the spot where Davy had found the suitcase and Battey led him to it. He stood looking at a low-lying cradle in a bend between two trees; then he looked around him and let his imagination darken the scene as if on a moonless night—and he saw a stooped figure drop the case between the trees.

Walking toward Jonathan Creek now, a man investigating a homicide, he still felt that he and the boy were the same person. Not the same man, nor the same boy, but both.

A line of policemen and women forced its way slowly through the trees and brush, and there was very little talking. They had turned up bottles, a chair leg, a rusted hammer head, mostly old junk, none of it relevant. McCord sniffed the air apprehensively and was thankful when all he could detect was the winter smell of freshly churned mud, the smell of a wetland—nothing more. The temperature was well below freezing and had been even lower before the rising of the sun—so maybe there'd be no smell—even if—

He cut off this line of thought and pressed deeper into the woods. His shoes were heavy with mud and his face and ears stinging with the cold. He came to the bank of Jonathan Creek, the same that passed by Highplain and debouched into the big river downtown. Here the creek marked the limit of McCord's District and also served as the boundary between city and county.

When McCord looked across the creek and a little to his right he could see a bluff rising ten or twenty feet above the level of the water. On this elevated land, beyond the bluff, a developer seeking to capitalize on the lower tax rates in the county had built an industrial park some years ago. He had laid down an infrastructure of gravel roads, electric lines, water and sewer pipes and fire hydrants, but few businesses bought in, and now nature was reclaiming most of it. Three or four large warehouses and other industrial buildings had been erected, plus a tannery and some small machine shops, but most had been abandoned. They had sunk in the weeds even as they sank into the oblivion that awaits unprofitable businesses—for this was the heart of the Rust Belt. So the land on the county side, which had been wild when McCord was a boy of ten, was reverting to a kind of urban wilderness today.

McCord could see none of this because he stood so low relative to the bluff, but he knew it was there. It wasn't his territory. Being in the county, it was the responsibility of the sheriff. The physical link between the two jurisdictions was the old Penn Central Railroad bridge.

This relic loomed above McCord to his left, a naked framework of ancient blackened steel, a thing that had put fear into him when he was a boy. It spanned the creek like a praying mantis whose limbs had been bent at angles by some malevolent force. If McCord wanted to cross into the county to visit the scenes of his boyhood explorations he'd have to climb the embankment that supported the bridge on either side and hop from tie to tie, trying not to notice the brown water twenty feet below. He had often imagined himself plunging between the ties, being ripped front and back and hitting the shallow water already half dead. Boy or man, he did not want to cross that bridge.

Returning to the used car lot he found a semicircle of cops standing in front of Davy's car, and Davy in the middle looking trapped. The patrolmen Angerman and Spars had found two things in his car, and these were now laid out on the hood. One was a white silk scarf. Holding it against the wind was a bottle of Estée Lauder toilet water.

"Have we got your prints Downtown?" Tim Sloan was asking Davy.

"Lordy, twenty-five or thirty times," Davy answered, nervous but boastful.

"You're going to be OK, then, aren't you?" said Tim.

"I sure am."

Turning to McCord Tim said: "We found these inter alia wrapped in his blankets."

Reitz snarled: "He's gonna tell us a lot more."

"No I ain't cause I don't know no more."

"You Hydramatic Kentuckian, you shiftless briar, fuckin white trash hillbilly scrotebag," said Sergeant Reitz with some heat, "gonna slam yer bony ass in City-County Consolidated and you can fuckin rot."

Head pushed down by guilty knowledge, little eyes sliding back and forth in their slits and fixing on the toilet water and the scarf, Davy said several No's and finally looked at McCord as to a reasonable man. McCord could see his eyes now glinting in their slits.

McCord shifted his gaze to the scarf, thinking of a line in Charles Carden's journal that went something like this: "Marie born today. What a strange but lovely being she is."

He saw right through it—saw what it meant—the white scarf. Sometimes a single piece of physical evidence can crack a case. This wasn't one of those times. All the scarf could tell an investigator was that a woman had owned it and somehow lost it. But it had a far-reaching effect and clear significance for Steven McCord, the man whose spiritual bedrock was his "clarity." The clarity shows you that the truth does not set you free but binds you in "bands of steel." He had read that poetic phrase somewhere and had decided to break free of the bands. He would sacrifice the clarity for freedom—for a life like the one lived by people who didn't have to look at such a thing as the white scarf.

From the used car lot he drove to his office. There his first act was to call the Great Valley Hospital and ask for the number of the ICU. He quickly searched for a piece of paper to write it on, one that his secretary wouldn't see. He wrote it on the cover of one of his law notebooks.

It was not very pleasant to realize that he had hushed his voice to prevent his secretary from hearing him. (Her desk was right outside his office door.) And that was only the beginning. He called home and asked Danny to tell Nora, when she came in from work, that he wouldn't be home for dinner because a law class had been rescheduled. He'd always known that this kind of business would force him to lie to Nora but he never expected to end up lying to his kids.

Before him lay two neat stacks of paperwork of the kind invented by the bureaucrats Downtown to prevent officers of his rank from doing real police work. Staring at these papers he couldn't decide to make the phone call so he dived into the paper. For half an hour he was swishing rosters, repair requests, overtime chits and such junk from the Do pile to the Done. He'd made an error in his request that the city send a crew to paint the "riot room," the third-floor attic that had been turned into a barracks during the riots of 1968. He had failed to specify a color. He wrote, "Any damn color you want" and threw the paper into the Done pile.

This activity did not suppress the shame climbing his chest, or explain why, if you snooze in your cage you are granted peace, but if you try to kick the door open you are tormented. He kept thinking: "I want to talk to her"—meaning Lindy Alden. He did not say "I want to destroy Nora's happiness and wreck my family," although both statements came to the same thing. He was kicking, kicking, struggling against the "bands of steel."

He called the ICU number and asked for Lindy Alden. She agreed to meet him after work—as if there were nothing remarkable in his request—and suggested they take a walk. "I'm a fast walker," she warned him. He said he'd keep up.

When he hung up the phone he could still take delight in her voice, as if hearing were as rich an experience as seeing or touching, and could be prolonged as readily by the imagination.

They walked along South Main where it led down the hill from the hospital.

She said she knew a way to get into the fairgrounds. They turned off South Main into the vehicle entrance, which was barred, then veered right to a pedestrian gate, which also looked firmly shut. Pausing before it she looked at him as if to say, "Try it." He pushed on the steel and the gate swung noiselessly open. They entered, and McCord closed the gate behind them.

They proceeded into a place designed for summer festivities now laid bare by winter, its pavilions, sheds and exhibit halls spreading out lifeless over a considerable area, gently swept by scattered snowflakes.

"Let's go to the track," Lindy said.

Passing to the side of the grandstand and through an open gate they entered the race track and turned right, putting the center on their left, and began walking briskly. An unexpectedly strong, frigid wind overtook them from behind.

McCord enjoyed the exercise, so much easier than swimming and so different. The wind and snow changed with each turn of the track, from a following wind that urged them along to a hostile force trying to slow them down, driving snow into their faces and humming in their ears—so that they had to turn toward each other to talk. He was keenly aware of the wind, the darkening gray sky, the crunching of the cinder track under their feet, and of his companion.

She wore white running shoes, khaki pants, a warm-looking black jacket and a red cap with upturned blue ear tabs. When he spoke she looked at him as if surprised to find him beside her, but her expression must have meant something else, maybe an innate liveliness.

He said half seriously, "Any more questions?"

She smiled the imperfect smile that was always in his mind and said: "Maybe later."

"May I ask one?" McCord said.

"Sure. If you're as nosy as I was yesterday I may not answer."

"This is personal but not nosy. Do you get depressed working with sick people?"

"Sick and dying," she said. "No, I wouldn't call it depressed."

"What would you call it? Does it make you hard-hearted? Do you still care?"

"Of course I care. The work shows me what I can do and what I can't. It makes me realize sometimes—"

When her voice trailed off McCord said:

"How little you can do?"

"Yes. I don't get depressed because I do all I can, but I sometimes feel it's very little."

"Suppose there's nothing you can do."

"Then I go on to the next patient."

"Did it ever happen that you couldn't do anything there either?"

"It happens all the time."

They had been walking fast into the wind, and he regretted the turn of the track that swung the force around behind them again. The going now was smoother and the chill on his face and hands less noticeable, but he missed the feeling of bending into the pressure. He asked if she came here often and she said it was one of her favorite walks, and that sometimes she ran instead of walking.

"You run how many laps?" he asked.

"Oh, four, five, at a half-mile each. I run when I need to discharge, but I can't talk while I'm running."

"Go ahead if you want. We can talk later."

"No, I'll walk with you. Why did you ask if I still care? If I didn't care I'd get a different job."

"But does it darken your life, being a nurse?"

"Oh no. I'm not the cause of the suffering. I just do what I can to help, and I get paid pretty well and I like the people I work with."

"But seeing all those sick and dying people, it must be hard to forget sickness and death."

She laughed in a burst of surprise and said, "I guess it is, and I don't forget."

"OK then, how do you handle it? Some cops harden, they desensitize, burn up, dehumanize, they go to the bottle or club their women."

"What an ugly bunch they must be."

"Not all of them. Some take it to church I suppose and some are just plain good people."

"But not very many, is that your point?"

"No, I like cops. That's one reason I decided to be one myself."

"But isn't a cop forced to think about violence and death more than anybody else?"

"I don't know about anybody else."

"You don't take care of sick people, that's one difference between us."

"No but I see death and worse."

"I agree," she said thoughtfully, "that there are things worse than death. I had a patient once, a sailor from what he called the Big War, who had a tattoo that said, 'Death Before Dishonor.' Yes—I have seen—things worse than death."

McCord grunted but did not speak. He saw the white scarf held to the hood of Davy's car by the bottle of toilet water.

Lindy Alden said, "Don't you develop some professional detachment? We are not gods. There is only so much we can do. If I were all-powerful the kid wouldn't die, at least not right now, and the old lady would get up and walk."

"And you don't feel bad about being inadequate?"

"Sure, but so what?" she replied. "Who cares how I feel?"

"You do."

"But the idea of detachment," she argued, "is that it keeps you sane and functioning. I'm sane and I function."

They went along in silence with the snow blowing past them, then turned into the wind again.

McCord said, "You know this place could be dangerous."

"I've thought of that, yes, but I'm fast."

He didn't press it but didn't like her answer. After a few more steps he said, "Find another place. I don't care how fast you are."

She smiled sidewise and said she'd think it over. Each time she faced him he felt as if lights had been turned on. He suddenly thought: "For all I know she's another ferocious Catholic." And it was a bit too facile to say "I do what I can do." Somebody in your care is dying an agonizing cancer death and you "do what you can do." If what you can do is zero you "move on" to the next victim. Still—the way she strode along so vigorously against the wind—sometimes wiping tears from her face—squinting as the snow struck her—and the way she had challenged him yesterday—all this, with that smile and that figure clothed in a silk robe, as it had been when she opened her apartment door, with her wet hair streaked back—"Jesus!" he said under his breath. He was glad he had not "confessed" to her. He felt nothing about feeling nothing. "Hell," he thought, "is when you don't feel it." How do you confess an absurdity like that? Hell is the extremity of suffering—and the absence of it?

Then as if he were a third person he heard himself saying: "The difference is you can do something."

She stopped and faced him with an expression that was neither a smile nor a question but more like a pause to wait for more. Then she caught up to where he was waiting and they marched on, beginning their third lap.

McCord said: "So you run five or six laps? How fast?"

"Seven, eight minutes a mile."

She looked mischievously at him and took off running. As he caught up she increased speed, and McCord paced her, pulling off his raincoat and letting it sail to the edge of the track, then his suit coat and finally his necktie.

"Are you a runner?" she asked without a trace of labor in her breathing.

"Swimmer," he replied.

"I hope your gun doesn't go off and kill us both."

He realized his gun and holster were advertising his profession. He was clamping the revolver tightly against his chest with his upper arm.

Viewed from the side her smile looked perfectly straight—and they clipped along at a decent speed, a little faster than before. He thought she might be revving up for more speed.

He said, "Hold er, Knute, she's a rarin."

"Where'd you get that?" she asked, and again she turned to him and again he was glad.

"High school," he said.

"You're puffing!" she accused him.

"Yeah. If you turn this into a race you'll have to visit the pool at the Y someday—and we'll see who wins that one."

"That's a deal," she said and added speed.

This prompted him to see her in a swimming suit, as he pounded along keeping up with her. Her footfalls were scarcely audible.

After running three laps they cooled down walking a fourth. He scooped up his clothes, pulled on his suit coat and folded the tie into a pocket; he tossed the raincoat over his shoulder. The wind was chilling the sweat that had begun to moisten his brow.

"How old are you, Mr. Swimmer?" Lindy asked.

"Forty-two," he said.

"You jog along pretty well for an elderly gentleman."

By now the darkness had come down. The only light came from a lamp high over the gate that led off the track. They moved slowly toward it and Lindy asked:

"You said, 'The difference is that I can do something.' Meaning you can't?"

For answer he said: "One of my guys came to me a couple months ago and said, 'Don't ever give me another one like that.' He'd found what I told him to look for, a ten-year-old boy. Found him stuffed into a storm sewer."

She made no comment on this, and he did not try to look at her. They were walking slowly across the darkened grounds, from one dimly lighted place to another.

He began telling her the story of the Carden case, giving special emphasis to the fact that it was not his responsibility, even though the murder occurred in his district, but the Bureau's. It was a measure of how little he knew that he had nearly finished before they reached the pedestrian gate by which they had entered the grounds. Here they stopped and McCord said:

"We had a piece of luck just before I called you."

He told her about the suitcase and then about Charles Carden's journal, about Marie, and about Basil Samuelson's report.

"There was something in the suitcase," he said and he could see her eyes in the light of the passing traffic, fixed on him, waiting. "We found a white silk scarf, and it's pretty easy to imagine that woman wearing it. I mean—to imagine the woman herself. You can see her putting it on, tucking the ends into the lapels of a coat. It's easy to see all that."

Her eyes were in his for a long time, until he put on his raincoat and pushed the gate. They started the ascent to the hospital, and neither spoke till they reached the parking lot. They were standing beside Lindy's car.

"Don't laugh," McCord said, "but tell me if you believe in hell."

"I not only believe in it, I see it every day."

"So—not a supernatural hell but one that's all around us if we look. It's where you find it."

"Or it finds you."

"Not a hell created by some insane god, with flames and lava and elegant tortures."

"Of course not. That was dreamed up to make a place where the cruel and destructive are punished, since they so seldom get what they deserve in this world."

"People need to believe in justice," McCord said. "But why is there so little of it? Why don't the cruel and the destructive get what they deserve?"

"What a strange question, Steven," she said using his name for the first time. He had not used hers.

"So what you mean by hell is suffering," said McCord.

"Of one kind or another, yes. The worst suffering. And yet, in the midst of that—"

When she didn't finish he waited.

At length she said: "Even then, you know, sometimes in the midst of the worst suffering—" She lifted her arms and let them fall against her sides.

McCord prompted her: "In the midst of suffering—what?"

"No matter how terrible it is—there's—"

She still did not complete the thought but McCord did:

"Courage—sometimes?"

And Lindy Alden said, "We can hope so. But think about professional detachment. Maybe you'd benefit from a little of that."

"Maybe I've got too much already."

"I don't think so."

"How much is enough? Move away and you're a block of ice; get too close and—you see my point."

She gave him one of her complex smiles, and McCord said:

"Maybe I could become one of those sane and functioning people."

"Aren't you now?"

He said, "Actually in some ways I guess I am."

He moved forward and held her by the shoulders, and she looked up into his face with consent in her eyes, and he kissed her on the lips.

Before McCord could go home he had to visit the 6th District station in order to establish a fact. The fact was that he had actually been at his office. Then if Nora asked, "Where have you been?" he could say he went to the station after his law class.

Obviously he couldn't ask the duty sergeant, "Did my wife call?" He said: "Any calls for me, Sergeant Freese?"

"No sir."

He unlocked his office, turned on the lights and the radio and stood listening to the dispatcher sending one of his crews to a breaking and entering in progress. A second crew volunteered to back up the first. He started his stopwatch.

McCord looked at his desk, and froze. His secretary had placed some new papers on it and the top folder on the right bore the label "Carden." He opened it and saw a sheet of paper marked "From Los Angeles." He unclipped the paper and lifted it. A young woman was staring into his eyes. As soon as he realized what he was doing, or what was being done to him by those intelligent, slightly ironic eyes, he closed the folder, but he could still see—he could not help seeing the face. He felt a convulsion threatening his throat. It came out as something resembling a sob, and his eyes burned—all of it amazing, inexplicable. This kind of thing never happened. He fled from this—sorrow—by checking his stopwatch.

Seeing that it showed five minutes he went to the duty sergeant's office and said: "Let's check on Six Three Four Alfa and Six Three Six." These were the crews dispatched to the breaking and entering.

The sergeant radioed the crews and told McCord they were checking the exterior of the building.

McCord thanked him and said: "I'll be at home."

"Good night, Lieutenant," said the sergeant.

He drove toward home. He could feel the thing like a bruise that the sob had left in his throat. A mild acid still glazed his eyes.

The radio squawked out the news that 634A and 636 were departing the scene, having found no evidence of a break-in. So he could forget about that and start thinking about dinner. He wondered whether Nora had left any food for him, but doubted it, given his message about a phony law class. Now he was hungry, but it depressed him to think of going to the Upper Crust for a hamburger. A man with a home, wife and family eating alone at a cop hang-out? No thanks. He slowed his car, to create time—and seeing the face of Marie Carden—her friendly, confident, pleasing face—seeing this lovely woman—

He wheeled around, pulling a U-turn on a busy street, and drove to the Shiloh Pike, then outbound, intending to do a little "terrain appreciation" on the side of the creek opposite to the floodplain where Davy had found the suitcase. From the Shiloh Pike he could drive into the industrial park and walk along the railroad tracks, as he had done as a boy, to the Penn Central bridge—that looming black ancient distorted praying mantis that had scared the boy he used to be.

He passed out of the city, drove outbound on Shiloh for ten minutes, and began scanning the right side of the road searching for the access road lead-ing into the industrial park. He had not been in the park for several years—it was, after all, in the county and therefore of no professional interest—and he was not at all certain where the access road touched the Shiloh Pike, but he kept going, and saw on the right a Sunoco station that awakened a dim memory—so he slowed down and switched on his blinkers, looking for the sign that would say: "Low Tax Industrial Sites." He remembered that much. But when he finally saw the sign it was almost obliterated by the fading and peeling of its paint.

Off to the right in the darkness, about four hundred yards away, he could feel the presence of the old Penn Central bridge. He turned into the access road, a gravel path now through waist-high brush encroaching on both sides.

His lights blazed on the unmarked skim of snow on the road; the weeds seemed bright too, crowding in toward the sides of his car.

McCord stopped and watched his flashers pulsing against the low walls of brush. He waited, as if expecting something to reveal itself, as if the pulsing lights were a prelude; then for no conscious reason he switched off both lights and engine and sat in the car, conscious now of the buffeting of the wind, which seemed more powerful than it had when he was running with Lindy Alden at his side.

There was a silent activity in his mind, wordless yet suspenseful, promising. He believed in those minutes that he knew the monkish experience of contemplation, holding his mind in readiness—the monk waiting perhaps for God, the policeman for a thrill. He was thinking: "I'll cross the bridge now, in the dark."

He drove toward the depression where Jonathan Creek lay concealed from his horizontal beams of light, and came after two minutes to a T. He surmised that the top stroke ran parallel to the creek, and that the railroad bridge was off to his right. He swung that way and saw, simultaneous with a sweep of fear or surprise in his chest, the black frame of the bridge half-disclosed against the dark sky, scarcely illuminated by the distant light of the city.

The road ended in a turnaround. From this point he could have thrown a rock and hit the place where he had stood on the other side of the creek. Leaving his car he struck out through thick weeds and saplings till he reached the tracks—which lay approximately where he remembered. Then he turned left and walked carefully toward the bridge, which he could not see, keeping to the center of the tracks where the crushed stone bed reached the level of the cross-ties. He stumbled once or twice but never fell.

The frame of massive black steel rose all but invisibly before him. He stopped. His heart was thudding against his ribs and he could feel his pulse surging in his ears. He took two more steps and stopped to listen for the sound of moving water but the creek was too sluggish and did not announce its presence. McCord needed no such announcement. His fear of the bridge—the fear of a boy of ten—revisited him in force. He turned back toward his car.

He drove away from the bridge, with the creek now on his right.

A vision captured his whole mind. He saw Marie Carden being pushed and dragged across the bridge by a man behind her and one in front. They were moving from the city side, Davy's side, to the county side where McCord now drove his car at a walking pace, in a dark field. They would be invisible to a physical eye but McCord saw them on the stage of his mental theater, framed by the black iron girders—he saw the open spaces between the ties and imagined the bruising and the fall if she should miss one step. This vision seized him as if Marie Carden were his own daughter.

But some rational voice told him they would not cross the bridge in the dark any more than he would. From the image he moved to the idea—that Marie's captors—he was now thinking of two killers—would not push her in this direction. But why not?

Davy had found the suitcase on the other, the city side, in the scrub woods covering the floodplain. So they would surely come this way to reach their car, which must have been parked somewhere near the spot where McCord now stopped. He felt uneasy, like a man caught in a lie.

Why would they park here? Maybe they parked on the other side, Hale Avenue, near the car lot—and walked—

No sooner had he visualized him, or them, walking down the sidewalk on Hale Avenue and going through the car lot—with their captive—than he realized this vision was even more misleading than the earlier one.

Reviewing the topography of the city side, from Davy's garden down the steep slope to the floodplain, choked with small-shafted alders and saplings, crisscrossed by foot trails—to the cold sluggish creek with ice moving out in thin sheets from its edges—surveying all this, and the bridge—he was compelled to reject his vision of Marie being dragged across the bridge. He had made it up out of nothing.

He drove around the grid of dirt roads, past the dark, low shapes of a few buildings, with dumpsters and derelict cars and pickups scattered around, and returned to the light stream of the Shiloh Pike, oppressed by a feeling of failure and wasted time.

If Marie Carden were still alive she could not afford the waste. This thought led quickly to another: there was no need to worry about that.

After the kiss Lindy Alden sat in her car and gave the engine time to warm up. She knew that if she started off immediately the steering wheel would drain the warmth from her hands and they would ache painfully. As she sat waiting it seemed to her that the man was still kissing her. His kiss was changing her life. These minutes of stillness and contemplation, as she grew warmer, gradually made everything simple. Up to now she could never be sure that what she desired actually existed in the world. Harry was telling her it did not. Now she knew it did.

That was where the risk lay. She could no longer dismiss it as the silly dream of a woman who never grew up. It existed because she had felt it on her lips and deeper in her body, and still did. The body was confirming the mind.

Whether you could build a life on it was still in doubt. Harry of course would say no.

In the McCord kitchen the lights still burned, but the rest of the house was dark and quiet. Charles Carden's journal lay open on the kitchen table where McCord had never put it. He was sure he had left it upstairs on his night table. He took his briefcase to his study alcove in the living room, and returned to the kitchen.

So—Nora was reading Carden's journal. He picked it up to see what she had read but found that his eyes distorted the page. He had perhaps felt some premonition in the car. He tried to focus and he saw scattered words, "love," "chaos," "wife."

He lifted his eyes and saw the room, yet not the room he knew. He stood still, anxious, expectant, and in the next instant a jagged green line jumped before his eyes, rose to a peak, and broke into segments.

He watched. He thought: "Love, wife, chaos," and saw the old man, and the white scarf. The picture of the room in which he stood warped and ballooned; then the lines of pale green light, almost white, resumed their jagged leaping and thrusting, and when he closed his eyes the green was stronger.

He had his warning. He knew what was happening in his brain and the coming effect on his body. Shielding his eyes against the glare of the fluorescent light at the sink he staggered to the hall, running his hand for balance along the wall till he reached the stair; he turned and grasped the rail and began pulling himself up with his right arm, working like an athlete to keep his legs in motion, pulling with his arm, shutting his eyes against the light coming from the upstairs hall. As yet he felt no pain.

But as the lines of light faded the pain took over, and when he vomited it was as intense as any he had ever experienced. Had that pain persisted it would have been unendurable. He thought: "What is unendurable?" He felt Nora's hand on his back as he bent over the toilet in spasms of gasping pain. He saw the vision of the railroad bridge and the figures struggling within the girders. He felt Nora's hands rubbing his back and he imagined her face and its solemn empathy.

For three days he lay in a dark room, getting out of bed only to drink or vomit, holding his hand over his eyes to block the light. The family kept the house silent day and night. No one played music or allowed a pot or pan to fall into the sink. The windows were opened during cooking to let the odors escape. A hint of food odor set him vomiting whether he had anything to deliver or not, and the retching brought pain behind his right eye.

Nora slept with him and came home during her lunch hour every day to ask if he needed anything. His answer was always no. She placed her soft warm palms over his eyes, with pressure on the rims but none on the eyeballs, and he pressed her hands.

While McCord Lay Sick—Nora

Three steel bolts ran horizontally through eight thick slabs of oak to clamp together the door of the McCords' house. When they bought the place Steven had said that if everything else was reduced to dust the door would still stand. The builders had cut a diamond-shaped window at eye level. In this window the central pane was clear but those all around it were of various colors, blue, purple, rose and emerald. Nora McCord had an affection for this weighty door which swung so easily on its silent hinges, and especially for the window. Each morning after breakfast, while still wearing only her robe and slippers, she would stop at the door to look out the clear central diamond. In one glance she could see the weather and read the thermometer fastened to a post on the porch. Then she would ascend the stairs to dress for the day.

The upkeep of the old house was a financial burden, and the neighborhood was declining faster than the house. But if the mother and father ever spoke of moving, Jill and Danny howled in protest.

On the third day of Steven's migraine Nora heard a light tapping at the window and knew right away it was Sergeant Gilbert Hughes. Obviously the caller knew Steven was sick, otherwise he would have rung the bell. He knew Nora had come home during the lunch hour to check on Steven, because her car was parked on the street in front. Therefore, it was Gil Hughes, who always visited when Steven was laid low.

Nora saw Hughes through the clear diamond and opened the door and pulled him in by his hand. Leading the way to the kitchen she asked if he'd had lunch, and he said he'd appreciate just a cup of coffee, if she didn't mind his radio.

While she was setting up the coffee maker Hughes toned down his radio. He laid his gloves and police hat on the table, and Nora held the radio cord while he shrugged out of his jacket. Now the gloves, hat and radio occupied the center of the old maple table.

Hughes remarked that the speaker resonated off the maple, and he toned the volume again. He looked up and asked: "Well, how's our boy?"

Nora reported that the boy was able to sleep now for longer periods, that this had been a severe episode, the first in more than three months, but the worst was past, and as usual the medicine didn't touch it.

Hughes made no reply. Looking around from beneath his white eyebrows he observed: "You painted the place."

The kitchen was a powder blue with white cabinets. Nora said they had left the choice of colors to Jill, and Jill did most of the painting.

"Yeah, feminine colors," Hughes commented, possibly with approval.

The chugging coffee maker and the rasping radio blended into a flow of sound pleasing to Nora's ear. She took an apple from a bowl and cut it up, placed it on a plate and set it on the table.

Hughes said, "Thanks, O'Leary," and began to move the objects around as if in search of a perfect pattern.

Nora said: "Now's the time, Gil. Don't keep me waiting. Say it!" She was feeling quite sparky.

"Yeah!" Hughes hooted. "Right. A battleship of a table you've got here, girl, solid maple and heavy as lead."

"Gilbert, you are a man of strong traditions."

"In with the old, out with the new."

Then his eyes went into a fixed stare as he picked out a broadcast for his full attention. In these blue eyes the whites were tinted with pink and there was perhaps an excess of moisture, as if from a strong wind.

"Get him a new doctor," Hughes said when the message had ended to his satisfaction.

"He's tried four," said Nora. "There's nothing they can do. 'Take this, take that,' to moderate the symptoms, but it hurts like the devil anyway, and it always lasts two days at least. This one is especially bad."

They were seated opposite one another letting their coffee cool.

Hughes said: "Must be hard to cure self-inflicted wounds."

"It's real," she replied. "You should see him."

"Real enough to send the message," said Hughes.

Looking at him with concentration Nora said: "I may know what you mean, but—"

"You do know. You know the man."

"Tell me anyway."

He got that abstracted stare on his face again and Nora caught, amid the numbers, the dispatcher's report of a "woman down."

At the end of it Hughes said: "Not our district, thank God. That'll be Olivia." He explained that Olivia was a professional car target. "Walks in front of cars about twice a year."

"Does she collect insurance?"

"Not anymore. She does collect Medicaid. One day she'll go too far, I keep telling her."

"And what does she say?"

"Mind my business and she'll mind hers. She's like a gambler on a losing streak and can't quit."

"Is she also—sick?"

"Sure she is. I tell her she could get crazy money from the government, they'd pay her to be a nut, just go to Wayne Avenue and act normal, but she tells me to fuck off. She's clean and sober, I'll say that for her, clean, sober and wacko. Lousy way to live your life but it's what she wants. Been knocked down three times that I know of."

Nora said smiling, "You seem to have a favorite subject today."

"I do?"

"Yes, Gilbert, you do."

"Like what?"

"Self-punishment, maybe."

"Aaah! Pay no attention to that, it's just a dumb idea."

Nora waited and the smile still lingered on her lips.

"Sure, I wanted to know how His Nibs was doing," Hughes said, "but the real reason was, I gotta sound the alarm."

He brooded, blew on his coffee, took an experimental sip, and finally looked square at her. "OK, O'Leary, I hate to look at it, I hate to watch it right before my very eyes, so to speak. Why do I have to be lookin at this?"

Nora watched him over her lifted cup but did not answer, or drink. She set the cup in its saucer, folded her arms and said: "Sound what alarm, Gil?"

Sergeant Hughes wished she wouldn't fold her arms like that. It was hard enough under the best of conditions to keep his eyes off her breasts. In a spirit of self-sacrifice he locked eyes with her and said,

"I hate to see it, O'Leary, and so do you."

"What do I hate to see?" she asked with a semblance of sincerity.

"Our boy drivin to the city dump."

"That's the alarm? Steven is 'driving to the city dump'?"

"Yeah. You're the one to scream stop. He won't listen to anybody else."

"You don't think he'd make a good lawyer?"

"Of course he would. You put your finger right on it."

"Too good a lawyer?"

"Yeah. If he was some incompetent moron, what would it matter what in this world he did with his life? But this guy, turn him loose in a courtroom, he could do real damage."

"And the worst damage, you probably are going to tell me, would be to himself." She spoke calmly and almost softly.

"Sure. Riddle the criminal so-called justice system with a tommy gun; in the process riddle your own misguided self. Don't tell me you disagree."

"Just a minute," Nora said cautiously. "Are you saying that you believe Steven intends to become a criminal defense lawyer?"

"He doesn't know what he intends, that's my opinion. He's run off his track. He's cold on the outside, your steel-eyed district commander, and on the inside he's totally friggin confused. He knows a lot of law, we all do, and he's a good talker—knows what to say and when not to say it—so he started on his law courses to take his mind off the blood and so forth—that's where he's kinda bewildered like a rookie—and I think—Listen, Nora, disagree with me."

"Go on."

"He thinks there must be a better life and I guess there is somewhere but he's—you say does he intend—maybe not but how else can he get free, which is what he calls it—be a lawyer and make big money? It all adds up. Be a snake."

"Let me just—not respond to that for a minute," Nora proposed reasonably, "and let me ask you a question. In your experience, Gil, have you never seen an honorable criminal lawyer?"

"Of course I have, but they're all assistant DAs."

Nora gave him Steven's argument about all the different kinds of legal jobs and he just made a face.

"I been over all that with him. He won't admit it but there's only one place to go, that's the criminal defense bar. He'll howl it ain't so but it is."

"And you think it's not possible for an honest man to do that work?"

"Sure it is, but not get rich. Our boy wants to get rich. They take the fee up front, never send out a bill. Take the clients who can pay the fee."

"If every policeman were honest," Nora argued, and she felt the heat rising in her head, to defend her husband even in this, "and every judge were wise, then we wouldn't need criminal defense lawyers, but since—"

"Yeah, yeah, that's what Stevie says, we need the vermin, but Jesus, O'Leary, so was Judas necessary, I mean Judas Iscariot."

"I know who you mean, Gil."

"Besides that," Hughes continued, "he's neglecting his job. He's jammed three law courses into his schedule so I'm—"

Nora made a sudden movement and Hughes looked at her in puzzlement. She stood up and watched him with an expression he could easily have mistaken for hostility.

Hughes asked: "Are you OK?"

She felt the blood draining from her head. When the dizziness passed she noticed that Hughes had a worried look on his face, as if he expected her to collapse; he started to get up but she went around the table and pushed down on his shoulders and rubbed the white fuzz on his big red dome. She told him to quit looking tragic, thinking:

"I'm the one who's acting tragic."

Standing behind him, as she had stood behind Steven to ask about the "lost hour," leaning on both his shoulders and rocking—so that he couldn't see her face because she didn't know what it might reveal—she said: "You say 'stop him.' I can't. Probably I would if I could. But I can't see into his mind. Can you?"

"Jesus I hate to say it, Nora Girl, but I can." He twisted in the chair and, wrinkling his forehead, looked up at her. "This is a guy who could be a captain. If the cards fell right he could be chief, deputy chief almost for certain. If I say, 'Stevie, go for captain,' you know what he says? 'I want a Mercedes.' A car, Nora, a toy."

He saw how upset she was but he had to keep going.

He said: "Most guys get tougher as they go along, or maybe I mean harder. I know I did. You help the widow and the orphan, come to find out the widow's a liar and the orphan tries to steal your flashlight. And there's the horrors, what Stevie calls horrors."

"Right," said Nora still rocking forward and back on his shoulders, which were thick and wide in her hands. She had a taut, hot expression in her eyes.

"And I used to think," Hughes said, giving his neck a rest by looking straight ahead again, "that this rookie Steve McCord was the toughest kid I ever worked with. Now, you know, I'm not sure. Is he so ambitious he just doesn't give a shit? Or is he maybe—is there maybe a narrow little streak in him that just can't take it?"

"Can't take the horrors?" Nora asked, because the same thought had crossed her mind.

"One bloody mess after another. The blood, yeah," he said meditatively.

"Does it bother you, Gil?" she asked, but her mind was running away on three law courses? Three?

Hughes replied: "Bother me? A little blood? I haven't got the character. You start out as human as the next guy, and the years roll along, pretty soon you are what you are. And that goes for me. Stevie—I don't know who he is."

The radio flashed an armed robbery in progress in the 6th. Sergeant Hughes rose slowly, and Nora drew back her hands. She helped him with his jacket, and together they fastened the speaker to his shoulder strap by its velcro tape. He put on his hat, squared it, and looked at her earnestly.

He said: "Stop him, Nora. I looked at it from every angle and I end up with, stop him."

"Yes," she replied hesitantly.

"I used to think he could take it. When he was twenty-five, thirty. I honestly think he ignored it."

Nora was half-inclined to agree—he had "ignored" it. Maybe it became harder to ignore as his children grew.

Hughes went on: "If I was God it'd break me up, it'd be my fault, but since I'm not, and I can't stop it, you know, I let it pass. There was this one guy in our outfit went to Stevie shakin and said, 'Don't give me any more like that.' It was a child stuffed into a storm sewer in the East End."

"I remember," said Nora.

"Stevie says 'OK I won't,' and I don't think he really gave a shit, he sure didn't hold the guy's hand, just sorta looked at him like, 'Weird.'—I better see about this stickup.—Sometimes I think, 'There goes your original Stone Heart.' "

He raised the volume on his radio and Nora heard the sandpaper voice of the dispatcher sending another crew to the stickup scene.

Hughes zipped his jacket but still didn't move. He said: "I just thank God he's got you. He'd be a friggin castaway."

Nora said without premeditation: "He's got me but I'm not sure I've got him. I hardly see him except at breakfast."

Hughes turned his radio all the way down and let his big sad eyes rest on her till he asked: "What are you sayin, O'Leary?"

Nora held him and looked into his eyes, which were those of a man whose heart had twice given him mortal warning, and she thought she detected something new in his glance; and maybe she stared at him too narrowly, for he turned aside, refusing, as it seemed to her, to meet her eyes. She pondered that, his turning aside, and she thought:

"He's ashamed." But she said: "Go to your robbery, Gil."

She knew that if he knew he would never tell. Nobody will ever tell the wife, at least nobody who cares. She thought: "He can't tell and I can't ask."

She kissed his wrinkled, bristly cheek and followed him to the door. She watched through the clear diamond as he walked stiffly, with a lean to the right, to his cruiser. He opened the door and, looking back over the top of the car, he waved but he didn't smile.

She turned and went to the alcove in the living room where Steven had set up a chair and card table as a place to study away from the noise of the kitchen. She lifted every book and scanned every paper, trying to categorize each thing, to fit it into a course, to see if she came up with three courses.

Gil had said Steven was taking three, but he had told her two. She couldn't help thinking that three would be a better excuse than two for his shifting the routine work of the office to his senior sergeant. Had he lied to Gil or to herself? With trembling hands she shuffled the books and tried to concentrate on the head notes to the case reports, but it was hopeless. There could have been the materials here for one, two, three, maybe four or five courses, for all she could tell.

"Why did he lie?" she asked. Her eyes burned but she didn't weep.

Bending over the table she dropped her head and saw her hair swing just before she closed her eyes. Her hair was still quite thick and glossy. She didn't mind the narrow streaks of white, and she thought Steven didn't either. He had always loved her hair—she remembered that—but that knowledge was a mere flicker in her mind now because she suddenly knew, without further evidence, that when Gil Hughes evaded her eyes he did it for shame. He knew or suspected, and couldn't tell. Thinking with increasing certitude about the lost hour she saw a vision of a woman with Steven. She got no sense of the woman's face but her body was lithe and young. Steven was giving her all she could take. She cried out and he gave her even more, and they laughed till the moment came when they were making hungry puppy sounds. Nora hated it but she watched it. Her contempt for Steven did not drive out her sorrow and pain. He was evidently willing to bring the house crashing down to satisfy his lust on the bitch—to risk children, home, their whole way of life. "Wait, wait," she cried. "I said bitch. No. That's not the way. She is—yes of course a bitch, a body, but it's the way of life that he's rejecting, our whole family and work and life, that's what he's— He doesn't want us!"

Her eyes fell upon a notebook and a phone number Steven had written. Without thought or hesitation she called that number.

A woman's voice said: "ICU."

Nora could neither speak nor think. She slammed the phone down. She knew what ICU meant but what did—

Nearly choking on her shame she cried aloud, "What am I doing?" Next she'd be searching his pockets. "How do I know he didn't say two courses when he—maybe he dropped a course. Maybe he said it last semester."

Disregarding the mess she was making of his books and notes, knowing he would notice it, she began shifting, sometimes throwing things this way and that. Then going back to the notebook with the phone number she turned the pages with quick cracking sounds, tearing one by accident and rushing on, till she came to a page headed "Winter term 1985"—the present—and there she saw a list of course titles—three of them.

Dropping the notebook she sat in his chair saying, "He said three—and here they are." She felt relief in her legs and chest, and a more intense shame for assuming that Gil Hughes "knew." She said aloud: "All right, he's taking three courses. What's the difference?"

Steven was upstairs sleeping, unless the pain had goaded him awake. She imagined the dark room where he lay, and realized the depth of her mistrust and despair—bordering on hate. The sweat in his hair, the smell of his vomit, the horrible barking sound when he bent convulsing over the toilet—none of this had ever upset her before; it was like wiping a baby's chin or changing a diaper: now it nauseated her.

She leapt from one form of torture to another—shame and chaos in her soul perhaps for the first time in her life, hate of the floozie, if there was a floozie, hate for them both together—

Withhold forgiveness, a clear idea—then: "Be somebody else"—other than herself as she understood herself, a person capable of fiery hate and icy rejection, a woman of no faith, a jealous maniac.

She suddenly stood with stark, wide-open eyes as if she were seeing the porn show again. Actually she was recalling the moment in her office at City Hall when she had reasoned that if it were "only an affair" she could forgive him and save their marriage.

"Fool," she said with venom, "pathetic fool."

She could no longer plan to forgive either the man or his slut. She saw the woman in City Hall, herself as she had been that morning, as a faithful imbecile who assumed he would still love her even while he played around with his floozie, and then like most men he'd come back and she, like a queen, would say something revolting like, "Do not kneel, Steven, we still love each other and that's the only thing that matters."

What garbage! She slumped in the chair and fought the tears — the chair he used while studying his precious law courses, one, two, three or twenty of them, in his snug little alcove right in the midst of his family. He'd promise to come to bed within the hour, then he'd study till midnight and Nora would be long since asleep, so they lost another night of love — and it all hung together, the cumulative changes that added up to his rejection of their whole life's structure and meaning.

"It's our way of life," she said aloud. "He's finished." She had perhaps known all this during her little "Queen for a Day" scene in City Hall but hadn't understood all it implied — that she herself had ceased to matter. Now she saw them writhing in each other's arms and heard their animal cries, and she believed she was sick. "I'm the one who's sick. He's innocent, confused but innocent!"

"God what am I saying? Is he — or isn't he?"

While McCord Lay Sick—Lindy

arry Kalzyn lost his nerve but only for a minute. He was running on faith. Naturally he felt a little queasy but, "Go ahead! She's a good-hearted, loving woman." And the passion that he knew was in her—the hunger—that was love too, that was her way of giving herself.

But he believed—and this was the "faith" that supported him—he believed she was still his wife, divorce or no divorce. "But so hot!" he whispered. "I could never really satisfy her."

He still believed it was his duty to protect her. He worried constantly about her living in this run-down building, to save money for Edward's education, when he'd gladly give— The very essence of his hope in life was to win her back. And he believed he could, because marriage is for life.

When he could think coherently about his "wife" Lindy he thought as follows: She had loved him in the beginning with a volcanic passion. His own love ran so deep he couldn't call it passion; it was nearer worship. So if she had loved with such abandon in their early marriage, and if real love may waver or change its temperature—but does not die, then—

Then knock on her door, Doctor, and spring the new idea.

The door opened sooner than he expected and it opened wide, with no security chain to stop it, and his first impulse was to chastise her about that but she hated lectures.

He said: "Huh—hello, Tulip."

"Oh!" she exclaimed in surprise and maybe disappointment. "It's you."

Harry smiled his huge handsome smile which according to his mother and sister took ten years off his age, and he held a bouquet toward her.

"No thank you," said Lindy.

"It's not a bribe. It's a bunch of innocent flowers." Harry brushed the blossoms across her breasts and remarked: "That's a pretty robe, Tulip."

She watched his eyes slip into their old comic ritual, and knew exactly what he'd say next.

And he said it: "Evidence! Conclusive evidence." This harked back to their early courtship; he had said that her figure was the best evidence he had ever seen of a benign creator.

Lindy did not retreat. "Don't come in," she cautioned him.

"Not till I have permission. Take the flowers."

Ignoring the flowers she said with a skeptical frown: "Have you stopped?"

"I have not yet begun to fight."

"Have you stopped, Harry?"

"If you mean with Edward, well, I haven't sent him any money for a long time."

"How long?"

"Oh, I don't know. He wrote a very nice letter and I can't just cut him off now."

"When did he write?"

"Well I can see by your screwed-up face that you're jealous. Maybe you should bribe him. I'll bet a hundred dollars would get you a letter or a phone call."

"Harry, if you talk that way about Edward you can take your flowers and go home."

He was no longer touching her with the blossoms but kept them within an inch. Letting his arm fall, letting the smile disappear, he said earnestly: "You are not losing your son, Tulip. What's happening is, he's in a growing-up phase. Young men know that college isn't life but only preparation, and they are uncertain about what kind of life they want and all they really know is that to be lost in obscurity and to be a nobody is the worst possible fate."

"Edward will not be a nobody," said Lindy.

She took the bouquet and went toward the kitchen, Harry following, exclaiming: "Evidence! Conclusive evidence!"

She smiled at that and filled a vase with water and fluffed up the blossoms. She placed the vase on the kitchen table; then she filled two water glasses, placed long-stemmed glasses on the table and poured brandy for two. Harry watched her doing all this as a man might watch a ballerina whirling in a spotlight. He set her chair and kissed her with unusual pressure but didn't make it wet. He smiled down on her and for some reason she said:

"Thank you, Harry," thinking: "He will never learn how to kiss a woman."

"You're so welcome, Tulip. I've got a proposal."

She saw his hungry, brown, prominent eyes rove over her face and breasts as he said: "My God, that robe."

She expressed not the slightest curiosity about his proposal, which disappointed him a little, but he went round and sat, and picked up his brandy, but put it down to reach across and take her hands. He bent to kiss them. Lindy raised her eyes and let them dwell for a second on the thick curly light-brown, nearly blond hair on top of his head.

Since the divorce Lindy had missed the tragic, funny, intense characters in Harry's big Polish family to the point of an aching, constant hurt. Harry's mother called her often from Chicago, as if she were still a daughter, so did one of the sisters, but Lindy found the contacts painful.

"OK, ready?" Harry asked with enthusiasm.

"Maybe, maybe not," said Lindy with a glare at him.

"Don't fall off your chair," he said.

"Harry, this is what I love about you, I mean used to love."

"Sure, I'm alive, I bring energy and joy, that's me. So here it is, my new idea, to save us both from solitude and gloom, save our marriage and create happiness. What do you think?"

"I think it's a terrific idea but what is it?"

"OK, this is big, here it comes. You and I, we make a baby."

The laugh she threw out so warmed him with sweet memories of happy times that it was worth all the opposition and conflict it foretold.

Harry said: "Do you know I haven't heard you laughing for it seems like years. Do you know how much I love to hear it? Nothing else in life—"

"Stop, Harry. You're out of your mind. That baby idea is old and you had my answer when we were married. You think I'll change now?"

"I don't know, but, you see, Tulip, that's why I came, to find out."

"Harry, you are preposterous. I've just met somebody and it's true I don't love him—don't love him yet—"

"But I saw love in your eyes at the Oak Knoll Grille—for me! Deny it."

"Affection," she countered, "friendship."

"Oh no, not friendship. I know you, Tulip, you're always meeting somebody but I am the permanent man. If you see reality instead of some erotic fantasy, and if you recognize what love is—confess it, this man's married, right—like most so-called eligible men, who— Well is he?"

Without waiting for her to speak Harry bounded ahead, saying:

"Knowing what love is is a brain thing. Love itself is in the heart, sure, but what you feel in the heart, I mean, the brain sort of tells you if it'll work. Saving a marriage, starting a family, these are things you can evaluate in your brain. Happy life is a family. Some things are good in themselves, Tulip, and some are bad."

"Harry, stop this jabber."

"Well, see, when the heart leads you to something that can't work or is bad, the brain says 'Eeek eeek.' "

"Who said it's bad? What if I want him and not you?"

"If he's married it's bad. Anyway you just said you didn't love him, for God's sakes."

"But what if I see him again, which I hope I will, and fall for him?"

She finished her brandy, took a drink of water that cooled her throat, and watched with a knowing change on her lips as Harry refilled her glass. She carefully pushed it across the table to within his reach.

"You mistake passion for love," Harry pronounced, placing two fingers exactly on the base of her glass and sliding it to one side. "Do you think I don't know you? I understand maybe better than you do. Passion, hunger, desire, fantasy—"

"Reality," she interjected.

"This is a critical moment in your life, Tulip. You're teetering on the edge of a knife and for some mysterious reason you won't answer me, is he married?"

"Not your business."

"What kind of life do you want? You have a passion for a married man, I have to assume that, you're not denying it."

"I don't have to deny it. You've got no right to ask it."

"Maybe even children. Does he?"

"I am not going to talk about him."

"I hear everything you refuse to say. Married with kids. Imagine you marry him or just shack up, that is to say, imagine you do to this man's wife and children what the famous 'home wrecker' did to your mother and you. You break up a family to satisfy a passion that'll soon pass. You spoil their life and carry the guilt forever. Don't forget, Tulip, I knew your mother. I saw the hurt and—"

"You barely knew her. She was already dying when you met her."

"Right, and she saw the illness as another way the world was crushing her with its malevolence."

"Why not! It was malignant, malevolent, what difference does it make. She was right."

"Please—the divorce—it stunned her spirit. You yourself said her ability to love even her own children had been blighted or something, by the loss of her husband, that her bitterness and resentment and tears of fury hardened her, and she could not love with her whole heart, because it was broken. Am I wrong? Love is joy, love is—"

Lindy looked into his great, deep, fond eyes and said: "You are right. She went to war against the world, out of sorrow and anger. I don't blame her either."

"Who's blaming her? Just take a minute, though, and contemplate the cause of all this, the woman you have always called the home wrecker."

"I have been contemplating that most of my life."

"So here's my point. One possible future lying before you is to be a home wrecker yourself."

"Do you think I haven't noticed that?"

"So you admit you love him."

"I do not love him, yet."

"So you'd be a kind of sister to the woman who destroyed your mother's happiness. That's one future."

Lindy said: "You know nothing about this man."

"True. How much do you know?"

"I know he wants a new life."

"He has a passion for you. I can understand that. But why is he still married?"

Lindy felt compelled to say: "We know another fact. He still loves his wife."

Harry's jaw dropped visibly and Lindy almost laughed.

He said: "Lindy, you are the real sterling. If we just gave you a chance, if we had a child and—"

"Gave me a chance by having a child! Are you mad, Harry?"

"Lindy, you're a woman with a heart. You would gradually—"

"No!"

"OK but what kind of man is this Lothario of yours if he'll leave his family?"

"About like me, no better and no worse—if he leaves them."

"And that's what you want."

"I don't know what I want."

"Well I do," said Harry smiling. "You want passion and love. I can give you a love that is deeper than your passion. Lindy, Tulip, dearest precious jewel, instead of a fantasy of wild athletic self-abandoning sex, try a different fantasy, a memory really, of you working in your garden."

Lindy yelped with laughter and Harry pressed right on:

"You loved it, and I loved to see you come into the house all dirty and sweaty and happy! Remember, happy? And I'd watch you go upstairs and I could just imagine you in the shower clean and contented with life."

He paused and then asked gently: "May I put a difficult question to you? You who are so honest and courageous."

"Harry, a garden, a baby, I could almost love you for being so ridiculous."

Letting this pass he said: "We both know what you want, to give yourself to love, surrender yourself."

"Oh? Is that what I want? Or is that your—speaking of fantasies—is that yours?"

"And I also know what you fear, Lindy."

"What do I fear, Harry, Doctor of my Spirit?"

"You should never be sarcastic, it doesn't come smoothly off your tongue. You fear a life with no one to love, to love you, to share your life with."

"What you mean," said Lindy, "is that I can't live without a man, but I happen to be doing just fine."

"And there is every possibility," Harry persisted, "I've been trying to tell you, that in a few months I will be as capable as any man and can give you all you need in that department."

Lindy saw a new moisture in his eyes as he stared at her, like a man seeking to understand or explain.

Holding her gaze with his own and speaking softly he said: "A married man. So sordid."

"Harry, dear Harry, what you want is life. That's what I want, and you're telling me that a garden can take the place of passion. You simply don't know what passion is."

"Living with a child you will love, with a man who adores you—my love and the child's will enrich your life, and you will come to love your life, and then by degrees to care for me again, because I will be good to you. And I am not impotent. I'm on this prostate medication but if I go off it for two or three days I'm completely male. You said, 'You give me what I don't need. What I need you can't give me.' That's all wrong. I can give exactly what you need."

Looking at him now with a smile he almost believed was real she said:

"Harry, you are the real sterling."

Harry said: "Tulip, please, for God's sake, don't wreck this man's family. It's not like you."

Two hours later, all alone but acting as if Harry were still haranguing her, she said in her mind: "Be still!" He had no right to lecture her on her own family's history or to put on that pious face and plead with her not to wreck some home that he knew nothing about. Maybe wrecking it would be the biggest favor she could do for that woman, the beloved wife.

What is love worth if the man goes out looking for somebody? "Nothing!" she cried. "That's his judgment, not mine. He's the one who—" Her clear thought was: "If he doesn't value it why should I?"

As for her so-called hunger, what did Harry know about that? He'd understand sexual desperation the day he experienced it for himself.

"And what am I supposed to do tonight? How do I get to sleep—I lie in bed and all I can think about is—a man—I'm giving him what he wants, giving, giving—"

The phone rang and she jumped halfway to the ceiling.

"Steven, Steven," she whispered.

She approached and let it ring, too scared to lift it, and thought of a girl reaching for a flower, then she picked it up and said hello.

"Hi Mom," said her son Edward, "it's me and I'm sorry I didn't call last week."

She was a little amazed at the joy she felt on hearing his voice. She calmed down and they talked for a good twenty minutes.

They had already said goodbye when Edward paused significantly and said: "And Mom."

"Yes?"

"You know he's really a good guy."

She didn't need to ask who he meant.

"He told me," said Edward, "he's hoping you guys'll get married again."

Lindy was silent, and not altogether pleased.

"He said you were interested," said Edward. "Are you?"

"No," Lindy said automatically.

"Why not?"

"Why should I be?"

"Well, like, he's a steady, sincere, generous, you know, man, husband."

"I know."

"And all I want is for you to be happy."

"I am happy," Lindy said.

"Well, OK, that's what matters, your what-do-you-call-it, happiness."

"Is it really?" she asked.

"I don't get you."

"Is that all that matters?"

"I mean not like philosophy or whatever, no, but when you look at your life, sure, you make certain decisions and sometimes you make a mistake, like divorce, but in the end you go for happiness, don't you?"

"I don't know," she said. "Do you?"

"Well sure. What else?"

"How do you decide what happiness is?"

"Gads, Mom, don't you know?"

"What if I can't have it?"

"That'd be tough, but you can have Harry, I know that much. The guy's still mad for you."

"I know it."

"And there's not a mean bone in his body."

"I know it," said Lindy.

"So you're telling me you don't regret the divorce? I sorta thought you did. He'd make you a good husband like before, when the three of us all lived together, and I was too young to know it but we were pretty happy, weren't we?"

After hanging up Lindy thought: "Did he tell him?" Did Harry tell Edward about the "married man"?

"God, no, he wouldn't," she pleaded. "He's not cruel. He wouldn't."

She felt shame inside her like a noxious tree bursting the soil.

"Damn it!" she cried. "He said"—(Edward had said)—"you go for happiness. You take it! Anyway the wife and family are not my responsibility. If he's chasing me it means he—well, wants me. That's clear. Everything else is—I don't know—I—"

CHAPTER 12

Strange Paradox

McCord awoke in the dark and sensed the approaching morning outside his curtained windows. The pain was gone, the relief was upon him. He was still weak but not sick.

Now he could reduce it to English—his "new idea," actually a sequence of ideas, which had assembled itself during the intervals when the pain abated—and having spoken it in succinct language he could examine it for flaws. So as he lay beside his sleeping wife on the fourth morning he sought to put it all together—what he had been thinking, as if in a dark fog, for he knew not how many hours.

"I remember sliding down the bluff, grabbing branches to keep my feet under me." Saying this he pictured the car lot and the slope behind it, and the course of Jonathan Creek between the floodplain on the city side and the higher ground of the industrial park in the county—and he stated what he called the prime fact, from which everything else proceeded: "There is no way for a car to get to the floodplain."

"But that is where Davy says he found the suitcase. Either somebody walked there and dropped it or Davy is lying. I think he's lying although I don't know why.

"If you kidnap a woman," he said silently and quite slowly, "you don't drag her through the streets and throw her on a bus. You certainly don't push her through a lighted car lot. You move her by car." He paused again and felt the hardening of his conviction that Davy was lying.

He was aware that the killer or killers could have left the woman somewhere else, alive or dead, and still dumped the suitcase behind the car lot. Or: somebody (including Davy) could have found the suitcase elsewhere and moved it to the floodplain. But why would Davy steal personal property from a suitcase he found somewhere else, bring it to his own back yard and then call the police?

He repeated the whole thing and added: "Why turn in the suitcase then lie about where he found it?" McCord had no answer for that and counted it a flaw. But he went ahead. The train was leaving the station and McCord jumped aboard to see where it went.

Having thought of a train, he thought of the Penn Central bridge, and of the county side, perhaps just because it was in close proximity, and said in his mind: "Those overgrown streets in the industrial park—with car access from the Shiloh Pike—" Not a complete sentence, but a complete picture.

Now he felt more secure in his reasoning—or in that part of the exercise that employed reason.

"If they were dumping evidence or a body—I think she's dead—I don't know—assume it—it would be easy to pull off the Shiloh Pike, drive a quarter of a mile into the industrial park and do their dirty business—so I can forget the picture of them pushing her across the railroad bridge because they never were on the city side of the creek."

He said: "If there is anything else to be found it'll be found on the county side." That was his most important sentence. He suppressed the next one—but couldn't suppress its preverbal form: Maybe they dumped her—somewhere.

This "new idea," shot through as it was with guesses and assumptions, was satisfying for giving him something to work on.

He was not yet hungry. When hunger came he would know all was well. His eyes no longer saw what wasn't there. They saw the black, and only the black. He lifted the blanket carefully—"Let her sleep"—and slipped out of bed. He pulled the satin edge of the blanket around her shoulders, and imagined her face in sleep.

He turned on the bathroom light so as to admit into the bedroom a pale illumination. Silently he opened a drawer and took out Levi's, shorts, socks, a flannel shirt and his old brown sweater. He dressed, and went past his children's doors carrying his clodhoppers and gun.

He consulted his watch by the fluorescent tube on the kitchen stove and stepped out into the cold, looking for a sign of daylight. The cold had deepened while he lay sick. He decided to brew coffee. There was no point in leaving yet. He ate a slice of whole-wheat bread which tasted surprisingly good, and sat at the table waiting while the coffee chugged in the percolator. The full lights of the kitchen canceled the prospect of a dawn outside. He adjusted the gun against his side, went to the hall closet, put on his red-and-black plaid jacket and a black watch cap and returned to the old maple table. He sat there dressed for cold weather, with his hand spread over the crank's journal. He saw Lindy standing naked before him—her white breasts and brown nipples so modest and plain, her belly only a little rounded, her hips amply curved, and her mons veiled by a red moss.

He slid into the car, flicked on his radio and keyed the receiver, which gave the rushing noise it was supposed to give, and opened the thermos of coffee.

His breath streamed over the smoking surface of the cup and he wondered where the light came from. The rising smoke seemed to derive a pale flow of light from the blackness in the cup. He tasted the coffee, started the engine, and turned on the headlights. Once again all hope of dawn vanished in the harsh beams of light. He backed into the alley and sipped the coffee, and knew he was well. Turning with one hand, flipping from reverse to drive with the same hand, he drove slowly, pushing forward into the pitching, reaching beams of light between the rows of trash cans.

To be the only man moving through the darkness was to be who he wanted to be. Now he was concentrated; there was nothing in his mind except cop.

He drove out of the residential neighborhood and went northwest on a big diagonal where the early traffic was already directing disciplined files inbound. In fifteen minutes he reached Valley Used Car Sales on Hale Avenue, and he sat in his car waiting for better light.

Impatient, hungry and somehow thrilled, McCord crossed the street. He stepped over the chain and went straight to the 1970 Pontiac Bonneville, and peered in at the pile of greasy Navy blankets where Davy took his rest. The cars, even the old ones, even the Bonneville, gleamed under the mercury vapor lights, and McCord decided he had enough light to make his way down to the floodplain.

He walked around Davy's garden and paused. The global traffic noise reached him from distant highways all around, filling the chill morning air. The routes into the city were displayed in his imagination with the exactitude of a survey map. But the interior light was stronger than the exterior—and he stabbed his right eye on a branch that he never saw. He gasped with shock and pain, cupped his palm over the eye, and stood there catching his breath and waiting for the pain to go away and his strength to return. This was bad luck. He was barely strong enough without this. And the stab had hit his shooting eye, which was better than the left. The pain was severe and didn't retreat. He stood there enduring it, getting gradually stronger, maybe, thinking however of the chain woven through the frames of the cars in the front row.

Looking back, his right eye still covered, he could see the traffic growing thicker and slower on Hale Avenue. And through the trees across the creek he could see the spasmodic white flashes of the traffic streaming along the Shiloh Pike a half-mile away.

McCord took a few steps and his clodhoppers made a gritty sound in the frost. His eye didn't hurt so much; the relief seemed too good to be true. But he moved by slower steps, descending from tree to tree and stretching his hands out in the foggy darkness marked with the vague shadows of close-set trees.

Reaching the place where Davy had said he found the suitcase he could already see the texture of the frozen mud at his feet. He stood there getting colder, wanting to move, but wanting also to survey this place again. He pulled on a pair of tight leather gloves and buried his hands in his jacket pockets. He was cold all through and the cold made him think of sickness. He pulled the watch cap down over his ears. The paths might be easier to see now, and the sky if he looked straight up seemed nearly as light as the eastern arc. Everywhere the trees proclaimed winter in stark hieroglyphs against the lightening sky.

He took a path he knew from boyhood, or some successor to that path in this flood-prone lowland, and came after three or four minutes to the silent creek. He beheld on his left the elevated framework of the railroad bridge. Elsewhere the morning had been windless, but here a frigid breeze rolled along the stream bed and sifted through the black girders above him.

He scaled the embankment, a struggle to gain more height than he lost by sliding with the crushed stones dislodged by his steps, and at length he stood panting by the tracks. He was not yet fully recovered, and felt his weakness in the quick shallow breaths he drew. Behind him the rails laid down on despoiled land a curve conceived in the mind of a civil engineer in the nineteenth century. Before him the tracks crossed the bridge into the county, to pass through the industrial park and emerge after ten or fifteen miles in farmland that was today exactly as it had been during McCord's youth—fertile and plowed from fence to fence, too valuable to despoil—yet.

As the light suffused the inner box of the bridge frame he stepped with some care from tie to tie, seeing the turbid colorless water motionless below, and said to himself again, no, they had not crossed this bridge with their captive. A misstep here and your leg is jammed up to the thigh between the creosoted wood ties.

Having crossed the bridge he stood in the county, on somewhat higher ground just opposite the place where he had stood minutes before.

He walked along a trail that paralleled the creek then struck out through chest-high brush till he reached another trail. He continued generally upstream till he could see on his right, across the creek, the rising land of the city nature preserve, which placed him some two hundred yards upstream of the bridge.

He came to the road he had driven in his car the night he got his migraine. He hesitated. If he took this road he'd soon reach the center of the industrial park, with its overgrown gravel roads decorated here and there with hydrants and street signs. Staring at the squat gray shapes of half a dozen isolated structures McCord made a decision.

He turned back. The suitcase was physical and real, the property of Marie Carden. The idea that turned McCord back was mental, had no physical reality. It contradicted an earlier thought, that Davy would not move the suitcase, steal from it, then call the cops. He had called; so the remaining unknown was whether he had moved it.

Crossing the bridge in the improving light he retraced his route and stood a few minutes later knocking with leather-gloved knuckles on the window of Davy's car. Now his hands were warm and he pushed the watch cap back on his head.

Davy's hand sneaked out of the blankets toward the bare-ended wire. McCord shouted his name and beat on the window.

They crossed the railroad bridge together and made their way to the two-rut road. McCord held Davy lightly by the shoulder of his coat. Davy moved as if to shrug off McCord's grip but didn't struggle.

Davy didn't like the look of this cop—black work shoes, red-and-black plaid jacket, black hat, blue jeans, and silence. Broad, tough face and hands big enough to squash somebody's head. Not a huge man, but those hands. Jesus! One eye bloodshot and dripping tears. A cop ought to be clean shaven and this flatfoot's mug was not. He knew that undercover cops went unshaven and tried hard to look like bums, which was what Davy looked like without any effort at all.

To Davy, McCord's whiskery jaw looked like a spade that had grown hair and his eyes looked unforgiving. When this lieutenant had been a uniformed rookie he'd be the kind who'd kick a bum off a park bench. That had happened to Davy more than once. You're lying there bothering nobody and some boy in blue weighing two ten and standing seven feet high kicks your butt just because you've got one.

Davy and guilt had never got along. He knew his station in life. Even when he did right he'd get fucked by the system and this guy was the system's guy. Davy stumbled along, one shoulder lifted higher than the other by "the system."

McCord released him and said, "I don't suspect you, Davy."

"Good, cause I ain't done nothin."

"But I believe you're lying about where you found the suitcase. I just can't picture anybody dropping it where you say you found it. I think you found it on this side, Davy."

"Didn't neither."

"Yes you did."

Davy thought: "Here comes 'maggot' and 'scrotebag' and 'briar hopper' and 'bum.' "

"Lying to a police officer investigating a case is a crime," McCord said, "but I don't suspect you of any other crime and I won't charge you with lying if you tell me the truth now. Show me where you found it."

Davy went motionless like a chipmunk sheltering in its camouflage. He didn't look at McCord. But he wished he could look straight at the copper and see his expression. Had he looked he would have seen a tension and expectation, hope, in McCord's blue eyes, and tears still streaming out of the one that was swollen.

"We're looking for a young woman," McCord said. "An innocent— beautiful—" His voice quit before it broke. He thought: "For Christ's sake what's wrong with me?"

He felt Davy's shoulder in his hand again. He looked into Davy's evasive watery pale blue half-buried briar-hopper eyes and he squeezed the shoulder and rocked the man by way of appeal.

"I'm sure you had a reason to lie," he said, "but there's a better reason to tell the truth."

Davy's eyes, which were willing now to look into McCord's, seemed older than his face, and his face seemed older than his years. McCord knew he was calculating. He had been calculating for forty or fifty years and ended up living in a car.

"Look," McCord urged, "we're not in my territory. I don't care what you do in the county."

Said Davy: "Now who's lyin."

"No I don't. So long as it's not too serious."

"Ha-ha-haaarrright! And if it is too serious, puketown for ole Dave."

McCord said: "Davy, for Christ's sake help me."

This was the sharpest probe in the homicide detective's kit. Drawn too early or too late it was unavailing. McCord waited, and lifted his hand, still feeling in his cupped fingers the mold of dry bones.

Davy heard the formula in all its latent power reaching clear back to the hills of Kentucky and to the porch of the family cabin—"for Christ's sake," a phrase it was dangerous, as he well knew, to interpret literally, and "help me," another figure of speech of uncertain meaning, depending on who used it. "Help me." And who was this guy who kept getting too close? He thought of this intimidating cop without looking at his face, he sensed his thrusting presence. Caught in a tangle of fear, hate and respect, Davy looked again at those eyes bluer than his own. He saw a pleading, a passion there. The guy's breath came out in steamy puffs.

"So you won't tell no deputy?" Davy asked.

"Have you hurt anybody, Davy?"

Hearing this, Davy again felt the lieutenant coming closer—too close. Davy saw that streaming eye.

Davy said: "You mean, did I—"

"It's a simple question. Have you hurt anybody?"

"Hell no, not me."

"OK. I won't tell the sheriff or any deputy."

" 'Kay then," said Davy and he led the way along the two-rut road to where it angled up a low rise to the industrial park, and they proceeded through weeds holding aloft a lattice of frost, soaking their trousers, till McCord could feel the weight and tug of the Levi's against his thighs. It was chill moisture, and the sun didn't warm it.

They advanced on a low worn-down building and for a moment McCord thought of it as their destination—but Davy went on by; they crossed a weed-infested square and aimed for a second building—and McCord picked up the smell.

"Stinks, don't it?" said Davy. "Good thing it ain't hot. Ha!"

McCord felt a sudden urge to stop, to control his anxiety—fear. He kept going and kept silent amid his wild imaginings.

They went half around the building and McCord saw that the windows had been covered with plywood. Yet the driveways leading to the loading bays showed signs of recent use. Davy said he got his leather here. He showed McCord how he pried one corner of a sheet of plywood loose and how he crawled in. He said he trimmed his strips of leather from the hides stacked inside.

"And you found the suitcase in there?" This question started pictures flashing in McCord's inner cinema of rotting cow hides stacked as high as a man.

But Davy said no, and led McCord down a cement stairway to the double drive below the loading docks, then past a row of offal barrels sealed with steel tops, and up a single-lane track that led out to one of the wider gravel roads. Where the track met the road Davy stopped and said:

"Here."

The weeds were beaten down. McCord saw a place where the suitcase might have rested. Davy cocked his chin and McCord followed him back toward the building, to a row of steel drums. Frozen streaks of offal ran down the sides. Davy approached a drum and took out a hunting knife, and McCord saw a glimpse of the scabbard hanging under his left arm.

Inserting the knife between the rim and the lid, Davy flipped the lid, replaced his knife and zipped his jacket against the cold. McCord did not feel cold. Davy kicked the lid away and reached deep into the drum and pulled out a wad of newspaper, unwrapped it and held out a woman's purse. At McCord's request he wrapped it up and put it back into the drum, and replaced the lid.

Davy said he had found it after the detectives released him, when he went back to look for more things, to make up for the scarf and perfume that the cops had taken. He took McCord to a place not far away where he had found the purse. He said there was nothing else.

McCord said, "Come with me, Davy," and they walked toward the Shiloh Pike and went into the Sunoco station. With his first call McCord cleared a joint city-county search with the field lieutenant at Operations. Next he described his findings to the Bureau and invited them to take part in the search. Next he reached his own duty sergeant, noting that it was just 7 A.M. and suggesting it should be possible to get six volunteers from the First Relief, then going off duty, and six from the Second. Thus he drew an ample complement of his own officers to augment the search party that he hoped the sheriff would organize. He called the chief deputy at his home, interrupting his breakfast, and found him willing.

McCord stood at the edge of the Shiloh Pike where the road he had explored gave access to the park. When a deputy drove up McCord asked him to prevent anybody from driving in and obliterating whatever tire tracks an evidence crew might be able to find. He regretted his own cruise in the dark on this ground. When the shoulder of the pike was lined with city and county cruisers, and the officers stood in silent solemn groups, the chief deputy spread them in a long line abreast and set them in motion.

They pressed slowly forward into the grass and rank weeds. McCord took a place near the center. In imagination he saw two men grasp a woman's body by the wrists and ankles, swing her once, twice, and on the third swing send her flying—so they made no foot tracks and trampled no weeds. He saw her body fly and heard it swish in the grass. He walked forward in the line and an inner voice cautioned him not to see, not to imagine, her body naked. The thrown body was clothed.

But the one he actually saw, ten seconds after the officer on his left shouted "Halt," was not.

She lay a few yards from the road, at the end of a trampled track with grasses bent both ways. So she had not been thrown. Everything else that could be done to her had been done.

An hour, two hours later, McCord remembered a passage from the journal in which Charles Carden wrote that he could not reconcile a paradox— that the universe was a mass of atoms, a physical system, mere physics. "But I adore this child." And now McCord saw the "child" the old man adored.

CHAPTER 13

Free Advice

After twenty years as a cop Steven McCord knew all about defensive wounds and binding wounds, rope burns, contusions and penetrations.

What he didn't know was why the world should be ordered in such a way as to permit one human being to inflict these on another. Driving from the search site he had Marie Carden's body in his eyes. Seeing the traffic and the stop lights, he still saw the wreath of frost around her lips and her open, frozen eyes. He wanted to relieve his mind by doing an hour's worth of administrative work before going home to shave, shower and eat breakfast, then he would dress in a suit and tie, go back to work and be normal. So he headed toward his station, thinking that the faces of the dead seldom tell much about the ordeal of dying. They may be wasted but this is evidence of the illness, not the death agony; or serene, but this merely declares the dying finished. If they are bruised, swollen, cut or wounded this may appear as mere damage if the viewer is not engaged, like the damage one sees on an animal carcass by the roadway. But it is actually a coded message to the engaged seer; the imagination fills in the pain and terror.

McCord's imagination now let him see the hitherto unseen in the new life he planned, a life free of certain experiences that were inescapable in the present. For the first time he gave a moment's conscious and clear thought to the idea that was driving Sergeant Hughes crazy—the absurd possibility that by entering the profession of law he, Steven McCord, commander of the 6th District, might someday find himself defending accused criminals. This "clear" thought placed McCord in a courtroom, arguing to a jury that the man or men who had murdered Charles Carden and his daughter were not guilty. He then revised this scenario and allowed himself to listen to a voice in his brain saying, somewhat more reasonably, not that they were innocent but merely that their guilt had not been proven beyond a reasonable doubt by admissible evidence.

This second, seductive version of the clear thought was, as McCord understood it, actually a defense of a noble system of justice that seeks to protect the innocent. In this kind of thinking "innocent" referred to defendants who could not be proved guilty beyond reasonable doubt. It did not refer to Charles and Marie Carden. Their kind of innocence was less important to society than the integrity of the justice system. So McCord understood that he had to choose—to act as if he were "society" itself, or some functionary of it, or a man.

Up to this point McCord had thought of law and lawyering as abstract, scholarly work. He would be drawn into intellectual problems. The work would pay enough to take him to Hawaii for two weeks in the winter and to Upper Michigan for a week in the summer. He would be free—not of work, worry and obligations—but of whatever it was that was producing the howl in his mind. The howl was an affliction so severe that he had begun to imagine himself screaming in the shower, something he had never done. What he needed to drive away the confusion was work. So he went to the station, arriving a few minutes before a black limo pulled into the front driveway and halted at the foot of the steps leading to the main door. These were four concrete steps.

A man grasping two canes got out laboriously from a back door of the limo, assisted by a chauffeur. He wore a dark blue topcoat with a black velvet collar. The coat, and the man's trousers and shiny black shoes were in that kind of sophisticated taste that calls attention to itself by being as inconspicuous as possible. The gentleman stood propped between his wooden canes and waited while the chauffeur carried a wheelchair to the top of the steps.

"All you have to do, Jason," said Wesley Hawkins, "is catch me if I fall."

Wesley Hawkins was a man of some seventy years who scorned such euphemisms as "disabled" and "challenged" and thought of himself with bitter vehemence as a "cripple." And with a cane slanting out from either hand and a look in his old shrunken filmy eyes that would ignite asbestos he prepared to ascend.

Jason, his driver and factotum, followed with arms outstretched. They were big arms, quite filling the sleeves of his chauffeur's suit coat. His neck was thicker than an ordinary man's thigh; his round skull was colored a steely gray by the stubble he shaved twice a week. His close-set eyes, of no particular color, moved diligently over Hawkins's back and legs, watching the wobbling rubber-tipped canes in particular. Jason was capable of moving fast, like the wrestler he used to be, and he could carry his boss in one hand, if the need arose, while lighting his cigarette with the other. It's true the boss had been reduced by cruel nature to a fraction of his former weight.

Wesley Hawkins rested on the first step and shouted back, "See, Jason?" as if Jason were a mile away.

"I see, Mr. Hawkins, but can you go on?"

"Going on right now!" Hawkins cried, and lifted his left foot to the next step. The canes shook and the man panted. The useless right foot slid up to the step. Hawkins reset the canes and lurched forward and upward, steadying himself at the new level and calling out:

"Always was afraid of heights. Ha! Acrophobia!"

"Yes sir," said Jason like one who knew the word. A cutting wind passed through his suit coat, made for looks, not warmth, but he could see that the old goat didn't even notice the cold. "Neither would I—" Jason thought, but didn't quite finish. This was the fate of most of his thoughts; they got off to a fine start and then melted in their own complexity.

It wasn't his employer's money, house or car that awed Jason—it was the old fart's photo-plate memory. He'd say, "Jason, you'd better get the car lubricated." Jason might or might not remember, but a week later the boss would ask, "How come you haven't lubricated the car, Jason?" And the boss's voice never trailed off. He never said "uhh" or "mmm" and told Jason not to.

"Uhh, you better rest," Jason advised. He knew his employer's limitations.

"I rest at the top," Hawkins breathed. He lifted his left foot, and the canes wobbled fearfully.

Hawkins was fully aware that he had sat helpless on his bed last night and allowed his nurse, the obese Mrs. Pumphrey, to unlace his shoes and pull off his trousers and shorts; that she had helped him lower himself to the toilet and get up from it—and yet now he was climbing these steps unaided. Mrs. Pumphrey believed he couldn't take a step without the assistance of her tremendous arms and the proximity of her steamy bosom. The monster was nearly as strong as Jason and he thought of her fat as camouflage for muscle. "Let her believe it!" he said to himself and he reached the third step.

His next obstacle, between six and eight inches high like the others, looked especially formidable. He stared at it, as he might stare at a stupid lawyer. He panted and sweated; he felt the blood trying to rise in his neck, but he did not loosen his tie. Never in adult life had he appeared in public with a loosened tie, except in the locker room at the Drumlin Country Club, which of course was the least public place in his social sphere. Rather it was a sanctum for him and his equals, of whom there were few in the city.

He mounted the step, reached the summit, and turned his rear to the wheelchair that Jason had placed five minutes before. With canes propped behind him he lowered his butt slowly, reaching the point of no return sooner than he expected, and fell into the chair.

"You made it, Mr. Hawkins."

Wesley Hawkins smiled, and networks of creases and valleys appeared all over his weathered face. Then Jason released the brake and spun the chair, and pushed ahead, and thus Wesley Hawkins, without appointment or warning, entered the headquarters of the 6th District and announced that he wished to see the commanding officer.

"You should build a ramp, Lieutenant," said Wesley Hawkins peremptorily.

"We're scheduled for a ramp," Steven McCord answered in a voice that had no timbre.

"Scheduled. A man in a wheelchair cannot go up steps with the aid of a schedule. A schedule is a scrap of paper."

Hawkins launched into a speech on the right of access to public buildings. He actually didn't give a damn what the city did or did not do for cripples. He was stalling, trying to collect his wits. This happened but seldom, this need to regroup, but the man he now confronted took him by surprise.

Hawkins saw the ruin of a man. He reminded him of Emerson's dictum that "man is a god in ruins." But this—could this disheveled—unimpressive—loser—be the man his sources in the Police Department had described as one of their elite, as a district commander nicknamed "Best Foot," a former homicide detective destined for promotion to captain—and perhaps not incidentally the husband of the third most powerful person in City Hall (after the mayor and president of the City Council)? Could he? Hawkins was caught between amazement and hilarity. The man was big enough but he slouched and looked depleted, like a homeless bum!—sitting there at a district commander's desk—a tramp!

While rattling on about the poor pitiful cripples and so forth Hawkins had an insight. He saw that this "lieutenant" looked like an actor playing the part of a bum—as if the makeup artist had slapped on "pale" and "haggard" and maybe "hungry"—with "abandon hope, all ye who enter here" thrown over the whole picture. In the first place he was dirty. Hawkins had seen the worn-out jeans spattered with mud, the muddy boots; he saw the threadbare plaid jacket that must be twenty years old, and the expressionless face that hadn't known a razor for a week.

That was the worst of it, the way his pallor contrasted with the blackness of the beard. But in the eyes there was hardly any contrast; no sparkle, no fire; the eyes were barely there. The man seemed to have no presence. Wesley Hawkins almost pitied those eyes.

He was having a private, self-satisfied dialogue with himself about this "ruin" and it almost compensated for his useless legs. He said to himself: "Pity!" But this little combination of four letters—yitp, or itpy, or pyit—in whatever order you like, these four tiny letters shifted his mind off its pillars— he knew not why. Or maybe he did. "I'm pitying a man—who can walk? Which of us is the proper object of pity?" He said all this to himself as he went ranting on about access to public buildings.

From his tirade he slid into a specific recognition that pity—rotting emotion—drove out love and respect. He hated it! He decided to let fly at this "ruin."

"As you are now, Lieutenant, I once was. I played handball, golf and tennis. My lungs were strong and my heart could have supplied a mother elephant with oxygenated blood. Look at me now!"

McCord looked, without showing much interest and zero empathy, and this suggested something amazing to Hawkins, that the man did not know who he was.

McCord said, "I will talk to somebody about the ramp. I agree that the handicapped should have access to this building. You know this place used to be a funeral home, it was never designed for—"

"I know it well, sir. I remember when it was a private residence, before the old man died. I have attended elegant parties, I have eaten a superb dinner in this very room."

This cut no ice with McCord.

But Wesley Hawkins now embarked on a narrative that McCord listened to with sharp interest.

"My health was generally good until quite recently, generally, with one small exception I will not address." He looked again into the wrinkled smirking face of a prostate gland and it almost made him gag. He continued: "But two years ago, sir, less than two years ago, I began to feel a weakness in my legs and pain in my lower back, which symptoms I mistook for the normal advance of aging, but that particular form of candor can actually metamorphose into denial. You will discover all this, sir, in due time. Then I found myself compensating in various ways for the pain, which in itself was not a major problem.

"And by so compensating I must have gotten myself into an awkward gait, especially going down stairs, because that was what hurt most. But not too much! I could endure it, I did endure it. People do not want to hear the complaints of aging men."

To which McCord said mentally: "Please stop talking."

"In any event," Hawkins was saying, "whatever the cause, I fell, and my back struck something hard, and that caused a rather severe pain, and I took to my bed for a day or two.

"My back hurt me in a new way. I am telling you this to explain how a healthy man just like you can be changed in a matter of weeks into what you see before you, sir."

McCord thought: "I can be changed faster than that"—seeing himself strutting in a courtroom.

"They operated, and found a tumor on my spine. It had hemorrhaged and the pressure on the spinal cord has landed me in this chair. But for a rigorous program of physical therapy every day of my life I would be totally immobile.

"Damn the ramp," Wesley Hawkins said in a sudden shift. "I must be imposing on you. Dressed as you are, it's obvious you did not expect to meet the public this morning."

"I did not," said McCord, and nothing more. He made no comment on Hawkins's sob story and he didn't explain his attire.

"Your duties must have taken you off the beaten path."

"Mr. Hawkins," said McCord, "you came here with something on your mind. If it wasn't a ramp, what was it?"

Hawkins said, "You are the district commander."

"Yes."

"And Laurel Street is located in your district?"

"Yes sir. You are here to discuss the murder of Charles Carden."

"So!" Hawkins said to himself. "He is quick!"

"Correct, sir," Hawkins said to the lieutenant. "I read about it in the papers. Charles Carden and I were law school classmates. Being older, he was a mentor to me. He was a veteran of the war, you know, while I was fresh out of college. I might have volunteered to fight but my father dissuaded me, so instead I went into an officer training program in college and the Japanese did me the favor of surrendering before I was needed. Do you have classmates who are especially dear to you?"

"I went to night school, Mr. Hawkins. It's not the same."

"High school classmates, then."

"Yes." Again McCord created a silence between them.

Now Hawkins examined the other's eyes with care. The right one was apparently recovering from some kind of jab or slap. He didn't know whether to pity or to hate those striking, intense blue eyes. Hawkins thought: "He's pretending boredom. Maybe he does know."

"I am not here, Lieutenant, to tell you your duty. I am here to say that Charles Carden was an extraordinary man, a human being among the rest of us apes."

"You have a poor opinion of humanity, Mr. Hawkins."

"And you have a higher one?—In this city and environs there are half a million souls and I doubt ten of them served their fellow men as Charles Carden did. He never took a case purely for the money. He took his cases for the good he could do even when defeat was foreordained. His whole life—"

"Mr. Hawkins," McCord interrupted, "in this department we have a unit called the Detective Bureau, and within the Bureau we have a unit called Homicide. Those are the ones you should be talking to."

"I was told that a district commander could exert a strong influence."

"You have been misinformed. I am a spectator in this case just as you are. It's the Bureau's case. If Mr. Carden were a homeless man living out of a grocery cart or if he were the mayor of the city, or my own father, it would still be the Bureau's case."

"You can surely impart a sense of urgency," Hawkins protested, "you can spur the detectives on to greater effort. Show them what I am trying to show you, that this man was—"

"Of equal value with a homeless drug addict or a strangled prostitute."

"Well of course! In the eyes of God and the law. But in the politics of your department someone assigns priorities, someone allocates resources and directs energy. Someone kindles the fire of determination and awakens zeal, to catch the killer. Every organization of whatever kind has its—"

"Right. And the proper man to inspire the detectives is the chief of detectives. And I'll be happy to give you his name and number, though he may be too busy to talk to you."

Hawkins allowed himself to think in a flash: "Woe unto the policeman who is too busy to talk to me." He stomped out this thought. He had seen one man after another overestimate his own influence. That way lay humiliation. He was looking at the "ruin" with a searching, voracious eye, thinking: "He knows who I am. He's showing how tough he is."

McCord spoke, as if to introduce a new idea. "You seem to know a thing or two about the Police Department, Mr. Hawkins."

"I know nothing about it," Wesley Hawkins shot back. In fact it had taken him less than ten minutes on the phone this morning to learn this man's identity and reputation. He looked again at the bum's costume, and he made a sudden guess that administrative work would bore him. He'd insist on being a real cop no matter what his rank. "But surely a district commander wouldn't go under cover!" Hawkins exclaimed to himself.

He repeated aloud, "No, I know nothing about the Police Department, but perhaps a little about organizations in general, hierarchies, bureaucracies. One duplicates another. Every ant heap is more or less like every other. In fact Charles Carden taught me all about that sort of thing during our midnight bull sessions in law school. He told us younger men, he said, 'Every battalion in the US Marine Corps is like every other. The structure, the mission, the methods are all identical.' "

"Except," McCord interrupted.

"Yes, yes, let me finish. The difference, and this is what Charles emphasized, is leadership. The leader virtually creates an organism within the outlines of some table of organization, and the table thereby becomes irrelevant.

"And that, you see, Mr. McCord, is why I am here rather than Downtown. The case needs a leader's drive and cunning. Let me shame you just a bit. I ask you to break out of a little box on a chart, for the sake of a good man murdered. I am not asking you to prowl the city in a tramp's clothes, stinking of booze and tobacco, sleeping under bridges, as a cover for your true role. No no. I only ask you to do what you can to energize the investigation. I am only—"

"You've made yourself clear. I've heard your request, and you have my answer."

"And you are dismissing me. Our conference is at an end. I advise you, sir, to—"

"The Bureau is investigating this case and I am not."

Now Wesley Hawkins felt right at home. The man was trying to beat him down, as if anybody could. He said, "I have other information."

"What information?"

"That you, Lieutenant, have the reputation of a tenacious and sometimes driven investigator."

"That's all in the past. Now I'm an administrator."

"Surely more than that. Of course you have administrative duties, but as a district commander surely you care about justice."

"This is a homicide case," said McCord, "and homicide is not my business."

"Not your business!" Hawkins cried. "A policeman who has no responsibilities when a murder is committed in his own district?" And Wesley Hawkins thought: "Look at him. I stung him."

McCord rose from his chair and Hawkins expected a confrontation, but instead McCord turned and stood staring out the window, showing Hawkins his back; and so Hawkins sat silent and left the next move to his adversary. It was about to burst from him, the question: "Do you know who I am?" But he suppressed it. Suppose McCord said, "No, who are you?" Would he then claim to be, what he was, the most influential and widely connected lawyer in the city—with allies and contacts where they would do him, and his clients, the most good? That was the last thing he would ever do.

He saw the breadth of the man's shoulders and the slenderness of his hips, saw him, in short, as an athlete in full possession of everything that he, Wesley Hawkins, had lost. Not a new thought: a repeated, hurtful thought; he saw men like this all the time, especially when he wheeled around the locker room at the Drumlin Club making light of his affliction and still drinking with the same old bunch. He also thought of this man's equipment, relative to his own, since the prostate calamity, and a tiny voice in his brain tried to squeak: "Doesn't matter! Power, that's what matters." Of course this was—as the French would say—garbage! Then he lost control and said something he wished he could retract, as in: "Your Honor, please instruct the jury to ignore that." But it was out.

What he said was: "Lieutenant McCord, given the chance I would strangle the killer. My arms, shoulders and hands are very strong. I am a powerful man from the waist up, Lieutenant. If you brought him to me I would gladly throttle him!"

McCord turned on him and said, as if instructing a rookie cop, "It is not my job to throttle anybody, not even Charles Carden's murderer. My job is to run this District."

"And solve crimes!"

"No. That's the job of—"

McCord never finished that repetitious sentence because Wesley Hawkins's eyes bulged and he shouted:

"Where is the girl? Where is Marie?"

This hit McCord like a projectile. Hawkins could see that. Still standing behind his desk the lieutenant looked like a man drowning. After regaining a degree of control he seemed to be reappraising Hawkins, perhaps, and watching the older man's hands—at which moment Hawkins realized they were trembling. He grasped the arms of his wheelchair.

McCord said: "We found a body this morning on the county side of Jonathan Creek. There's been no identification yet but I think it is the body of Marie Carden."

Hawkins gave a cry of anguish and for a second, in the enclosure of his shock and anguish, he shrank from a major player on the city scene to a wretched, grieving lover. His power and prestige in the public arena and in the arena of his mind were all based on law books, a silver eloquence, cleverness and quickness, connections and deep knowledge—yet he had failed this girl through neglect, laziness, and the importance of his own children—who didn't need him at all.

He was close on cursing all mankind—and God. That was what he wanted to do. "I curse the killer and all mankind and I curse God!" He nearly let it come out.

McCord walked slowly around the desk and approached and put a hand on Hawkins's shoulder. Looking up Hawkins did not see the "god in ruins," he saw a rugged cop with an unshaven face and he noticed the thick strong hands on the man.

Wesley Hawkins said, "I am Charles's friend. I loved Agnes before Charles ever married her. I wanted to marry her myself but she chose Charles. I held that baby in my arms, I made her smile, I was a second father—I am that girl's godfather."

His voice quit working. He averted his eyes and thought of Marie, and knew instantly the agony she had suffered.

She was only sixteen when he last saw her, and now he included himself in the circle of the accursed, for neglecting her, for devoting himself so fiercely to his own children, the same who later called him a buffoon and a laughingstock for marrying a young lawyer. "You divorce Mother and marry a floozie! You, the great intellectual, led around by your peter." He forgot whatall they called him; all he remembered now was Marie as a baby, Marie at sixteen—and his guilt seethed inside him.

She had needed a steady, practical mentor to guide her and to counter the idealistic and dreamy influence of her saintly father—somebody to teach her what the world is really like—and he had failed and forgotten her. He gave all his attention to his own brats, who understood nothing about his second marriage or his needs. No, as soon as Marie went to California he forgot she existed, didn't even answer her Christmas cards, didn't send a dollar or make a single phone call to ask: "How are you doing out there?"

He told McCord: "I was among the chumps who ridiculed Charles Carden. I was so stupid and class-bound as to say to him, 'You'll never get into a country club this way. Clean yourself up. I'll buy you a good suit. Practice law!' He was kind to me and did not answer as he could have. The Drumlin Country Club for Christ's sake! What I saw in his eyes was reproach and disappointment. He could control his words but not his eyes." Hawkins added as an afterthought: "At that time I was addicted to status, advancement, money, power. And I still am."

He was staring ahead; he felt McCord squeeze his shoulder. Staring at nothing he saw everything about Marie's ordeal. He cursed his imagination and loathed its fertility. He cursed the man who was choking Marie in the scene playing in his brain. The man hurled her to the ground and threw himself on her naked body. Hawkins turned away but the vision was inside his eyes. The Marie that he saw was only sixteen. The man was tearing her clothes and punching her with his fists. Hawkins heard her sobbing, saw her pitiful nakedness and her futile attempts to pull away, to hide herself, to bend so her breasts could not be seen. The murderer of her father jerked her up and grasped those soft and tender breasts and squeezed to make her scream. Hawkins saw all this.

When he regained his wits he found the room silent, and McCord sitting sidewise on his desk, with one leg swinging and the other braced against the floor. He was watching Hawkins with patient eyes.

Hawkins hesitated as if he feared the answer and asked: "Had she been assaulted?"

"We'll have the answer to that later," said McCord.

"But did you see cuts, bruises—"

McCord stared at him. His eyes were changing but he did not speak.

Hawkins was held, horrified by McCord's eyes. He drew a great breath and shouted: "Jason!"

The chauffeur entered and Hawkins felt a jolt when he took the chair by its handles. The chair began to rotate and Hawkins held up his hand. The chair stopped and turned back to face McCord.

Hawkins said: "After she moved to California I took Charles to lunch. Agnes was already dead. Did I say that Agnes was his wife? That I loved her first and always regarded Marie as—not that she wasn't Charles's daughter, but I said, 'Agnes is her mother.' Marie, daughter of Agnes.

"Charles's usual lunch was a baloney and cheese sandwich. I said, 'Man, you've got to eat vegetables.' And he said, 'I eat carrots. They're cheap.' So I took him to the Bicycle Club where they really fill your plate, where the talk is good and so is the food. Everybody is a hotshot. If you're some kind of plodding insurance salesman you don't get in; the members are chosen for their style and brains, for companionship and good cheer. And status of course. Ha!

"But they do have a certain minimum standard, and when I picked Charles up at his house I almost said, 'You can't walk into the Bicycle Club in those clothes.' I kept my mouth shut and took him. Regardless of my reputation, I took him.

"And I'll tell you, Mr. McCord, there was one member who knew who he was, and that was the mayor. Remember Mayor Green? He came up to us, shook Charles's hand and said what an honor it was to see him at the club, and please would I bring him often. I still thought, 'What's OK at the Bicycle Club will never work at a country club like Drumlin—never!'"

Hawkins repeated: "Everything I have lost, you still possess. Youthful vigor, good legs, health, the love of a good woman—I presume here, sir, I just presume. A future. I have no future compared to you. Because of all this," he continued, "you scorn the role of the foot soldier. I did so myself. I was fool enough to lecture Charles on it. I said, 'Charles, you are wearing out your life on petty projects that have no effect. Do the big things! If somebody gets thrown out by his landlord, so what! Don't waste your time and talent on these small misfortunes.'

"And you, Lieutenant, are rising in the world. And so you say, 'Let the Detective Bureau do its job and I will do something so much more meaningful, I will study law and become a big shot.' Well, Lieutenant, I myself am a big shot and I can tell you, sir, success and power are not what they're cracked up to be. Go after that killer. That's the meaningful thing. Catch him, and if you give me half a chance I'll strangle him for you— Jason, let's go."

As the chair began to turn McCord said, "Who told you I was studying law?"

Hawkins lifted his hand and the chair stopped and turned back.

Hawkins smiled and said, "The same ones who told me you are one hell of an aggressive police officer, the kind of man the city cannot afford to lose. Now, Lieutenant, do your duty."

But McCord said: "I'll tell the chief of detectives about your concern."

"No, sir. You fail to recognize that this is not a common run-of-the-mill case, and Charles Carden was not some negligible old dodo."

He fished a business card from his inside pocket, wrote on it and gave it to Jason, who gave it to McCord. "I am helpless, as you see," said Wesley Hawkins. "Think of Charles and Marie Carden and do your duty."

Toasted Balls

A fter Mr. Pomposity left him alone McCord dug into a mountain of routine work—and got stuck on a use of force report that bothered him; and then his secretary buzzed with a call from Tim Sloan.

"Lieutenant?"

"Yes Tim."

"The coroner says he'll be doing the autopsy this afternoon. Do you want to come?"

"Are you kidding?" McCord retorted. "I've got time to stand around watching an autopsy?"

"Sorry. I thought you had a special interest in this one because of Nora."

"I'm poking my nose back in my own business, Tim. I've got enough to do running my little patch, you know?"

"Yes sir. So you're out?"

"I'm out. I'm getting sucked in and there's only one cure."

Tim said: "Well then—"

"I'm fuckin tired of it," McCord managed to say in a steady voice. "Know what I mean?"

"Sure," Tim conceded. "I guess we all get tired of—you know—of the—"

McCord was thinking, "But I'm lucky, I can get out." He said: "I had enough homicide, Tim."

"I know what you mean."

"You remember that black depression in her forehead, and that little triangular hole and we couldn't find anything to match it, no weapon lying around."

"Yeah, that little triangular hole," said Tim speaking as one who remembers a fact once forgotten.

McCord went on: "The discoloration and swelling? Remember the bruises around her ankles? How you could look at her face and go berserk?"

Tim decided to be quiet.

"You know how wounds talk. You saw the defensive wounds on her forearms, didn't you?"

"Sure."

"Yeah, so did I," said McCord decisively. "Don't you think she must have been cold out there, being naked?"

This may have puzzled Tim Sloan and it certainly stopped him. After a pause he said: "I'll tell the coroner not to wait for you."

"Tell him. Don't laugh, Tim, but you're a good man."

"Goodbye, Lieutenant."

"Bye, Tim."

McCord returned the phone to its cradle gently and rocked back in his chair staring at one mental picture after another, creating his own case file labeled "Carden, Marie, dead." This was bad enough but he made a stupid mistake when Nora called a few minutes later to ask how he was feeling.

Instead of just thanking her and saying he felt better he said something—he was never sure exactly what he said—about the world being unchanged, that he had pissed away twenty years but the world, or at least the city, was just as bloody and unjust as when he started. Whatever he said about hopelessness he said it while seeing Marie Carden.

Nora asked: "So you expected to change the world?" Her voice was soft even when her words were hard. That was her unique style; nobody else spoke so melodiously while giving you the business.

He said: "Did I ever tell you you've got a musical voice?"

"Yes. Thank you."

"I like the melody and I like the sound."

"Fine, Steven, but do you like the question?"

"No. Yes, I expected the world to change by one or two atoms at least."

"Maybe it has. Who can measure an atom?"

"It has not. We found her body this morning. It told me everything I knew it would."

Nora was silent.

"Toast my balls for twenty good years till you could blow away the ashes with a chicken fart, and this is how it turns out."

Nora still said nothing. He knew her eyes would be concentrated on some point a yard or two away and that she'd be waiting, not for anything he might say but for a click in her mind. She would take in the fact of Marie Carden's suffering and maybe form an image of her body, and find a place for it in her thinking, and then she'd find a place for Marie herself—with God. She would conclude: "She is with God."

Nora said—speaking with care, as if to find the level of truth that he could accept: "Of course we try to do work that is worth doing, in your case work that must be done, work that could possibly make a difference, maybe just an atom's worth."

McCord said, "Zero."

"But I think that you expect too much if you look around and all you see is horror, because there is more than that, and because you don't look into your own soul. That's the place to search."

"I do," he said, "and it's not a pretty sight."

"Neither is mine," Nora said, "but if nobody fought for justice there would be no justice. It is not given to us. We have to fight for it. That is what you—"

"Right. And these guys raped and beat her to death, and it'll happen again tomorrow to somebody else. So where's the justice?"

"Steven, ask yourself, what is the best way to live?"

"That's what I'm doing," he said.

He couldn't remember how that conversation ended, if it ever did, but that same night he was washing dishes at the sink, looking into darkness toward a vague cone of light under a street lamp in the alley, and his eye rested on the gray unmarked police car beside his garage—while Nora cleaned up and packed the leftovers in plastic bags—and the kids were upstairs and Danny's music sent bass beats shuddering through the frame of the old wood house. McCord shook his hands and picked up a towel and wiped, and turned and said to Nora: "How's our bond rating today, O'Leary?"

As if she'd been touched on the shoulder by an unknown hand Nora stood quite still, holding a bag of chicken wings. Without looking at her husband she put the bag in the refrigerator, pulled back a chair and sat at the table and opened Charles Carden's journal.

McCord waited with mixed apprehension and curiosity.

Nora flipped pages, looked up at Steven and said, "Here it is. He doesn't say, 'The world never changes' or 'My work makes no difference' or anything like that. Here's what he says. To me it's like a poem. He says, 'If I resist evil I resist chaos.' This is after the business about the 'slime on the rocks.' "

McCord gave a grunt that sounded more derisive than he felt. His answer was: "I'm kicking the case."

"How can you kick it when it never was your case? It's the Bureau's case. You said so just today."

"I am kicking it."

"Three years ago," she said, "you would have been all over it."

That was when he took command of the 6th.

He replied: "Three years was a long time ago."

"And maybe you were a different man then," said Nora closing the book.

"You mean a better man. What you don't understand is, I'm not the whole Police Department."

"Of course not."

"Well you don't understand that."

"You are changing, Steven. You are always gone. That's what I can't understand." She leaned forward staring down at Charles Carden's journal, pressing her hands together between her knees and rocking with a scarcely visible motion. She was wearing her sister's old red bathrobe. He couldn't see her eyes.

"If the old geezer had seen," Steven said dodging that last, "what I saw this morning—" He searched for language but there was none. He settled for: "If he had seen his daughter—Maybe he wouldn't even be able to talk, to even think what it means to resist chaos."

"Resist evil."

"OK."

Nora said: "If he had seen her maybe he'd go mad, but he would never give up." Having said this she looked up at him with something in her eyes that was not sympathy, not a plea.

"You know how to stick it in," he said.

Nora had spoken in fear of her husband's temper, but had been determined to speak. Seeing his color rising, and his struggle against anger, she told herself that an important moment had arrived and she must meet it honestly.

Nora said: "I told you I would not interfere in your decision."

"I guess you forgot that."

"I didn't forget. You say the world doesn't change, but my world is changing and now I have to say what I think."

"So you lied."

"No, I meant it. I intended to stand aside and watch you, and hope. Don't talk to me about lying."

"I shouldn't have said that. Sorry. What was it you planned on hoping for, that I'd stay and buck for captain?"

"That your decision would be in character, as I understood your character."

"As you understood it. Past tense."

"As I understood it then."

"Not now."

"Now, Steven, I don't know. You seem to be sick of your work and I wonder, are you sick of your family too, and of me? I think that if you become a criminal defense lawyer, knowing your judgment of those men, you will destroy yourself."

"Do you think everybody the DA charges is guilty?"

"Of course not."

"Do you think criminal defense lawyers are necessary?"

"Yes, Steven."

He could hear the patience, amounting to gentleness, in her responses.

He asked: "Do you think the criminal lawyers are worse criminals than their clients?"

"No, but you do."

"Anyway, whoever said I was going to—"

"No one yet," Nora cut in.

Said Steven: "Maybe if I see what I saw this morning another time or two I'll turn out like Reitz."

She said only: "Reitz does his job."

"And I do mine. I'm not a homicide detective."

"When you were," she said, "you knew what you were doing."

"What are you saying, Nora?"

She hesitated, knowing that he had a point. Nobody could be the whole Police Department and if he tried he'd go crazy. "I'm saying," she pressed slowly on, "and I don't know exactly what this would mean, as to what you actually do, but I'm saying I don't see how you can turn your back on that girl's suffering."

"What?" Steven said so softly she could barely hear—and she saw that he was on the edge.

"Imagine," Nora proposed, despite her fear, "that the killers, the torturers, are caught. Who would you rather be? The policeman who catches them or the lawyer who defends them?"

Nora felt her body trembling as she heard the quaver of rage in his voice.

He was saying: "There's a whole system of so-called justice and it never gets any better, and therefore if you're a part of it, it doesn't make the slightest difference which part you are. I happen to know a lot of criminal law. I see judges caving in to the defense every friggin day, partly from a heavy work load, partly because they're stupid, spineless and lazy."

"Some of them," Nora said.

Paying no attention to that, Steven said: "So why should I be the one that eats dirt instead of drinking French wine and never touching anything except with tongs? Since it'll go on forever. Hey, O'Leary, poke a hole in that."

She answered by meeting his hot, furious eyes but she didn't speak.

"And I'll tell you who turns their back on that girl. Want to know? Hey!" he shouted, "do you want to know?"

Nora sat mute and met the challenge of his outraged eyes.

"You!" he said. "I know what you think even if you haven't said it. Maybe you're ashamed to say it. I'll say it for you. 'She is with God.' Am I right? Is that what you think?"

"Yes, Steven."

"Well I'm sick of living with that bullshit! She is not with God, Nora, she is in a drawer at the coroner's and her guts have been pulled apart and her face peeled back and her genitals scooped for semen."

Nora said, still holding his eyes: "That is her body."

"Right, her body. What about her spirit? Two or three days of terror, torture, rape, assault, a hammer in the face to end it—I think they had some kind of hammer—her spirit, what does that do to it? Right, a body is material, the spirit is what counts. What happens to her spirit in the hands of those killers?"

"I understand that she was—"

"No you don't."

"Steven, please," she said softly.

"I should spend my next twenty years if I live that long chasing killers and rapists when it doesn't make a particle of difference because there's more where they came from. And anyway it's not all that important, is it? In fact it's not important at all, it's meaningless, according to you, since the victims just shoot up to heaven, never mind the ribbons of blood trailing from their ankles, and adore God for allowing killers and killed to play their part in His big comic opera."

Nora's eyes narrowed, a rare event, and she hesitated before saying: "Steven, God works through us. If you should decide to—"

"He doesn't. If He did He would have sent somebody to Laurel Street with orders to kill those killers first."

"Steven, you are one of those he sends."

"Too late and too seldom."

"You are asking for a perfect world."

"No, just for a little more progress and a little less rape and murder."

"So—you're giving up?"

"Christ, don't look so stricken. I'm just starting a new life that makes some sense."

Nora closed the old man's journal. She asked: "Don't you agree with Charles Carden, then, that resistance itself changes the world?"

"I do not."

Nora leaned back and seemed to ponder. Steven watched and waited, and felt his anger smoldering in his chest.

Then Nora said: "If you cheat on me, Steven, you might as well go ahead and be a criminal lawyer because I won't care."

McCord stiffened—and stared at her, and his mouth went dry as ashes. He said: "If I cheat on you I can go my own way, and you—"

"I won't even look at your back."

"And if I'm faithful," Steven pushed forward, "and I still go my own way, what then?"

"You mean the lawyer business?"

"Some kind of lawyer, yes."

"If you become a criminal defense lawyer, since there is no money in the DA's office, you will—"

"You already told me. Destroy myself. But you don't seem to care if I get destroyed some other way."

"I care, but if you cheat on me, do whatever you wish, and it won't matter to you what I think, will it?"

Again she saw that he had let pass an opportunity to protest his innocence.

Nora resumed: "Because the man I married was not a cheater or a coward."

"A what?" he said moving closer.

"The man I married did not turn his back. You see, Steven, I am changing too. I see things in a different light these last few days."

He didn't dare ask why. He said: "You still haven't answered my question," and felt like the man she claimed he was becoming.

"What question?" Nora asked.

"The one where I asked, OK, if I don't cheat on you and I decide to—"

"Oh, that."

"Yes that. If I choose some other kind of law, just to get away from the game your loving God plays, what then?"

Nora gave a gesture of indecision and said: "And you haven't answered my question either."

"What question?"

"I haven't asked yet," she said, "but you know what it is."

Of course he did know but said he didn't.

She said, "OK, Steven. You have to make two decisions, don't you? One is whether you're going to resist evil or profit from it. The other is—"

Finding herself unable to voice the next question—"Will you stay with us?"—thinking of the children—seeing a "plain strewn with rocks" before her—she placed her elbows on the table, rested her face in her hands and closed her eyes.

The next sound she heard within her darkness was the back door closing. Then she heard his car start up, and that was all. Then she noticed the unheard music thudding through the house.

For half an hour she didn't move or open her eyes. Fearing the throes of jealousy she tried to blank the images of Steven's "relationship" with a woman she tried not to call a bitch. As a sick woman might feel her fever rising Nora felt her heart going faster, and soon her legs began to dance under the table. She could not still them. She skidded her chair back and got up, and listened to the beats of Danny's music. She ran upstairs and pulled on a pair of slacks and a sweater, and told Jill she was going for a walk—which she was.

She plunged into this "walk" and reached out with a stretching stride and marveled at the cold, but she did not go back for warmer clothes. She was too busy constructing a future for herself and the kids. The bitch was listening.

At first Steven drove aimlessly. Or if he had a destination it was someplace where he wouldn't hear "coward" and "resist evil or profit from it" zinging between the hot panels of his brain.

He put a sentence together and listened to it in Nora's "melodious" voice: "You have to decide whether you're going to resist evil or profit from it." She seemed to be demanding that every day justify itself, that the years already spent didn't give him any title to freedom or development; and that whatever abilities he had possessed as a rookie of twenty-two were all he'd ever need in this life.

He realized he was cruising his district. He went into 2 Beat, and turned on his radio to learn what was happening. The dispatcher sent one of his men to Nailer Court on a domestic violence complaint. McCord drove there to check on the officer's response time. The cruiser was already on the scene. But the next call he checked was different. McCord waited at the scene almost ten minutes before a cruiser arrived. Then he threw open his car door and met the officer with a stream of invective he didn't know was coming and couldn't stop. Even as he realized he was making an ass of himself the vitriol kept pouring out, and the officer, a black rookie, looked at him astounded. "So this is the famous Lieutenant McCord." That was the thought McCord attributed to him. A martinet and a blowhard—yelling in the middle of a residential street at ten at night. McCord drove away hissing "Ass, ass."

He knew he'd be reliving this scene ten years hence and going hot with shame. He vowed to seek the man out tomorrow and do it right: ask where he was when the call came, and what he was doing, and what he did on the way. McCord's brain boiled. He squirmed in his seat and kept repeating the ass word, as his aimless driving somehow took him closer to Lindy Alden's apartment.

He drove down a half-lit street by the old tire plant, remembering when this area had been home to machine shops and small factories supplying parts to the GM plants. Most of the buildings now were boarded up with gray, peeling plywood; the houses where the GM and rubber plant workers had lived were either gone or stood empty, grim testimony comparing the present to a very different past. There were more cats than people here now. He stopped under a street lamp and began the kind of effort that is usually called thinking, but it left no trace; he didn't even know what he had been concentrating on; he felt the strain and that was all. He drove to Lindy's.

The wings of the Normandy Arms were all connected on the inside and McCord didn't go to the door nearest her apartment, in case he was recognized. Pulling open the outer door he thought again that he'd call the commander of this district (he was in the 3rd) and suggest he tell the landlord to install a lock-and-buzzer system. Then of course he acknowledged he could never do that. But he was always thinking of Lindy's safety, and getting her out of here had become an element in his brooding. He mounted the stairs through the mystery smell and thought of her rooms, fantasizing about a different apartment, one they would live in near the university, a neighborhood he liked that was also near her hospital. He was thinking of a place with one or two guest rooms—for his kids and hers, if she had any. He was walking down the pale path in the middle of the burgundy carpet, hearing the TV noises and the junk music that pressed against the doors on either side, thinking:

"It's too late"—too late to knock on her door. She had to rise early to reach the hospital at seven-thirty. Too late to stop his tirade against the rookie, and too late, according to Nora, to make a better life.

A revelation came to him from nowhere: he saw why Nora was acting half crazy, calling him a coward and condemning him with something like: "You are turning your back on that girl's suffering. You are just the man to defend her torturers." It was because her heart was breaking—because she saw him destroying their way of life.

Lindy opened the door and Steven said impulsively:

"I'm sorry, I'm sorry, I'm sorry. Here's what happened. Will you listen?"

"Yes," said Lindy Alden.

"I was sick with a migraine for three days. Then today—today is the fourth day—"

"I've been counting days too."

"—today I could have called, and should have, I just didn't. It was thoughtless and I'm sorry."

"You were sick for three days?"

"In bed in the dark."

"And why didn't you call today?"

"I just didn't. I wasn't thinking of you." That slipped out and he was glad, because it was true.

"Too bad I was thinking about you," Lindy said. She wasn't smiling.

"I'm sorry."

"OK. Don't say it again. Can you come in?"

"Please."

Lindy went down the hall to reset the thermostat. The place was cold. She must have been in bed but her face showed no signs of sleep.

Lindy looked toward the kitchen, with a suggestion in her expression, and began to walk that way, and McCord followed; but when she stopped to turn on the light he intercepted her hand.

They were very close when their eyes met. Looking at her McCord thought she didn't know what to expect or what to hope for. They were just at the entrance to the kitchen, which was dark, and the light struck her face from the hallway. Her beauty was half in shadow yet more suggestive and powerful. It had an absolute power over him. He held her and gazed at her with a need that was like a thirst; and her generous eyes—the music of those eyes, so light in their brown color, and far apart, and her nose and mouth, the whole composition of her face, so calm and expectant, soothed him and strengthened his desire.

He held her in suspense and there was certainly a question in his eyes, and as yet no answer in hers. He drew her body against his own, and the whole front of him awakened to her presence. He couldn't see her face, she was in his arms and pressing against his body.

He was jolted by a flash of Marie Carden's body in the sere weeds, and to darken that he kissed Lindy. He knew the joy of realizing that she was returning his kiss, that she was not passive; and soon her kiss was as aggressive and hungry as his own. He pressed her back against the wall and took her face in his hands, and prolonged their kissing. He knew by the taste of her mouth that she had not been asleep. For the first time he noticed that she was wearing a silk sleeping suit; he saw its red collar. He lifted her breasts with both hands, feeling their changing shape and the awakening of her nipples through the membrane of silk. By this evidence of his hands, by what he could see in her eyes in the half-shadow, by her style of kissing, of giving and asking with eager, repeated strokes—by all this he knew that she wanted what he now realized he so ardently wanted. And the voice of the betrayer spoke in his mind, saying Nora had never wanted him as desperately as this woman did.

He reached down somewhat awkwardly, to put an arm behind her knees, to lift and carry her, fearing she might not allow this—losing contact with her eyes—

"No, don't," she said urgently.

So he straightened up and saw her expression of regret, recovery, refusal.

She was saying, "Stop, please."

She put her hands on his cheeks and kissed his lips gently, in full control of her hands and her lips, regaining control of her breathing.

He said, "OK," and when she took his hand he allowed her to lead him to the kitchen. She turned the lights on and he looked around at a clean, well-organized place, small and efficient.

She said, "We can't."

He pulled in a heavy breath and repeated, "OK."

"I want to give myself to you," she declared, half conscious of vindicating Harry with this confession, "and to find you inside my body, I want all that."

McCord filled in the empty part by saying, "But we can't, right?"

She kissed him again in the same gentle way, looking into his eyes sorrowfully, or in a plea for understanding. They stood there not knowing what to do next.

In the beginning he was too frazzled to follow her narrative or even to see that she was trying to explain something. He caught the phrase "big mistake" and this oriented him. Then she mentioned her son, Edward, who was away, it seemed, at college in the East. By the time he could take this in, McCord had regained his wits.

She told him that Edward, her only child, was the son of her first husband whom she had married at seventeen and divorced three years later. When she kicked him out she had a young child in the crib, three dollars in her purse, and no education beyond high school.

McCord asked why she had kicked the husband out. Her only answer was: "I took it as long as I could stand it." McCord didn't press.

She said that her father had left her mother when she and her brothers were kids—two younger boys and Lindy, all less than ten years old. "My father just walked off," she said. "I remember that day; I remember my mother telling us kids, 'Dad's gone and won't be coming back.' "

McCord nodded, responding in his own gesture to the gravity in her eyes.

She and Edward moved into her mother's one-bedroom apartment; the mother took care of Edward at night while Lindy studied to qualify as a nurse's aide. Once she got a job in a hospital she began taking courses toward an RN, working as an aide at night and going to class in the daytime. "My mother saved me," she said.

"What about Edward's father? Didn't he help?"

"He paid support for three months and disappeared."

"OK. Go on. Or do you mean marrying the guy was the big mistake?"

She shook that off and continued. While working as an aide she found herself talking with a doctor, a man considerably older than herself, who seemed to recognize that she was a human being even if all she did was change sheets and empty bedpans.

"I married that man," she said, "for the wrong reasons. He loved Edward and said the boy had tremendous promise. Bright, quick, articulate, capable of hours of concentration. It's true that Edward would read literally by the hour or study dinosaurs from a book—and this man, my new husband, Harry Kalzyn, took him to a museum in Cincinnati to see the bones."

McCord asked: "What was his name again?" and she said it was Harry Kalzyn and spelled it.

"I've heard that name," McCord said.

Lindy continued: "My husband said he wanted to give Edward every advantage. He said, 'I will be a father to Edward.' That was how he proposed. He said, 'I consider him my son, with your permission.' He put me through nursing school and through the master's program, full-time study, I didn't have to work nights. He sent Edward to private school and gave him swimming and tennis lessons and sent him to summer camp in Michigan. He was terribly generous and he loved us, but I was in the wrong toward him."

"You're saying you didn't love him?"

"I cared for him. Affection, companionship, I provided that. But I failed him at the end, when our situation changed. I was not fair to him. I started by accepting his terms. We both knew what they were. And in the end I could not—because of the change."

"Could not what? What change?"

"Don't ask me that."

"OK."

"His health, I'll put it like that. I wanted real marriage, Steven."

When she used his name he felt as if he'd been kissed. He said: "You wanted love."

"On both sides, complete love."

"And you couldn't give it, or he couldn't, or both."

"I convinced myself I loved him for a while and that when two people love each other they can find ways to express their love, no matter what the handicap—but when things changed I saw I had been lying all along because I could not keep on—on the level of affection and companionship, not even at that level. If love can't endure change, it isn't love."

"I don't agree with that," he said, "but I think you're saying you never did love him."

"I accepted his terms, and they were generous. He was generous throughout. I failed him because there was something dishonest in me, I didn't have enough to give. When we divorced a year ago he promised to send Edward to college and I refused. He said, 'He's still my son, with your permission.' And I said, 'Not any longer,' it was not possible. I said Edward and I would manage and he said, 'You'll never be able to give him the best,' and by the best he meant Harvard, Yale or Princeton, but I still refused his money. He saw that as a sign of my hating him and his money, but I do not hate him.

"He argued with me that I was sacrificing Edward to my disgust with his body. I said of course I was not disgusted and I—"

"Were you?" McCord interrupted.

"That isn't the word. I said Edward and I were grateful, but 'I can't take any more of your money.' It really cut him, I could see that. But I had made my big mistake and all that horrible stuff started there, and I knew I could not undo it, but— A mistake like that cannot be undone, Steven. Do you see that?"

She had taken his hand in both her own—imploringly, he thought, and he believed she was telling him the thing he wanted least to hear.

McCord watched her, and listened. "Can a mistake be undone?" he asked.

"The initial mistake," she repeated, "once you make it, you can't stop what happens."

"And he of course was a perfect husband," Steven said. "It was all your fault."

"He bears some of the blame but don't underestimate my capacity for— wrecking somebody's life. He went into it honest, and I went into it dishonest, and that's how we came out." She spoke in a tone of remorse, with a rueful smile on her lips.

McCord again noticed her full lips and her not-quite-perfectly-aligned teeth, and he had never before seen a smile that moved him as this one did.

She said: "I can feel you going deeper in me by the hour, and I love the feeling. It's the most beautiful, reassuring thing that has ever happened to me." Now she smiled all the way and he saw how one side of the smile seemed to be mocking the other.

"But," she said squeezing his hand and getting red in the face, "I can't afford another big mistake."

She had a thought she did not express, that it was better to live alone, go to bed alone and wake up in the same company, to touch herself when no one else wanted to embrace and caress her, better than—

Aloud she said: "It is better to be strong and alone than married, even to the one you love, if your marriage depends on cruelty."

McCord rose and moved uneasily around the kitchen, looking mostly at the floor, but glancing up once to meet her eyes. He said: "How do you know it would be cruel? What makes you think there's anything left to wreck?"

"Steven," she said quietly, "you still love her." Her eyes with their calm honesty made him turn away and he saw Nora and thought: "But what's left?"

He said—placing his hands on the table and leaning close—"I do love her. What kind of husband would I be if I didn't? But Nora and I are growing apart. We've been on separate tracks for a long time. Or—no. She's on the same track and I'm the one who's veering off in a new direction."

"Why, if you love her?"

"Other reasons, other plans, hopes. Nora has the world all figured out but the world I live in is a mess. If you think you understand it you're crazy."

Pacing the room and looking everywhere but at Lindy, McCord launched a new idea. "Suppose," he said cautiously, "that I made a big mistake too, twenty years ago, and the consequences are still—

"Suppose when I see that white scarf, instead of seeing a girl wearing an elegant piece of silk around her neck I see a scene out of hell—and now—her body—

"No, I can't undo the mistake, you're right about that, but 'undo' looks to the past. Are you saying there is no future? That I'm stuck with that mistake till I die? Are you caught in a net and no matter how you struggle, you'll never get free, because of your big mistake in marrying the doctor for your son's sake? Assume you were dishonest to him. Call yourself anything, even a whore."

Lindy winced and McCord added quickly:

"Wrong word, sorry. I mean let's say I accept what you say, you were dishonest, or did what an unscrupulous woman would do, because you believed you had to do it. Does that mean you live with the mistake and never hope for a better life? Does my mistake mean I'm caught in a net?"

"I don't know," Lindy said and McCord sat down and reached across the table for her hand, and she gave it. He told her about Marie Carden's body and explained its "meaning" as if every line and mark could tell what Marie herself could not.

Then they both fell silent, and remained in this deeply communicative silence for several minutes. McCord was thinking that by saying "I don't know" she had expressed a profound sympathy and spoken the only possible truth. Lindy Alden was thinking she had found someone she could love and that he had been lost to her before she found him.

Lindy asked, "How old is this girl?"

"Woman really. I found the entry on her birth. She's twenty-nine."

"What 'entry on her birth'?"

"In her old man's journal. I'm reading all his thoughts about life, his philosophical gropings."

She smiled again and said, "Now I know why you're so interested in professional detachment. Because you don't know what it means."

After another silence—and they still held hands—she asked:

"Your big mistake. What was it, exactly?"

"Being a cop, what else?"

"Not your marriage then."

"No—I don't know. It's all kind of wrapped up in one package. I'm a cop and I'm married to Nora. But you said I didn't have to stay caught in a net. I'm pretty sure you said that, or did I—"

"I said I just don't know."

"But I don't see how a big mistake has to be the end of life as we know it."

"I hope not."

"But it sounds like your idea of honesty is, I walk out your door right now."

"Yes."

"But our mistakes don't rule our lives forever. That would be too cruel, right?"

"I guess so, Steven. I don't know."

She kissed him again at the door and said goodbye. She watched him down the carpeted corridor.

She foresaw, as if she were looking into a chamber of stone, a life of solitude, of the never-ending search for new friends among women. She could expect one of two futures. They would never see each other again, or she would wreck his home. She would smother her hopes, or her conscience.

It was a night of dark, deep cold. When he took off his right glove to fish for the car key, and unlocked the car, his hand grew chill and stiff. He started the engine and sat there in the cold while the engine warmed up. He looked at his watch, holding his wrist up to catch the street light. It was one in the morning. He turned on his radio but he wasn't listening to the dispatcher. He headed for home.

He strained to re-create her exact words about cruelty. He spoke aloud, which was his way of making certain one sentence connected to the next. He said: "She meant we couldn't live with the cruelty."

He didn't express it in words but he felt as if a support had been removed and he was slipping. Before tonight he could have foreseen a bleak and pointless life, a continuation of his marriage with Nora less the love and happiness, or the new life—maybe with Lindy. "After one kiss." He thought of their first kiss, in the parking lot, as a turning point.

He wished he could take her in his arms and tell her he loved and admired her, for her courage, her honesty, her vocation as a nurse, her cinnamon-colored lively eyes. He would have turned the car around but for a need to think it through again. He kept driving. There was some gentle presence of Nora in his heart.

The radio emitted an emergency tone and the dispatcher sent a crew to First and Majestic for a "woman down in the street," and McCord swung his car to the right and drove to the scene. Now his cop brain kicked in, and as he approached the intersection and saw the horizontal shadow on the pavement, a "woman down" indeed, and a man standing beside her in the headlights of a stopped car, he had a sudden intuition that the woman was Crazy Olivia, the 6th District's professional car target.

McCord and the ambulance arrived together. He set the flashing light on his car and blocked the street with it, and trotted toward the prostrate form.

The man standing there cast a terrified look at him and McCord believed it was Olivia and that she was dead. It shot across his mind that Sergeant Hughes had told her less than a month ago that she was flirting with death. She told Hughes to fuck off.

The body lay across the center line. The engine was still running in the stopped car, and McCord saw the pale, frightened face of a woman behind the wheel.

Seeing Olivia's tan raincoat McCord thought: "She must have been freezing."

The ambulance crew verified in several ways that she was dead; they exerted no heroic measures. McCord knew that once they had started CPR they could not quit till they got the body to the hospital. The lead medic said twice, "She's dead."

McCord talked with the medics and the police officers, he called for another cruiser to help with traffic, he glanced once quickly at Olivia's gray, wasted face before they covered her, and then he left for home.

He was still two miles from his house when he saw his wife striding fast down a dark sidewalk, with a gait as if she were climbing a hill, although the street was level. He noticed this rushing gait before he recognized her, it was so dark between street lamps. So he was past her when he brought the car to a skidding halt. He got out and looked over the roof but she was gone. He shouted, "Nora, it's Steve. Nora!" He couldn't find her so he yelled again, "Nora, it's me, Steve."

Then she emerged slowly from the shadow between two houses and approached him. She yanked open the passenger door and flopped into the seat. As he slipped in beside her she looked at him. Her lips were blue with cold and he thought she might be trembling.

Maybe it was his cop brain that spoke, or no brain at all, but he almost shouted: "Jesus, Nora, what are you doing walking at night in this neighborhood?"

She stared fixedly at him. She said: "Shut up."

And now he could see that she was shivering. He slammed the door and the car went dark.

Ball and Chain

Amidst his day's work, which included a tense meeting with a drug store manager whose place had been stuck up twice in a month, McCord spent most of his nervous energy digging himself deeper into confusion. It wasn't exactly "Which woman do you want?" It was closer to: would he lose both? Had he already lost Nora? Would Lindy send him away? Was he unworthy of both?

"The answer is yes." He said that to himself and was impressed with the truth of it. But this Yes made an unnatural compound. The man who said "You are not worthy of either one" was obviously a strong, bold man who made judgments. The man to whom it was said was a wreck. And McCord was both men. Pondering this he exclaimed: "Bullshit!" And then the buzzer on his desk interrupted him.

It was his secretary and she said, "Nora's on the line, Steve."

Thinking "Here comes a flame-thrower" he picked up the phone and said, "Hi, O'Leary."

"I hope you slept well," she said, not hot but cold.

Recalling his turbulent night spent on the couch in the living room he improvised: "Like a wee babe."

"Will you agree, then, to a truce for a day?"

"Why a day? Why not a week?"

"One day," she said firmly. "Because today is special."

"What's special about it?"

"You mean you haven't heard?"

"Heard what? I haven't heard a damn thing."

"Maybe I should let somebody else tell you."

"Tell me what, damn it?"

"Maybe Danny wants to tell you."

"Danny can use the telephone."

"He hasn't called?"

"Nora for Christ's sake cut this out."

"OK. Danny joined the Army today."

"What the hell are you talking about?"

"The United States Army. He reports a week after graduation, and thank God there's no war on. You or I have to sign a consent form and I think it should be you."

"Wife, thou shittest me."

"I shit you not. Get two bottles of champagne on your way home, if you plan on coming home."

"I'm coming home all right."

"One day," she repeated. "Now I have to—"

"Wait!" Steven shot back. "Why two bottles? Is Robert coming?"

"Robert can't but Tim's coming."

"Oh? Well good. Tim's my guy. But why'd you invite him?"

Nora said: "You'll find out. Anyway he's honest. Get some chip-and-dip, and don't spoil your son's party. You're such a good actor, so act normal tonight. Did you know you had a scent on you last night? Very feminine. And if you want to leave after dinner, leave. Bye, I have a meeting."

"Tim, you're so cute!" Jill cried. "You've got snow in your hair."

"Yeah," Tim acknowledged, looking embarrassed while Jill brushed out the flakes with her fingers. She was nearly as tall as he. Taking the lapel of his jacket she began to peel it back over his shoulder, revealing his customary attire of black shirt and trousers and a wide black belt.

"I was supposed to go bowling," he said to Steven, "but Nora called and told me, you know, the news, so I—"

"Told you!" Jill exclaimed. "Didn't you know?"

"Well sort of," Tim admitted.

"I mean, you were the one all along," Jill persisted. "Weren't you?"

"Well, I don't know about that."

"Sure he was," said Jill turning to her father. "He advised it. It was actually his idea."

Danny piped up from behind Steven: "It was Tim's idea. It never entered my head."

A knowing smile crossed Nora's lips and Jill, completing the uncoating of her favorite, said from behind his massive back:

"Of course, Dad, Tim's the one who convinced him to do it."

"What?" said Steven. He had seen Nora's smile without understanding what it meant, but she certainly was not expressing anger.

Tim was denying responsibility, saying: "No I didn't convince him, not at all, no siree." His slow, sensitive eyes opened a channel of candor and confession between himself and Steven and he said: "He asked me what I thought. I said the Army, per se, it'd be a good start is all I said, sort of."

Danny whooped, "Sort of!"

"He asked you for advice?" Steven gaped, and he recalled Nora's calling Tim honest—which he certainly was, but—

"I better go bowling, really, Nora, sorry, Jill, there's guys meeting me at Kramer's."

"We won't let you go," Nora said. "Don't you see, we want you to celebrate with us."

And from Danny, who still hung in the background: "Celebrate? I could be crushed by a Russian tank."

"But you'll look so handsome," said Jill, "lying there in your coffin with all your medals."

With another guilty glance at Steven, and only after Steven said, "Stay, Tim, really," Tim consented.

Jill gave a little wiggle of satisfaction and followed her mother into the kitchen. Danny lingered for a moment then sensed that the two older men wanted to be alone; he followed.

Tim pressed his wet hair back and rubbed his hands on his trousers. He said: "The kid called one day and said could we talk." He rubbed the water out of his eyebrows and looked at McCord, awaiting his reaction.

McCord said, "Fine. That's fine."

"He said, 'in confidence,' you know."

"Sure."

"I told him since he was under age you'd have to sign for him anyway, so why not talk it over with you, and he said, you know, 'Later. I want Dad to know but I'm just exploring.' "

McCord seemed to see Danny going somewhere to meet Tim in secret.

Tim continued: "He said like, 'What do I do, work at McDonald's?' And he said, 'I'm green as grass.' Then I said, 'A cop's life, Danny, you better keep your eyes open.' "

"Wait," said Steven. "What do you mean, a cop's life?"

"He wants to be a cop and he thinks a tour of duty in the Army is a good preparation maybe."

"A cop?" Steven echoed.

"Yes."

"Really?"

"Yes sir."

"You mean he's got a clear idea?"

"I don't get you," said Tim.

"He knows what he wants?"

"Sure, be a cop, a soldier first for two years then the academy then a street cop."

"God what a fate!" said McCord but something in him leapt and he lost control of his face.

Tim saw a smile such as he'd never seen on McCord before. Then he felt the thud of McCord's fist on his chest; then he heard Nora call from the kitchen and he said in a low voice:

"Also, I got some business to discuss."

"Go ahead," McCord consented.

"You're not hounding the Carden case anymore but like you say, it's your territory, so I thought you should know right away, the prints, one of the prints I took from the Carden house, Gardner found a match. Actually two."

"Who's Gardner?"

"New guy in Technical Services. Hard worker. He heard about the girl and worked himself blind going through old files."

Tim reported that what Gardner had found was a nearly certain correspondence between two prints from the Carden house and two from the apartment of an old woman murdered for a pitiful sum two years earlier on a street near Laurel.

"No identification," Tim concluded, "just a match."

Steven said contemplatively, "I remember the old dame. Nasty."

"Yeah, unnecessary roughness. Something else too, Lieutenant." Tim took an envelope from his leather-bound notebook, removed a photograph and handed it to Steven.

It showed a small steel ball connected to a chain. A ruler in the picture showed the ball to be about a quarter-inch in diameter and the chain an inch and a half long.

Said Tim: "From the autopsy."

McCord looked sharply at Tim to learn his state of mind. He saw in his eyes a gravity bordering on the mournful; and when McCord returned the photograph he accepted it with a studied solemnity.

Replacing the photo in his black leather-bound notebook Tim explained: "Sure, it's a ball and chain, but what is it? I want to ask Nora and the kids. Get a female and a juvenile perspective."

"You don't know what it is?" McCord asked.

"No. Do you?"

"I'd be guessing."

"So would I. The doc didn't know either. We're all guessing."

McCord asked: "Where'd it come from?"

"The worst place you can think of," said Tim and patted his belly.

"Jesus. So you want to ask Nora and Jill what they think it is?"

"Yeah, and Danny. Women and kids see things we don't. I thought maybe—unless you think it'll upset, you know, scare—the females. Cause sooner or later they'll find out why we asked'm."

"Sure they will," McCord agreed. "They'll insist. I know my women."

"Yeah, so if you think it'd be too—you know."

"Nora'd be all right," McCord said, ruminating on the proposal. Speaking slowly he said: "Jill—she could take it—but she's so young. Do we really want to—Danny'd be OK I think. It's Jill I worry about. I don't mean worry, I mean should we spring something like this on her so soon?"

"Yeah. She's a kind of a bud that hasn't blossomed yet. We better not."

But thinking of his reverence for the principle of "clarity" and of his daughter's character McCord said: "We'll ask Jill too.—OK." He paused to reconsider, holding Tim's eyes, then reaffirmed his decision: "Yes. Jill too."

Putting his hand on Tim's shoulder he said: "Wait till after dinner."

The two policemen went toward the kitchen.

Turning to McCord, Tim Sloan said: "Gardner, actually, he wanted me to tell you personally about the prints."

"I'll thank him tomorrow," Steven said. He was thinking of the old lady. He asked what else was in the evidence locker from her case and Tim told him prints, fibers, hair, boot-print casts and some other stuff.

McCord and Tim Sloan downed a whiskey while Jill set the table and Danny got the champagne from the Frigidaire, then they all gathered at the table. At Steven's place instead of a plate he found a printed form and a pen. He read the form carefully amid silence all around, then, after sweeping the group with his eyes, he put the form to one side and twisted the wire on the bottle, and worked the cork free so it popped and hit the ceiling. He filled each glass then sat down and clicked the pen open. The others watched from the heights, as it seemed to Steven, as if he were in a ceremonial place, and each person was holding a lantern of bubbling golden light while he wrote "Steven X. McCord" in one space and "Father" in another.

Then he rose and lifted his glass, looking at each face in turn, wondering what it would feel like to look at Nora innocently, till he came at last to his son. Danny's lips were compressed as if another second under his father's eyes would break his composure.

"To a soldier!" Steven proposed.

They drank and Jill asked earnestly,

"Right, but Danny Boy, what are you going to do until graduation?"

Danny complained that the champagne was not cold enough.

Jill said with expert knowledge: "It's not beer, you dope."

"*Cod*," Danny groaned in disgust. "What do you know about it?"

"That may sound like 'God,' " Steven explained to Tim, "but its 'cod,' as in codfish."

Extending her glass toward Tim, Jill said, "Let's drink to our guest."

Glasses chimed all around and Tim Sloan declared as he held his own aloft, "I'm drinking to the Cordettes."

"Jeez, Tim," Danny complained, "are you still on that?"

"Sorry. You're right. You're not Cordettes anymore. To the McCords!"

"And to the one who signed the paper," Danny said and turned red.

Steven touched his son's glass across the table and then all the others.

He smiled at his son with a blazing salutation. Danny looked at Steven, but his father's undisguised approval broke his stare. He looked down and his color deepened.

McCord's mind drew him into a trap. It showed him in quick succession that Danny was grown up, was almost gone, would soon be writing letters from Germany or somewhere; that Jill was almost a woman, sitting there in a woman's body, smartest in one sense and best-fitted of all the kids for the blows and unknowns of life; and that Nora was self-sufficient.

Being fast and irresistible his mind introduced the inevitable and fully justified issue of this series: that he was free.

"Free!" he thought, "to do—to begin a better life,"and he looked around the table—but he did not feel exhilaration or—freedom. What he felt was a crippling remorse together with a strong, confounding hunger, which seemed to press him toward Lindy Alden, even as the remorse showed him Nora's virtues in a bright illumination—and even as his family seemed more precious and—necessary.

Lifting his glass, which was all but empty, he thought, or some voice that was really free declared, "You could destroy all this." To create "all this" had taken twenty years—and he could ruin it in one day.

He proposed another toast, looking directly at his wife. "To Nora O'Leary, mother of warriors," and Jill joined in with the cry, "To Mom!" Danny turned to his mother unconstrainedly—there was no barrier or gulf between them—and drank to her. Tim, for whom looking at Nora was the prime aesthetic experience of his life, lifted his glass with a dignified affection.

But Nora tried to understand the strange look in her husband's eyes. Was he trying to say they were still husband and wife—though he had denied nothing?

Steven was chastising himself for his "mother of warriors" toast. He kept saying things that were either lies or imperfect representations of his thoughts. If he had spoken from the heart he never would have uttered that stupid phrase. He tried again, saying, "To Nora," and lifted his glass, and found it empty—so he smiled at her, a smile, as Nora saw it, full of pain and longing.

She thought: "Maybe a few more nights on the couch will do him good."

And Steven thought: "She is a good, faithful—beautiful—strong-looking woman!"

"*Cod,*" said Danny with a little explosion, "let's eat, OK?"

And they dug in, Steven with all the rest. He wanted to catch Nora's eye but she was giving all her attention to Tim. He looked at his son, who was busy eating; at Jill, but she was tapping Tim's arm trying to get into the conversation; and again at Nora, but at just that moment she broke into a heartfelt laugh at some remark of Tim's.

Steven looked at his plate, meat, mashed potatoes and green beans, and thought of his boyhood, of dinners at home and of his mother. Nora was still laughing.

McCord thought: "Christ, she's tough."

Jill cleared away the dishes and wiped the table with damp paper towels till it shone like a skating rink. Danny slumped with his feet poking out under the table. Nora poured herself a brandy. And Steven set the coffee machine chugging, while he watched Tim Sloan remove the photograph from his notebook.

To the kids Tim said: "You guys and your parents are a police family." There was a stern tone in his voice and the kids picked it up immediately.

Standing at the counter, Steven also sensed a new, thick gravity in the room. Nora looked at Tim with readiness, or respect in her eyes.

Tim said: "I'm going to put something on the table. What we say now, what we do, and this goes for all of us, is secret."

McCord assured Tim: "This family can keep a secret."

Tim laid the photograph on the table. He said: "Nora, you start. Take a look at the picture."

With an interrogatory glance at him and another longer one at the picture Nora asked: "What is it?"

Tim didn't answer. He held his hand out for the picture and passed it to Danny, admonishing the boy: "Don't say anything."

Danny looked at the picture briefly, just a glance, then pushed it back across the maple table to Tim.

"It's a quiz," and the calm and deliberate Tim Sloan opened his notebook and tore off four sheets, dealing them out to each person, leaving one at Steven's vacant place.

Steven set the coffee pot down on the table. He poured brandy into his glass and offered some to Tim, but Tim put his hand over his glass. Steven pushed his cup and saucer to one side, accepted the picture, looked at it and gave it back.

"The question is the one Nora asked," Tim explained. "What is it? This plays like a game but it's real. Write your answers and fold your papers."

"Give it to me," Jill said. She gazed at it and immediately wrote on her paper.

"I know what it is," Danny said.

"Write it down," Tim ordered.

Danny wrote and folded his paper. He slid it to Tim who anchored it with a forefinger.

Nora asked to see the photograph again. She examined it, then turned it so the numerals on the ruler in the picture were upside down, but her face showed this maneuver had no effect. She wrote her answer and passed it to Tim. Steven wrote last, and the photo was placed by Tim in the middle of the table.

"The end of a lamp chain," Tim read.

Nora explained: "I mean the chain you pull to turn it on."

Danny said: "Lamp chains are beaded. This one has links."

Jill said, "That's right."

"Maybe some have links," Nora said doubtfully. "It's the right size."

"Where'd you find this, Tim?" Jill asked.

"Tell you later. 'Chain from the zipper on a woman's purse or a coin purse.' That's yours," he surmised looking at Jill.

She said: "I had one like it once."

"All right. 'Purse chain.' That's your writing, Lieutenant?"

"If you call him Lieutenant again—" Nora began, but Tim said immediately:

"This is business."

"It's mine," Steven confirmed. "I mean the chain you pull the zipper with."

"OK. Here's Danny's. 'Zipper chain, windbreaker or leather jacket.' Have you ever seen one like it?"

"Yes. Are you going to tell us what it is?"

Tim said, "I don't know what it is."

"Are you going to tell us where you got it?"

Tim said, "Later."

Standing alone in Charles Carden's bedroom, hearing from time to time a murmur of Tim's and Danny's voices from downstairs, McCord pulled the chain on the lamp beside the old man's reading chair. It was a beaded chain.

He studied the books piled on the table and picked up *The Complete Poetry and Selected Prose of John Donne*. He chose the book because it had been much handled. He let it fall open in his hands and it showed him a spread of heavily marked pages with penciled comments in the margins such as "No!" and "A gifted mind gasping for truth as we gasp for air." The passage that elicited these comments was a sermon; and McCord had no interest in sermons from any century or any mind, however gifted.

He flipped backward and his quick eye alighted on "To His Mistres Going to Bed." He was astounded to read:

> "License my roaving hands, and let them go
> Before, behind, between, above, below.
> Oh My America! . . . My Emperie,
> How blest am I in this discovering Thee!"

McCord gulped this in and dropped a few lines down till he came to:

> "Full nakedness! All joyes are due to thee,
> As Souls unbodied, bodies uncloth'd must be."

As he paged through the book it seemed to McCord that the preacher had been one kind of man and had converted himself into another. Suddenly he was rushing into a panoramic vision of a life with Lindy. Was it plausible? Could it be?

Could they share an apartment with guest rooms for their kids, and would they still love one another after a year? He half-consciously assumed they loved one another now. Would Steven really drive a Mercedes and stand up in court to prevent the conviction of guilty men, playing a necessary and honorable role in an adversary system of justice? Even if their marriage was not based on cruelty, could he ever convince Lindy that it was not? Could he convince himself?

This startled him, coming amid a flood of belief that everyday life with this lovely, generous woman would lift him up as nothing else could. And he answered the question: "She is good; she loves me." He now believed he understood last night—she stopped him but he knew she wanted to surrender to love. "Give her time," he said.

The idea reasserted itself: he could lose both women. One for cheating and the other for—cheating! In the end Lindy would never consent to cruelty, he saw that; and Nora would forgive him but never love him again.

In his fantasy of life with Lindy he'd come home with a briefcase full of work. After dinner he'd go to his study to prepare for a trial. He'd work for two hours and then, to relax his mind, wander around the apartment, come into their bedroom and find her reading. She'd look up and their eyes would meet, and the shared conviction would pass between them that they were the luckiest couple in the world. He'd give her one chaste kiss and go back to work, in the knowledge that she would be waiting.

"How blest am I in this discovering thee! To enter in these bonds is to be free." She was his "America," his "new-found-land."

He named each of his children: Bob to medical school, Danny to the Army, Jill to college after a few years and a sure success in some career—and Nora reposing in her unassailable certitudes. "Why go on living this half life?" he asked. "*Destroy* is an ugly word but—" There was no oxygen in his life.

"Don't be stupid. You have everything a man could want. Except what I want! Nora is beautiful, and willing"—and he dwelt for a change on Nora's body, realizing what the difference was: Nora's was glorious, Lindy's broke his heart.

He imagined Lindy standing naked, facing him as if in a kind of confession. Her square small shoulders and her sensitively shaped breasts, with their brown nipples, and the gentle swelling of her belly and the rounding of her hips made a beauty he could dwell on forever. She was a healthy and capable woman—so why did it "break his heart" to think of her slender, finely formed body?

He put the book down and went to a window thinking, "Defend criminals?" He noted that he had mentally said "honorable." Was it true?

He looked down on a deserted street, narrowed on either side by a row of dimly shining cars. A motorcycle passed down the dark defile carrying two black-jacketed men. "I wonder if they were bikers," McCord thought.

"Dad?" Danny stood against the light in the doorway.

McCord said: "I wonder if they were bikers."

Danny said, "It's pretty cold out there."

"I just saw a bike go by."

"There are a few guys at school who run their bikes all winter," Danny reported. "That's my idea on the ball and chain."

"What idea?"

Danny backed into the hall and lifted his arm, looked at his watch and said, "I'll show you. We've got time. Let's go to the Montgomery Mall."

"Is Tim ready?"

"Yes."

"Didn't find anything?"

"No," said Danny confidently. "We're wasting our time looking at lamp chains."

The father and son went thudding down the carpeted stairs and met Tim, who said:

"Danny and I thought we'd try the mall."

They went down the hallway leading from the old man's study to the front door, where McCord paused, parted the curtain and looked out. He asked his son to go out, close the door and ring the bell. Danny tried but the bell was broken so he knocked. Between the parted curtains Steven saw his son standing under the porch light in full view.

"Did you see me?" McCord asked his son as Tim locked up and rattled the old knob in its socket.

"I could see the curtains were spread a little but that's all."

McCord thought what a thin thread connected the girl to her destiny.

They went down the cement steps to the sidewalk by the light of Tim's Mini-Mag. Danny rode with Tim in his red Trans-Am and McCord followed in the unmarked police car. Twenty minutes later they parked side by side on the asphalt plane outside the mall.

McCord could remember when rows of corn had bent in the wind in this exact location, when fields rose and dropped with the land, divided by growthy hedgerows of pawpaws and willows, saved from sterile symmetry by a meandering creek held together at its banks by the spreading gaunt roots of innumerable varieties of waste trees. Strewn here and there by the course of the creek giant sycamores stood at their appointed stations like monumental sentinels. To level the undulations of nature, bulldoze the hedgerows, channelize the creek and chainsaw the sycamores had been the present's comment on the past.

The pavement was damp with melted snow and the wind was northwest and strong. The mall spread across their path like the citadel of a toad god.

McCord was walking in the middle, Danny on one side and Tim on the other. "This alone should be enough!" he exclaimed silently. They drew near the mall, where it blocked out the sky with its angled shape and its lights. "A man who has everything a man could want—except what he wants! is—what?"

McCord stopped. The other two went ahead for a pace or two then turned and waited.

McCord had to say something and what came out was: "Now, Tim, we'll find out what this rook's big idea is."

Knowing that parents get stupid about their children Tim just smiled and waited for the lieutenant to rejoin them. Danny suffered in silence.

Lost in thought as they took the next several paces, unaware of wind or wet, unaware of the looming mall, McCord was struck by a bolt of happiness.

He thought: "Resisting evil I resist chaos? What chaos? It was a great dinner, Miss O'Leary. Danny's decided! There is life after high school." And he could already see Danny in uniform, trying to be something that is not easy to be, a good soldier, and he clapped him on the back making a big pop against the boy's nylon jacket.

"Jeez," Danny groaned and rolled his eyes, and they entered the mall.

Pausing at a haberdashery window McCord stared at a suit. The style was reserved yet new. The cut was perfect. The cloth said money. For only four times as much as he had ever paid, he could wear this suit and be somebody different. He saw himself carrying a leather briefcase a little too slim to be useful, emerging from the courthouse as clean as when he went in, for the simple reason that dirt cannot find a purchase on such a suit. He felt himself guided by a new, more ambitious mind, one capable of a ruthless suppression in the pursuit of its goals. The mind knew, and didn't care. It went on. The idea that a body bludgeoned and lacerated by a torturer is restored when God "hisses," as Donne had written, and the stunning thesis that God's justice rules the world—these ideas only fed his ambition. He had no time to waste on a plunge into puerile delusions. Opposite the pole of faith, just as the old fart said, lies the pole of chaos. You either have a children's theater or something utterly pointless like a boat journey through the gilded bowels of the toad.

Danny and Tim waited just ahead. McCord wandered on and came to a gift shop, a place without a theme except the frivolous spending of money. There were little cast statues of fat boys in red suspenders, stuffed animals at absurd prices, and little fake violins and little fake pistols. Though none of these objects was inherently depressing he felt his spirit draining away as he looked at them. He heard the tinkling, scratchy water-noises of the promenade, and saw the sparse crowd drifting toward the exits; and the pavements seemed to be, and indeed they were, emptying and stretching out in longer prospects before him, with sparkling signs in letters and logos on either side, stretching in a long seemingly roofless corridor of consumption, inviting him ever deeper into this Common Ordinary Shopping Mall with its glittering fountains and inoffensive music.

Danny led them into a store called Leather City.

Tim asked: "What are we looking for?"

"A leather coat," Danny replied. "Jacket length or knee length, big zipper in front with a pull-thing big enough to handle with gloves on, big square pockets on both sides, and pockets on both sides of the chest, with zippers. It's the zippers."

"Pulled by a little ball," Tim guessed, "on a little chain."

"Right."

McCord asked: "Have you seen such a coat?"

"Yes," said Danny. "Some of the bikers at school wear coats like that."

"So there are kids in your school," Tim observed, "paying two, three hundred dollars for a coat."

Danny said there were.

Tim said to McCord: "There's your problem right there."

"But it isn't just kids who wear these coats," McCord said.

"No, I see em on the street," Tim assented.

"Me too," said Danny. "If you wear a coat like that, shoulder straps and wrist straps, a belt and huge pockets, with the ball and chains flopping around on your chest—"

"And the leather," Tim put in.

"Then you're somebody," said Danny.

"Especially if you're nobody," said Tim.

While Danny spoke to the sales clerk McCord imagined the cycle cruising by 128 Laurel in the night.

McCord and Tim started searching while Danny followed the clerk. Few of the men's coats had the right kind of pockets on the chest. McCord looked at every coat on his side, and Tim scanned the other; and after five minutes Danny whistled, and spread a coat before him, and McCord saw the ball and chain at each of the two breast pockets.

McCord said politely to the clerk: "What time do you open in the morning, sir?"

The man said ten o'clock.

McCord smiled and thanked him and said to Tim and Danny:

"Ready?"

Laying the coat carefully over a glass counter Danny thanked the clerk, and they left the store.

Walking three abreast along the deserted arcade they passed a succession of electrically lighted distractions that none of them noticed. And they didn't speak. Danny's chest was crowded with triumph and foreboding. Tim was putting his story together. McCord knew what it would be.

Turning at the exit, passing a security guard who watched them lazily, they each used a separate door. So they passed out the doors without halt or hesitation, and continued across the lot at the same pace, with nothing to say and nothing to stay for. Danny zipped his jacket against the rain and lifted his shoulders. The rain was thin but it blew over the lot in boreal streamers, whose hidden structure was revealed as they passed through the zones of light at each lamp post.

Tim's car awaited the men in a power crouch; the gray police sedan hulked beside it.

Danny said: "He won't be wearing it very much longer."

"He will if he's a biker," Tim opined. "It's cold on a bike right through April."

"I don't think he's a biker," said McCord.

"Why not?" Tim asked.

"It's a pretty long coat to be wearing on a bike."

Danny and Tim pondered this till McCord said:

"Tim, you'll tell Sergeant Reitz?"

"Yes sir."

"And suggest he get out here at precisely ten in the morning?"

"Yes sir."

"He probably won't need the suggestion, but just in case."

"I'll tell him," Tim assured McCord.

"And Tim, can you take Danny home?"

"Sure."

They stood there. McCord reached into his pocket for his keys and rattled them like bones.

"Jeez Louise!" Danny cried, "is anybody gonna explain?"

Looking at Tim, McCord gave a slight nod.

Tim turned to Danny—and the light wasn't very good but McCord saw that his son's face shone with moisture, and his hair was darkened by it, and he looked as if he expected a blow.

"We found it in her stomach," Tim said.

"Oh!" said the boy. "Her stomach? Whose stomach?"

"Here's the way it must've happened." And Tim told the Carden story.

Danny's eyes seemed large and sensitive in the feeble, rain-filtered light. They leapt to his father, and Danny saw in his father's unflinching eyes a lesson of gravity and truth, as if he were saying: "Just listen to Tim. He's describing our world."

And Danny listened to Tim's explanation of the ball and chain and how they got into a dead woman's stomach.

Alone, McCord drove into the billows of windblown rain. He thought: "What I'd pray for now, if I prayed, is cold weather." His windshield glass moving frontally along the freeway at sixty miles an hour forced its path through an atmosphere black with night and alive with water. And though the night was bitingly cold and the month was still February, his city was a kind of border town between North and South, and he feared that spring was moving in from the South in the sky above the rain.

The wiper blades left a narrow streak on the left stroke and a wide smear on the right. This added to his driving woes when he banked off the freeway and left the ramp and entered dark streets where the lights were fewer and dimmer, and where pedestrians might be staggering drunk in the gutters or a car might skid past a stop sign into his way. So he slowed down and found that his guts were taut and his neck aching from unconsciously hardened muscles. He relaxed his grip on the wheel and ran his free hand up and down his right thigh, massaging the muscle.

He was in the industrial flats near the old carbarn where he had met Basil Samuelson, the cab driver. The hospital where he'd been born stood visible, lifting its lights on the hill to the left—the hospital where Lindy worked. He passed warehouses and old machine shops, a big bakery that had sent the aroma of baking bread through his boyhood, a coal-fired power plant and the street leading to the church his parents had attended—his own church till he was through high school.

He turned in at a driveway by a low brick building, swung into the lot in back and parked.

The rain darting against his face like little ice arrows made him shield his eyes, and the act of lifting his arm admitted a wave of cold into his coat. He walked quickly, trotting the last few yards, to the cement stairs that led up to a metal door beside a loading platform. He stood exposed under the blue-white light and rang the bell. He moved his feet constantly and thrust his hands deep into his raincoat pockets. He swept the lot with his eyes. There were three vans and just two cars including his own. The door opened and he was admitted by a man he had known since his days on Homicide. His hands were stiff with cold. He removed and shook off his coat, and went to the men's room where he ran warm water over his red hands and dried his hair with paper towels. He looked in the mirror and found his features sharper, his eyes bluer and larger than he expected, and his face—he stared for half a minute—his face seemed—cruel. Here was an impression he had not expected to give, and he wondered if he gave it to others. What did they see when they saw him? It must have been the influence of the cold and sleet. His ears were red, his eyes shining with the internal struggle to send warmth outward to his extremities and face.

He urinated and when he was finished he stood there waiting for more. When it didn't come he ran his thumbnail lightly, slowly up his buttock, and a new stream was released at leisure. He said, "That proves you're over the hill." He rinsed his hands again in warm water and let the heat soak into his fingers and wrists, pushed his hair into rough order, then went down the fully lit hallway to the duty desk. He asked to see the protocol on Marie Carden.

He read it quickly, having seen "a thousand" such forms; then he asked to see the ball and chain. The clerk scanned the exhibit list, wrote McCord's name and rank, and went to a locker. McCord heard a padlock click open and slide out of the hasp.

The clerk gave him a purple envelope. McCord looked closely at the ball and chain, and bunched them up to see how small he could make them.

According to the protocol the ball was three-eighths of an inch in diameter and the chain seven-eighths of an inch long. It was made of chrome. He dangled it, then enclosed it in his hand and held it for a moment. He gave it back. The clerk returned it to the safe, and McCord asked to see the body.

He wanted to stand alone beside the body but knew this would not be permitted. He followed the clerk into the big room, to the row of locked drawers. The man unlocked one and slid it out. The light in this room was quite strong; glass tubes recessed in the ceiling sent out a generalized fluorescence which bounced in a pervasive confusion off the white walls and the granite facets in the terrazzo floor; and the sheet which the man now drew back also sent its whiteness pouring into McCord's eyes.

Her face had no expression, unless one searched for her history in it. There was no death agony, horror, pain, fear or triumph, and no ecstasy at an ultimate revelation. Rather her face was ideal, and perfect despite the effects of the assault, like the face of one who has kept her identity. That was McCord's idea, that hers was the face of a woman about to be awakened, waiting for her life to resume. When it did, this perfect, ideal face would suggest what she knew. But in a little while McCord saw the damage more clearly, the color and the shapes that merely evince a kind of damage that cannot be seen. Then the "perfect" and the "ideal" face changed altogether, in his vision, and he lost his balance. The blood drained from his brain and he saw the room whirling. He reached out and steadied himself by gripping her arm.

He thanked the clerk and went back to his car. Next he was sitting in the car and noticed that the engine was running.

He may have sat for several minutes shivering and then cut the engine. The rain ran down the glass in thin streams of crystal light, and followed the slanting blades to discharge itself in augmented streams where the blades ended. Then the flow of water and light dispersed at the bottom of the glass, and McCord watched.

He had wanted to kiss her. It was as if there had been no autopsy. He knew that her lips would not be the lips of a live woman and that kissing her would open a door to madness; he was quite sane; he would never do it.

He was shivering and did not think to start the engine and turn on the heater. He saw the perfect, ideal face within the half-destroyed face and imagined a young woman who had loved her father. For a second he looked carefully at that unusual triangular dent in her colorless forehead, but this wound held his attention simply because it was evidence, or might be, if they could find the instrument that produced it.

He wished he had looked at her hands, which would perhaps be unhurt. He thought of going back and looking.

He seemed to see her hands reaching out to take his face between them, and he was stricken with love. He didn't know whether his pity was turning to love, or his passion to pity, but he began to cry. It was safe to cry because no one could see.

As the earth is said to have a molten core, and the mind resists this improbable fact, which may seem even more remote on a night when the rain jets down in little stabs of ice, so a man may have a hot center and never know it—or learn only at a certain passage in his life. McCord was crying with convulsive force, holding both hands over his face and moving with irregular bends of which he was unaware. What he felt was a liquid heat where his hands pressed against his face, and a burning and swelling around his eyes. He might have been crying for Marie Carden or for his own life. As every person does who cries, he learned there was some power that could take control of him, but he didn't learn what it was. His throat hurt with the sobbing; his heart protested against the fierce strain.

When he could finally sit back and breathe normally and rub his aching throat he had no idea what had happened, or how long it had lasted. The rain still beat and sparkled silver on his windshield, and he heard the dark, drumming waves on the roof of the car.

He caught a quick breath and endured a jerking sob of the kind he remembered from childhood. He saw that some of the blurring on the windshield was located in his eyes.

He knew it was coming back, he felt it trembling in his throat and chest, and it struck him again with greater force, rising up from a place deep in his soul and shaking his whole frame. For a few seconds it blinded and choked him, and he didn't know who he was.

Lawyer or cop? He did not hear it in words but felt its effect as if he had. This question did not reach him in English. It lay concealed.

The sobbing shook him again and he let it go on—till it was over—and then he knew.

CHAPTER 16

Razors and Broken Glass

When the three men went out on some kind of search related to the ball and chain—her friend Tim, her son and her husband—three men launching an expedition from the family sanctuary—when they left the house Nora felt aglow over the two older men honoring Danny. She felt Steven's approval of the boy and was sure Danny felt it too. Here was what Nora had missed in the degrading suspicions of the past week, the identity of her house and family as an inviolable haven and seminary for the children, a home for herself and Steven, where the strife and chaos of the world could be understood by comparison. Here the kids could gather strength, nurture courage and learn to know the good when they saw it.

"I can learn too," she thought. She had plenty to fear but the most fearsome thing was the hate in her own breast for a "bitch" who might not even exist. The real destroyer was not the bitch but her own jealousy. If she poisoned her own mind she'd eventually lose the ability to distinguish good from bad and purity from pollution. "So—don't—pollute it!" she said bearing down on every word.

Nora had passed the entire evening without sensing the presence of the bitch at the family table. The dinner was an echo of the happiness she once possessed. She knew it was real. About the lost hour and the ICU telephone number she knew nothing during that celebratory evening. Of the shame she thought she saw in Gil Hughes's face, nothing. Of her husband's new indifference to love, nothing. But now that the men were gone this "nothing" weighed on her chest like a lead-lined coffin—like—indifference.

"Why don't I confront Gil? Go there and say, 'Gil, if you are my friend, tell me.' But no, I can't pull him into this mess. This is my fight."

But when the three men went out together in their search or quest or whatever it was, she saw her son growing up and Steven being his father. That gave her a ride.

Nora and Jill cleaned up, then Jill went upstairs to do homework and Nora brought her briefcase in from the hall closet and opened it on the table. She plowed through a folder of letters to the president of the City Council, penciling notes at the top of each one; then at about ten o'clock she checked the back porch light, left the kitchen light burning for Steven and Danny, and went upstairs.

As she undressed she felt the familiar, half-welcome desire to place her body at Steven's service—only half welcome because this impulse sometimes got out of control to the point of torturing her. Just now it was a gentle, sweet hope that sent new life flowing through her limbs and fresh images of love into her mind. In some moods, in these early stages of desire, she wanted to "serve" him according to the idea of "loving service" that she had been taught when quite young, before experience had shown her that love is for two.

Tonight her mood changed as she found herself prolonging her toilette by washing herself as she might do if she knew Steven was waiting for her. She brushed her hair and felt a flicker of pride in its glossy black abundance, white streaks and all. She put on her pajamas and went to bed to read *Oliver Twist*, and found that what she was actually doing was waiting for Steven. If he were here, regardless of all the bitches in the world, she would find a way to make her willingness known to him. Their lovemaking seldom began this way but when she took the initiative, however hesitantly or subtly, he always understood.

"I will give my body and my sweet love."—She anticipated a tender, yielding intimacy. "I will please him with my breasts, which he loves so insatiably, and I will slowly spread my legs in hope."

Now, reading Dickens, she allowed her left leg to trail over into Steven's territory. "Not very subtle!" she thought—and this should have made her laugh but didn't. She felt herself pulling him, suggesting he roll over and cover her.

When she had finished a chapter she looked up, and a clear thought came to her: "I don't want that."

What she did not want was to punish him again by sending him downstairs to the couch. Sleeping alone was not Nora's idea of—anything. Throughout their marriage, from the hard days when Robert was an infant and they were living on a patrolman's pay, through her early years doing clerical work at City Hall, bearing the children, starting and stopping work—from the time she began to take on real responsibility in the civil service, and to take pride in her new assignments—from then till now, sleeping with Steven whether they made love or not was her source of deepest joy. She'd be making dinner, getting the kids to bed, thinking of the moment when Steven would slip into bed with her, and they would each open a book, or she would put on her earphones and listen to one of her favorite pieces of music. Her course at community college on music appreciation had not achieved its aim of opening the whole range of classical music to her—but she loved her favorites, especially Vivaldi, and often listened to the same work twice or three times in a row. Thus the hour from going to bed until sleep was a precious time, and Steven's bodily presence—her music, her reading, Steven's breathing if he fell asleep first—made it so.

After the first few weeks of marriage she had evolved a new style of prayer in which the Act of Contrition, the Lord's Prayer and Hail Mary gave up part of their space to a freer form of meditation. She needed her own way of expressing gratitude or worry, of dealing with fear and disappointment. She thanked God for Steven and the children, for her family's prosperity and good health. And during this time she discovered that whenever she gave thanks for Steven, or prayed for him as an individual, she was addressing Jesus, the Son, not God the Father. This puzzled her, and she decided at length there was no harm in it, and it came naturally, and she had continued it till now. This was the only differentiation she ever made among the Persons of the Trinity. When she wanted to place herself or family in God's hands, it was "God" she addressed. When she meditated on marriage she walked with Jesus.

Thinking of all this she remembered the moment in Vivaldi's "Spring" when the violin strikes twice, and with strong strokes strikes twice again, and again. Whether this was meant to be menacing, as it sometimes seemed to Nora, or the prelude to an all-body drama under Steven's carefully applied strength—whatever the reason, these vibrating strokes of the violin were the sounds of music Nora loved best. She thought of them now as she closed her Dickens and prepared for prayer.

This preparation was modeled on Teresa of Avila's "Prayer of Quiet," in which the saint endeavored to bring her mind to peace before praying with her whole soul.

Tonight Nora could not do it. There was no "quiet" and the "strokes" in her mind did not come from a violin.

Vivaldi was Nora's supreme musician of love. Imagining "Spring" she wanted Steven beside her. She could not pray. She couldn't stop thinking. She threw the blankets aside and went downstairs. Her feet were bare and cold, her heart was racing—perhaps from jumping up so abruptly. She paced around the dark living room where the floor was carpeted, and she thought: "Bitch!" The jealous fury she feared was starting to boil up inside her, maybe because she could still hear the Vivaldi in her head.

But she whispered: "That will ruin me. Hate, jealousy, 'He betrayed me,' all that is—razors and broken glass! Marriage, family life, all wrecked, if I am weaker than my hate. He is betraying me!" she cried in protest. "Am I supposed to deny it?"

Rocking back and forth in a chair she admitted: "I do hate. She is a bitch and he is a lusting animal. I hate them both."

Shaking in her sweat, she felt a steely iciness under her sleeping shirt. She tried to calm herself to pray the simplest prayer, and finally was able to press the words out: "Guide me!" she whispered.

And guidance came, a simple, irrefutable revelation. Forgiveness is not enough; she must love. "I see that," she said. "I must love. I will take less for myself and give more to Steven."

She rose and crossed the dark room into the half-dark hall, approaching the lighted kitchen resolutely, knowing exactly what she would do.

Her briefcase still lay on the old table that Gil Hughes called the Maple Battleship. She took out a yellow tablet and wrote:

Dearest Steven—

You have told any number of little lies but I can see that you can't force yourself to tell the big one. I honor this in you, Steven. I hope it means you want to hold our marriage and family together. I treasure both, and I treasure you, my dearest. I know that I am not all you need—but I ask, Is anyone perfectly complementary to anyone else? It seems to me that since our first night when we danced at Lakeside we have been good for one another. You are a daring person and passionate, but I am more passionate than you recognize, and I am steady, and I give you all my love.

Please, let's bring this into the open and discuss it. Please, show me my suspicions are groundless.

—Nora.

She folded the paper, wrote his name on it and placed it in the center of the table. As often happened, the billowing grain in the wood carried her back to the day they bought the table, their first purchase for their first apartment. They went to a used-furniture store on East Third Street and—

She heard a noise from the living room. But Steven and Danny would come in from the alley, from the back. She went quickly to the window over the sink, but there was no car in Steven's slot by the garage. Somebody was in the living room—she heard the click of the latch as the door was drawn shut. She went toward the hall—but she was in light and the living room was dark, she'd be visible and the other would not. She thought of Charles Carden and his daughter and her heart went wild. She saw a shape or shadow moving in there, and she stood frozen where the hall and living room met.

"Who is it?" she demanded in a shaking voice.

"Jeez, Mom, you'd think I was a ghost," said Danny stepping forward.

"What are you doing here?" Nora choked out.

"Coming home, what else?"

"Why did you come in the front door?" she demanded, taking hold of herself.

"Jeez, why not?"

"Where's your father?"

"I don't know."

"What do you mean, you don't know?" she asked hotly.

"Cripes, Mom, he went somewhere in the City car. How would I know?"

"Then how did you get here? Did Tim bring you?"

"Yeah, Tim. Are you OK?"

"I'm perfectly OK," she responded in a still, cold voice. "School in the morning, Danny."

"Yeah, I'm on my way. Night, Mom."

"Good night, Danny." And she thought: "Always somewhere else. Never home."

Nora returned to the kitchen table. She was momentarily distracted by her freezing feet and by the rain against the window glass, and the water gushing down from the eaves. And she saw that her handwriting was misshapen, but she wrote steadily and surely.

Steven—I have waited for you to deny it, or to tell me there is nothing to deny, or to say *it is over*, or to ask forgiveness, as I ask yours for my shortcomings, because I know I am not the mistress of your dreams—but you have not done anything but wrap yourself in guilty silence. I see that you can tell all the little lies but not the big one. How honorable of you. So, Steven, leave. Leave tonight. I do not want to see you in this house tonight.

She took the first note and replaced it with this new one, then she turned off the back light and the kitchen light and went upstairs.

She roamed. The bedroom could have been a hundred yards long, so endlessly did she roam and pace and stare at the walls and watch her feet flying over the rug and across the strip of wood flooring where the rug ended. She did not pray, or hate, or see porn pictures. She was in a frenzy but it was a frenzy not of hate but of thinking. Her thoughts moved in spurts into one future life, then another, then yet another.

Some strange noise intruded on her thoughts and she listened. It was a murmur of voices, the kids were talking—arguing? It wasn't just talk, it was something urgent or dire. Jill's voice lifted to an unnatural pitch; Danny's had a low, pleading quality.

A ray of fear shot through her heart—that the kids were arguing over their father's infidelity. They knew something was amiss—Steven had slept on the couch—but how could they know any more than that? She opened her door and stood in the hall watching the streak of light under Jill's door. The girl was speaking fast, in disturbed or frightened tones, but Nora could not pick out the words. She opened Jill's door and stepped into the full light of the room.

The girl was sitting upright on her bed with her blankets piled around her waist. She stopped speaking and looked at her mother as if in alarm.

Nora saw her against the background of her music posters, including one that Nora strongly disliked, of a rock musician in a spotlight on a dark stage. His pelvis was thrust forward and he held his guitar high up, and his face showed either ecstasy or pain. It was an obscene picture, in Nora's eyes.

"Do you know where they found it?" Jill asked in an unsteady, disbelieving voice.

"Found what?"

"That ball and chain thing. Do you know?"

Then Jill told her. Nora listened, with orison in her mind, a prayer beneath the level of language, even as she listened to every syllable of her daughter's narrative. The orison was a plea to Jesus to give Jill the courage to face a woman's life.

Mother, daughter and son talked for an hour before Nora insisted they go to bed, repeating the formula that dated back to kindergarten, "School in the morning, kids."

She retrieved her note from the kitchen. She put it in her book beside the first one; and though she was shaken by her talk with the kids, about danger and cruelty, she still couldn't sleep beside Steven tonight. She gathered up a pillow and two blankets, and dumped the whole armload in the hall. Then she shut the bedroom door. She pulled the covers to her chin and shut off the light, and looked at darkness.

At a time close to midnight, when she could neither sleep nor read, she turned the light on again. She heard a noise so slight it could hardly be taken for a knock. But that's what it was! He was knocking on the bedroom door, very softly and timidly. A thrill raced through her body, not of happiness, but of anxiety or dread. She listened intently and heard a somewhat louder knock, then another, and she rose slowly from her bed and stood motionless beside it.

She approached the door and stood by it, waiting. She opened, and her shadow obscured him for a moment, and he seemed hugely misshapen.

When she moved to one side she saw that he was holding the blankets and pillow under one arm and had lifted the opposite hand to knock a third time. His face was not clearly illuminated but his eyes shone as if they were larger and had more light in them than she expected.

"I went to the morgue, Nora," he said. "I saw her body."

"Is that what you did."

"Yes."

"How often have you done that?"

"Done what?"

"In your whole career, how many times have you visited the morgue in the middle of the night to look at a body?"

"Never," he replied in a husky, cracking voice.

"Exactly," said Nora.

"What are you saying?"

"I am saying, Steven, that I don't believe you."

"Oh — of course. Why should you believe me? But — listen — the old man was right, I can see it now. You remember he said —"

"I remember."

"Well now I see a way to change it — by two atoms, no more, but I can see —"

"Do you think I care what you see, or what you say?"

He looked at her as if he half understood, and she closed the door. But the picture stayed in her mind of Steven bent slightly, holding the bedding, pushing his head a little forward as if he was waiting for her to say something else.

CHAPTER 17

Testimony

A scene kept whirling through Wesley Hawkins's mind. It was not a dream for it came when he was awake, as he was now, at ten in the morning in his office on the twenty-eighth floor of the tallest building in the city. He was expecting a visitor and that was probably why it popped up just now—because the visitor's name—Steven McCord—set in motion a succession of linked ideas. These led straight—or circuitously, it made no difference—to "the scene."

On a dimly lighted stage in a theater with no audience—the whole seating area was black—there stood a cage tall enough to hold one man. The man was Mrs. Hawkins's illustrious son Wesley at his present age of sixty-seven. Somehow Wesley Hawkins, standing in the cage, felt his mother's remote presence. He stood illuminated from above. If he looked up he was blinded. He could only look at the stage around him.

They were dancing a ballet to the groaning of a bass violin and a saxophone bigger than a piano. The dancers were men, some dressed in black leotards and T-shirts, others quite naked. They were of various ages from about twenty to eighty and the older they were the more likely to be naked. This was not a dance presented for the sake of the dancers' beauty.

The theme was—

Suddenly a dancer dropped, quivered on the boards and went still. Then another, and another; one by one they gave it up, until the spectator in the lighted cage saw the point.

There came a knock on the open door of the office and the secretary said: "Lieutenant McCord is here, Mr. Hawkins."

"Ah!" Wesley Hawkins exclaimed. He began the arduous project of standing up. Grabbing the leather pads on the arms of his chair he took all his weight on his arms and shoulders and lifted till he could lock his good knee and bend forward from the waist, extending his hand across his desk to greet this big policeman tightly packed into his K-mart suit.

"Cheap suit, excellent man," thought Wesley Hawkins as they shook hands—a sort of duel of masculinity as they gripped and regripped and assured each other that they were happy to meet again. Hawkins said he had been pleasantly surprised to receive McCord's call an hour ago; McCord said he was glad that Mr. Hawkins had an opening this morning.

Wesley Hawkins saw how different the man was when he wasn't playing the role of a bum. He had come to life, standing there in his cheap suit—but he wore a good conservative black-and-red tie, Hawkins noted. The man's hands and face were red from the cold wind sweeping the city; his eyes were a little moist and his hair tousled but somehow not sloppy. But for the suit, Hawkins thought, they might both have been members of the Drumlin Country Club meeting on business.

Wesley Hawkins offered coffee and McCord turned politely to the secretary and declined. Most guests would speak directly to Wesley Hawkins. "He is good with all sorts of people," thought Wesley Hawkins—by which of course he meant people of lesser status. He also noted that the policeman did not search the room furtively for the wheelchair. Many of Hawkins's visitors, of all degrees of sophistication, could not stop themselves doing this.

He indicated a chair, and McCord sat, and opened his briefcase on his knees. The briefcase, of the kind called an attaché case, was not of the best but was better than the suit. Hawkins examined the suit with care and concluded it was not quite so cheap as he had first thought; but it was not of a style Hawkins or his law partners would think of wearing.

McCord drew out a file folder. He paid no attention to the office, which had been designed and the furniture chosen by Wesley Hawkins himself to impress clients, colleagues and opposing counsel. To clients it said: "Expect to pay dearly." To colleagues: "You see who's on top." And to adversaries: "You will be treated like royalty before being whipped like a peasant."

Wesley Hawkins had paid ten thousand dollars for the desk alone, when that sum would buy a Cadillac. There was an oak credenza that had stood in Charles F. Kettering's dining room in the city now called Kettering; and there were brass lamps from the estate of another founder of General Motors Corporation. Only the carpet was new—selected for Wesley Hawkins by the top-of-the-heap decorator Omer Rich. The pictures on the walls were the usual scenes from the Old Bailey, plus signed photographs of Harry Truman,

Dwight D. Eisenhower, Gerald R. Ford, and three governors and four senators.

This was the office of the man in the illuminated cage.

He now said: "I am delighted you called, Lieutenant."

McCord smiled; he said nothing, just smiled. Hawkins appreciated the coolness, the economy. McCord passed a portrait-sized photo to Hawkins and said,

"This is a copy of one sent to us by the Los Angeles Police Department. I thought you might want it. It is yours to keep."

Looking on her youthful face Wesley Hawkins was stricken with love and remorse. His mouth shut itself. He spun in his chair and looked out on the city where a woman so splendid, so young and free, could be so abruptly thrust into a hell on earth. When he turned again to face McCord he brought himself under sufficient control to express his thanks.

McCord said: "So far the coroner has been unable to locate any relatives either here or in California."

"I believe there are none," said Wesley Hawkins.

"So, if you wish it," said McCord, "I will suggest that the bodies be released to you."

"I do wish it, I certainly do."

"I'll tell him you were the friend of the father and godfather to the girl."

"Yes. I hadn't thought this far ahead. To the funerals. Yes, by all means. Assuming no relatives are found. I don't believe Marie ever married."

"She did not," McCord said, "and since you are the closest we have to family I will report on our progress from time to time, if you are interested."

"Interested? You know the answer to that."

"All right," McCord said closing his briefcase and placing it carefully on the carpet beside his chair. Looking squarely at Hawkins—like a man who says, "You asked for it," he began: "We have a certain piece of physical evidence, and in view of your relationship with both victims, and since there is no family, I am willing to tell you what I think it means, but I can only do so after receiving your promise of confidentiality."

"You have it, sir."

"If this were to leak out it could destroy our investigation."

"Sir, I am a lawyer of nearly forty years' experience. I do not violate a promise of silence."

"I will be forced quite soon to share this information with a small number of people who are not law enforcement officers," McCord continued. "I don't want to do it but I must if I am to exploit our best chance of success. Therefore, Mr. Hawkins, if I should hear this on the street I will have no way of knowing who let it slip out. But since I have your promise, and considering your bond with the Cardens, father and daughter—"

"And Agnes, the girl's mother."

"—considering all that, I repose perfect confidence in you."

"Thank you," said Hawkins, thinking: "Talks like a man who has observed and listened to lawyers."

All this time McCord held a much smaller photograph, which Hawkins managed to keep under surveillance without looking straight at it. But all he could see was the blank side. It had come out of the same folder as the picture of Marie Carden.

"We have a few facts on which to base a narrative that includes a fair degree of speculation," McCord declared. "I can recite this narrative if you like, but keep in mind that I have scattered guesses among the facts."

"Please go ahead." Wesley Hawkins leaned forward and interlaced his fingers.

McCord said: "Mr. Hawkins, this is not an easy story to tell or to hear."

What Hawkins saw was a set of intense, lively, disciplined dark blue eyes set wide apart, under blond brows, in a face still reddened by the wind. It was easy to imagine this man exploding. In which case, stand back.

Hawkins prided himself on his quickness in reading the human book. He saw before him the face of a man who had decided to be a policeman when very young, for the best and the worst of reasons. He saw a rugged specimen who in a different era might have been a brawler. Had he been a young immigrant in 1900 he might have gone into the boxing ring, won two-thirds of his fights over ten years and gotten his brains pulped. Hawkins saw a tough man who hadn't shed a tear since he was a baby, hard, but alive to detail and nuance.

Steven McCord said: "Marie Carden shared an apartment with two other women in Pasadena. She flew out of LAX early on the morning of the murder, changed planes at O'Hare and arrived here at eight-thirty in the evening. She left the airport in a Cliff cab at nine and arrived at her father's house at a quarter to ten. She told the cabbie she had come to visit her father and seemed extremely happy about it. As they drove through town she would say things like 'That's all different' and 'I just don't recognize the place anymore.' But she went silent when they entered her father's neighborhood, where she grew up."

"That has changed too," Wesley Hawkins interjected dismally.

Both men sat without speaking for a few seconds till McCord resumed:

"She knocked on her father's door. The bell does not work. Somebody opened to her. She apparently listened to some story, because the cabbie heard both her voice and that of a man, but not a very masculine voice, the cabbie said. He was standing at the curb waiting for her to go in. Maybe the man who opened the door told her he was helping her father fix a pipe. Maybe that the old man was not well.

"I don't think it was the father who opened the door because the cabbie said there was no exclamation of greeting, no happy talk, only a low murmur of her voice and some man's—then she went in."

"That is how things happen," Hawkins said while inspecting his folded hands as if they held some relevant information.

"What things?"

"Oh, we think we are doing the natural thing, a thing of no consequence, but we are entering the unknown. Unknowing, we enter the unknown."

McCord gave a noncommittal grunt and said: "I believe that her father was already dead and that as she entered his study—the kind of room that used to be called a parlor or sitting room—as she entered, she saw what I saw the next morning, her father tied in his chair with blood spilled down his front, tremendous quantities of it. You may ask why I believe she was taken into the study."

"I assume you have a reason."

"A slender one," McCord admitted. "I believe there were two assailants and that they would have sent the less threatening one to answer the door, or to wait in hiding till the caller went away. But that would be risky; it would excite worry about an old man living alone. So the less threatening one went, to pose as a friend or neighbor or relative and give an explanation."

"But in so doing he would let himself be seen."

"True, and there was a porch light, but such light as there was in the doorway came from behind the killer. In any event we know that he did open the door, maybe because Marie Carden knocked more than once. The cab driver called me just this morning with that information. She knocked a series of four knocks three times. He can repeat the rhythm of it from memory."

"This does not explain your belief that she was taken to the study."

"Yes it does. Marie Carden stood five ten and weighed one thirty-eight. She was not remarkably big but neither was she frail. Also she was an athlete, according to her roommates in California, a runner and swimmer.

"Now suppose the killers were a kind of duo—a relatively small man who thinks he is brainy and a larger one who accepts the brainy one as his leader. The one is proud of his brains and the other of his muscles. Each supports the other's pathetic delusion. If this were the case—and it is a common one—

then Brainy, who makes all the decisions, would size up this woman, note that she was young and attractive, and he'd see that he would need help in subduing her. And help was available in the study, where Muscles was waiting. So he leads Marie into the study to show his partner what he's got, a young woman all alone, and to get help in controlling her."

"Plausible," said Hawkins meditatively.

"It is not demonstrable, Mr. Hawkins, but it may be something slightly better than plausible. The reason is that this young woman never was completely subdued. She put up a terrific fight and it lasted right to the end. I'll tell you why in a minute. At this stage, seeing her father's body and the goons grinning at her, I think she was driven mad with grief and rage. As you see, much of this is guesswork.

"I think they dragged her upstairs to an unused bedroom, which must have been her old room, dragged her there hoping she'd be easier to handle if she couldn't see the body. And they did handle her."

Wesley Hawkins looked into the eyes of the woman in the portrait. He almost said "Stop!" His jaw was clamped hard.

"They raped her in her own bedroom after a violent struggle, then took her downstairs. My guess is the smaller, brainy one—if they were the kind of duo I've described—went to get their car, wherever it was, while the muscle man held her captive near the back door.

"That they took her away is a virtual certainty. That they did it by force is suggested by the physical scene and evidence found in the house. That they would drag her down Laurel Street is scarcely conceivable. They took her away in a car, and we have a pretty good fix on the tires on that car. We also have two fingerprints from an earlier home-invasion murder of an old person that match prints we found in the Carden house. And we have something else."

McCord passed the smaller photograph across the desk. Wesley Hawkins studied it and looked up inquiringly. McCord then opened his briefcase again, took out another photo and passed it over. It was a picture of a leather coat spread on a table.

McCord watched Hawkins as he studied first one picture then the other.

Hawkins surmised: "So you must find a man wearing a coat like this, with one chain missing from the chest."

"Exactly."

"Do you have this thing in your possession?"

"The ball and chain?"

"Yes."

"Yes sir, we do. It was recovered in the autopsy."

"Jesus Christ I see it all," Hawkins groaned.

"Yes. Another struggle when they came to assault her again, or transport her somewhere, and she still had the strength to resist, and she—"

Wesley Hawkins cut in: "She yanks the ball and chain off a man's jacket and she doubles over or somehow conceals her movement—it must have been in a terrible struggle if he didn't notice she had taken it—and she swallows this—" Hawkins waved the photo of the ball and chain by its edge.

As if to test him McCord asked: "Why do you say she bent double? Why—"

"Because!" Hawkins cried. "Had they known, you would never have found this! God damn their miserable souls to hell!"

"Precisely," said McCord. "Your estimate of these men, of how far they would go, is the same as mine. She had to do it secretly, otherwise they would have—"

"Stop!"

"So—yes. We sent a detective to the leather store at Montgomery Mall but nobody had a clear recollection of who bought the coat. One sales clerk remembered a big guy who paid cash; that's all. And these coats are sold in other stores too. We are looking for a man wearing a coat like this one, probably a man who paid in cash—but on his particular coat one ball and chain will be missing."

"But you have no time to lose!" Hawkins exclaimed in discovery. "He'll put the coat away in the spring."

"Unless he's a biker," said McCord. "But I agree, our best chance is to get him soon. That's why I rejoice in this freezing weather. Yesterday's rain scared me but this ten-degree icebox we're in now is perfect. Pray for ice."

"Do you realize what this means?" Hawkins asked almost in a whisper.

McCord waited.

"About her—character. Do you realize?"

McCord met the other man's eyes but said nothing.

Speaking slowly, piecing his thoughts together, Hawkins said: "A woman taken captive by her father's murderers—after reading in the papers all her life about—newspaper stories about—you know. Any woman would be forced to see the possibility, at some point—that she was doomed."

He looked at the spread of three photos between his big, nervous hands, and shifted the pictures around, and kept staring at them, till he went on:

"But most would not believe it. Most, I venture to say, Lieutenant—maybe all but a few—would refuse to believe in their own death. They would—am I being unjust?"

"I don't know," McCord said.

"They could not face it. They simply would not. I hope this is not unjust. I know if I were a woman in that—I couldn't! 'Give them what they want! Do everything, take all you want, just let me live!' "

"I know a case," McCord said, "in which the woman had been repeatedly raped, and the assailants then demanded fellatio and she refused. They beat her, they believed, to death. But she lived and told her story to a jury. When her assailants made their demand she said, 'Never, for a person like you.' I have always thought it was odd that she couldn't find a word for those men, that she used the word 'person.' "

"And you, sir, use the word *man*."

"I do."

"But are they really men?"

"The law," said McCord, "defines them as men, the same as you, me or Charles Carden."

Said Hawkins: "I do not."

And McCord said, "Neither do I."

Wesley Hawkins bent again to the photographs, and looking up after a moment he said: "Marie's integrity carried her through, in a certain sense, to death, but it was a life decision. She resisted, Lieutenant. Do you see that by swallowing this object, when she had every excuse for surrender and despair—she did not surrender!"

"I see that," McCord assured him. "That's exactly what I wanted you to know."

"She was sending a message," Hawkins declared, "to anyone who would listen. A message that even as she was being reduced to an object, a mere object, sir—to them, a piece of warm meat—in her last hour, when nothing else but peace would matter to a lesser—to me, perhaps—to most people, just peace!—when nothing would matter but release—"

Hawkins paused to ponder these ideas. "Pain, torture, degradation."

McCord said: "She had internal injuries consistent with severe beating. Her face had been hit at least twice with a hard object."

"At that moment, into this amoral universe," said Hawkins, "she sent her message, that she was still resisting. Beyond hope, but not beyond resistance, do you see? A coded but clear message. 'I am not defeated.' Can you see it?"

"I see it. An act of faith, not hope for life, which was gone—she knew that—but hope for something else."

"Yes! Faith! Hope! In this worn-out amoral universe we inhabit."

"That somebody would care," McCord said. "After being used for their filthy pleasure and beaten to break her spirit, with the stink of their bodies in her nostrils—" He didn't complete this.

Hawkins was overwrought and he saw the changes coming on in McCord's face. The policeman's facade of a cool forensic technician was cracking. McCord said in a voice that was much too loud—so it seemed to Wesley Hawkins, a voice that threatened to run away with its owner:

"This was her way of testifying at the trial. Her way of accusing the killers and proving her accusation."

Hawkins caught the fever and said: "When I try to imagine details such as the stink of their breath and their hideous squeaks and howls of gratification I go sick for the human race."

"The race is sick," McCord pronounced in a normal voice.

"My God, Lieutenant, not all of it, not everybody. Are you and I sick?"

McCord stared at him then went on: "You said 'amoral universe.' But she must have thought that if she sent her message there was a chance somebody would hear it. If the universe is amoral, or immoral, or nothing but a bunch of atoms—whatever they are—with no particular reason to exist, no cause, direction or aim—if she thought that, she never would have sent the message."

"A cry for justice."

"Even if she thought justice was impossible," said McCord, "which it is, she might still have felt some glimmer that somebody would recognize as—I can't put it into words, I don't even know what I mean, except courage."

"I know what it means," Hawkins said.

"Then go on."

"It was all those—ideals. A cry for justice even when justice has already been eaten alive by the crimes; a refusal to surrender when she was at their mercy, of which they had none; and a signal to others that her spirit was unbroken. Sir, I thank you for telling me. One act of courage on that order is worth an entire lifetime of—" Wesley Hawkins stopped speaking. He waved his hand vaguely and looked around his office.

McCord rose and asked for the two smaller photos. He put them in their file and clicked his briefcase shut. He said: "Absolute secrecy."

Hawkins nodded agreement and began lifting himself. He knew this made his face go crimson and that people sometimes grew impatient. He was not embarrassed. He stood and put out his hand and asked:

"And you, Lieutenant, did you get the message?"

McCord said with a laugh, "Oh yes, I got it."

2 Beat

The 3rd Relief, comprising some twenty officers, was assembled for roll call in a room crowded with folding chairs. The time was a few minutes before three in the afternoon, and Sergeant Hughes, resting his belly on the lectern, was admonishing the "brutes" while McCord watched from the back.

Hughes's eyes rambled, his voice rumbled. He was saying: "Lieutenant's orders, got it? This is critical. We want this insect. You catch this one and you'll be doing the best work you ever did and maybe ever will do.

"But lemme say it again. Secrecy, ladies and gents. Absolute secrecy on the coat. You can't tell your wife or husband. You can't tell your barber or beautician."

"Hey Huge-es!" a man called from the back of the room, "can I tell my boyfriend?"

Hughes paid no attention, but continued to unfold his litany. "You can't tell your mother—those of you who've got one—or your father. That leaves about sixty trillion people in the world and you can't tell them either. Is there anybody who understands I'm saying something real simple? You can't tell anybody."

They were in the basement of the ex–funeral home that sheltered the 6th District headquarters. McCord was the only one in civilian clothes. Behind him there was a door with windows admitting the dull light of winter. True or not, it was legendary among the cops that the six steps leading up to ground level from this door had been the entrance and exit ramp for the morticians, who received a body whole and ugly, and sent it out eviscerated and pretty.

Still treating the "brutes" like dimwitted children Hughes asked if anybody could tell him why his orders had to be secret.

Greta Gabriel, a patrol officer who had been known as a "can't-work-alone" for her first two years, but who was turning that reputation inside out, spoke up from behind McCord: "If he knows we know," she called out, "he dumps the coat."

"And that coat is our best chance," Sergeant Hughes said. "So look for a coat on this pattern"—holding up a photo—"missing the ball and chain on one side of the chest or the other. If you see a coat with both zippers on the chest stop him anyway but don't mention the coat. Keep him till we check him out. If you see this coat and a zipper is missing you're looking at a killer. Put your own safety first. Call for backup, that's the first thing you do. Then make the collar and again, find some other reason if he demands one.

"He might be black or brown but we think he's white and got a partner. But you're looking for a coat, not a man. And don't forget the partner.

"We think he or they killed Old Lady Schneider two years ago, eighty-year-old lady with ten dollars in the bank. We've got prints that match. I'm not going to describe what they did this time—to the Carden daughter. OK? You don't need that, right?"

Nobody spoke; of course they knew.

Hughes said more quietly: "Don't read the autopsy protocol on Marie Carden. That's my advice. It'll ruin your day and maybe your life. Just look for the coat, and keep your response cards handy. If the lieutenant yells Bullseye drop everything but your pants and go to your concentration point. Any questions?"

Greta Gabriel said: "Do you have a copy of the protocol?"

"Leave that alone. Just watch for the coat and if you see it, send out a ninety-nine because this is not a job anybody should try alone."

McCord made a movement and all eyes converged on him. He said into their silence:

"Hughes and I are going to recruit a few civilian volunteers as lookouts. If even one talks about the leather coat it could derail us. It makes me nervous. This whole thing makes me nervous. And I've got to repeat something Huge-es said. The first thing you do is holler a ninety-nine; don't make this grab alone."

Hughes repeated it was secret, and nobody groaned "We already know that." Hughes said, "OK, scram," and the room was empty thirty seconds later, except for McCord, Hughes, the other two sergeants on the district staff, and Jim Dotson, the patrolman who knew 2 Beat best. At ten past three Tim Sloan and Sergeant Reitz arrived and the meeting addressed its business.

Which civilians could be trusted to act as lookouts? Each man made one or two suggestions, and they settled on a list of five—all of them cashiers or managers at convenience stores. And there was a sixth civilian.

Borrowing a term from Charles Carden's journal McCord thought of the killers as men of chaos. They had two drives only—money and lust. Possibly also drugs. If they were white and if they lived in the 6th District, they lived in that subsection of it known as 2 Beat.

Within the boundaries of the beat there were still a few machine shops run by old krauts, a few used-car lots, and some dry cleaning shops and 7-Elevens and Quickies. There were three magnificent Protestant churches which retained much of their original splendor, or seemed more splendid than ever amidst the surrounding decay; there was a plasma center where the poor sold their life's essence, barbecues and bars and a gleaming hospital—but nothing to do the city's tax base any real good. About a third of the businesses had gone bust or been abandoned. The beat embraced some of the oldest and crookedest streets in the city. It was home to a unique mixture of blacks, native whites and briars. Many of the briars had actually been born in the city but, like their parents, still thought of Kentucky as "down home," while the native whites talked like briars. In 2 Beat it was the briars, not the blacks, who gave the police the most trouble.

McCord guessed that the killers ate a lazy man's diet of readymade sandwiches, that they snacked on Hostess pies, candy and chips, and that they bought girlie magazines. If so they would frequent the 7-Elevens and Quickie stores.

The plan, therefore, which the meeting set in motion, was to distribute pictures of the leather coat to about half the seventy-five officers in the district and to every officer in 2 Beat. There would be no broadcast and no coordination with Downtown.

McCord relieved Dotson of his regular duty and told him to roam the district at discretion. Tim Sloan volunteered to do all he could, while keeping his regular job. And McCord said he would do the same. He assigned Hughes to recruit and brief three of the six. McCord himself would take the other three.

It was a job he couldn't do in a suit and necktie. He'd stand out like a banker in a bowling alley. He changed out of his suit into jeans and an old shirt and jacket. He drove to 2 Beat, where at the age of twenty-two, newly married, he had started his career. He'd been firm in the conviction that he would never operate a turret lathe or horizontal planing mill at a GM plant, or turn himself into an NCR drone. He had a different life in mind, and he started living it in 2 Beat.

This tract of urban misery, want, waste and vice turned out to be the incubator of his manhood and seminary of his philosophy.

It was in 2 Beat that he walked up to a wooden house near Highplain. The porch was crowded with black and white kids from the neighborhood. This was where a burned boy hung out, a boy of ten or eleven who wore plastic wrappings as sleeves, and no mask. McCord had seen him once or twice but never spoken with him. It took him a few weeks to acknowledge that he felt a brew of emotions including revulsion and pity, and uneasiness, when he thought of this boy. His mother, a slender middle-aged woman whose dugs gave a pathetic lift to the gray undershirt she wore, told McCord that she had found a baby in a playground and that her son knew where it belonged. So he sat on his heels and conferred with the boy, searching his eyes, to find or give reassurance. He said, "Will you show me where the baby lives?" The boy did not speak. McCord remembered the longing and perhaps hope that he saw in those suffering eyes.

On that same street two cars collided. One of the injured was a woman of thirty, with waved blond hair, soft, hurt eyes and a round, naive face. She was trying not to speak about her pain. Her eyes strained out of her face looking to McCord for help. The ambulance took her to the hospital, and when McCord left the accident scene a half-hour later to collect her statement he found her lying on a gurney in the emergency room. When he finished the interview he went to find a nurse, and was told that nobody was free to help the woman. He went back and talked with the injured woman for a few minutes, and she began moaning. He went again and got the same answer: nobody was free. All this was 2 Beat in his mind.

The next summer McCord was dispatched to a report of a baby locked in a car. The city was under siege by the sun; only a week before this a baby had been roasted in a locked car on the roof of a parking garage. When McCord arrived the mother was beating on the window and yelling orders to William—who turned out to be a basset hound, locked in the car with the baby but much calmer than the mother. Patrolman Steven McCord, the young man so clearly present to the lieutenant, his successor, told her the dog was not panting and therefore the temperature in the car was not too high. The woman shrieked, "If you break the window my husband will kill me!"

McCord sensed her deepening frenzy as he and a newly arrived officer tried to jimmy the door, but it would not unlatch.

The dog took on his mistress's fear and began moving around and stepping on the baby's face, then the baby began crying lustily. The mother found her scalp under her hair and dug in her nails, screaming.

McCord drove his club through a rear window, spraying glass all over the interior. They took the baby out and McCord blew the chips from its face.

The girl in the coal bin was another chapter in McCord's education. McCord and Gil Hughes were dispatched to a subdivided mansion on a vague complaint of "guns and knives." The complainant was an old white landlord whose tenants were all black. The landlord was not to be found but McCord encountered a girl on the second floor landing, in the dark. Limned by the blaze of McCord's flashlight the girl seemed like a priestess in a fire-lit ceremony. All she said was: "Rent man done call the po-lice. I gone!"

McCord and Hughes decided to start with the cellar. They crept down the stairs, Hughes first, each carrying a gun in one hand and flashlight in the other. "Be careful now, you're a married man," Hughes said over his shoulder. And McCord added: "And one in the oven." Down the creaking, foot-worn stairs they went. The basement was in blackness but for their probing lights. McCord took one side of the coal bin and Hughes the other. McCord understood that to do this job you couldn't go tactical; you had to use your light, and you had to say "Police. Do you need help?"—when somebody in the dark might just put a hole in your chest. In a minute McCord heard the bin door creaking open. Hughes shouted: "Freeze!" McCord reached him in three steps—his heart was pounding at his ribs like an air hammer—and he shone his light into the bin. He saw a black woman with no shirt, wearing shorts, sprawled against the wooden wall, squinting at the light. Her face was bloody with cuts and scrapes and her eyes were barely alive.

The landlord came quietly down and said: "Did you find her? Is she dead?"

Another time McCord and Hughes were searching a drugstore. The electric alarm pierced their eardrums. They determined that the sales area was empty, and there was no basement. This left the space behind the prescription counter. This too was unoccupied but there was a door, leading they knew not where. McCord imagined a man crouched and waiting to blow his face off. He opened the door and swung his light, and nobody shot him because nobody was there. He kept his face and his fear.

One evening while it was still daylight Sherry Bellavance flagged their cruiser. She had lifted her arm before Hughes could shout his usual greeting to prostitutes: "Go home!" McCord eased the car to the curb and Sherry Bellavance bent to speak intimately with Hughes. Her clavicles started out of her skin and she rested her little stick-like fingers on the window ledge of the cruiser. But Sherry had an angel face, pale and sorrowing; this was her stock in trade and it was hard to imagine what else she had to sell.

She confided to Hughes: "You should arrest Burton."

"Why's that, Sherry?"

"He beat me. Knocked me down and stomped me."

Another woman's face appeared beside Sherry's, her friend Hazel, who said: "He rolled her down the yellow line."

"He took a five-spot," said Sherry, and her face collapsed, "from you know where."

She struck her forehead lightly against the window ledge and cried.

The streets and alleys of 2 Beat were the framework of McCord's history. 2 Beat as a place of human habitation was the scene of the myth of his life. As one man may be formed by playing high school football, another by two years at sea, and yet another by war, so McCord was formed by his early experiences in 2 Beat.

Cruising now in the unmarked gray sedan, walking the alleys in downtrodden clothes, half hoping some lunatic would try to rob him, Steven McCord, lieutenant and district commander, felt as if he were being borne along by an irresistible current in a stream whose banks he could not see. Ever since the demon had snatched him outside the morgue he had tried to find a true sentence that would reassert his control. The best he could do was, "I got the message."

A vision of his daughter came to him out of nowhere and thrilled him with its vividness. He strode along, more like a man out for the exercise than a searcher. He tripped over a crack in the sidewalk and let out a gust of laughter. He knew exactly what Nora would say if she could peer into his brain. He had heard her quote Pascal on this very point: Chase after your desire and you will never be satisfied; only give up desire and you will be satisfied completely.

He tramped along, almost enjoying himself. "I'll get the bastards," he said aloud, "and everything'll be OK." He touched the grip of the revolver under his left arm and thought: "Thou shalt kill" and snorted with laughter. A new sentence formed itself: "Blow their fucking brains out." It sounded too easy and he didn't quite mean it anyway.

He was heading toward a 7-Eleven to talk to a cashier but on the way he passed the Main Game, a moron parlor, and he ducked inside long enough to ascertain that Leather Coat was not there. The patrons instead of committing real murder were doing the next best thing by blowing people up on a computer screen. McCord felt better when he regained the street.

The wind moved against his back, hurrying and cheering him because it was cold and icy. Reaching the 7-Eleven he saw three cars in front, one a police cruiser. He entered the bright interior and neither Carol, the woman at the register, nor the two cops paid him the slightest attention, and he gave them the same treatment. Carol had learned not to speak to men she knew to be cops if they were dressed like bums.

McCord and Carol went to a storage area behind the soft drink cooler. He showed her a photo of the leather coat and explained its significance—and the need for the utmost secrecy. He told her to call the District if she saw the coat, or his own beeper if that line was busy; he told her not to display any special interest in the man if she saw him. At the end of his pitch he asked her: "Will you keep your eyes open for this coat?"

"Sure, Steve. I'm glad to help. Don't tell me what he did. I don't want to know."

This woman, aged about fifty, overweight and near the bottom of anybody's economic totem pole, was pretty well known to Steven McCord. He had never seen her angry, never heard a complaint. She seemed to like her job and she always smiled and frequently laughed. McCord wondered: "Is this real?" Was there more to the "clarity" than he thought?

Walking to his second stop, another convenience store, he thought: "It's OK. It's going to be OK." His mind was unclear on what exactly was OK. "But first blow their brains out." He recruited his second civilian and moved on.

His third stop was Granny's. He drove there thinking: "Granny is maybe the best chance we've got."

"I'll be damned, I'll be switched. The lieutenant comes aknockin like the king who dressed up as a peasant. I recognized you, Honey, before you turned the corner."

"Before I turned the corner. Jesus, Granny, if you can see around corners in the dark I'm hiring you."

"No, Stevie Boy, ain't hired out in forty years."

"Come on."

"Why, how old do you think I am?"

"I'd say forty."

"Oh you doll, come inside, Babydoll."

McCord entered and Granny said:

"Now hug me. Your wife'll never know."

She slipped into his embrace and it was scarcely possible to find her little form in his arms. He embraced her carefully. She smelled like an old woman, or, more accurately, she had the cosmetic scent he had associated with old women since childhood. Side by side within the aura of her lavender perfume, still embracing, they walked down a narrow hall to the kitchen—and he said:

"I'm not here to harass you."

"Me? I never worry about the cops. I'm starin into the grave, Stevie, I seen the solid bottom, I seen the walls. Think I can scratch my way out with these?"—and she held up her twisted white hands—with their splotches of brown or orange color and bulging blue veins. "In I go, and they fill it right up with the brown earth. I should worry about harassment from the cops? Ha!—You take cream and sugar? I forget. Let me hold your hand, you ain't come under my roof in years."

"I never did come under your roof," Steven said.

"You naughty boy!"

"Except on city business," McCord said.

"*City* business. Just remember I got business too, and it ain't none of the *city's* business neither."

McCord sat down and said he'd take his coffee black. Granny began to measure out the coffee then turned and drew very close, so he could see her whiskers and the map of veins in her eyes. "Do you have any idea, you bozo, how glad I am to see you?" She grabbed his shoulder and pushed back and forth. Her hand closed over the strap of his holster.

McCord said he was glad to see her too, and patted her bone-bundle of a hand on his shoulder.

McCord took in the room, looking for the sketch of the hand—to him a remarkable drawing, the work of a young prostitute named Susan. Nothing he remembered from his rookie days was any clearer than the hand. He said: "What's this talk about the grave, Granny? You look pretty fit to me."

With her widow's peak and widow's hump, loose stockings hanging around her ankles, high black leather shoes and a flowered house dress thrown over an animated skeleton, she did look lively.

She hollered: "Fit for what, you redneck? If you knew what it was like livin in this little wicker body— All I ask is, don't get me talkin about food and bowel movements like them old bags I know.—I got Dunkin' Donuts. Want one?"

"Yes please."

"*Yes please*, oh ain't he the goody-goody. Tell me who you think you're foolin."

"By saying yes please?"

"No, you damned katzenjammer, by that silly camouflage, them old rags. I can tell right where your gun hangs."

"Sure you can, you just found it." Then McCord took off his jacket, exposing the gun and radio. "You know," he said, "I've been off the street so long nobody knows me. I'm not so obvious as you think."

"And wasn't you on homicide for a while?"

"Not for a while," he said, "forever."

"Homicide don't wear no uniforms," Granny declared.

"No."

"Now there's a job I couldn't never do, homicide."

McCord said, "Me neither."

"So—you come for something besides the coffee, right?"

"Yes, I came for help."

"Always help a cop, and never expect any help back." She went into a reverie. "Been through night court and day court and City-County Consolidated before it was the little tea party it is now, I done looked at the judge in the morning what I sold my face the night before.

"One thing I'll never do and that's purple my hair. That's where I draw the line.—How's my old bear Tim?"

McCord said Tim was working on the same case he had come to talk about. He accepted the coffee and put the smoking cup to one side and spread the photos on the table, one of the coat, one of the ball and chain.

"Police work!" Granny cried and fished for her glasses. After examining the pictures, sliding her magnified eyes back and forth and lifting the frames to regard McCord bare-eyed, she said: "Gimme my assignment, Chief."

McCord said: "Would you be kind enough to memorize what you see? I can't leave these here."

"Kind enough," she repeated. "What's got into you? And he don't trust me with the pictures."

"I trust you. I trust you never to mention this to anybody, ever."

"Do you trust my memory too?"

He held out his hand and she delivered the pictures.

McCord asked: "What did you see?"

Folding her glasses by pressing them between the fingers of one hand and the back of the other, Granny recited the details of both pictures. McCord spread them out again and pointed with the tip of his pencil to the zipper pulls on each chest pocket. He instructed her on the ball and chain. She bent forward, and McCord saw the bald patch where her hair opened to show the pink skin beneath.

"This man," McCord said, "doesn't just break the law, he breaks people."

"God, this place!" She lifted her arms and seemed to look all around. "There's so much cruelty anymore! When I come to this burg in the twenties it was a boil of sin, that's the very reason I come. But— You know, I run off with Joe Longfellow—I still like the name. Carry milk to the pigs? hoe out the gutters and get cow plop splattered in your eye? Not me, Mister. So I run off with Joe till I found out more'n I wanted to know about men. So I went home a week later, ring and all, praying I wasn't pregnant, and my pop says, 'You made your bed, lie in it.' My sweet daddy.

"And so I come here just before the Crash. Let me tell you I never even thought about cleanin house or runnin a carpet sweeper at the Hotel Gibbons—nosiree—see I knew how this little magic organ pleased Mr. Longfellow, pardon the expression but that was his name. Was mine too! I got into this work cause I was too smart. I stayed cause I was too dumb. I'm still in cause it's too late."

She picked up a photograph, settled the glasses on her nose, and studied it. McCord drank his coffee and wondered about her mind as she stared away at nothing for a minute, making a gap of her mouth and unconsciously swinging her jaw from side to side. For a second she looked grotesque.

"What ever happened to Sherry Bellavance?" McCord asked.

Granny snapped out of it and said, "Oh that ugly Burton, that misfit, he beat that little bag-o-bones, tossed her in the alley, took her pathetic fake jewels. She'd come here for sanctuary. You know my place is a haven, still is today. Sure I take my five-spot every trick but they get a haven in return and clean rooms. We allow no evil parasites in this house. I got a gun—"

She pushed herself erect, cast a piercing, authoritative look at McCord, braced herself against her chair, and then shuffled to the cupboard. She opened the door, and McCord saw the sketch of the hand. She took out an old Colt .38, a snub-nosed Detective Special, and waved it in the air without turning around—then after a moment's hesitation, as if forgetting what she was doing, she put the gun back.

"People look down on a whore but I always said, 'Give'm a place to live, where they can take a bath in private. Let'm do what they must so they won't do what they shouldn't.' I don't hate men, in case you think I do, no sirree. There's the good and the bad."

McCord repeated gently: "What happened to Sherry Bellavance?"

"I told her, I said, 'Stay here. You'll be better off here.' What's a fiver on a twenty-five dollar trick? But no, she went off again with her Burton. They just believe in goodness, that everybody's got some. You'd think they'd know evil when it strikes'm but they don't. There was this girl named Susan stayed here."

"I remember her," said McCord.

"I had her draw me a cross to soothe her troubled spirit, show she had other talents, and she did, she stuck it inside my closet door, I said, 'There, Susan, nobody'll see it there. We don't want the girls thinkin I'm some kind of missionary.' I said, 'I can look at it and fall back into the days when I was a little slip of a blond thing, pure as honey, scoopin manure and ridin hoppity-gee on my daddy's knee.' You don't want to talk about that much but you better not forget it. Your daddy give you a hoppity-gee ride, you better remember, no matter what, come what may."

"And she sketched a hand," McCord reminded her.

"Good sketch, I still got it," Granny said. "Sherry—I don't know what happened. They dragged her away blubberin and swinging at'm all snot-faced, eyes like red-hot embers, and now she's gone—where dopers go."

Granny closed her eyes. She recited: "Straps on the shoulders—pockets here, pockets here—zippers."

"And what's this?" McCord asked showing the picture of the ball and chain.

"Why it's one a these," she said confidently putting her finger on a chest pocket.

McCord nodded. He decided her mind was OK.

Granny said: "And what you're after is a john wearing that coat with a zipper missing from the chest."

"Yes, Granny."

"Oh I love that smile and them blue orbs! Are you still married or do I have a chance?"

"I am, Granny, I am."

"Lands, what a lucky girl!"

McCord asked to see the hand that Susan had sketched. The paper had turned brown, and McCord accepted it carefully. It showed the right hand of a strong working man—gripping a bar of wood, maybe the handle of a hammer or hatchet—gripping firmly—what? He had always imagined the picture represented a policeman's strong hand grasping his night stick.

He kissed Granny's forehead and left the house. Walking fast to his car, wanting to get home, McCord first thought of Granny's emaciated and no doubt many-colored body under her bag of a dress. Then he could see in his mind Marie Carden stretched before him, and then with a shock he saw Lindy lying naked on her bed. Her patient eyes were upon him—awaiting him with a gentle happiness.

He did not go home. He went to Lindy's.

He felt a strong impulse to tell her what he had tried to tell Nora last night.

He didn't mention the ball and chain, but said he had gone to the morgue to see the body, and it was more like a living woman's than he expected. He said he had seen hundreds.

Lindy nodded. He saw in her face, in her broad strong features and her cinnamon-colored eyes, bent so earnestly on him, a sympathy that cut through everything they didn't know about one another. He believed she understood his narrative better than he did. He felt he could tell her about weeping in his car.

She said she was glad he had wept.

As if it followed, McCord said, "Yes, but I nearly passed out. I held her arm to keep upright. I didn't tell you that. I got dizzy, and I reached for her arm." He could feel it in his hand.

Lindy asked if he meant her bare arm. Or had he touched her through a sheet?

"Bare," said McCord. "The man had thrown back the sheet, for me to see. I think I was crying out of pity, and I was, that was part of it."

"You mean in the car?"

"Yes. And helplessness. Maybe I'll get the killers but maybe I won't. What if I never do? What if I spend—and never—"

He fell silent. They were on the couch in her living room, each turned toward the other.

"I felt my life was a wreck, it was hopeless," he said. "Maybe it was self pity."

"And the pity for that woman, and helplessness," she said as if to remind him of his own words.

"Right. All of it."

"But, Steven, your life is not a wreck. You are in a crisis but you're are a strong man," said Lindy.

And McCord snorted: "I better be. She sent a message and I'm the one who got it."

The perplexity showed in her face, and Steven explained:

"I'm the man who stood there looking at her wounds, at her body, at her face. They tried to rape the courage out of her. I'm the man who got the message. I know who I am. I saw her wounds."

"Yes, but Steven, won't this burn you up?"

"Well, has nursing burned you up?"

"Not yet, but I've seen many who are changed by it. I know a doctor who elicits pain, you know, by pressure on a certain spot or by twisting a limb, for diagnostic purposes only, but then he does it again. Once he did it a third time, not looking at the patient but at me, like a co-conspirator. So—be careful, Steven.

"I used to work for a hospice, with the dying," Lindy continued. "I came out of one patient's house, a woman dying young of cancer with her family and friends all around her, and I had given the pain-killer, and I sat in my car and sobbed, and couldn't stop it."

"So you aren't burned up," he said.

"No. But if it's a drug addict, no matter how real their suffering is, I don't care half as much. Some part of me says they've got it coming."

"So they do," said Steven. "But this woman didn't have it coming."

"No. Be careful."

He said, "Don't worry about me," and touched the gun under his jacket.

"You know what I mean," Lindy said.

They didn't say much more after that. Neither knew what to say.

This time she let him lift and carry her. While Steven undressed she went to the bathroom, and he stood waiting when she returned a moment later. He unbuttoned her silk sleeping shirt then kneeled and pulled down her trousers, and touched her mons with a light kiss, and held her hips while continuing and varying his kisses. He did not press her from the front but could detect in his hands the soft undulating of her hips, so he made his grip stronger and his caresses gentler but quicker. She began to make the cries that were his chief reward, sweet and almost inaudible, then stronger.

Suddenly she took him by the shoulders and tried to lift him. She said, "Come on," lifting, and he got to his feet after freeing her ankles from the trousers. When they reached the bed she drew him down on her, so he could see the divine face looking up at him, and he said, "You're my goddess." She whispered, "I want you to take me," and he said, "I will."

He found her ready and went in too fast. She cried out in pain or shock and lifted a hand to touch his face. She said, "Gently, Steven," and he gladly complied; the gentle and the slow intensified and prolonged the bliss. It was bliss already. He collected his wits and sought the twisting, ascending road that would carry her up the mountain. If he concentrated on this ascent, on her ascent, he would not get too self-confident or stumble off the path and fall from a cliff. He wanted both to fall from the summit. He wanted the highest cliff for Lindy and knew that if she attained it she would pull him down with her.

In this seemingly selfless ascent, in which his whole desire was to carry this woman to a higher place, he was detached from himself and conscious of himself as a person apart. This was the meaning of ecstasy. He was a man, perhaps a man he knew, controlling the striving of another man, perhaps himself, for the sake of a woman's ascent. Whoever he was in this striving, "he" loved her with all his complex being. She was to him a goddess with a divine capacity for physical experience, and he was the mortal man for whose sake she had come to earth this night. Through the body they were moving to a bliss of the spirit.

Then McCord made a mistake. He looked down at her face. The beauty of it now lay in the joy it showed him. She was his; he was her chosen man from whom alone she could derive such mystical and physical joy. But her face thrilled him too deeply and he felt the beginnings, deep inside, and low, of the climax he wanted to postpone.

But it was not too soon, for Lindy had already begun. He could tell at first by her cries, which changed their tone, then by the tilting and tightening of her sheath. New pressures disturbed his concentration and confused his purpose. These were too powerful to withstand. Steven and Lindy plunged from the summit into a wild stream together, and slipped through roiling rapids and over falls, like lovers holding hands in order to die together; and it was a long-drawn dying, or living. In the end they came to a tranquil pool, and Steven found that Lindy's arms were around him and she was kissing and praising him.

When they said goodbye the praise was still continuing, simply in the look in her eyes, and it was not possible to tell the difference between this and love.

Transcendent Love

Thinking of her sexual life—of life with Steven—Nora McCord cast her glance across a spectrum of possible lives and paused to think about one with no man at all, a life that perhaps fell short of purity but didn't depend on anyone else's anatomy. Such had been the fate of the only saint she had studied in any detail, the only one she loved, Teresa of Avila.

After her initial transgression when, as a girl or young woman, she may or may not have lain with a man (and was clapped into a convent by her father), Teresa observed the church closely and saw its imperfections. She devoted herself from that time forward to creating an order of nuns who would seek God, not pleasure or comfort, and to pursuing the "way of perfection" in her own spiritual life.

Nora was convinced of this keystone fact—that if Teresa had been a satisfied wife, "satisfied" once, twice or three times a week!—she could never have explored her "Interior Castle," her mystic style of communing with Christ, and she certainly would never have experienced the ecstasies that she believed God sent her.

Nora opened her book of photographs of works by Gianlorenzo Bernini and turned to the sculpture that had captivated and confused her since she was fifteen. It showed Teresa at the feet of a boy angel. She was seated, nearly supine, on a slope of some strange rocklike material that looked like huge leaves turned to stone. The angel was small, winged, softly built and prepubescent, with curling locks of thick hair, and his body was not quite covered by a billowing garment that left his wings free and exposed one shoulder and nipple. He was smiling benignly, or perhaps mischievously, down on Teresa as he extended his left hand, and he seemed to be lifting a fold of the saint's cloak. In his right hand he held a spear with a barbed point, poised for a thrust into the saint's body.

Teresa was a woman in her twenties—emphatically a woman, a female dweller on this earth, certainly not the image of a saint. She was wrapped in a cloak and only her left hand and foot appeared below the fringe, limp, as if in surrender.

Nora believed the angel had already delivered one or more thrusts, for the saint was twisted left, toward the viewer—toward Nora. Her thin lids were closed over large eyes—and her lips were open—not for a cry but perhaps a moan—because the pain was so intense.

Nora thought of Teresa's eyelids as tender and vulnerable, and of her breath as untainted but urgent. She seemed to be awaiting the next thrust. And though Nora could not see a flame, the saint had written that the spear was tipped with fire.

Relating this incident in the book of her life Teresa wrote that the spear entered her heart but probed so deep it reached her entrails, and all but pulled them out of her body when the angel withdrew it for a new thrust. Her pain surpassed any she had ever known—and she assured her readers that she'd reached the extremity of pain before this; but the agony of the spear's entering and withdrawing was unlike any other.

Unlike in intensity and effect. For this pain animated her with a sublime love of God. Physical suffering advanced into spiritual bliss. Spiritual pain made her moan, but was so desirable she hoped it wouldn't end.

Reading Teresa's account of this and similar incidents that followed, gazing at the statue, Nora could not discern any difference between pain and rapture, or between physical and spiritual.

Her eye kept returning to the small, innocent hand of the angel which seemed to be preparing to open Teresa's cloak—and to the indefinable smile on his girlish face. To Nora it seemed that the artist was depicting a living woman giving herself over to an act of disrobing and burning penetration. Nora knew the difference between Teresa's own interpretation of this, as a message of God's love and the bliss awaiting the saved in Paradise, and the modern meaning of those same terms—disrobing, burning, penetration. And Nora defined herself as a woman of her own times who was nonetheless capable of a sixteenth-century sensibility.

She could sense the breath issuing from Teresa's half-open lips and hear the groans of her half-turned throat. Under the rippling folds of Teresa's garment Nora imagined her body twisting left as the pain-induced love coursed through her limbs. And Nora felt the growth and flowering of love in her own body. It was not for Teresa's work as an abbess but for her raptures that Nora loved her; it was the raptures that reached over the centuries to touch her. It was a touch she did not think of resisting, expressive of the saint's power. And since she accepted Teresa as extraordinary, unlike herself, she was not jealous. Teresa united in one person the mystic and the achiever in this world, a capacity for love and work far exceeding Nora's. She was a worshiper who communed with the Christ to whom Nora could only pray, whose only answer was silence. But this same woman also outmatched the Spanish Inquisition in an era when "illuminists" were burned alive—and Teresa was nothing if not illuminated. She was a mere nun but her purity outraged the corrupt priests and monks; her enemies denounced her to the executioners, but she proceeded with the work of restoring honesty to the church. The Inquisition grudgingly let her be.

The archpriests who menaced Teresa were the same men who burned alive the illuminists who claimed they had seen God. Could it be that the priests believed nobody had seen Him because they had not? These robed enforcers knew what lesser mortals did not, that it was better for an illuminist to burn than to go on living in the sin of false visions.

Better because the flames would consume the lower fringes of the sinners' garments first, giving them time to repent; and repentance however late was the only path to salvation. So the priests tortured their victims out of charity; they knew what God wanted even if no one else did. Hating the inquisitors and executioners, Nora loved and venerated the saint who had helped mend their church in spite of them.

Conscious of her lowly status, Nora still felt a double affinity with Teresa. She wanted ecstasies for herself and her desire was explicit. The ecstasy she wanted was sexual. Wanting it herself, she believed Steven wanted it too; and she feared he was getting it from his bitch.

"But I can give you that!" she cried aloud. "You want 'wild nights'? Don't you remember when we were wild? Is the past dead for you?"

"It's not Steven's fault," she said a moment later, closing the book, with the open mouth and closed eyes imprinted in her memory. "It's my body's fault."

The ecstasy Teresa evoked with such metaphoric power showed Nora a landscape she had not set foot upon since the first year of her marriage. She gave Steven everything she could and took from him in equal measure, but love and making love were two different things. She loved Steven with her heart and soul; she made love with her body. She did it with gentle compassion. She had studied him, and could touch him with consummate skill and tender restraint; he responded; he cried his love when they reached their predestined, most intricate phase—and she took her own pleasure eagerly, and it rocked her body, it stunned her mind; it even surpassed her hopes—but it was not ecstasy. She never lost herself in the transforming bliss Teresa described.

Exhausted in this labyrinth, sick with a sense of inadequacy, she found herself dwelling on another aspect of Teresa's legacy.

She, Teresa, was a woman of power, and the taste of power was sweet to Nora McCord. Nobody was threatening to burn her alive but there was a lot invested in the game she played too. And she was honest in admitting what she loved about it. She loved the power to do or leave undone, to help or abandon, create or destroy. It did not trouble her that her stage and audience were small. Teresa's had been a convent of about thirty women in an obscure town in Spain. What mattered was the action and the outcome. And just now Nora was preparing an action that would produce an outcome with tremendous effect on the city. She would have to crush one man, or at least bend him to her will, but even he would be better in the end whether he knew it or not.

Nora had to walk carefully, since she was still on the civil service list, but she was de facto whip of the City Council president's faction. It was her job to line up votes for a series of critical contests with the mayor, with whom the president was at war. There was a vote coming up next month on the demolition of a government-built slum in the 6th Police District. The Council president needed the vote of a certain Alderman Dennis Crowley, an unreliable, unpredictable, impulsive man who sometimes voted with the mayor and sometimes with the Council president. The president and Nora had met to discuss Crowley: how to get his vote for the demolition. It wouldn't work to argue that the place was a hideous warren and should be torn down for that reason alone. In fact no argument would work on Crowley. So Nora proposed fear. "There is no blacker pit than a real job," she said.

The president's face lit up. He said, "Yeah! The private sector. He'd die out there."

So they intimidated him with the interim census data, which Nora had obtained from a friend in the federal building. Crowley was white and his district was turning black, was already fifty-five percent black, according to the new data. Crowley had been watching this trend for years with apprehension. "This is much worse than I thought," he said unsteadily. Nora predicted: "You can win once more, Dennis, then you're out." And she told him he was lucky that two or three black activists who wanted his seat were still a little premature, and would cancel one another out in the next election.

Nora then asked Crowley how he intended to vote on the demolition and he equivocated. She asked what he thought of the proposal to drive a freeway through the site, to carry traffic from the suburbs to the downtown business district in ten minutes instead of thirty. He equivocated again, and she could see the wheels turning behind his eyes.

Her third question was easier: How would he like it if the committee on re-districting drew him a new district? He could keep much of his white support and bring in a large bloc of white voters from an adjacent district, whose black alderman would get Crowley's black neighborhoods. The black alderman happened to be an ally of the Council president and was already on board.

Alderman Dennis Crowley was too cautious to give a straight answer so soon, but he thought he was looking at the light at the end of the tunnel.

And Nora McCord, watching this scenario play out, imagined herself presenting the proposal at a meeting next summer of the redistricting committee. It happened that the chairman of this important body had been making hungry eyes at Nora since the day he met her, and was held in check, she believed, only because he was afraid to go overt with the wife of a cop, especially one with Steven's reputation. But his admiration was not hidden. Nora's demeanor was that of a married woman who will tolerate distant fealty and nothing more.

But—imagining the meeting—she felt his eyes crawling over her body, and she was ashamed that she had chosen her dress that morning with him in mind, a dress that would warm his infatuation and arouse his hopeless lust.

Yes, it would be a good meeting.

Nora had a wild thought: "I'm displaying myself to that creep—and enjoying it!"

Teresa had deployed her political skills to reform the Carmelites by turning the nuns back to the service of God. "What am I doing?"

Her imagination presented the image of Charles Carden, a man purer than she. He was crossing the great atrium of City Hall to fight for the poor. She felt her old affection—and she said almost aloud—to him: "I am trying to make this a better city. We'll clear that slum and we'll— *That's* what this is for!" And she detected a note in her voice of anger, arrogance. This shocked her and she fell on her knees and clasped her hands in fervent prayer. She asked God to make her more like Teresa. "I do not compare myself to her except to learn more about my shortcomings. But help me to emulate her, to work for the good. If I can't be Teresa I can surely work to be as good as

Charles Carden, by trying to achieve for others what they cannot for themselves."

She paused. This "prayer" shamed her by its falseness. She knew what she really wanted and it was not to be as good as Charles Carden. It had come clear to her in just the past few minutes. She said to herself: "Steven wants wild passion and he's gone where he thinks he can get it. More than passion—I have that—more than steady love and the good wife and mother business, he wants, I want—I want ecstasy, to be taken out of myself by taking Steven into my body wild. Now I have an orgasm and it's good, it's nice, but compared to—rapture, bliss! What is it but a momentary spasm? It doesn't drive me crazy. Oh Steven, I want it and want to give it to you. God, why not give it to me? Please!"

She rolled on her side and lay weeping, knowing she could not be changed. She was too normal. She had something good to give, but it was not a form of madness. "I am too sane," she thought, as one who might say, "I am too reasonable." But she believed or tried to believe that what she gave him was more precious than mad bliss, it was love.

Staring along the level of the floor she admitted that the other woman might love him too, perhaps with more heat because her love was new. Nora saw that her only way was the way of transcendent love—the love that would release him to find happiness elsewhere if he could not find it at home.

"I have to love selflessly. Desire is selfish and selfishness is to die. I have to love him, and love for him. Be the best I can be in this life, and put his happiness before my own, even if it means losing him." She held to the ideal of transcendent love and searched for the glory in it.

Now came the final, crippling blow. We are commanded to love our enemies, so she had to love the other woman as she loved Steven. A moment later, breathless with the cruelty of this commandment, she cried in her mind: "Love her? Love the bitch?"

CHAPTER 20

Confession and Refusal

Unconscious of the blustery wind, of the night and the passing traffic, McCord stood outside the Normandy Arms undecided. It was just nine o'clock, too early to go home if he wanted to arrive after the kids had gone to bed. And he saw the living room couch—and wasn't sure he'd go home at all. But he did not move toward Lindy's door.

He drove to 2 Beat, parked his car and began roaming, thinking, not really searching, going from one puddle of light to the next and sometimes pausing to listen in the dark spaces between. He was dealing with a self-destructive impulse to confess—to Nora—and this confession would divulge—not that he was a stone; he had already told her that; but that he had done the unforgivable. When he listened, that was what he heard, himself telling Nora. He didn't know where confession would lead, unless it was to the riot room, which might be better than the couch.

He drove to the 6th District station, talked with the duty sergeant for a few minutes then climbed two flights to the attic, which had been fitted out as a barracks. It was McCord's policy that each officer keep a shaving kit and change of skivvies in a locker up here. The roof sloped sharply down on either side, and the cots were pushed as far under the slopes as they would go. A back-to-back double row of lockers divided the space down the middle, and two bare light bulbs hung from the ridge pole. A blanket was draped over a wire at the far end to accommodate women officers.

Except by the victims of hangovers—and male cops with woman trouble—this "riot room" had not been used since the disturbances of the 1960s. McCord had slept here only once, during a manhunt. He looked down the long center, along the rows of lockers, with a dismal feeling creeping into his heart. But his contrition was compromised, or confused, by another vision of Lindy Alden.

Whoever first invoked the image of a willow to describe the body of a slender woman could have been speaking of Lindy. McCord saw her again stretched on a white sheet. Her finely formed breasts were spread soft over her chest. Her long tapering waist disappeared into the widening curves of her hips; and her mons lay modestly concealed by a light, airy covering of pale red hair. Her long white thighs, tinted with rose, lay open, exposing the somewhat redder inner surfaces of her knees; and her feet tilted slightly outward. Seeing all this in one glance, he also saw her eyes fixed on him, full of trust, but now the trust was suffused with happiness. That was the confusing part—her happy, trusting eyes. Would confessing to Nora mean betraying Lindy?

He bade the sergeant good night and drove home.

He parked beside his garage and looked at the peak of his house raising its black shape in the night sky. He saw liar's curtains descending on him and encircling that part of him that he called his soul. He said "soul" because the years of brooding on final questions had scattered the idea of immortality without offering a substitute for that word. What was darkening was his soul, whether immortal or subject like the rest of him to the laws of the physical universe.

He wanted the new life but was ashamed to seek it. He wanted Lindy and couldn't have her. He wanted Nora and didn't deserve her. Nora appeared in the kitchen window looking out, and a gaping hole opened in McCord's gut.

She wasn't there. The room was lit and her papers were on the maple table, and he heard the bass notes of Danny's music throbbing through the house. He opened the Frigidaire and took out a bottle of Schoenling beer.

"What's her name?" Nora demanded in a breaking, unrecognizable voice.

He turned and saw her standing in the hall, in the dim light. She came forward and he saw the face of agony, shame and rage.

She screamed: "Name of the Rat Woman! Name, name, name!"

McCord moved carefully, put the unopened bottle on the table and turned again to face her, and she was still coming. She took his shoulders in her hands, dug her fingers in and cried: "Rat Woman! Does she have a name?"

McCord saw in her staring, sleep-deprived eyes such suffering as he had never seen there.

Still squeezing his shoulders she said: "They showed Teresa her place in hell. A little oven too small for her body, and to get there—they made her go there and crawl in—her place in hell!—to get there she waded barefoot through a hallway running with stinking water full of—rats!"

Steven looked at her silently out of his own agony and she screamed in his face:

"I don't recognize you. Why should I want your pity. Wipe it off your face. What's her name? Has she got a name?"

He said, "Lindy Alden."

"How cute! Lindy. *Lindy*. Isn't it cute, Steven?"

McCord said: "I've been unfaithful to you."

"Don't confess to me. I'm not a priest." And "God Almighty," she whispered, "he has everything. His health is good, his children love him, his wife loves him not that he gives a damn, he's not a drunk, got important work to do in this world, a hundred friends, and he must fuck, fuck, fuck his Rat Woman."

"Nora, please."

"Quiet!" she screamed, and her hands shot up into the air. "Don't say please to me, don't say anything. Say please to your rat. How long have you been lying about that woman? You never were a liar, but as near as I can figure out you discovered somewhere along the way that our religion is not true. Now you go around saying you live your life according to truth, but you don't know what the truth is."

She stepped back and cocked her head as if to examine him and said: "Isn't it funny, you've finally achieved your big ambition and changed the world. You've destroyed your family. You've damaged my love, the most important thing in my life, as if you cared. You've lost my respect and God only knows what your children will think. But maybe they'll adjust!

"People forget what was good and grow accustomed to—shit—pardon me but I can say shit like anybody else. They come to accept anything, that's known as adjusting to reality, giving up your ideals, and so your children will surrender their idea of the good, of family, faith and truth, and they'll say, 'Well, we were mistaken about Dad. We thought he was special but he's pretty much like all the others. He's got his new squeeze and I guess that's what he wanted, and he didn't really give a shit, you know?'

"That's what they'll think, Mr. Whoever You Are. In time it'll seem perfectly normal, a year or two. They'll look back on their first life as a dream. Yes, you've finally changed the world."

She fell into deep thought, as if thinking back over what she'd said, paying no attention to Steven.

He confessed that he had lied, betrayed her, and risked his children's happiness.

"Risk?" Nora echoed. "It was no risk. It was deliberate and calculating. You created all this knowing where it had to lead. A *risk* is when you take a chance. You're still lying, only this time you're fooling yourself. Teresa sinned too, probably a sin of lust, but she— Do you know who I mean?"

"No," said Steven hoping the screaming part was over.

"You wouldn't. She wasn't your kind."

Nora was leaning against the refrigerator with her head down. Her face was like an icon, a sacred object symbolizing their commitment to each other and their whole life. Whenever he saw her face it was the face he had seen the night they danced at Lakeside, and the beauty of it reached to the center of him.

"I don't care if I go to hell for it," Nora said, "but I hate you." Her face was red and swollen; there were tears smeared on her cheeks; her eyes were half closed now, and she said:

"You would never abuse her trust. After all, she gives herself to you, how could you use her as a mere object? You see I understand your philosophy although you try to conceal that too. I know that for you suffering has no meaning at all, so you could never dream of inflicting pain on your Rat Woman, it would be pure pain, never to be washed away. And so—isn't this your philosophy, Steven—we must be so very careful not to add to the sum total of suffering, since there is no God and we have somehow landed on this earth under our own power. We must love our little Lindy with the cute name and the luscious body, not merely use her, mustn't we—because life means nothing! Oh, she's a lucky woman. I'll bet she's beautiful, and young. Is she young, Steven?"

"She's about thirty-five or six."

"Thank goodness she's not twenty-six!"

Nora thought a minute and went on: "But you aren't fucking some policewoman or court stenographer, are you. You're doing much better than that. Let me guess. Is she a lawyer?"

"She's a nurse."

"Oh, not a doctor? You're so ambitious, I thought you'd aim higher."

Nora began to pace the room. She would take three or four steps then stop to stare with glaring eyes at some nearby object, then turn and take two or three steps—and fling a glance at her husband—then seemingly forget about him and resume her solitary thinking.

She said absently, "Open your beer."

He stood still and didn't answer. Nora pulled a drawer and threw the opener at him so quickly he couldn't deflect it before it hit him in the chest and fell to the floor. Staring at it McCord sensed the old love filtering through his pity and admiration. He had never pitied her till now. The pity itself shamed him—it was shameful that a man such as the one he had become in the last year should pity a woman such as Nora had always been. Mixed in with this he realized he was on the point of injuring Lindy Alden beyond anything she deserved.

As if she could hear his thoughts Nora said: "You created all this—whoever you are."

She sounded calmer and McCord again hoped the worst was over. Deep inside him beneath his despair he knew the worst still lay ahead, and that he had changed their lives. His mind kept working as if it could grope to the end of something. He thought that Lindy was not quite the person he had believed she was, that she too was willing to seek happiness and let Nora and his children pay the price. "Just like me," he said aloud, but Nora paid no attention.

In his mind McCord said, "I thought she was better than I was. But we are the same." Thinking this he knew he wronged Lindy.

He saw Nora coming again and he prepared to meet her fury.

She demanded: "What do you think I see? When we make love, which we never will again, what do I see? Those nights when Rat Woman has her period and you do me the favor of jumping me, what do you think—answer me!"

She grabbed him again and pushed him violently back and forth, and he took it. He knew the answer but didn't speak.

She cried: "I see you writhing on top of Rat Woman. Surely you know that. You could figure that out."

"Yes."

"Then say it."

"You see—what you just said. Nora—"

Either her face was scarcely human under torture or he lacked the humanity in himself to see it in her.

"But you're suddenly a better lover," said Nora with a strange leering smile. She swung at him but he intercepted her hand, and held her by the wrist. She didn't struggle or protest but kept on:

"Rat Woman must be a slut of wide experience. She's been teaching you what sluts learn. Slut!" she shouted.

McCord let go her wrist. He knew there was no point in telling her he had only lain with Lindy once. He was hoping and half-expecting that she'd fall weeping on his chest and confess that she still loved him. That seemed to be the only way out for them at this moment.

She turned away and he resisted the impulse to take her in his arms.

"But sometimes," she said, pausing, turning to face him again with wide-open startled blue eyes, "sometimes I ask myself who could this woman be, what kind of woman has such power over you, and I am forced to admit she might have some twisted kind of character to her. Maybe she's suffered losses of her own and sees in you the same sturdiness I did, and falls in love with you and can't be expected to resist you. I couldn't resist you, why should she? Do you follow me? I mean that she's deceived in you, as I was.

"And I think she must be intelligent and somehow good, or you wouldn't have fallen for her, and you're both tormented by the whole divorce question, especially if she's been through a divorce and if her husband left her, cheated on her. Does she have kids? So the two of you get caught up in long sick dialogues about me, your family, and you talk yourselves into believing that you're suffering for your love. It makes you feel so righteous. And wow! What a noble couple! What agonies you go through getting ready for your next fuck. She must be way out there on the bell-curve of passion. Am I right? You touch her and she squeals and squirms and attacks you and swallows your cock, and when it's over you talk about how you were off in some unknown country, how you never had anything like that from anybody else, how mystical and sublime it all is, how violent!

"I understand, Steven, I have always understood, that I'm sort of in the middle of the bell-curve, perfectly OK of course by most people's standards but maybe not what you really need. I don't go mad and scream and that disappoints you—but you don't know what bliss I feel when we make love. Or don't care. I wanted you as my husband but you wanted me as a woman. But I have passion too, Steven. No woman could love you more than I did."

McCord spoke with caution, and fear: "More than you did."

She didn't respond.

"I love you, Nora," he said.

"How lucky for me. I wonder how you treat those you hate."

She dragged her chair from the table as if it weighed a hundred pounds, and sat and fiddled with her papers. She absently clicked away at her calculator, producing a scroll of tape that she didn't bother to examine. She said, "I don't like her perfume," and laughed in two or three short bursts, and looked up at him and said: "For a policeman you are very careless, Steven."

McCord said as if it followed: "I'm back on the Carden case now."

"So I heard," said Nora.

"Heard where?"

"Janey Hughes told me and Gil told her. I'm not totally alone, thank God, I've got Janey. See, Steven, Janey is honest and truthful. It's so refreshing. But why the sudden change, Steven, on the Carden case?"

He told her about the "message" from Marie Carden.

She pondered this for some time, giving him an appraising and even sympathetic look, and said: "You are, maybe, too complicated."

He stood on the same spot, with the bottle opener between his feet. He wanted to say more about the message.

Nora said: "This isn't all your fault, I'm aware of that. I have been sleepwalking through our marriage. I have been too devoted to my job and too fascinated by the little ripples on the surface, unaware of the deeper currents. When I said, 'You created this,' of course you did, but I did too. I ask your forgiveness."

"Don't. I have nothing to forgive."

"Yes, I ask forgiveness. I am sorry I've been preoccupied with this miserable, struggling, rusty old city. The city could get along fine if I were dead, but I owe everything to my family, and I haven't given enough."

"Nora, please."

"And I never tried to understand how you see the world. Instead of listening for the sincerity in your voice I just kept telling you that you were wrong. I've been waiting for you to come back to faith and now I see you are not coming. I think you're making a fatal error. And now I have to ask whether a sincere error can actually be fatal in the sense I mean. So I ask your forgiveness for my arrogance, Steven."

"You are not arrogant."

"It's kind of you to say so, but you are wrong. You'll understand someday, when your guilt has cooled and some new bitch explains to you what an awful wife I was, and you'll agree with her.

"But Steven, let's stop a minute before we go over the edge. My love is not completely gone, and I am ready to offer it all over again, stronger than before. And who knows? Maybe with more passion, inspired by fear of losing you. I have only one condition, that you never see this woman again. Just promise that you won't and I will accept your promise as if it were given to me by the man I married. Do you promise."

He said, "No."

"Damn you!" she cried.

"May I explain something?"

"No! What could you explain? Out!"

While he packed a suitcase Nora remained at the kitchen table with her hand covering her eyes. She noticed there were no bass notes coming down through the house and wondered if she had screamed and alarmed the kids. How much had they guessed from his sleeping on the couch? But she did not dwell on the kids. She dwelt on, and in, her own misery.

A slowly widening stream of anger began to flow into the wretchedness of her conscious mind. Hearing him coming down the stairs she lifted her hand, blinked at the light, and watched him entering from the hall.

"You attack my faith," she said, pressing forward as if with a knife. "You are so sure of yourself. Not that you know all the answers. You don't need answers because your whole system claims there are none. OK, live in that wasteland if it feels like home to you. But don't expect me to understand how you can prefer it to a world of the spirit."

"I don't prefer it," Steven said, and she heard nothing in his words or voice that meant anything to her.

"And I never attacked your religion," he added.

"Another lie. You said I was the one who turned my back on that girl's suffering, because I believe she is with God. Or don't you remember? You said, quote, She's not with God, she's lying on a slab in the morgue because I just saw her. My God, what a pointless, vile, hopeless vision of life."

She saw him hesitate and then heard him say: "Please, Nora, let me explain something."

Was she turning cold or was she growing hotter than ever? She heard herself saying: "Explanations mean nothing to me, you liar. There is nothing you couldn't explain. I asked for your promise and you refused, so just leave me alone."

She closed her eyes, and heard the door open, then close. It was a sound she had heard a thousand times, but never like this. Instead of crying she gave full freedom to a frightening idea.

What if she had listened? When he said "May I explain?" was it possible he only wanted to go back to this woman—she withheld the "rat"—to tell her it was all over?

Nora stirred in her chair. She glanced distractedly at the work papers and the tape spread over the dark maple grain; then she was looking at the refrigerator and stove, and her eyes swept this whole historic room where they lived as a family—she saw the oven where Jill baked her pies—and she thought:

"If all he wants is to tell her he's coming back to us—or—is she pregnant? God, please, no. And he can't abandon her—yet—there is still goodness in him. He simply isn't the kind of man to throw her out—a good man whose passions are so strong that he—"

She fell into a less articulate style of meditation. Ideas, thoughts that could be expressed in words, and forgiveness, were now gone and all that remained were yearning and love.

McCord was driving down the familiar alley, which affected him as if it were a photograph of Nora dancing at Lakeside Park—and not a corridor of dark garages and gray trash cans. He thought: "I have to do it. I will do it. Christ, I'll do it."

CHAPTER 21

In the Riot Room

"How'd you know I was up here?" McCord said morosely, half awake and half frozen.

"Never mind," Sergeant Hughes answered. "It's eight-thirty and you're late for work and I'm coverin your ass as usual."

"Thanks. Anything?"

"Nothin. The naked city's peaceful as a tea room. You—course you don't know what peace is anymore. Have a nice sleep, did you?"

"I froze."

"Yeah," said Hughes, "but any dreams? Any little worries about what a fuckin mess you're makin?"

McCord didn't answer, just stared at nothing, till Hughes said:

"You didn't know hell looked like this. You thought it was a friggin inferno with guys hangin from wires by their scrotum."

McCord didn't respond to that either. He looked around, probing every dark dimension of the riot room, thinking he was looking at a fair approximation of the place reserved by an imaginary god for real punishment. Sitting in his skivvies on a canvas cot, huddling under an old war-surplus blanket, McCord said the place couldn't be hell, it was too cold.

"You're the landlord," said Hughes. "Turn the heat up."

It was an unheated attic but McCord didn't bother to contradict Hughes.

"So—couldn't sleep?"

"No I could not."

"The cold?"

"I just told you."

"Oh! So it wasn't your conscience."

McCord pulled the blanket closer and didn't respond.

Hughes sat across from him on the opposite cot, settling his paunch comfortably and leaning his elbows on his knees, thus pushing his face halfway across the little aisle and poking his eyes a little way out of their sockets to challenge McCord—blue rheumy eyes full of kindness, certitude and censure.

"Go back to her," Hughes counseled.

"She threw my ass out," said McCord.

"Go back."

"Did you hear me?"

"Listen, Stevie," Hughes began almost gently, "these women have got something we don't. They are steady and they are solid. You're in a swamp but these women, Nora and my Janey, are the dry land. She'll forgive you because she's the best woman God ever made except for Janey. She's smarter than you and me put together, she's a beauty—did you ever see another figure like hers, you fuckin bozo?—and I swear to God I don't know what came over you, except you been followin your peter."

"You seem to know all about it," McCord cut in.

"Nora called Janey this morning."

"Terrific."

"Why not? They hang together and they know the value of a family and a home. And let me tell you something, your old training officer tellin you a piece of the truth because I'm smarter than your dick. A fuck once a week that blows your tubes is all anybody needs. It's not necessary to find some super pussy that sends you off into the next world."

Said McCord: "Once a week? Are you that old?"

"So you're sayin you got yourself a red hot bimbo."

"She's no bimbo, Hughes. Watch yourself."

"Oh! Excuse me. Didn't mean to insult your floozie."

"Watch it," said McCord in a low, menacing voice.

"I should watch it? What about you? Do you know the risk, the cost?"

Giving him a glaring stare that lasted a long time McCord finally said: "I know the risk and the cost."

"And you figured somebody else'd pay. Like Nora and the kids. Not your royal self. Cheat a woman like Nora? What's out there that you don't already have at home? You've got the best, strongest wife there is, you moron. Janey said she sounded a lot better than you look."

"How would Janey know how I look."

"Don't give me technicalities. If my cat dragged you in I'd throw you back on the street."

"Thanks."

"An electric cunt does not make a woman, you fuckin bonehead."

"Look, can we drop the insults?"

"In a minute. Let me ask you, what kind of woman sleeps with a married man?"

"Maybe you wouldn't know."

"Yeah, maybe I do know."

"So you're no cleaner than I am?"

"Stevie, ask yourself, if a woman sleeps with a married man, with kids, with a wife—"

"I know all that."

"You know! Then what are you doing? 'Not a bimbo, not a slut.' Why not defend your wife instead of the slut?"

Controlling his anger McCord said: "Nora is a class all by herself, I know that. There's nobody like her."

"OK then. The kind of stuff you want, you can get it at Granny's for an hour's pay. Why fracture your whole world? I thought you were pretty smart but as of now I doubt it."

"Smart has got nothing to do with it."

"Stevie, explain yourself. You've got Nora, the kids, the—"

"Leave it alone!" McCord shouted.

"So is it just—you're an animal?"

"Yes."

"OK we settled that. Now the lawyer thing. Are you still—"

"I already forgot it," McCord declared. "Criminal defense lawyers are scum and I'm just scum of a different kind."

"Good. Progress. And the bimbo, forgotten?"

"Listen, you sack of shit, I could take this from Janey but not from you, after what you just confessed. So shut up. I'm finished with her. I—I've decided I—"

"Decided what?"

"The one you call a floozie, who's actually a pretty decent—"

"You're all done?"

"Yes, god damn it. We made love once and only once and now you can keep your insults to yourself."

Hughes grunted his satisfaction and then asked: "Now what's this crusade on the Carden case?"

"It's not a crusade," said McCord gathering in the blanket.

"Yeah, I see you're still cold, you poor duck. Also late for work. But talk, go ahead, Carden case."

"There's nothing to say. It's a routine investigation by the Bureau, and all I did was activate an old search plan which was drawn up by a certain paunchy red-faced bulgy-eyed sergeant. I pulled one man off the street, Dotson, and that's all. No big deal."

Hughes's livid, rounded face broke with a huge smile, followed by a bellowing laugh. "Right! Routine! The district commander prowling at all hours of the day and night like a rookie with a hard-on, chasing all over hell and gaping at a body in the morgue. Routine!"

"Exactly. Glad you agree."

"If I was you," said Hughes, "I'd just do my job. Set up your bullseyes and trip wires, pass out your pictures and all, but do like Burl Ives says, stick with your wife and family. If we make a grab we turn the puke over to the lawyers, and that's all we're meant to do."

"And the lawyers," McCord began, "and the judges—"

"I know. Do you think I'm blind? They don't give a shit. But watch out. Go on a crusade, you're gonna fuck up, no question. Either you'll shoot Mr. Puke when you shouldn't or you'll get all scrambled in your head."

"Say, Huge-es, I haven't been a cop for twenty years for nothing."

"Haven't you? I told you before, take it—"

"You told me everything before."

"—take it easy. You seem to think you're in a duel to the death with Mr. Puke. You kill him and justice reigns. We both know if you kill him, unless you do it *precise-l-ly right*, according to the rules, they'll wreck your career.

"Stray one single degree from the exact prescribed way and the lawyer machine turns and opens its jaws for you, the hero. You could end up in jail. You been a cop for twenty years, OK, what world are you in? A little more humility, a little more realism. Your mission isn't justice, your mission is to make the grab and put his ass in City-County Consolidated and let the lawyers do the rest."

"They won't do the rest."

"Sometimes they do. There are some lawyers who want justice as much as you do."

"They'll never bring him to justice. They don't know the meaning of the word."

"Look," said Hughes patiently, leaning farther forward so he had to look up to face McCord, "I realize they think justice is when they make his life a little inconvenient. They see their job that way. They're all hot for processes. Follow procedure and that's what they call justice. But who are we to rain down righteousness from the sky? Are we gods, are we the president? We are fuckin cops, Stevie, we play by the rules."

"Just like them? Play by the rules and call it justice? Anyhow, I intend to do it by the rules."

"Do what?" Hughes shot back with sudden vehemence, almost alarm.

"Like you said, make the grab."

"What are you tryin to tell me? You make the grab in accordance with the law."

"In accordance," said McCord, "with the real law."

"There's no *real law*. There's just the law. That's our book. Everything else is— Everything's wobbly, the whole world," Hughes lectured, "fluid, jelly. 'Without form and void.' Like it was never finished, created but not completely. Me, I go through the motions, I go to church to please Janey, I cross myself and don't even feel like a hypocrite, it's for a good cause. A place like 2 Beat don't make sense to me any more than it does to you. I'm lookin for sense somewhere and I never find it.

"When I was a boy in Edgemont the two worst things you could be, the lowest, was a dope peddler or a queer. My mother'd say, 'If a man comes to the playground and offers something nice, run like the wind.' Now I bet they don't even confess it, they just say 'Hey, this is me.' If they did confess the priest would say, 'Well, pal, give me three Our Fathers and three Hail Marys and an Act of Contrition. Skip the part about amending your life, ha ha,' and *sk-k-k-k* he shuts the panel and off you go. Where's your *real law*?

"I got my family, I got no holes in my stomach yet, heart's not so good but I made my share of grabs and did as much for justice around here as half the ones that go bust. Nothing personal, Lieutenant."

"I am not going bust."

"When you talk about the real law I wonder. But hey, only once, really?"

"We made love once, and for all I know if I call her again she won't answer."

Hughes dropped the corners of his mouth and put on an expression of: "What do I make of this surprising new fact?" But when he spoke it was in a different spirit. He said: "You're not callin her again, right? Right?"

"Yeah," said McCord in a flat voice.

"Say, 'I am not callin the floozie again.' Say it."

McCord seemed not to hear. He said: "I saw her—" intending to say he saw his wife in pain. "And the other one, who you call a bimbo—"

"Forget I said that. Maybe she's another Mary Magdalene."

"And it's true I've made a mess."

"But don't worry too much about the other woman, she's got it coming."

"Now get out and let me think," said McCord.

Hughes rose and said: "Janey told me, 'If you don't bring Stevie home for dinner tonight, don't bother coming yourself.' "

"Thanks. I'll come."

"Now, one more thing. One little detail, OK?"

"What?"

"Just a detail. Did she cry?"

"Who?"

"You think I care about the bimbo? Nora, did she cry, yes or no?"

"No," Steven answered, seeing again how she had leaned against the refrigerator.

"OK," said Hughes, "that's even worse. Do you realize what the family means to her?"

"Yes. Quit this, for Christ's sake."

"One more," Hughes went on. "Do you realize what you mean to her, lies and all?"

"I can see that she's—" McCord's voice trailed off.

"In agony. Right?"

Steven said Yes in a tone of confession.

During dinner that night at the Hughes manse Gil was mostly silent and Janey spoke of the McCord marriage delicately and only twice, both times obliquely. She said, "You and Nora are a couple, Stevie." McCord thought: "We were." And Janey said cryptically, "I love her, Stevie." McCord couldn't answer but he nodded.

Much of the time he felt alone at the table. He couldn't drive Marie Carden from his mind except for short periods when he would forget her existence, then unexpectedly he'd see her in her captivity. He saw what she endured. This had a form, and was not a void.

When he turned at the door to say goodbye all he wanted to say was thanks. He found he couldn't speak, looking into Janey's calm eyes. He didn't know which grief was stifling his voice, Nora's, Marie's, or his own.

Janey looked up. She reached and took his face in her hands and said: "Go to her. I told her it was only once. She said that made no difference, but don't listen to what she says, just go to her."

CHAPTER 22

Harry's Glimpse

One second, and Harry Kalzyn's life turned. In fact you could have split the second in half, into quarters or fifths, and the effect would be the same. His lungs sucked a gasp of air and his heart lost all its blood, and he walked away a frightened man.

The whole thing started when his office phone rang. The caller was a surgeon who had just completed an operation on one of Harry's patients. He asked if Harry could meet him in the ICU.

To Harry ICU meant Lindy.

Harry's office was located in a separate wing of the hospital, a five-minute walk via corridors and one elevator ride—five minutes to a chance of seeing Lindy—even if he couldn't find an excuse to speak with her. So he grew nervous and happy as he made the little trip.

After talking with the surgeon and looking at his patient's chart he searched the ICU, wondering if anybody would notice—since everybody knew he was Lindy's ex. She wasn't there, so he went to another place where she might be at this hour, the cafeteria. It was mid-afternoon and he wanted some fruit juice anyway, or so he told himself, but what he got was something quite different, not juice but poison.

Lindy was sitting with a group of five or six nurses crowding around a table meant for four, and she was the center of their attention. When he glimpsed her she was laughing, and she added something to whatever she'd just said— he couldn't catch it—and it sent the nurses off on a new wave of laughter, and one even clapped her hands. Lindy's color was up and her voice carried a strong and melodious sound to his eager ear.

The trouble was, this scene virtually duplicated one several years past. In the earlier scene, on the day after she accepted his proposal of marriage, she had sat at the center of just such a group as this, showing her ring and—it seemed to Harry, who happened to come in at just that moment, not entirely by accident—that she was spreading happiness all around, that hers was so abundant she must share it, because she was happy in love—with him! That "ring" scene animated his mind from that day onward as the fruition of his hopes and emblem of their future life. It was a good part of the reason he had never fully believed in her decision to divorce him because, as he kept repeating in his mind, real love doesn't die.

With her left hand extended toward the center of the table and her face "radiant," in Harry's eyes—she looked up and saw him. Letting her head fall between her shoulders she looked at him as if he'd caught her at something naughty. She tilted her head mischievously and wiggled her fingers at him—and that moment was the summit of his marital happiness. He was certain of her love and confirmed in the devotion that still guided his life.

And this time, too, she looked up unexpectedly and saw him; and this time, too, in an unguarded moment, in her surprise, she revealed herself. What he saw in her face was: "I'm caught," and she was anything but mischievous. What he saw was shame.

He turned quickly, to spare her, and walked into the main lobby, almost falling on the way, but it was not in his nature to do anything so melodramatic, not even involuntarily.

He knew what that shame signified. The woman he loved so deeply and inescapably was plunging down a dark and dangerous street, toward a wrong that would compromise her for the rest of her life.

If she were saved it would be by her lover's abandoning her. The pain of that would change her. And if he took her, he would degrade her, as she degraded herself. In either case she would be changed—maybe not into some other person, but injured and guilty, especially when she thought of the wife and children whom her lover still loved, or, worse, if he should let her see his own shame and remorse.

Walking across the lobby Harry appreciated perhaps for the first time how his confidence and hope of a reconciliation depended so critically on his faith in her essential goodness. And now unless he was wildly mistaken about the look she had thrown him—now his faith—

He couldn't bear to carry the thought any further. He felt physically weak and morally stricken. He felt in his heart and soul something so terrible he couldn't name it or face it. Because of all this his love became even more intense and—bleeding. He thought "bleeding," to describe his love. He thought: "How can she do this to herself?"

CHAPTER 23

In Memoriam

McCord made his plan for the memorial service, briefed his officers—and felt uneasy. The chance of the plan's turning up anything useful was pretty slim. It was, however, based on a real possibility, that the man or men who had brutalized Marie Carden would yield to a sick desire to see her lying in her coffin. But even if a murderer came and mixed with the mourners—a chance in ten thousand—how could he be identified?

Sergeant Hughes's job was to arrange for a videographer from Downtown to be posted behind a second-floor window across the street from the parish hall where the service would be held. Tim Sloan would stand beside the videographer as lookout and radio relay in case McCord or any officer needed to communicate with the videographer. Any and all radio talk would be conducted not on the District's regular net but on the B Channel, which was secure.

McCord placed one officer, Greta Gabriel, wearing plain clothes, at the back of the audience. Greta Gabriel was a tall blond woman whose severe beauty shone with a special luster when clothed in the blue and silver of police power. She was less conspicuous in her civvies. McCord instructed her to be alert for any sign of morbid or aberrant interest in the proceedings, especially the bodies.

From her post at the rear Gabriel could pick out the young males during the music and the eulogies and track each one as he went to the front to view the bodies at the end of the ceremony. Wesley Hawkins, taking the minister, the Reverend Mr. Boulton, into his confidence, had already arranged for the seats, the lectern and coffins to be placed so that mourners approaching the coffins would turn left around the lectern and then move past the coffins and file away to the left. In making the turn to view the bodies they would of necessity turn to face the audience, which is to say they would face Greta Gabriel at the center rear and Steven McCord on the left side of the seating area.

Patrolman Dotson, also in plain clothes, would station himself to the right, keeping watch on McCord for one of two hand signals. If McCord lifted his left hand to his ear it meant "Approach me." His right hand up meant "Track that man," where "that man" was the one at that moment moving away from Marie Carden's coffin.

The two coffins were placed so that the mourners would pass by Charles's body before coming to Marie's. McCord and his officers would observe any unseemly hesitation over the second coffin.

As the mourners filed out of the building and down some steps to the sidewalk the videographer would film every face.

The scene of this event was the parish hall of a black congregation that had moved into one of the majestic old Protestant churches in McCord's district. In arranging the event Wesley Hawkins had approached the Reverend Mr. Boulton, a man who fully appreciated Charles Carden's advocacy for the "voiceless." The pastor had offered his church but Wesley Hawkins asked instead for the parish hall, on the ground that a smaller space would be more appropriate. In fact, less than thirty feet would separate the eyes of McCord, Greta Gabriel and Dotson from those of a mourner gazing on the body of Marie Carden.

With utmost gravity Wesley Hawkins had urged the pastor to maintain a perfect silence about his request that the coffins be arranged as they were. Both coffins were open but anyone who wanted to view the bodies would have to march the route laid out by Steven McCord, and thus face the audience. The pastor gave his word.

McCord would park his unmarked sedan just a few steps from the parish hall door. Dotson and Gabriel would come in a marked cruiser which they would park beside another cruiser a few blocks away behind an abandoned tavern. The driver of the second cruiser, who would remain with his vehicle ready to move, was Patrolman Lennox. This cruiser and Lennox would play a critical role if McCord put his plan into effect. His object was modest: to learn the name and address of any man who aroused his suspicion, without alarming the suspected one.

Wesley Hawkins had arranged for the undertaker to place a notice of the service in the papers.

In McCord's instructions to his officers the essential element was: "If we focus on a man, do not let him know it."

The service was set for 10 A.M. two days after McCord took up residence in the riot room.

The morning was sunny, bright, and cold. The time was nine-thirty and time to go; but some gentle, unidentified power, strong enough to hold him, prevented McCord from leaving just now. He put on his winter coat but still did not leave. Breaking his own rule he dialed Lindy Alden's apartment on his office phone and left a message: "Babe, it's Steven. May I see you tonight? I'll call around six." He hung up and noted—and it was no surprise—that his hands were trembling.

When he slid behind the wheel of the gray sedan and got on the radio he instructed his special crews to shift to the B Channel. With that act he lost all identity save one: McCord, cop. He stopped one street short of the parish hall and ascertained by radio that Tim and the videographer were on station and Dotson and Gabriel were en route. He knew too that Nora would be on her way but this was mere knowledge, like knowing the sun was shining and the traffic was light. He was too deep now.

Or so he thought. He found himself asking how the undertaker could hide or soften on Marie's face the marks of her ordeal. He imagined her in her coffin, wearing her white silk scarf across her forehead like a nun's wimple, with a loop of it covering her disfigured jaw.

He parked the gray sedan and, in spite of the cold, left his winter coat in the car. He proceeded toward the hall wearing only his suit, shifting his left shoulder to place his revolver comfortably. He saw Nora coming toward him and he kept walking at the same pace. The sight of her had an impact as if they'd been separated for years and he now saw her looking younger. She lifted her hand and smiled, and McCord returned the greeting, feeling strange and tense, before he mounted the steps to the parish hall and walked in to the music.

He saw Greta Gabriel near the center rear of the audience, and checked the layout of the coffins and lectern, which was correct; then he took an aisle seat on the left of the audience.

There were about forty metal folding chairs in six rows, and the rows were filling with mourners, most of them black. Greta Gabriel was looking at nothing and everything, except for Steven McCord.

Patrolman Dotson, in a gray tweed sport coat and black sweater, was on the right and forward, where McCord could plainly see his blond crew-cut head. Nora had taken a seat somewhere in the rear. He turned and saw her, and she smiled again with actual warmth in the smile. He didn't know what this might mean. He wondered if she had been looking at him before he turned, thinking: "Turn around, Steven."

As the organ billowed out its soft solemnities the seats filled, and McCord glanced over his right shoulder, scanning the audience. Loudspeakers carried the music in from the church, and McCord wondered idly how the organist knew when to play and when to stop. He caught another glimpse of Nora, looking as if she were meditating on the dead and death.

McCord let his gaze slide, not making contact with anybody but seeing everybody in the way a sailor sees a light at night, by sliding past it. There were several males under sixty in the room.

The moment came when he had to face forward and listen. The Reverend Mr. Boulton was extolling Charles Carden's life of selfless service. He kept his Christianity under restraint, perhaps knowing plenty about that part of Carden's character. He concluded with: "Not every man who abandons God is abandoned by God. This was a good man, my friends, and never forget, God is a good God."

The local alderman then took the lectern, and while he was arranging his notes McCord swept the room again quickly. The men were fewer than the women, and among the men more than half were black. Believing the killers had been white McCord found he was looking at the white faces, and at one in particular that interested him. He could not study it. He turned again to face the speaker.

The alderman was an elderly black man named Dave Brisbane. He had been the football coach at Dunbar High School when McCord was a seventeen-year-old halfback at rival Stivers. He built on the theme of selfless service and added color blindness to the lists of Charles Carden's virtues. And he mourned the death of a young woman who had come from California to visit her father.

The next speaker was Wesley Hawkins. McCord wished he could look again at the "interesting" face. His memory constructed an image of a man shorter than middle height, whose head and shoulders suggested a slight build and a weight of about one-fifty. What, perhaps, had arrested McCord's eye was the man's haircut, a Prince Valiant style with black "bangs," to use the term applied to women's cuts, solid masses of straight hair reaching halfway down the forehead and describing a level line above the eyebrows. These were very prominent, almost heavy; and the hair was a near-black kind of brown with yellow or red highlights painted on its plasticized surface. Below these bangs and below these eyebrows a pair of dark eyes looked out with an expression that to McCord suggested self-satisfaction. He thought a man would have to be very proud of himself to fix his hair like that.

All this time McCord was vaguely aware that Wesley Hawkins was talking. This perception did not block out his mental examination of his photocopy of the "interesting" young man. The haircut seemed to say not only that the man admired himself but that he admired the wrong things. McCord realized there was no telling his age. He could be twenty or forty. Dwelling on the nose, the lips, McCord realized what was "interesting." The man was pretty. Maybe not beautiful, certainly not handsome. McCord wanted a frontal look and especially a look in his eyes, but couldn't get one.

Still half listening to Wesley Hawkins's eulogy McCord's brain clicked on another impression. He had seen a tall, large, light-skinned black man sitting two rows behind Prince Valiant, and now he realized it was Basil Samuelson, the cab driver. There was something pleasing in this recognition. He listened to Wesley Hawkins.

"And so, my friends," Wesley Hawkins was saying in his rounded, trial lawyer tones, "I return to the question I began with. Why are we here? Fifty of us, approximately, mostly unknown to one another, citizens of a troubled city within a troubled nation, gathered on this cold, brilliant morning to remember one man getting along in years, and his daughter just beginning to get along in life—not, as the tender-minded would say, to celebrate their lives, but, speaking harshly, speaking straight, to mourn. We are here to mourn their deaths, to enter a deep and almost smothering consciousness of our loss.

"But there is within us, thanks to these two people, Charles and Marie, some cause indeed for rejoicing, that we and they are of the same created humanity. Men like Charles, young women like Marie, can make us glad simply by living.

"I referred a moment ago to justice. I said that when I think of Charles Carden and Marie his daughter I think of justice, and now I will tell you why.

"The ancient philosophers, religious thinkers and poets, searched the human character for the cardinal virtues, those qualities in men and women that enable them to live a meaningful life, to flourish in a world where morality and law are mostly a dream.

"The ancients saw that men and women who lived by prudence, temperance, courage and justice could live the best of all possible lives.

"Prudence blends reason and traditional wisdom, giving each its due weight. Temperance puts a check on the appetites, which would otherwise run away with us. Courage, when instructed by reason and temperance, empowers righteous anger.

"And if justice means that every person gets what he deserves then I say that justice embraces all the other virtues. Because a just man or woman will work to create a world in which the poor are succored, the hungry are fed, the sick are tended, the bereaved are comforted and the cold are clothed.

"Charles Carden worked for social justice, for a fair chance for everybody at the goods of this world.

"In addition to social justice there is another kind, we call it criminal justice, a very inadequate and misleading name. Those who take from others—money, property, or peace of mind—or life—must be given what they deserve. This is the role of righteous anger. Without it no society can offer a decent life to its citizens, because the strong and the brutal would always prevail."

He stopped, and McCord thought that this was a man who could barely stand, yet he held his audience in perfect control by the authority of his sonorous voice and his gaunt, masculine, tortured features. For the first time McCord could see the pain of the man's legs visible in his eyes.

Leaning on the lectern and enhancing his voice somehow, making it both deeper and wider, Wesley Hawkins repeated: "Justice is: Every person gets what he deserves. The sick woman deserves help and compassion. The poverty-stricken school child deserves a chance at a good education. Marie Carden deserved to live her life. And her killer, in justice, deserves—to be removed—from—the human community."

He looked with his angry, judging eyes at nearly every person in the room. McCord sensed the wrath in those eyes as they penetrated his own. He wondered if Wesley Hawkins had looked directly at the young man with the Prince Valiant haircut.

Then the speaker said: "The Reverend Mr. Boulton can teach us how to temper justice with mercy. Mine is a simpler task. Let justice be served—in this our city of violence, our nation of moral anarchy. Let us remember that Jesus drove the moneychangers from the temple with a whip, for defiling a holy place. And the killer or killers of this good man, the torturers and murderers of this innocent woman have defiled humanity and taken from Charles and Marie what only God has a right to take, life. The wrath of God is to be feared by the wicked, but the righteous wrath of man can also be terrible, swift and certain. My last word is: Justice."

This word filled the little hall—and the organ sounded a slow, celestial fanfare. At first McCord didn't recognize the melody, so hesitating and solemn was the pace of its unrolling. After several bars had reverberated through the room he realized it was the most familiar spiritual of all, "Swing Low," rendered with a poignant charity.

The Reverend Mr. Boulton, speaking in a voice just loud enough to be heard as accompaniment to the music, told the people they could now bid goodbye to Charles and Marie.

While the mourners lined up McCord moved to the back of the hall, and touched his left ear. The line began to move slowly toward the coffins, so all McCord could see of Prince Valiant was his slightly curved back in a green windbreaker. When Patrolman Dotson reached his side McCord asked if he had noticed the "interesting" man. He had. Did he know him? No. Never seen him around 2 Beat? No.

McCord gave Dotson the key to the gray sedan and said: "Take Greta and follow him. You go on foot, Greta drives. If he gets into a car, jump in with Greta. I'll call Lennox. Got it?" ·

"Yes sir" Patrolman Dotson said. "Prey car first, Greta and me following in your car—I mean if he has a car—and Lennox follows us in his cruiser."

"Right. I want Lennox to stop him on a traffic violation. So Lennox will have to pass you at some point."

"Yes sir. You'll call Lennox?"

"Yes," said McCord. "If it's a car ride you'll have to direct him. And you decide when he should pass you. I don't want the suspect looking in his mirror and seeing a cruiser till the last minute."

Dotson signed to Greta Gabriel and the two left the hall, Dotson first, Gabriel a minute later. If the plan worked Greta Gabriel would proceed surreptitiously to McCord's gray sedan and wait till she saw Dotson going one way or the other on the sidewalk. If Prince Valiant got into a car she would pick Dotson up and they would follow Prince Valiant, and direct Patrolman Lennox in his cruiser to follow or intersect them, keeping him at a safe distance, beyond the range of Prince Valiant's mirror.

The first mourners had now made the left turn around the lectern, where Wesley Hawkins, the Reverend Mr. Boulton and Alderman Brisbane stood talking in quiet voices. Hawkins and McCord made eye contact once and neither betrayed any sign of recognition. McCord saw his wife join the line of viewers. He admired her erect carriage and straight shoulders, her dark auburn hair under the small black velvet hat she wore only in church. And seeing Nora he thought of her children, his own, and wondered what they thought of him now.

Prince Valiant was still moving with the line slowly toward the turning point. McCord stepped outside and keyed his mike, telling Patrolman Lennox, who was still parked, to be ready to home in on the gray sedan.

Looking around him McCord could see the stairs leading to the sidewalk, and the building across the street where the videographer was stationed. He could see neither Gabriel nor Dotson, which was fine. When he returned to the music and the crowd in the hall Prince Valiant was making the left turn toward the coffins.

He watched. Having now a frontal view McCord guessed the man was about twenty-two. From this angle his haircut was even more striking, framing in tinted, glossy hair a face that was almost beautiful, if a girl's face can be beautiful on a man. He was bigger than McCord had guessed, probably five-ten and one-sixty.

With a start that was the next thing to a thrill McCord noticed what was different. Prince Valiant's skin was flushed, almost crimson. Yet McCord was certain he'd been pale at first sight—that the chalky pallor of his skin had contrasted with the hair. Now there was no contrast. The face was a deep red, and the hair—dark but with its artificial blond or red tints—harmonized with the complexion.

McCord thought: "That's his reaction to the word 'justice.' "

As Prince Valiant drew up to the first coffin and stared down at Charles Carden, McCord joined the rear of the line. He lived in fear that Prince Valiant would suddenly look up and see a man in a suit, who was certainly no lawyer, doctor or businessman, staring right at him. McCord spoke to the black woman in front of him; they talked about Charles and Marie.

Glancing again at the "interesting" face McCord saw no expression; none. Charles Carden had no visible effect on him. McCord and his companion took two steps forward while Prince Valiant moved to his own right and stood over Marie Carden.

The effect was instant and visible. It was a glinting, utterly captivated stare of enlarged, enslaved eyes. The man's head moved forward like a turtle's sticking out of its shell and his lips pressed upon one another and bowed outward. Not knowing exactly what he was seeing McCord knew it made him sick.

Then a remarkable thing happened, although it's likely no one noticed but McCord. The blood drained from the man's face, and he seemed to go into a standing faint. McCord thought he might collapse. Instead he moved on, slipping past several people as quickly as possible, like a man who needs air. He reached the door and was gone.

"Sir," said a mellow voice close behind McCord.

He turned and saw Basil Samuelson holding out his hand, looking level at him with an offer of friendly renewal of acquaintance. Seeing the cab driver McCord made an instant decision. He had intended to follow the funeral cortege to the graveside service, but having seen Prince Valiant rush out he changed his mind. He would manage the tail himself.

Shaking the huge hand of Basil Samuelson he said: "Do you have your cab?"

"No but I have my own car," said Basil Samuelson in surprise. And yet, Basil Samuelson reflected, he wasn't surprised at all. He expected something intense and active from this man whose sharp, glaring features were suddenly focused on him.

"Can you give me a ride?" McCord asked still gripping Basil Samuelson by the hand.

"Yes sir."

"Right now?"

"Yes, of course."

McCord headed to the exit and when he was out in the sunshine and trotting down the steps he saw that the gray sedan was gone and neither Dotson nor Prince Valiant was in sight.

"Quick," said McCord, "where's your car?"

Samuelson led the way, pressing his unathletic corpus to unusual exertion, as McCord followed, pulling out his microphone and saying:

"Three One One, this is Six Dash One."

Greta Gabriel responded promptly: "This is Three One One. We are eastbound on Third approaching Ludlow."

Samuelson unlocked the passenger door of an old Chevy and McCord slipped in. He turned up the volume on his body set so Samuelson could follow the action. And he said to Samuelson:

"Third Street eastbound," and Samuelson kicked the car into gear; they pulled away.

McCord called Patrolman Lennox and was gratified to learn he was underway and had the gray sedan in sight. McCord cautioned him against following too closely.

As McCord visualized the sequence now the prey car was leading Greta Gabriel and Dotson, who led Lennox, who was being followed at some distance by McCord and Samuelson. McCord could not yet see the cruiser but knew its position from the transmissions between Lennox and Gabriel. The prey car was now about a mile east of the parish hall, still eastbound on Third.

Over the next fifteen minutes Prince Valiant stopped only once. He got out of his car—McCord listened to Dotson's narrative—went into an apartment building and emerged ten minutes later, then reversed his course. Now the snake turned, pulling its tail behind, going westbound on Third. McCord ordered Lennox forward and told him to make a traffic stop as soon as he observed anything resembling a violation. He ordered Greta Gabriel to stay a block behind the cruiser and stop when Lennox stopped, but to keep him in view in case he called for backup.

McCord and Samuelson were less than a block behind the cruiser when Lennox set his red lights flashing. McCord saw the rack lights come alive; he saw a car pull over, and saw Lennox get out and approach the prey car—an old Dodge—and then McCord said to Samuelson:

"Hang back."

Samuelson slowed, and pulled over at a crosswalk, while McCord watched. Meanwhile Dotson radioed Downtown and asked for a check on the prey car's license number.

McCord said as if to himself: "All I want is to see his face again."

Basil Samuelson looked aside for a long moment. His benign eyes seemed to rest gently on McCord. He asked, nodding forward: "Did he do it?"

"I don't know," McCord said.

Basil Samuelson had cut his engine, but he kept the steering wheel in his hands, moving his big thumbs up and down slowly. McCord could hear a wheeze in his breathing.

"The man who spoke about justice," Basil Samuelson began and paused.

"Yes, Wesley Hawkins, a lawyer."

"Is he a friend of yours?"

"An acquaintance," McCord said.

"Tell him we all, even he, have cause to fear justice."

McCord turned in his seat as if to hear more.

"Tell him justice that is not tempered with mercy is not God's justice."

"He might agree with you," said McCord.

"And tell him it's not true that the world has no morality of its own and no laws built into it."

"I'll tell him you said so," McCord assented, "but what he said was that morality and law are a dream. What's wrong with that?"

"I think he meant they don't exist. I think he's an apostle of despair, but he knows full well that only God can bring justice, and he doesn't believe in God."

"He believes we have to create justice for ourselves, justice, morality and law, or none will exist."

"It doesn't work that way."

"I think it does."

"Man cannot do it. He can only obey God's law or disobey and fall into despair."

"And if this guy," said McCord gesturing forward, "raped and killed that woman, what would you do about it?"

"Me myself?"

"You, just a man, you yourself."

"I would help catch him. And if I was doing God's work I wouldn't be 'just a man.' "

"You are helping me, and I thank you. But if you caught him, what?"

"Turn him over," said Basil Samuelson.

"To the police?"

"Of course."

"And do you believe that justice means giving each person his due, what he deserves?"

"Who does not believe that?"

McCord said: "I believe it." And thought: "What have I done to Nora, that she did not deserve? What did I do, thinking I was getting away with it? What do I deserve?" To Samuelson he said: "I want to see his face again. Please circle the block."

So they went around a block and approached the prey car from its front, and McCord got another fleeting glimpse of Prince Valiant.

Patrolman Lennox stood at the window of the Dodge.

"Slow, but not too slow," McCord urged Samuelson.

Their speed dropped to fifteen and they glided by the prey and the officer. Prince Valiant was looking courteous and submissive—so McCord imagined—and he was smiling. McCord saw the smile and wondered how he could manage it.

Then he checked himself, having no proof. He called the station and ordered Sergeant Hughes to draw up a request for seizure and search of the Dodge, to compare its tire treads to the impressions taken in the mud behind

128 Laurel. The clerk Downtown radioed McCord on the license, saying the car was registered to one Emily Lonvillion of Cleveland, two hundred miles northeast; it was not reported stolen.

Still coasting at fifteen, well past the prey car, Basil Samuelson said patiently, "Where to now?"

As if he hadn't heard, McCord said: "I just wanted to see his face again."

"You can't tell much from a face," said Basil Samuelson.

"Maybe not, but if you know what he did you can look at his face and try to figure out why."

"You said you didn't know whether he did it."

"That's right," McCord said, "I don't."

Then he took Samuelson's huge shoulder in his left hand and rocked the man heavily left and right, saying: "Thanks for the ride, Mr. Samuelson."

And Basil Samuelson said: "You can't have either justice or mercy till you get him. So, Mr. McCord, get him."

"Mr. Samuelson, are you maybe feeling righteous anger?" McCord asked with half a smile.

"Sir, I am. Are you?"

McCord recalled the icy rain streaming down his windshield; he recalled his convulsive weeping. He said: "Yes, I am. And in ten minutes I'll know this guy's name and address and his record if he has one."

"But maybe he didn't do it," Samuelson said as if to remind McCord.

McCord replied: "And maybe he did."

CHAPTER 24

Street Man

Viewing the videotape McCord saw Prince Valiant as a bouncing young fop trotting down the stairs between the hand rails—glancing left and right, squinting against the low winter sun, descending with quick choppy steps that made his knees pop in his trousers while his hands glided above the rails.

The camera could not register the gaping fascination that McCord had seen as the man stared into the coffin with eyes starting out of his head, as if he saw her staring back—or—maybe it was McCord who was carried away by his own imaginings—and maybe the madness was in McCord, not the other, who could be innocent—a ridiculous little dandy but not a—and maybe the nausea that assailed McCord when he watched him looking at Marie's body was the product of McCord's own—wish! He wished, he fervently hoped this was Marie's torturer—"Because—" he whispered, but stopped before saying, "Kill him!"

He rolled the tape again and saw Prince Valiant pause as he reached the sidewalk, then go off quickly to his right. Next came the unstoppable Patrolman Dotson, only fifteen seconds after his prey—then Greta Gabriel, who strode off fast to the left, toward McCord's car—and regardless of what anybody else might see or miss, McCord had seen the bulge in Dotson's sport coat. Dotson too scanned the sidewalk in both directions, paused to let his prey gain a little, then set off in no great haste. After the gray sedan passed, here came McCord himself down the steps, looking perhaps a little worried, then Basil Samuelson descending carefully, as one does who fears falling, sliding his hands along the rail and choosing his steps judiciously.

Then McCord and Samuelson exchanged a few words and went off toward Samuelson's car.

After the viewing McCord felt a dangerous new heat rising in his soul. He stopped this with a deliberate echo of Sergeant Hughes: "I am a cop. Just a cop." To steady himself he picked up the phone and called the commanding officer of the East Side district where Prince Valiant had visited an apartment building. The lieutenant told him the place harbored two and maybe three drug dealers. In his mind McCord said, "Excellent," because now he could close his hand around Prince Valiant's wrist anytime he chose.

That closing hand meant imprisonment, and he said half aloud: "No, I am not turning my back on that woman's suffering." And "suffering" painted pictures from which he fled by rising from his desk and going to the duty sergeant's office (Hughes had gone home) and asking him to send an officer in street clothes to relieve Dotson; and he asked the sergeant to summon Dotson as soon as relieved.

McCord then climbed to the riot room where he changed from his suit into Levi's and a flannel shirt, and from his funeral shoes to clodhoppers. He hung the old Colt revolver under his left shoulder and returned to his office carrying his windbreaker.

Realizing he'd made a mistake he called Downtown and stopped the process of seeking a warrant on the car. Serving the warrant would alarm Prince Valiant and perhaps send him scurrying out of town. Far better to keep him under surveillance as long as it seemed worth the expenditure of manpower. Sooner or later he would be seen wearing a black leather coat— McCord pictured it as black—but the store clerk had told Sergeant Reitz that the coat also came in brown—with a zipper missing—or he would meet a man wearing such a coat—or such a man would enter the house or building where the Prince lived—or none of these would happen and McCord would be forced to end his surveillance and admit that his suspicions were unfounded.

No. Don't scare the Prince. Cancel the warrant and be patient—and prowl the streets—"since I don't have a home to go to."

Patrolman Dotson gave McCord the keys to his car and then read aloud from his notebook and McCord wrote down what he said. Prince Valiant's name was Vincent Willey. This name was not in the phone book nor was there a police record on it. He lived not in 2 Beat but nearby at 727 Majestic, not far from the "Irish Video," an old mansion recently restored by a rich lawyer, ornate and brilliantly lighted at night, but still surrounded by what the papers called urban blight. Should a comely young woman, in the bloom of her youth, health and beauty, emerge from one of those decaying habitations you would be entitled to wonder. But of course they did, both black and white.

Still copying Dotson's report, McCord wrote that the connection between Prince Valiant and the owner of his car had not been established. McCord said he'd speak to the Bureau about that, thanked Dotson, and, when alone, sat staring at his notes.

He glanced at his day book and saw that he had a law class scheduled at five. It was a relief to cross it out.

He left a message at the Bureau for Sergeant Reitz and then noticed that he was hungry. He drove to the Upper Crust, the cop hangout in 2 Beat. He ordered a ham sandwich and a glass of milk, and stepped to a nearby table to talk with two detectives. Two of his own uniformed cops came in and McCord greeted them too. Finally getting a chance to eat his lunch he found that he didn't want it. He ate half the sandwich, drank a glass of water and left for Majestic.

He cruised past Number 727. It was an old brick apartment building with three shops at street level, a DoNutHut, a dry cleaner and a game room. He was tempted by the game room, and he reasoned that he'd look different in his present attire from the suited, neck-tied gent who attended the memorial service—but he resisted the temptation. Nor did he turn the car for a second pass. He parked a good distance away and began to roam the streets. The image of the black leather coat went with him. Hope had greater power over his actions than the logic that said his chances were near zero.

While he roamed, his mind surveyed his situation with diligent care, guided by one sentence: "I am the man who stood by her body." He had gone to see her in response to her "message." He imagined the contrast had he never seen the ball and chain or deciphered its meaning or looked into her damaged face. Had he ignored the message he would have been some other, lesser man, taking notes on a law lecture.

When she swallowed the ball and chain she must have been hoping that such a man as he existed. If he were really the kind of man she believed in, he would act for justice. Since he could not torture and brutalize her killers without brutalizing himself, he would have to find a way to kill them.

He said in his mind: "I'll make the arrest." If they surrendered, he would miss his chance and leave it to the system with all its corruption. If they resisted, his chance would come. He intended to make an arrest that he hoped would set up a killing. He could see no difference between this hope and a simple intention to kill. If he intended to do it, and did it, it was murder. If so, he was a murderer.

He recoiled—halfway, or less—from this logic. He ran through the sequence again and it came out the same.

A cutting, cold wind lifted the leaves and trash in the gutters of Majestic—he realized with alarm that he had somehow circled back to Number 727. What was the point of assigning a man in street clothes to watch the building if he was going to parade back and forth and arouse suspicion? So he set out walking back to First. He did not feel the cold. The street lights came on and he checked his watch: Still too early to see Lindy. He kept walking. He was elsewhere, tracing his logic compulsively. If the man in the leather coat had come forward on the same sidewalk he would not have noticed.

At the curb on First, with the lights and noise streaming past him, he paused to look left at the dead electric sign over Shipman's Barbecue, closed four years ago when the owner was killed in a shootout. That man, father of a boy beaten to death by cops, had also been forced to kill.

To McCord's right the parapet of the bridge stood above the traffic, rising in gray concrete lit by amber lamps projecting from aluminum poles on both sides of the roadway. Twenty years ago McCord had drunk beer under that bridge with his friends from 3rd Relief. They would gather at midnight to drink and skip rocks on the metal surface of the river. Home for McCord at that time had been a "studio" apartment that had suddenly turned dingy and depressing the moment Nora agreed to marry him.

For a minute the twenty-year-old Nora O'Leary filled his mental theater with a lustrous, youthful presence. Then, reliving an even more remote time, he was walking with his father, a big man full of laughter and convoluted jokes, along the levee and his dad was saying, "That screw, Stevie? It's a test of strength. If you can turn it they'll ask you to play football for Ohio State."

His father lifted him, and McCord, aged five or six, grabbed the big iron wheel and strained to turn it. He remembered the thrill when his father lifted him to his shoulders; he remembered the rust on his hands after he tried to turn the unyielding wheel.

Finally it was full dark, and late enough. He walked rapidly to his car and drove to the Normandy Arms.

Lindy Alden was leading him into her kitchen and McCord was saying,

"No, I can't, it's very kind of you but I—"

"What a strange thing to say," she exclaimed and turned to face him. "It's 'kind of me' to offer you dinner?"

"I just mean that I see you as a good, giving woman. You're somebody I admire and I—"

"Steven," she said, thinking of a garden and a baby, "what's all this *good* business? How would you feel if I started telling you how good you are?"

"I'd say you were exaggerating."

"OK then. Please stay for dinner—if you can."

"I can't. I'm living alone now but I can't."

"Oh! I'm so sorry."

"Yeah. So am I. I never expected this to happen to me."

"And you never dreamed it would be so horrible."

"No I didn't."

"Did you tell her that we made love?"

"More or less."

"The poor woman. I know exactly how she feels."

"So somebody cheated on you?"

"Of course."

"Why 'of course'?"

"Men—you know."

"Yeah, I do."

"But if it's any—if it makes any difference," Lindy said, "I don't feel it was an accident."

"An accident that—" he began to ask.

"May I say it again?" Lindy asked, as if to say: "Please listen." She said: "I don't feel our making love was an accident."

He said smiling: "We were meant for each other?"

"I am beginning to hope so."

"So was I."

He could see that she understood the "was" in his answer, then doubted her understanding, and finally confirmed it. All this displayed itself on her face as it passed through her mind.

"Well then," she said, "of course, you don't want to stay for dinner."

"I only came because there's a chance I could be killed in the next few days, a very slight chance, but I wanted you to know that I feel this powerful—feeling for you, and admiration for your honesty. You are lovely to me, Lindy."

"I am not honest and neither are you."

"That's true, I guess, but I meant I would have grown to love you, I could see it coming, but I can't. If there was even a near-zero chance of my dying I had to tell you. Maybe this is a little confusing."

"No," she said with the lopsided smile he loved, "I understand perfectly, you might have loved me but you don't, and now you tell me you might die."

"Yes, that's about it."

She probed him on "the next few days" and his danger, and begged him to be careful and safe, and he agreed that safety is a very good thing. He assured her that he'd die of old age in a nursing home.

When she had run out of exhortations to caution, Steven said:

"Besides, you don't want to get mixed up with a murderer."

Calmly, but with grave interest, she asked for an explanation of that. He told her his "logic" on killing with intent and she said:

"Is that really murder?"

"Almost," he said. "Yes, I'd call it murder."

"Then let somebody else do it."

"No," he said moving his head slowly from side to side and watching her closely, "I'm the guy."

"But not my guy. You're saying it's over. So if I begged you to back off, and you loved me, maybe you would. Since you don't, you won't."

"I won't."

"Have you told your wife?"

"About the murder idea? No."

"Tell her. See if she begs you to stop."

"She might," he said uncertainly, "but I doubt it. Anyway I won't back off, not for her, not for you."

"And you 'can't' love me. You say that as if you're unable to."

"I'm not free to. I'd better not see you again."

"Because you might fall in love with me."

"Right."

"But you still love her."

"I never stopped loving her," he said.

"Even while we were making love?" She spoke without anger, as if knowing the answer.

"Yes. I wanted you and had a powerful feeling for you and I still do, but so long as I love her I can't say I love you. I'm sorry. I've been in the wrong toward you."

"And her."

"I like your direct way of speaking."

"And now you're going to walk into a—what may turn out to be a shooting match with one or maybe two killers, who have killed before, is that what you're telling me?"

"It could happen, probably not, but maybe."

"So if they kill you I'll have the consolation of knowing that you might have loved me if you hadn't married your wife."

"Lindy," he said slowly, "I'm terribly sorry."

She said, "Goodbye. Don't be careless."

She walked him to the door thinking: "A garden, a baby—or Steven."

She saw her hand closing around the doorknob. "This is hard, isn't it, Steven?" she said. "And don't we deserve it."

Standing alone in the hallway where he had pressed her against the wall, and she had said No, she thought:

"If I had said No the second time I'd never have known him. God, if I cry every night of my life, I'd never give it up. Yes, he's gone, and I'll never see him again. OK, I understand, that's the price."

"Well, yes," she said a minute later, as if to crystallize it, "she's got him and he still loves her and does not love me, so I— Yes, I'd do it again."

Back at the station McCord parked in the back lot, took a metal box from the trunk of his car and carried it down through the assembly room and into the men's locker room. He went to the cleaning locker and got a big rag which he spread out on a bench. Unlocking the box he opened it and took out a gun rug, which he unzipped and laid open. In the fold of the rug was a 9mm Ruger P85 semiautomatic pistol. Taking the old Colt revolver from its holster he placed it beside the Ruger.

The comparison was striking. The Colt: six shots, muzzle velocity 945 feet per second, and manual cocking. The Ruger: sixteen shots (fifteen in the magazine and one in the chamber), muzzle velocity 1225 feet per second, and automatic cocking except on the first round.

He cleaned the old revolver—the Department's authorized duty weapon—and hung it again in his shoulder rig. Picking up the semiautomatic pistol he ejected the magazine then jerked the slide back and sent the chambered round flying to the right, where it hit a metal locker door with a clang and rolled on the floor. This round, like the fifteen in the magazine, was a semijacketed hollow point, for adequate penetration and good deformation. He retrieved it and put it on the rag beside the magazine.

Setting the slide in the back position he searched in the breach for the steel flange that would release the recoil spring without making hamburger of the finger with which he was probing the dark interior of the frame. He probed and pressed and couldn't find it.

He carried the gun to a light and tilted it, and saw his mistake, and pressed the flange, and eased the slide forward and away from the barrel. Back at the bench he sat down and spread the components on the rag—the black frame, stainless barrel, slide, recoil spring and spring rod. He cleaned the bore with powder solvent, which gave off its peculiar banana smell that seemed so incongruous. After he had finished the bore he took a toothbrush to the grooves, then began reassembling the weapon. He had neither fired nor cleaned it for two or three years.

He took it to a shadowed corner of the locker room and aimed it at the wall, to see how quickly he could find the white locator dots, two in the rear and one in front in the middle.

Having spent a few minutes at this exercise he went back into the light, yanked the slide back, set it, dropped the free round in the chamber and released the slide. It jumped like an eager cat and seemed to try to get free of his grip. He rammed the magazine into the butt and checked to be certain the Safe/Fire lever was set to Safe.

He stowed the cleaning gear and replaced the semiautomatic Ruger in its box, and returned the box to the trunk of the gray sedan. Then he climbed to the riot room.

CHAPTER 25

Storm

McCord hung up the phone and said to Gil Hughes: "Gotta roll."

Hughes looked a little bug-eyed and started to rise from the dinner table.

Janey Hughes looked at McCord in consternation and said: "You aren't leaving, are you?" She had just spread before them a dinner of pot roast, mashed potatoes and gravy and green beans, and a full glass of beer by each man's plate.

"Sorry, Janey," McCord said, "business."

"Is that what I think it is?" Hughes asked.

"The man in the leather coat," McCord said. "He's at Granny's, with a partner."

Hughes started barking at McCord as though their ranks were reversed. "You're doing the perimeter; I'm going in there—the house."

McCord laughed and contradicted him: "You're bossing the perimeter. I'm going in there."

"Bullshit!" cried Sergeant Hughes as his features took on a red rage. "You're so full of god damned gooseberries, you fuckin rookie—Sorry, Janey, this god damned—"

"Put on your coat and shut up," McCord said and added to Janey, "I'll keep him on the perimeter, don't worry about that."

Hughes protested: "If you go in, I go in."

"Hell you do," McCord shot back. "You're boss of the perimeter."

Hughes fumed in silence but clipped his radio to his belt, and Janey held the speaker unit and its wire up against his body. As he shrugged his jacket on she attached the speaker to the epaulette. Talking over Janey's shoulder to McCord he said:

"Morgan'll be there and he can take the perimeter. I'm going inside to keep you from making a dumb mistake."

"No," said McCord, "that's final," while Janey Hughes held his speaker and cord aloft. He put on his jacket, but since it was not a police garment it had no epaulette. Janey attached the speaker to the collar on the left side.

McCord said, "Tim'll be inside with me."

Janey smiled up at McCord to signal her approval of this plan. She turned again to her husband, zipped his jacket nearly to his chin, and kissed him on the mouth.

Hughes said, "Thanks, Doll."

Janey turned and stood on tiptoe and grabbed McCord by the ears and gave a vigorous twist.

"Yikes!" he cried.

She pulled him down and kissed his forehead and blessed him with her mild eyes.

Looking into Gil Hughes's pale blue eyes McCord said: "Ready, Boss?"

Hughes said "Ready, you damn rookie" and spanked Janey on the rear and led the way to the front of the house. The two men went into the freezing night and crossed the yard to McCord's car.

Janey extinguished the light in the living room and peered out the window. She saw her husband's arm reach out of the car and clap a black object on the roof. The object began flashing red; the headlights came on and the car pulled away.

Janey Hughes sank to her knees, closed her eyes and pressed her intertwined knuckles against her lips. As she had done a thousand times on nights such as this she prayed to her Savior, first renouncing any rights or claims, asking to be taught submission to His Father's will. Thinking of what Marie Carden had endured, a hell she could not possibly have deserved and one that no human being, except the hideously twisted, could have dreamed up, Janey confessed to harboring critical, rebellious thoughts. She had never found out how to suppress these thoughts. They halted her prayers. Kneeling on the carpet, silent and motionless as the furniture, she admitted, again, that "God's will" must mean something she was incapable of understanding or approving. Were a mortal man to stand passively by and watch Marie's ordeal—as God had certainly watched it, if He were the omnipotent God she believed Him to be—she would condemn him as worse than the devils

doing the raping and beating. Here was a test of her faith, and her faith recoiled from it.

At times of severe stress she admitted that her faith in the Son was all that
saved her from the grave sin of denouncing the Father. If hell existed then
surely one of its torture chambers was reserved for heretics like herself whose
love of the Son counterbalanced her distrust and even animosity toward the
Father. She believed in Him, it wasn't a question of belief or disbelief. But
when she contemplated the suffering of a woman raped and murdered and
even tortured she could not believe in His goodness; He receded from her
into a smoky darkness.

Tonight she prayed to the Son for Gil and Steven: "Keep them safe
tonight. And don't let them do what they'll regret, what will poison their life,
kill without need, kill or beat in rage and hate. Please, Jesus, guide them."

Her knees cracked audibly as she rose, helping herself up by pulling on the
arm of the couch. Returning to the kitchen she blinked at the light, put on
her glasses and went to the radio that her husband kept by the phone. She
turned it on and listened to the dispatcher sending a crew to a property-
damage-only collision in the Central Business District. Then the radio emitted a screeching tone that lasted three seconds, then: "Bullseye Six Four. I say
again, Bullseye Six Four."

She did not know where 64 was but it must be in the 6th District. She had
heard Steven's end of two phone conversations five minutes ago. The first one
began when his beeper sounded. He had left the table and walked to the
phone and dialed. She heard him say:

"Granny, Your Loveliness.—Exactly as the picture showed?—With a—
Good, good.—Alone?—OK, describe them.—Leave the house.—Well,
you've got a coat!—All right but stay in the kitchen. I'll be there in ten minutes."

Then Steven had dialed again and she heard him say: "This is McCord.
Broadcast Bullseye Six Four in five minutes. Six Four."

In Janey's imagination cruisers from all over the 6th District began con-
verging on a point called 64. She did not need to know what "Leather coat"
meant to understand that somebody had walked into a trap and that Steven
was closing it.

"Pull the perimeter in as tight as you can," McCord shouted over the siren.

"Yeah, yeah," said Hughes. "Slow this buggy down."

"The more people you get, the tighter," McCord said. "If these guys run—"

"I know, for Christ sake."

"But don't place anybody where he can be seen from a window."

"OK. Not so fuckin fast." And he added, bemused: "So Granny's got a bullseye in her pants and her whole fuckin house is a bullseye. Ha!"

McCord roared out a loud laugh and punched Hughes in the thigh.

They streaked down a commercial street and the flashing red was reflected back at them from plate glass on both sides. McCord sent the car sailing over the old arched bridge that crossed the little river at Highplain, then began threading the kinked residential streets that had been laid down before electricity and cars were invented. The gray sedan with its throb of red and its glaring headlights probed its way westward across the district toward 2 Beat and Granny's.

Hughes said: "Slow down, you lunatic. Granny'll be OK till we get there."

McCord's eyes were on his driving and he didn't answer. A car pulled out of a driveway ahead and he skidded to a halt, so they sat there for ten seconds and Hughes argued: "Calm, Stevie, cool. Granny's OK and the old man and his daughter are already dead. It's done, Stevie, it already happened."

"I think I know that," McCord said and flashed his high beams and punched the siren. The gray sedan swerved around the other car and proceeded on.

Leaning toward Steven, watching the streets, Hughes said: "You say you're living by *the real law*, as you modestly call it. Does that mean what I think it means?"

"What do you think it means?"

"Don't be cute. Tell the truth. Do you intend to kill this guy?"

"Depends," said McCord.

"You think because he deserves to die that you—"

"Yeah, he does, him and his little partner. Granny said Leather Coat is with a sidekick she calls Little Lord Fauntleroy. They're upstairs with two girls."

"How do you know this Fauntl-whatever is the same guy as—"

"I'll confirm it, you moron. That's one reason I'm going in."

"You confirm it, then what?"

"Then we see what happens."

"OK, Stevie, suppose they're all four sitting on the couch in the parlor, each bug with a whore under his arm, and you say, 'Ladies, outa the way,' and you blow their brains out."

"Excellent. Perfect."

"Sure, perfect. How are you going to feel after that? I mean—"

"Pretty good, I expect."

"—I mean how's it feel to be planning a double murder?"

"I'll tell you if I ever do it. Just don't give me a sermon on the theme that these guys are human beings."

"I wouldn't go that far but I'll say this, they're suspects, Stevie, is all they are. We put the collar on, and that's all. Hear me?"

"Yeah."

"The elements of the offense of murder—one of the elements is intent to kill."

"Is that a fact?" McCord said.

"All I want you to do is put a clean collar on these insects, OK? Let that be your intention, because it's all in your mind, the intent. Will you promise me that?"

"Sure, old man."

"Cause if you step in the shit tonight you're going to need a friend, and I don't mean me, although I am your friend."

"I know who you mean, but she threw my ass out."

"Look, Stevie, don't make it harder on her by committing double murder. Imagine how she'd feel if her bonnie lad turned out to be a cold-blooded killer."

"My blood's not cold," said McCord coldly.

But Hughes thought he had found his opening. He pursued it: "No, I wouldn't say they were human, but I know one guy who'll be splattering shaving cream and spit all over the mirror in the morning saying they are, or were."

"Don't count on it," McCord parried, but Hughes heard a fault in his voice, or thought he did.

Hughes said: "Even if you do this by the book, Stevie, if these pukes bleed you'll want that friend. Believe me, I been there."

"You mean kill? You mean it's so awful?"

"That's what I mean."

"Did anybody ever deserve it more than these pukes?"

"Stevie, don't be stupid."

They reached the big river, turned left and followed a boulevard that passed within two blocks of Granny's house. Granny's was on Bluff Avenue. Slowly now and soundlessly they moved under one street light after another—till they came to the corner of Bluff Avenue. Here McCord turned away from the levee and halted behind a parked police cruiser with four cops inside.

Hughes said: "It's all in your state of mind. You don't murder if you don't intend to."

"One other thing too," McCord said.

"What?"

"Come out alive. I'm not going to take the first bullet."

"Don't. You don't have to."

McCord vowed: "I'm walking out of that house ten minutes from now with six holes in me."

"Counting your nose as two," Hughes surmised.

"Exactly."

"You don't have a hole in the end of your bozo?"

"That makes seven," McCord said.

"OK I won't lecture you in front of the people, but sit one minute and think. Why not find their car, disable it, throw a cordon and wait for the bugs to crawl out."

"I told you I need to confirm identity."

"We do it outside. Why not?"

"If they see us disable their car—"

"We cruise around till we find it. If it's visible from the house we don't mess with it, we throw the cordon and wait."

"We've got too many fat sergeants and girl cops," McCord argued.

"What the fuck you mean?"

"Dark. Run. Dodge. Hide. Gone."

"That's a possibility. It's still better if we—"

"My way's better," McCord said climbing out. "Seven holes," and he went back and opened the trunk.

Hughes followed and demanded: "What now?"

"Nothin," McCord lied, opening the metal box. The trunk light shone dimly down on the gun rug and both men heard the rip noise when McCord unzipped it. He opened the rug and took out the 9mm semiautomatic.

"Holy shit," Hughes breathed.

McCord rammed the pistol into his belt and started off.

Hughes grabbed him with considerable force and whispered—so as not to be heard by the four officers who had gotten out of the car parked just ahead: "If you need that thing you need more manpower in the house."

McCord pulled away and said, "Good evening, officers," and continued on his way.

The four cops, three men and Greta Gabriel, were bent against the cold, adjusting belts and hats, not talking, looking pretty dark with just a few glints off their badges and, in one case, their glasses. Greta Gabriel had obviously come from home; she wore a civilian jacket with her badge pinned on, and no hat.

Hughes said: "We're throwin a perimeter. You people are part of it."

McCord was walking fast along Bluff Avenue, with Granny's four or five houses ahead. Before reaching it he turned right into an alley.

Here the only lights were the ones hung over garages by the homeowners; no city lights, and few of the garage lights. He walked past trash cans, open garages, closed and locked garages with double doors and padlocks chained shut, piles of junk, a mattress leaning against a garage—thinking: "At least it doesn't stink in this weather"—walking—till he saw a dark figure approaching. He kept on, and so did the other, and they met where the alley was joined from the left at a ninety-degree angle by another, shorter alley that led back to Bluff Avenue. They were now behind Granny's.

"Hi Lieutenant," said Tim Sloan.

"Hey Tim. Take a look at that door."

Tim glanced to his right at an elevated porch and dark door.

"I'm going in the front, and I'll let you in that door," said McCord.

"OK."

"You'll be at the back end of a hall that runs from the front to the back of the house."

"I know the layout," said Tim.

"You're a steady customer no doubt."

"No sir. Went there once strictly on duty. Nice place, ugly girls."

"Yeah, they're a pathetic lot. OK. Shut off your radio but keep it in place," said McCord as he shut his own off and removed the speaker unit. He put this in his pocket.

Tim was wearing a black watch cap and police jacket over a black jump suit. He clicked his radio off. The jacket had side vents, and out of the right vent a revolver butt projected and caught a gleam of light.

McCord asked if he had a backup gun.

Tim said, "I won't need one." He showed McCord his revolver, a .44 Smith & Wesson magnum, heavy black frame and long barrel. "*Res ipsa loquitur*," he said.

Thus both men carried weapons that would have been against regulations during duty hours but were OK off duty. Neither trusted the approved .38 to stop a desperate man.

McCord said: "So you know the parlor is to the left of the front door. I'll come in to the entranceway and the parlor's on my left."

"Yes, and the stairway's straight ahead, facing the door as you come in, the dining room is on the right, the kitchen down the hall."

"I'll go to the kitchen," McCord continued, "and I'll make sure Granny stays there. Then I'll let you in. When I give the word, go through the swinging door from the kitchen into the dining room. If they're already in the parlor I'll stand in the hall for a second where you can see me. You'll have a clear view of the entranceway, the bottom of the stairs, and the parlor. I'll move into the entranceway and you'll hear me talk, if they're downstairs. I hope they're still upstairs."

"OK, I go to the dining room and do what?"

"Back me up. Keep me in view. I'm not busting in the house with ten cops because these bugs might go nuts and grab a girl. For the same reason I won't draw if I don't have to. I want Granny talking in the kitchen and making everything sound normal from upstairs—they were upstairs ten minutes ago—while you and I get into position. Use your judgment. If you think we need more men, close the circle. If you think I'm having trouble, do what's best. If the doorbell rings let Granny answer it and turn people away."

"When do we go?"

"Five minutes. Give the bullseye a little more time."

Tim thrust out his hand and consulted his watch. In the darkness McCord could see its green hands and numerals glowing.

McCord said: "There are two of them, plus two girls and nobody else in the house but Granny. Granny says Leather Coat is big, over six-two and two hundred pounds. His partner who thinks he's the brains of the outfit is smaller, maybe five-ten and a hundred and sixty. I saw him—I think I saw him at the memorial service. Granny says they're brothers." Conscious of the passing minutes, McCord described Prince Valiant.

Then he said: "I'd send the whole relief in but that could turn to chaos. I'd rather have one accurate shooter with me than twenty of anybody else. There'll be two girls in there, Tim, plus Granny."

"Send Granny out."

"No. I think I can use her to separate the girls from the two men. She can call from the kitchen, call for a girl. I want to get the girls clear of the bugs."

He reached out and rested a hand on Tim's shoulder, and turned to his left. Tim went silently to his own right, up the wooden steps to the little porch which stood about five feet above the alley. As he went toward Bluff Avenue McCord noted that the windows were lit up throughout the first floor. He caught a glimpse of Granny pacing the kitchen, with suspense and trouble in her eyes. He tapped on the window glass and she jumped like a puppet, came close and peered out with big frightened eyes.

Arriving at the front corner of the house McCord took one step out on Bluff Avenue and looked for Prince Valiant's Dodge—and found it. He retreated two steps into the alley and shifted the Safe/Fire lever on the Ruger from the white position to red. He was elated, dizzy with seeing the car and knowing what it meant. He reached a hand to his back and felt the handcuffs looped over his belt; he felt in his right pocket for his sap, and in his left jacket pocket for the leather folder and badge. It was the gold shield of a lieutenant, pinned on his chest by Nora at his promotion ceremony. He started for the porch. An unmarked car was pulling to the curb half a block away, dousing its lights. As McCord entered the zone of light from the porch a thrill of contest fear shot through his trunk from anus to throat. He mounted the porch steps and stood at the door.

Detained by an idea, a kind of riddle, he paused, realizing that Hughes had never before spoken of killing a man. When McCord joined the force it was an incident still fresh in the lore; but as a rookie McCord had believed he could not ask about it. Throughout his first year he waited for Hughes to bring it up but he never did. Men would sometimes say "He never talks about it," but McCord didn't get the meaning of that till now.

The door swung silently. Stooping in her gray shawl, with her head cocked back and her thin, yellowish-white hair lifting in the breeze, Granny looked a hundred years old. She reached out a multicolored, bony hand and took McCord's hand and pulled. He entered and closed the door with a single click. McCord and Granny were in the entranceway, just inside the front door, with the stairway before them.

"They're upstairs," Granny whispered, bending so close he couldn't see her face. She took his other hand and squeezed and asked: "Are you all alone?"

"No," said McCord. "Is the house still clear?"

"Just those two and the two girls," said Granny.

Placing his arm around her he moved her to the kitchen, bade her sit down, then returned to the hall, which was lit by one bare bulb, and opened the back door. Tim and McCord went to the kitchen.

The three bent close to one another and McCord whispered:

"Granny, I want you to talk as if you were on the phone. Keep talking. Talk for five minutes, talk for an hour. Just talk."

She gave a brisk little nod—and shook her finger at Tim and said: "I know you. You're Tom the Terrible."

"Tim," he said. "Yes, you know me."

She shifted in her seat and pulled her shawl at both edges and said to McCord: "He's a good boy."

"He sure is. Now if you hear anybody come down the stairs—if you hear one of the girls, sing out, call a girl by name and ask her to come to the kitchen."

"They won't like that. They'll think I want my fiver."

"Do they owe you a fiver?"

"Sure. Each girl will owe me the minute they come down. If they go back up, they owe me again."

"Call them to come here. That's important. I want to separate the girls from the two men even if it's only for a half a minute."

McCord pondered his next statement and the others watched him closely.

Addressing Tim he whispered: "If one of the men—if any man moves from the parlor or the bottom of the stairs—I mean if anybody goes toward the hall, any man, and looks like they're heading for the kitchen, stop him. You'll be the one to stand between them and Granny."

"My savior," said Granny.

Tim patted her on the head.

"If the bugs come down," McCord resumed, "we make the grab down here. If not, we go up, but first we call Hughes to send a man for Granny. If we have to go upstairs—" He stopped and asked Granny: "Do the stairs squeak?"

"Oh my lands, do they."

"OK, if we have to go upstairs we'll call for two more men. I'd rather do it down here because there's only one approach, via the stairs. If we go upstairs we'll be looking at a bunch of doors."

"Five counting the bathroom," said Granny. "Six with the closet."

"Too many doors," said McCord, resting his gaze on the thoughtful, somber eyes of Tim Sloan. And to Granny: "How long have they been up there?"

"Fifteen, twenty minutes."

"OK. We wait on this floor for a while. We shut off the lights in the hall and the dining room. All other lights stay on."

Granny nodded gravely and said, "You are good boys."

McCord bent and kissed her forehead. It was smooth as glass and just as cool.

They heard footsteps and a creaking of old boards from the room above. Said Granny: "That'll be Dorie's room."

"Go to the dining room," said McCord to Tim. "Darken it." To Granny he said: "Start talking."

"Lands!" she said in full voice. "Dad had them pigs and I saw the old sow lying like she was dying, heaving, while them twelve piglets sucked on her, and I thought, 'If I stay in Zanesville that's me, only less tits to go around, and maybe some pig for a husband.' "

Her old teeth made an appearance, hanging like stalactites from receding gums.

Tim passed through the swinging door to the dining room and turned off the light. He looked toward the parlor, which he could see was still empty, and saw the hall light go out. The entranceway at the bottom of the stairs and the parlor itself were still lighted.

Starting toward the front of the house McCord heard a girl talking, and steps descending on the creaking, crackling boards. The girl laughed and a man's voice said, "Later!" McCord heard the crinkling of a paper sack. He went to the front of the hall and looked left into the dining room but it was too dark for him to see Tim. He waited till he sensed the man and girl were near the bottom of the stairs, then he turned right, and saw them going into the parlor. The man was broad across the back; he wore a calf-length black leather coat with a loose belt. The girl was hanging on his arm.

The man put the paper sack, probably with a bottle inside, on a low table and turned. McCord saw his face, his gray skin and features too big for his head, a flat nose, a mouth open to expose his bottom teeth, which were small and separated one from another. His eyes looked out from under a shelf of bone bristling with black hairs. His coat had two breast pockets and only one had a pull-chain on the zipper.

McCord moved closer, keenly aware that when he stood at the foot of the stairs he could be seen from above, but could not see up there without taking his eyes off the man in the leather coat. He glanced quickly up the stairs then took one more step.

Granny's gabbing came steadily from the kitchen. McCord said in a loud voice:

"Hey, Buster." He reached into his jacket pocket, produced the leather folder and flipped it to display his badge. He started to speak but cut himself off to allow Granny's voice to be heard as she called:

"Dorie Honey, com'ere a sec."

The girl and the big man stared at the badge for half a second and there was terror in the girl's eyes but none in the man's.

McCord said, "Go to the kitchen," but the girl was frozen. McCord at this moment was aware that if she moved she would cross his line of fire. He said to her: "You're not in trouble. Just go."

The girl swayed, it seemed, as if in a strong wind, and clutched the arm of the man in the leather coat.

To him McCord said: "You are under arrest for murder."

Looking at McCord with perfect calm he slowly extended his left arm till it encircled the girl's shoulders, and pulled her roughly to his side. McCord reached for his gun. Using that same moment the man in the leather coat dropped his right hand, and when it came up it carried a semiautomatic .45 pistol.

He rammed the muzzle into the girl's cheek with such force that McCord could see her jaw open and the gun separate her lower from her upper teeth. She cried in pain. Her head tilted and her eyes sought McCord with terror and supplication.

Granny called out: "Dorie Honey, come on."

A door closed upstairs and voices sounded in the upper hall, a man's and a woman's. The woman let out a cackling laugh. The man called, "Hey Jerry, wait up!" The stairs had not yet started to squeak.

"Don't come down!" the man in the leather coat shouted.

McCord moved one step to the right, putting his shoulder against the frame of the stairway entrance. He did not have time to hope or to worry. A sound like no other filled the house as a blow from the stick fills a kettledrum. An energy wave flashed by McCord, and the head of the man in the leather coat exploded. The girl screamed as blood and brains spattered against her cheek, and the man in the leather coat pitched off his feet backward.

McCord pivoted right and faced Prince Valiant, who stood at the top of the stairs holding a girl by the hand, gaping. Recognizing McCord, perhaps, he screamed, "Jerry! Jerry!" Trying to be heard over the girl's hysterical cries he screamed again: "Jerry!"

"Let her go," McCord shouted.

Prince Valiant jerked the girl's arm and sent her tumbling down the staircase. McCord saw she was going to hit him and at the same moment he saw what he had never seen before, the insolent yellow flash of a gun firing on him.

The girl's coiled body struck and spun him and the snap of a passing bullet shocked his ears. He tried to regain his footing but stepped on the girl's arm, which turned his ankle. The girl screamed and McCord lurched against the banister. But he still had the same intention. He lifted the big Ruger and fired, but this first shot was double-action, a single pull of the trigger both cocking the hammer and releasing it to fly forward. He knew this shot would go wild, but it was instantaneous and its purpose was to rattle Prince Valiant. It worked. The little torturer lost all control and jerked his trigger four times more and they all went wild. Prince Valiant seemed to believe that a close shot was a sure shot—but it is not always so, and jerking the trigger will seldom do the job.

McCord learned the lesson of Prince Valiant's panic. He went to a calm zone in his mind. The ringing and buzzing did not distract him. He knew what to do. He had to aim, to align his sights even at this close range and to form at least a rough sight picture. The picture would consist of his placing the white dot on the front sight post in the center and level with the dots on either side of the rear sight notch—making a level row of three evenly spaced white dots. He would then bring the center dot under the target, all in half a second.

The whiplash of Prince Valiant's shots snapped in McCord's eyes. One shot burned his right ear, but he did not forget his intention. He cranked off another scare shot to give himself a fraction of a second in which to aim. One aimed shot is better than a whole magazine fired in jerks. He would stand and fire.

First he saw the face of the man who had stared with sick eyes into Marie's coffin—except the eyes now were those of a man standing in a bonfire. Then McCord saw the white dot. Then, as he brought the dots into sharp focus the face went blurry, as it should. Then he dropped the dot a foot and moved it three inches right. The picture was complicated but not distorted by the target's forward lean. McCord had a good sight picture with the dots in focus and the face blurry. He began his trigger squeeze, not knowing and not trying to predict when the hammer would strike the firing pin, trying only to preserve the sight picture in its present form.

Before McCord knew it the Ruger roared with a horrific sharp metallic cry within the roar. The blast and recoil lifted the gun, obscuring the body and face, and when the gun dropped back down and McCord searched for the target all he could find was Prince Valiant's feet, the soles of his quivering shoes.

Untangling himself from the girl's limbs McCord went up the stairs, pausing to see if the feet were motionless. He stood two steps from the top in the smell of burnt powder—a semisweet smoky odor, a compound of organic and inorganic chemistry. He looked at the body and felt a nauseating identification with the man who had inhabited it, for he too had looked down on a body from which he had driven all life.

Prince Valiant's face was already pale, if not white, and seemingly innocent. The fancy hair was still fancy. A small wound, a skid mark without color, marked the bullet's entrance. McCord mounted the last two steps, squatted, with his gun pointed at the face, and rolled the body.

The exit wound, terminus of a cone-shaped blast of energy, all of it caused by a semijacketed hollow point 115-grain inert missile shaped like a volcano—this exit area was crammed with shreds of fabric permeated with blood, tissue and minute chips of bone. McCord did not bother to check for a pulse; he didn't care to touch the man's skin.

He descended into the mad screaming of the girl in the parlor and the soft, patient moaning of the one on the stairs. Granny rushed past, toward the parlor. When McCord reached the bottom, having stepped over the moaning girl, he joined Granny at the screamer's side. The girl was rapidly losing her voice, so her screams were hoarse and even more mad than before, a reptilian croaking. A purple bruise showed where the muzzle of the .45 had been jammed between her upper and lower teeth.

"I'll be back," Granny said.

McCord knew where she was going. The girl had tried to rub it off but it still covered the side of her face and was scattered through her hair. She looked at McCord and whispered, "Get it out of my ear" and then went silent for a moment, but only a moment.

He tried to take her hand but she flailed at him and howled.

Granny knelt beside her and wiped her face and hair with a wet towel. A moment later McCord noticed Tim standing by with two more towels. As . Granny soiled each one she threw it aside and took another from Tim.

Still kneeling, McCord turned to see two uniformed officers taking in the scene with quick, darting looks. The front door lay behind them, shattered in its frame. One cop shouted a question to McCord which he didn't hear, and he called back,

"All secure. Call an ambulance."

McCord got to his feet, glanced at the man in the leather coat, and went to the girl on the stairs, moving from one set of cries and croaks to a different, milder one. Bending to this second girl McCord saw a big drop of blood appear on her forehead, then another. He understood that this was his own blood, and touched his ear to confirm it. He wiped his hand on his trousers and bent closer to the girl, who was calming down.

"Tell me if you are all right," he said softly, as if a secret were to pass between them.

In her turn she also whispered: "Yes."

"Are you hurt?"

"Yes."

"Tell me where."

"My shoulder, my arm, my elbow."

He examined the arm, without touching it, but his concentration failed; he was not thinking of this girl but of his daughter.

The girl said, catching her breath between sobs, "Did you kill him?"

"Yes."

"Why? He was such a sweet guy."

McCord said, "He wasn't so sweet."

He mounted the stairs again, took out his handkerchief and spread it over the tips of his fingers, and pressed into the carotid artery. Some warmth reached his fingers through the cloth but no signal of a beating heart. When he removed his fingertips the neck gurgled and refilled the depression his fingers had made. He dropped the handkerchief and stood up, and looked at the face, which did look sweet. But the eyes were expressionless. Still they had one power; they could create an emotion in McCord that was neither regret nor satisfaction, but something heavy and silent. He stared at those eyes for several heartbeats; he could measure time by the throbs in his chest and ears. He realized he was still holding the Ruger. He flipped the Safe/Fire lever from red to white and put the gun in his belt.

When he went down again he found the girl leaning against the wall holding one arm in the other and watching him, following him till he stood over her, and her eyes were lifted to him with awe and fear.

McCord went to the kitchen and called the field lieutenant at Headquarters and reported the shootings. He called Sergeant Reitz at his home and set in motion the processes that would lead to the seizure of Prince Valiant's car and a comparison of its tire treads with the impressions taken in the snow behind 128 Laurel Street; to a fingerprint comparison, and to a search of the dead men's clothes and of the apartment on Majestic. When he returned to the parlor the medics were treating the girls and an evidence crew had begun its work on the scene.

The man in the leather coat lay with arms and legs spread, and his shirt exposed. His bowel and bladder had let go, and the room was the worse for it.

McCord turned at a tap on his shoulder.

"So, Stevie, are you OK?" Sergeant Hughes asked.

"And Tim, yeah, we're both OK," McCord replied. "But I'm going to be here a while. Why don't you catch a ride with somebody from Third Relief?"

"We'll wait up for you, Janey and me, no matter how late," Hughes promised. "Come."

"OK," McCord said, and he tried to read Hughes's expression. Did Gil Hughes think he was looking at a murderer? Would he tell Janey and would Janey tell Nora?

"We'll tell Nora you're OK," said Hughes reaching out with his fist and giving McCord a light punch on the chest. He said: "I'll call Public Works and see if they'll send a carpenter to board up the front so Granny's pipes don't freeze."

"I hadn't thought of that," said McCord. "I can feel the cold in this place."

Hughes was watching him attentively. Hughes said, "Yeah. So come see us when you're free."

McCord said, "Don't worry." He was aware that he was talking, and that it was all pretty ordinary.

McCord and Tim Sloan stood together a moment later, watching the medics, then McCord said:

"We are going to be interviewed and asked whether we have discussed this thing, and we want to be able to say no, so let's not discuss it."

"Yes sir," Tim assented.

"But thanks, Tim. Thanks."

A lieutenant from Homicide questioned McCord for an hour. A sergeant and a videographer showed up and they went through the whole process again, with McCord re-enacting while the videographer hopped around filming everything from two or three angles. He filmed the bodies, the hall, the dining room, and Granny. She said that at last she was in the movies. A separate team interviewed Tim after the first told McCord it was time for a trip to the hospital. An Internal Affairs lieutenant who had been hanging around listening invited McCord to meet him Downtown at eight-thirty in the morning. He didn't come along on the hospital trip.

In the Emergency Ward a nurse stripped away the dressing that a medic had placed on McCord's ear and applied a new one. Next a lab technician tested McCord's blood for alcohol. Then the Homicide team drove McCord Downtown where he helped reduce his statement to writing, and signed it. He got back to his car, still parked near Granny's, at one in the morning, and drove to the Hughes manse.

Janey Hughes was knitting a red scarf for her little grandson, but her mind ran free over her whole universe. If her needles clicked she didn't hear it. All she heard—at intervals—was the dispatcher sending police crews here and there all over the city. If he called out an address that she knew was in the 6th District the action of her hands would cease, she would focus sharply on a point in thin air and then, having satisfied herself that this broadcast was unrelated to the bullseye, she would pull a new length of yarn from the basket at her feet and go on knitting. For a full half-hour, maybe more, after Gil and Steven left the house to catch "Leather Coat" she heard nothing of any interest.

The first real thing that happened was that the dispatcher sent two ambulances to an address on Bluff Avenue. She could picture the street, running from the levee boulevard toward the slums—not the worst street in town but a place that had been pretty rough even when she was a child.

"Two," she said meditatively, aloud. "Two."

There had been no preceding broadcast about an accident on Bluff Avenue. So the ambulances were being sent for—probably, considering the neighborhood—a shooting.

She put on a pot of water to boil, and turned the radio up so she could hear it over the whistling to come. She got a tea bag and put it in her grandmother's World's Fair cup and resumed her knitting.

There was no anxiety in her fingers—they were nimble as ever—but her mind must have known something was coming, because she saw a vision of herself on her knees. The whistling of the kettle interrupted her thoughts. She poured her tea and put it on the kitchen table where she could reach it.

Now the radio blasted her with an irrelevant broadcast and she turned angrily and reduced the volume again. Her face and scalp prickled with the shock. And her fears took over her mind. She thought: "One for Gil and one for Steven." Then the dispatcher told somebody that a coroner's wagon was on the way, and Janey knew for sure where it was bound.

Steven had ordered Gil to the perimeter but it would be just like him to disobey if he heard shooting and go charging in like an old war horse. She started knitting faster and made a mistake. She undid it and blew a long breath out between compressed lips. Then she heard Gil's voice and she dropped her work and turned the volume up. It was Gil all right, ordering somebody to secure a car at the same address on Bluff Avenue. "Secure," whatever that meant. She didn't care. It was Gil's voice!

She dropped to her knees and felt a release of joyous gratitude that had been confined within her for the whole day, for a week, a year, for her whole life. Gil had a bad heart and high blood pressure but he was safe tonight! She let her happiness issue forth "like a mighty stream" which spread over her entire family, her two sons, her daughter, her grandson Jimmie. It was a style of prayer that had no use for words, it was pure, distilled consciousness of grace.

But she was confused. A flooding sense of gratitude for the good, and a refusal to acquiesce in the bad. That heretical combination was willful, nonsensical. Also—maybe—dangerous. This confusion and, perhaps, fear crept in as the pain in her knees became more intense than she could bear this side of hell. She struggled to her feet, coming face to face with the radio, and stared at it as if it were an animal.

The clock showed nine. Gil and Steven would not be back for another hour at least, she guessed. She put the uneaten dinner in the oven ready to heat up when the men came home. She put a bottle of whiskey and three glasses on the table.

She had added a whole six inches to the scarf before she heard the front door open and shut. Gil kissed her but he wore the crooked mouth that she saw only in troubled times.

He told her what happened, and said he'd asked Steven to come when he could, but it would be a long wait. He encouraged her to go to bed but she refused. Gil lay down on the couch in the living room. Janey called Nora and told her that Steven was nicked but OK.

"It's black and bitter," said Janey pouring reheated coffee into Steven's cup.

She asked the men if they wanted their dinner. Gil said yes and poured the whiskey. Steven finally looked at her and smiled as you might smile to comfort a sick child.

Gil drank but Steven just sat there as if he were alone.

Janey went to Steven and began pulling his jacket. He smiled again over his shoulder and leaned forward, and pressed one arm back, then the other till she freed him of the jacket. She draped it over his chair—saw one gun in a shoulder holster and another in his belt—and got to work on his right ear, which had soaked its dressing and was starting to drip blood. She told Gil to serve the food. She caught up a napkin and gripped Steven's ear; she took his hand and showed him how to apply pressure, then began to cut out a dressing.

She asked who the dead men were.

"Killers, rapists, torturers," said Gil Hughes. "And maybe the killers of the old dame on Locust Street."

Janey remembered this murder.

"We'll know more about that tomorrow," her husband said. "But Reitz talked to a guy in Cleveland who said they've both got more than one name. So who are they? What are they's a better question."

Hoping to reach Steven, Janey covered his hand with her own and said, "Steven, I'm glad you weren't badly hurt."

He gave her a silent, perhaps an understanding smile.

"That ear'll save a hundred grand in lawyer fees," Gil said. "Tim had to shoot because the big bug jammed his gun into the girl's face. Stevie had to shoot because the little bug fired on him first and kept on firing. I don't see any way this could mean trouble for anybody."

"That's not why I shot him," McCord said to Janey.

"Yeah yeah, justice and so forth," Hughes said hastily, "but if you went in there and said, 'Sorry, Insect, you're on the way to City-County Consolidated' and he said 'Good idea, officer,' you wouldn't've. You shot the bug so he wouldn't kill you. Not to mention the little tart in his line of fire. Tell me I'm wrong."

"He's right," McCord said turning again to Janey, "but there's the other thing too."

"I don't know what you mean by the other thing," said Janey, "but it sounds to me—" Looking into McCord's face she had a flash of the young man he had been twenty years ago, and she wondered what was different. She saw the same eyes that could express the whole range between sympathy and indifference; and she remembered his naive effort to conceal his admiration for Gil. "It sounds to me," she said, "from what I know, that you were justified."

"I was," said Steven. "But an action that is just—sure, this was a just action, Tim and me—but doing what's just isn't the same as justice."

"Huh?" Gil grunted.

Still speaking to Janey, McCord said: "Justice would be if the whole thing never happened."

Janey understood him. "If they had never killed the father or laid their hands on the daughter. We'll never see that kind of justice in this world."

"Right," said Steven, and to Gil he said: "See what I mean?"

"Sure but so what?" Gil glared at his wife and his friend as if they were demented. "The justice I care about is, Stevie and Tim don't get slammed by the lawyers for killing these pukes. Was the big insect a mortal danger to the little whore and Stevie? Did the little bug try to kill Stevie? Who fired first? If Stevie had stood like a statue presenting his shield would he be alive now? That's justice as far as I'm concerned. When the dicks draw their trajectory diagrams and the little whore calms down and tells how she got that bruise in her cheek, and when we compare fingerprints and tire treads and all that, and the ball and chain—I mean what more do you want?"

"Sure," said McCord, "but why is it so—" He didn't finish but Janey finished for him:

She said: "Why is it so awful."

"Sickening," said McCord, and Janey saw a flicker of life in his eyes, maybe anger.

"Not because they're our brothers," Hughes declared dogmatically.

"No, but maybe because they could have been," Janey said, "if they had only—tried. You have to try."

"To be human?" McCord asked her.

"Yes."

Janey and McCord stared at one another as if they would pursue this strange concept but Gil Hughes burst in with:

"Jesus, will you cut the soap opera? What sickens me isn't killing the pukes but what they did to the old man and the girl. They had their chance. All they had to do was drop the gun. You and Tim did what had to be done, it's that fuckin simple. Nothing sick about it."

"You're right," McCord said contritely. "I didn't mean 'sickening.' I meant fucking bad. You didn't do it, so—"

"I have too done it."

"OK, OK. If it's right you should do it, and I did it, and I don't feel so good about it."

"Would you do it again or let the little puke blow you away?"

McCord laughed but not with the sound of mirth. He asked Janey to call Nora and she said:

"I already did. She wants to come over but she said, 'Ask Steven first.' She wants—Stevie, do you see—"

Steven lifted a hand to stop her. He got up and pulled on his jacket and kissed her on the forehead, noting how different her skin was from Granny's. He pounded Hughes with his fist, lightly on the shoulder, and went out.

As he drove, it seemed the car was a capsule inside which shots and screams were in endless ricochet.

Lying under three blankets on his cot in the riot room he shivered and trembled.

Is Love Enough?

He fell into a half-sleep charged with echoing noises that resembled screams and bangs; he awoke into the depressing gloom of the riot room. His reward for waking up was that he saw a vision of Marie Carden bound, waiting, with the big goon standing over her while Prince Valiant went to some nearby street for the car. McCord could not stop looking into her eyes. In these eyes he saw what they had done to her, and her knowledge of what they planned to do. He had a vision of the men dragging her out of her father's house to the parking space by the garage. And even as this vision proceeded he could also see Marie's inner vision of her father seated in his chair, bound by rope and lamp cord, bloody and lifeless—the man who had raised her, her protector.

Inhabiting Marie Carden's mind in this way McCord moved toward a deeper vision of the world that he and Janey Hughes had spoken of, a world in which there is no implanted justice that is part of the design.

He washed, shaved, put on a suit and drove downtown for his appointment with Internal Affairs. Walking from the parking lot to Headquarters he was walking in Granny's house from the parlor to the bottom of the stairs, having seen the effect of Tim's magnum bullet on the man in the leather coat. The screams from behind drove him on toward the whimpering girl. He crouched; she asked if he had killed the sweet man. He climbed the stairs, watching the bottoms of Prince Valiant's shoes to see if they were still quivering.

He tried to drive this out. What he got instead was a repeat of the mean little yellow flashes of Prince Valiant's gun.

He was about to enter the building when he was approached by a man who looked familiar, a brawny, thick-set man with a shaved head, wearing a black suit.

"Lieutenant," said the man, "this is for you from Mr. Hawkins."

"Oh yes, Jason. Thank you." And McCord took the envelope Jason proffered. He paused in the lobby to read its contents.

Lieutenant McCord:

Since I prodded you, and am to that extent partly responsible for the news I heard this morning on the radio, I am emboldened to offer one thought. In the aftermath of last night's incident you may be all too keenly aware that the killers were human beings like us. But even we, sir, you and I, would not be entitled to live had we done what they did to Charles and Marie. Being human may be an accident of nature; it is also a responsibility. Be well, be secure, be content. You did your duty.

                —W. H.

When one of the investigators asked why he was armed with a 9mm pistol instead of the standard .38 revolver he answered: "I carry the Ruger for personal defense. I have a wife and three children." When they asked why he hadn't thrown more cops into the house he gave the answer he had given to Tim in the alley. When they asked why he had attended the memorial service, and how often he had done such a thing, he answered that Charles Carden was a friend of his wife. He added that he had never met Carden or his daughter.

He could see they weren't serious. Especially he could see it when one of his interrogators, a man with an anticop persona—slovenly, disorganized, indifferent and cold—smiled as if to say, "I know what you did," and then said: "Our questions are all pretty pointless, eh Steve? You did what you wanted to do, and it appears you did it just right."

To which McCord replied: "I wanted to make an arrest."

"Well, they never gave you a chance, did they?" the interrogator asked.

McCord said: "I've told you what happened," and that was all he said.

As the evidence rolled in throughout the day it became obvious that the two dead pukes were the killers of Charles and Marie Carden, and probably of the old lady murdered in her home two years before.

That evening McCord showered and shaved in the locker room of his station. The shaving especially was boring, and silent. He listened for gunfire and screams but all that was elsewhere. His mental arena was silent and dark but he kept listening.

He drove to the Upper Crust for dinner. When three of his cops came in and joined him at his table they all had a satisfying conversation. He thanked them for showing up for the bullseye. One patrolman congratulated McCord on having such big ears instead of a bigger head. An old sergeant suggested he spend more time on the pistol range. To this McCord responded that he had fired his first two rounds only to warm up the barrel.

Coming out with this group McCord stood in the parking lot and watched each man get in his cruiser. They saluted as they drove past him—in cop style, well short of the military—and McCord returned the salute. He stood there a moment and let his mind run, but it kept running to the same place, its predetermined destination for the last several hours.

Entering by the back door at about nine o'clock he saw that Nora's papers and adding machine were still spread on the kitchen table. This meant she was upstairs showering and laying out her clothes for tomorrow, and she was coming back. He sat down to wait, listening to the bass notes of the kids' music throbbing their way down the frame of the old house. He saw Marie Carden's captive eyes. He noticed for the first time that when he thought of Marie Carden his next thought was of Lindy Alden. So it was tonight.

When Nora came in he got up—as if he were meeting her in a hotel lobby or somewhere—and she turned to stone—looking at him with frozen eyes and pitiless expression—so it seemed to him—while he stood waiting. He knew that in this moment she was deciding their fate. He believed she still loved him and that in her heart, if anywhere, love would prove stronger than reason, anger, jealousy or hate.

At length Nora's freeze broke and she gave a tentative, perhaps doubtful smile and said rather softly: "Sit down, Steven."

He did so, and she sat opposite, leaving the papers and adding machine to one side.

He began swinging his leg under the table but was otherwise still and silent, looking at her and waiting.

Nora said: "Janey told me. Do you know that she prayed that last night would not ruin your life?"

"I'm the only one that can ruin my life, and I almost did."

"Yes," Nora said as if to stop him. "And your ear?" Her gaze shifted to his wound and back to his eyes.

"It's a nick, that's all."

"And Tim is all right?"

"He's fine. He's also a good shot. Otherwise we'd have stepped into a mess." Saying this McCord realized it did not express his real feeling. What actually happened—if not a mess—what was it?

"Yes, I'm sure he's an excellent shot. A good man with a gun."

"He is."

"And that 'little brother,' Janey said, tried to kill you."

"I killed him."

Nora believed this had been difficult for him to say; she looked into his steady eyes and did not try to mask her love.

"It was pretty brutal," McCord said.

Seated with her back straight, leaning forward, with her hair still darkened by her shower, Nora watched him, searching his eyes.

McCord knew she wanted something clear from him. He was on the point of speaking when she said:

"Steven, I am so glad you are alive. But—are you troubled?"

"If I did the right thing why should I be troubled?" Having said this he paused, thinking perhaps she'd answer, but she did not—except that she reached across the table and took his hand. Her hand touching his sent a flow of assurance through his body.

He said: "Yes, I am troubled. I expected I'd have to pay a price but I didn't know what it would be like. What I'm finding out is—I feel almost like I shouldn't have done it."

"You did it—to save your own life. That's what Gil told Janey."

"Oh sure."

"Isn't it so?"

"Sure it is."

He told her what Gil had said last night—Gil's defense of him and Tim Sloan. He said: "That's the story the Department is buying."

"Steven," she repeated, "is it true?"

"Yes. It happened just like that."

"I cannot believe there's any sin in it. Gil says you gave the man a chance to surrender. Instead he took a hostage and jammed a gun in her face."

"True. I'm talking about something else. It happened just like I planned. And it was justified, just like I planned. Janey understands. Gil doesn't."

"Steven," she began with the deep honesty in her eyes that he venerated, "I understand too. We are not made to carry a burden like this alone."

His answer was: "I need you, Nora."

She said: "That's not what I meant."

"I know what you meant, but it's you I need, Nora, you."

She came around the table and McCord turned in his chair to meet her. She embraced him and he buried his face in her breast.

Nora said: "Would you like to sleep here tonight?"

He looked up and she saw that he would—but he didn't speak, just looked into her eyes, with his own eyes filled by—not tears, but remorse or love.

"If you had been killed, Steven, the children and I—to lose you would be—"

McCord felt his jaw clench. He thought: "I am so lucky and so cruel"—to Nora, to the children and to Lindy, who had said: "Don't we deserve it."

As Nora held him—thinking, weighing, he believed, love against justice, hope against bitter knowledge, Steven grew calm. She stepped back and he took her hand, which she gladly gave. He could have been guiding or reassuring her—the way he held her hand—but the truth was otherwise. He felt as if they were walking through a storm together, not of rain or sleet but of blind, buffeting waves of pressure.

"Thank you," he said. "Yes, I'd like to sleep here tonight, if you'll forgive me. I don't deserve it but I ask your forgiveness."

They slept in each other's arms but did not kiss. He felt the stillness of her body, except for her breathing, in his embrace, and her warmth.

With the second night came the part he did not like, about our not being made to bear certain burdens alone—but he knew he must go through it; he did not try to stop her.

"If you refuse to surrender to God you'll be turning your back on the only reliable guide we have," Nora said.

"I have you," said McCord.

"There will be a part of you I cannot reach, but if you pray that part too will be healed. If you refuse you'll never know God or your own soul. And you consent to this diminished, scurrying life for the sake of some truth, as you call it, that you can't verify or even describe."

"That's right," he said.

"Then why reject our faith?"

"Because it is not true," said McCord.

"You admit you can't know that."

"I meant to say I do not think it's true."

"Your so-called truth is a faith too, but it has no grounding and gives you no consolation."

"I choose it," he said looking directly at her and almost smiling.

She saw in his dark blue eyes evidence that he was sleeping somewhat better. She said: "Yet I love you, Steven."

"And I love you, Nora. That you should forgive me is—"

"Don't say anything more about that. I have already forgiven you because I believe you love me."

He did not feel it would be fair to ask if she loved him.

Later Nora said: "You have a saint, though, Marie Carden."

He said it was true.

But Marie's were not the only eyes he saw in the days that followed. Marie's were living. McCord also saw dead eyes. Once or twice he felt himself rolling Prince Valiant's body over and then he saw the exit wound. One afternoon in his office he thought he heard the little whore screaming in mad terror; then he saw in his mind what his eyes had never seen, the impact of his bullet on Prince Valiant's body and his look of horror and protest in the instant of death.

Coming home at night he was more tranquil. The evidence kept piling up on the two-year-old case and now the brothers were implicated in yet another murder, this one in Cleveland.

Nora said: "I admire Marie Carden too, but what will you live by?"

"If I put it into words," he admitted, "it melts away." He could not say that he believed he must live by raw courage.

Nora echoed: "Melts away. Not a very good sign."

"I have what I think I need," Steven said and this was a new realization.

"What do you have," she asked, "besides pride?"

"I'll start with that."

"And are you too proud to come back to me in intimacy?"

"I love you," he said, "and I want to love you as your husband, but we are more truly different now than ever before."

"But I want you," said Nora. He saw her hands clasped before her breast, and he found something very lovely in those hands.

He said: "Can we be married again if we're so different?"

"I don't know," said Nora. "Is love enough?"

Steven doubted it, thinking of his feeling for Lindy, which confused him.

"I'm afraid you'll leave me again," Nora confessed. "I don't know if I can trust you."

"There's no reason you should believe me," he said, "but you can trust me. I'm all through with that."

"But we are so different. And I think there is no true love without God's blessing."

"Nora, I'm sorry. I just can't accept that."

"And you won't try?"

"No."

She rose from the table slowly, held out her hand and said, "Then we will have to try pure, desperate love."

They went upstairs hand in hand and the tread of their feet on the carpeted steps clashed at first with the rhythm of the thuds pulsing through the walls. Then the two rhythms seemed to be reconciled, and the couple found they were marching in time with the adolescent music. They squeezed hands and laughed.

"A wedding march," Nora whispered.

The tormenting conviction that he had no right to make love to her was driven clear out of his mind by the intoxication of the flesh. He detected its subtle approaches, and thought: "Is it possible? Is this real?" He took her breasts in his hands, kneeling above her, filling his hands with the warm fullness of her womanhood. Then the taste of her skin and lips brought the whole of their marriage to his consciousness, one touch opening the story of their lives. If he had ever contemplated living elsewhere, he forgot all that in his passion for Nora. Nora was his home.

Her swelling movements and the electrical darkness of her inner body were the same as before—and he seemed to be approaching ecstasy. He was desperate for Nora to follow him, and believed he could bear her along, so they would arrive at the same place and time. That was all he wanted; he did not worry about himself.

But he noticed, after first denying it, that she was lying inert under him. He didn't know how long she had been so. He kissed her and tasted her tears.

Looking down on this, the loveliest face he had ever seen, he begged forgiveness. A voice in his mind told him silence was better. He wiped away the streaks of water running down the sides of her face. Feeling the moisture on his fingertips he wondered how, by what aberration of character or twist of intellect, he could have betrayed her. Yet at that same moment he thought of Lindy and understood. Then, feeling compelled, he broke the silence and said he loved her and again asked forgiveness.

She said: "I forgive you, Steven, I love you. But I don't know if love is enough. I don't know—can I trust you?"

He said: "Yes, yes," and he believed that if love is not sufficient, life is unjust at the root. But that would mean an embedded principle of injustice, amounting to a principle of cruelty; and he would not go that far. "We have to love one another," he said. "If we do, we'll be OK."

She didn't speak. He saw her hands rise to cover her face. She began sobbing and it went right through him.

ABOUT THE AUTHOR

DONALD PFARRER's novel *Temple and Shipman*, which told the story of the fatal beating of a black suspect in police custody, was praised on National Public Radio for its powerful dramatization of the dilemmas of race. His *Neverlight* and *The Fearless Man* were cited by leading publications in this country and the United Kingdom for their nuanced depiction of Americans fighting the Vietnam War.

Pfarrer was awarded the Bronze Star with Combat V and the Purple Heart for his service in Vietnam.

On returning from that war he covered the antiwar movement for the *Milwaukee Journal*, then shifted to reporting on crime and politics. His work for the *Journal* earned the American Political Science Association's award for excellence in public affairs reporting.

He is a graduate of Harvard College and the father of two daughters. He lives with his wife, Anne Burling, in Cambridge, Massachusetts.

1/7/09